"It is corny," Father admitted with a laugh. "It's the corniest, most wonderful story in the world. The story of all our lives." He looked at each of us in turn, smiling so delightedly that I just wanted to throw myself into his arms and give him a hug. "You see, although I dialed the wrong number, I didn't want to ever hang up. I heard your mother's voice and something very strange happened to me."

"Something magical, too," Mother added.

"We recognized each other," he said then.

There was something almost religious in the air. They were talking to each other without words, and it thrilled me as few things ever had. To see them so in love, to know how much they cared about us, made me feel that nothing would ever happen to us, nothing mean or frightening or terrible.

But things did happen.

Awful things.

# THE INNOCENT DARK

## J.S. Forrester

Dell Publishing, Inc. * * * New York

Published by
Dell Publishing Co., Inc.
1 Dag Hammarskjold Plaza
New York, New York 10017

Dell ® TM 681510, Dell Publishing Co., Inc.

ISBN: 0-440-03852-9

Printed in the United States of America

First printing—January 1983

Once again, for Chad

Human life does not move with the regularity of a clock. In living there are gaps and silences when the soul stands still in its flight through abysses—and then there come times of trial and times of struggle when we grow old without knowing it.

Hamlin Garland, *Main-Travelled Roads*

It's like a lion at the door;
And when the door begins to crack,
It's like a stick across your back;
And when your back begins to smart,
It's like a penknife in your heart;
And when your heart begins to bleed,
You're dead, and dead, and dead,
    indeed.

*Nursery Rhyme*

# 1

It was a time of terror, a time of nightmares.

Six years have passed since then, yet the events which occurred soon after my twelfth birthday are as vivid today as if they happened yesterday. But for the longest time—the first twelve years of my life, in fact—it seemed as if everything were just as perfect as could be. If Mother and Father kept any secrets from us, we never knew about them. Besides, they were so much in love that what did secrets matter, anyway? I don't think they were of use to anyone, because secrets pull people apart. Sometimes that happens without their knowing it, and maybe that's what happened to us.

But when I was little, the only secrets I knew about were the dreams of the future I kept locked in my heart. I guess that sounds mushy, and maybe you're thinking a girl like me would be better off worrying about boys and new clothes and whether or not the pimple on her chin will ever go away. But I never thought of those things. Or if I did, I think it was when I was much younger, more innocent too, I guess.

My brother Jason, eighteen months older and so much bigger and stronger than me, had plenty of secrets. But he never shared them, either. Whenever I caught him looking moody, and as he got older he seemed to act that way a great deal, he always pretended nothing was wrong. He really had me fooled, too. I thought his moodiness had to do with growing up. Changing is another word for it, I guess. I wanted to ask him about those changes, why the fuzz over his lip suddenly didn't look like peach down anymore, why his voice sometimes slipped and cracked like Mrs. Darby our housekeeper dropping a wet plate and all the pieces of china scattering like frightened insects across the floor.

But whenever I brought up those subjects, he always shrugged, saying it wasn't important, there'd be plenty of time for me to find out. That's why, on my twelfth birthday, or actually a few days before, I decided to ask Mother about all those things that were confusing me.

There wasn't a better person in the world than Mother. Whenever I had a problem or needed someone to talk to, she was always there for me. She never said she didn't have time, or don't bother me I'm busy, Quinn. No, she always put down whatever she was doing and we'd sit together and have a girl-to-girl. That's what she used to call it, and the words themselves always gave me a good feeling, like sipping hot cocoa on a cold wintry day.

"Now you just sit right by me and speak your mind, Quinn," she would say, clearing a place for me alongside her.

When Mother held me I was safe and everything was right, just the way it was supposed to be. And she always smelled so good, too. There were roses in her perfume, but it wasn't a heavy smell, sticky and sweet like candy you take out of your mouth to see how much it's dissolved. No, Mother's perfume was light and delicate, just like the little wild roses that grow in a part of the Bottom near where Jason and I have our secret place.

When we had our girl-to-girls, Mother would tell me what it was like to be a woman, and how beautiful I was going to be when I was all grown up. Even if one part of me was afraid to believe that, maybe because I was afraid of being disappointed, it was still wonderful to hear it from Mother's lips.

She said I was a gamine. When I looked it up in Father's dictionary, the big leatherbound one he keeps in his study with all his other books and papers, I liked what I read. So Mother thought I was a pert, playfully mischievous girl. That made me glad because pert was a bouncy full-of-life kind of word, which was so much nicer than being thought of as sullen or dull.

"But will I still be a gamine when I'm like you, your age I mean?"

"I don't see why not, Quinn. It's a wonderful quality, quite rare these days. Most women lose it because they're not half as clever or pretty as you. Men will always seek you out, believe me. There's something about a woman who's boyish and full of the devil that attracts a certain kind of man."

I snuggled closer to her, making her perfume my perfume, her soft womanliness part of me as well. "What kind of man?" I asked.

"The kind who'll let you be a free spirit, who'll let you be open with your feelings and be your own person. But I wouldn't worry about that now, Quinn. You still have lots of growing up to do. Even though it's sometimes painful and confusing, I think it's the very best time in a person's life."

"You mean you'd be my age again if you had your way?"

Mother's smile was so radiant it lit up her entire face.

"Only if I had a brother like Jason," she said. Then a cloud came into her eyes, and for a moment I couldn't tell if she was feeling sad or cross. "But I didn't," she went on. "I had a sister."

"Aunt Gwen," I volunteered.

Mother nodded. "Unfortunately," she admitted, "your aunt and I never really did see eye to eye."

What exactly did that mean? I wondered. Every time our Aunt Gwen came to the Valley for a visit, Mother was always very nice to her. Father was nice, too, making jokes and even tickling her the way he sometimes tickled me, saying that she and Mother were so alike there were times when he couldn't even tell them apart. That was Father just being polite, of course, because Mother and Aunt Gwen were as different from each other as me and Jason. But I guess Father meant it as a compliment, especially since all you had to do was look at Mother to see how beautiful she was.

Father always enjoyed telling the story of how they'd met. Once a year at the very least, and never with any warning or particular reason, he'd suddenly clear his throat and get all serious and businesslike. Jason was the one who invariably guessed it was time for the "mating ritual," as he called it. Whenever he used those words anger would flash in Father's eyes. But it was anger like summer lightning—gone before you quite realize what you've seen.

"Mating ritual my ass," Mother once said. She promptly put her hand over her mouth and blushed, apologizing to me, and saying vulgarity should never be a lady's strongest suit.

To tell you the truth, I didn't know what she meant. How could a "suit" be strong, or even weak, for that matter? But this was even before I turned twelve and she gave me her special grown-up present, and at nine and ten and eleven I didn't ask half as many questions as I guess I do now.

Anyway, when Father told his story he always turned it into something that sounded like a fairytale, even down to the "and they lived happily ever after" that comes at the very end. He was still in law school, he explained, when they first met. A friend of his from one of his classes had given him the telephone number of a girl he knew. Father was supposed to call her up and ask her out. At least that was the plan. Only things didn't quite work out that way.

What happened was that Father was so nervous about asking this girl out on a blind date that he either misread the phone number or dialed it wrong. Instead of getting Sue, or whatever the girl's name was (every time he told the story I think the name changed, though I can't remember for certain), he got Mother.

"Then what happened?" Jason would always say. A giggle would inch its way across his mouth. Sometimes he couldn't even control himself, and he'd just burst out laughing.

Father returned his grin in kind. Then he'd look across the table to where Mother was sitting at the opposite end. "Rebecca Howe Lefland," he would pronounce, saying her name like it was the most beautiful poem any man had ever written.

"Bennett dear, please," Mother whispered. "You're embarrassing me in front of the children."

I could never help sighing and smiling, feeling all tingly with goosebumps all over, just to see them that way. That's what love was all about, I knew, the way Father gazed across the table, capturing Mother's beauty in his eyes, holding it there like it belonged to him and no one else.

It was a wrong number, but Father said there was

something in Mother's voice that made him clutch the telephone receiver for all he was worth.

Jason began to giggle, and though he tried to stop himself from laughing, he seemed to have the hardest time.

"You don't have to stay if you don't care to hear the rest of it, son," Father told him.

Jason, who still had peach down then, and a clear high-pitched voice nearly identical to my own, squished himself down in his chair and lowered his eyes. "Sorry," he muttered.

"Sorry for what?" Father said sternly, though there was a good-natured twinkle in his eyes even as he continued to reprimand my brother.

"He thinks it's corny, Bennett," said Mother. She reached over and put her hand on Jason's shoulder, her long slim fingers trailing down his arm the same way her favorite ivory nightgown trailed along the floor.

"It is corny," Father admitted with a laugh. "It's the corniest, most wonderful story in the world. The story of all our lives." He looked at each of us in turn, smiling so delightedly I just wanted to throw myself into his arms and give him a hug. "You see, I didn't want to ever hang up. I heard your Mother's voice and something very strange happened to me."

"Something magical, too," Mother added.

"We recognized each other," he said then.

"But you hadn't ever met before," I started to say.

"A different kind of recognition, Quinn," Mother replied. "A subtler kind."

In my confusion I held my tongue, listening to the silence all around me. There was something almost religious in the air, the "ritual" Jason had spoken of earlier. They were talking to each other without words, and it thrilled me as few things ever had. To see them so in love, to know how much they cared about us, made me feel that nothing would ever happen to us, nothing mean or frightening or terrible.

But things did happen.

Awful things.

Secrets and more secrets like spiderwebs covered with sticky dead things.

Yet when I was little, *real* little I mean, eight and nine and ten and even eleven, I couldn't possibly imagine how anything bad could happen to us. We were Leflands, Father and Mother's children, and Father looked across the table and burned with love, not just for Mother, but for all of us.

"I couldn't hang up," he said in a whisper.

Mother sighed, and later Jason told me it was a sigh of longing, whatever that meant. "So true," she said. "Neither of us were willing to put down the receiver."

"So we agreed to meet," Father went on.

But first they must've spent hours on the phone, just talking to each other, learning all about themselves. Father was in his early twenties then, I believe, and Mother was a few years younger. She'd come to the city just a month or two before, and as she explained it she didn't know a soul.

Finally, in what must have been the wee hours of the morning, they agreed on a place and time to meet. Father said he would wear a flower in his buttonhole, a red carnation I imagine, or something similar. He'd be at a certain streetcorner at a certain time. Mother would recognize him by the flower. If for any reason she didn't like him or changed her mind, all she had to do was keep walking. He'd never know who she was, and so no one's feelings would be hurt.

"And you walked right by him, didn't you?" Jason said with a giggle.

"Of course I did," Mother replied. She kept a straight

15

face, even as I looked at her in shock. "Now don't you worry, Quinn. If I hadn't stopped to pluck the flower out of your father's buttonhole, none of us would be here today."

So she didn't walk past him. She'd liked what she saw, Father that is. They went to some wonderful dark romantic place, a restaurant I think it was, though one year he said it was the skating rink at the park. But it didn't matter that neither of them could ever get the story straight. What mattered were the feelings they had for each other, not the details of where they went and what they ate or drank.

I looked back and forth, from one end of the dining table to the other. I knew one thing. I wanted to grow up to be as beautiful as Mother, to meet a man as handsome as Father, to fall in love with a stranger with a red carnation in his lapel, to live happily ever after.

"And so you fell in love," I spoke up.

"Even if I didn't want to, I couldn't have helped myself," Father said.

"Besides," added Mother, "I can be very persuasive, especially when I set my mind to something."

"And needless to say," Father concluded, "that something was me."

The last time he told that story was just a few days before my twelfth birthday. For weeks and weeks, probably even months I guess, I'd been storing up all these questions, wanting to know about things that only Mother would be able to explain. Jason wasn't going to tell me, even though I'd asked and asked and probably made a nuisance of myself.

"It's not my place," he once said.

It was one of those mysterious phrases I couldn't make heads or tails of. Place for what? And if it wasn't his place, whatever that was, then whose place was it?

"Ask Mother," he suggested. He made it sound more like an order than good advice. "Women know more about these things, anyway."

The things he was talking about were changes, a person's body doing strange things, acting differently than it ever had before. Those changes had begun to happen to me, and at first I was very frightened. Mother probably thought I was still too young, and so she hadn't gotten around to explaining things. I thought I was bleeding from the inside, that maybe I was even dying. I suddenly had this terrifying picture of myself in a hospital somewhere, having been rushed there in an ambulance with a siren screaming down the highway. There were needles in my arms, and tubes going every which way, machines thumping and clicking right beside my bed. Everyone I cared about was huddling around me, and I was spending my last hours on earth with them.

But I didn't want to die. There were too many questions left unanswered, and too many reasons for wanting to wake up with a smile each morning. I thought of the "mating ritual," the wrong number that had blossomed into an *ageless* love (I got that word out of Father's dictionary, and I think it describes things perfectly). I wanted that for myself, and death was suddenly like the boogeyman, an enemy you banish by opening your eyes and turning on the lights.

So I went to Mother to have her explain what it meant, the cramps and the bleeding, the napkins and all that other personal business I shouldn't be talking about in public. She wasn't in a very good mood that day, I remember, kind of nervous and jumpy, unable to sit still or concentrate on anything. Anna Darby the housekeeper referred to those times as Mother's "sick headaches," and we all knew that if we left her alone she'd soon come out of them and be her old self again.

But I guess I was just too impatient. Frightened too, because of the blood part and making a mess of myself. Why she hadn't prepared me is anybody's guess, though later Jason insisted it was merely an oversight, a big word that seemed to cover a multitude of sins.

"Can't it wait, Quinton?" she demanded.

Whenever she called me Quinton I always knew I'd be better off leaving her alone until the headache passed. But the awful truth is that I was scared of dying, bleeding to death I mean, and I was too ashamed to run to Mrs. Darby for help.

"Oh that," she said when I told her what was wrong. "Darling, that's nothing."

"But if it's nothing then why am I bleeding to death?" It came out with a little cry of terror. I wish Mother had held me close then, like she so often did when we were alone together. But she was lying in bed, a damp compress across her forehead. She didn't reach out for me. She didn't even tell me to come closer, to sit on the edge of her bed with its lovely satin counterpane. Instead, she just waved her hand in the air, so impatient with me I wondered if I should turn around and leave the way I'd come.

"Oh, Quinn, don't be such a baby. God knows it happens to everyone."

I sniffled back a sob. "What happens?"

"Having your period, darling." Despite her sick headache, there was a moment of laughter in her eyes. She seemed amused by my predicament, that something as natural as menstruation (that being the word I learned that afternoon) should cause me such concern.

"Then I'll be all right? I mean . . . I'm not hurt inside, like a cut or something?"

"Of course not. But can't we talk about this later, when Mother's feeling better? My head is splitting, Quinn. I can't think straight at the moment."

She closed her eyes, just like it was a signal for me to leave. I tiptoed from the room, pausing by the door to look back at her. The damp compress had slipped to the side, and there were deep hurtful lines revealed across her forehead, furrows of pain and maybe even unhappiness. Yet the rest of her face was composed, her long silken lashes fluttering ever so lightly like the dream of a butterfly on a warm summer's day.

Secrets and more secrets, words spoken in darkness, waking up in the middle of the night certain someone is standing over your bed, ready to reach out and stifle your screams. But in a few days I was going to be twelve years old, and I never believed that happiness, the warmth and comfort of family, would ever be destroyed. I never even dreamed my life would change, and all the things I'd come to love, to take for granted too, would no longer be the same. Not ever again, for as long as I lived.

I knew I shouldn't have spied on them that day, the day that came right before my twelfth birthday. But I just couldn't help it. If that sounds like a poor excuse, then I apologize, but they were talking so loudly, so angrily too, that I just had to listen and find out what was wrong.

You see, I couldn't remember ever hearing them argue before. Mother and Father always spoke to each other with kindness and concern. Even when Mother took to her bed, as she did when she had her sick headaches, she never lashed out at Father, short-tempered because she wasn't feeling well.

It was that mutual respect they had for each other that struck me as the glue that held all us Leflands together. It was one reason why I'd always assumed Jason and I were different from other children our age, because of that ageless timeless love Bennett had for Rebecca, and she for

him. Love like that is such a rarity that it cements relation-
ships together as few things ever can.

But then the words came, the horrible mean angry words.
I was so frightened to hear them shouting at each other that
I wanted to rush into their room and stop them before it
was too late.

It was the night before my twelfth birthday. Outside my
room the great horned owls who live in our Valley were
shrieking through the darkness. I'd heard them calling to
each other so many times before that it didn't scare me,
even though all the lights were out and everything was as
dark as the bottom of a cellar. I was snuggled under all
these wonderful quilts Father said were heirlooms that had
been passed down from one generation of Leflands to
another. So there I was, warm and toasty under at least a
hundred years of family history.

Then I heard them. At first I didn't think much of it.
They seemed to be talking, normally I mean, and I closed
my eyes and buried myself down into the pit of my bed,
wondering what the birthday party would be like, and the
special gift Mother had told me she'd bought. She said it
was going to be a grown-up present because I wasn't a
little girl anymore. I couldn't be sure if that was because
of the changes, the physical ones, or if she meant I was
more mature in an emotional sort of way. But whatever
her reasons, I was so excited about the prospect of opening
my presents I could hardly keep my eyes closed.

From the far end of the hall where they had their
bedroom, the voices grew louder, more insistent too. Something was wrong. Maybe Mother wasn't feeling well, maybe
that was it. Jason's room was right next to mine, and I
wondered if he could hear them, too, and if he was getting
worried the way I was.

I sat up in bed, shivering when the covers slipped down
off my shoulders. Father prided himself on being a practi-

cal sort of man. When everyone retired he made sure to turn down the heat, saying it was a waste of money and natural resources to keep the furnace going when we were all asleep. But it was getting chilly as a result, and my teeth started to chatter.

"—not this time you won't!" Mother suddenly cried out.

There was a buzz of frantic whispering after that, as if they both realized they were making too much noise. But it was too late. I'd heard them and I just couldn't help myself. When I got out of bed my feet searched blindly for the slippers. They were white and fuzzy like two baby rabbits, little-girl slippers because I wouldn't be a big girl until the following morning, when I was officially twelve. Then I threw on my robe and made my way to the door.

The moment I stepped into the hall they were at it again. Something caught in my throat. A sob, maybe, or something even worse. It was like fear, but not boogeyman-fear, scared of dark places and monsters lurking in the shadows. It was fear of things changing, of our lives being touched by something we had no control over.

I guess I should have knocked on Jason's door, instead of just continuing down the hall. But if it was wrong to spy, to eavesdrop on them, then I take full responsibility for what I did. It was their tone of voice, you see. They weren't speaking with the voice of timeless, ageless love. They sounded as if they hated each other, and I was terrified of what it might mean.

"You think you've been very clever, Rebecca, don't you?" Father was saying when I reached their door. "But I see right through you, my darling."

"You see nothing, Bennett, because there's nothing to see."

"The boy suspects. You've made him curious."

"No, it's not true," Mother insisted.

21

"Gwen remembers."

"She does not!" Mother shouted. "She was much too young. It's all a dream for her."

"No," Father corrected. "Not a dream, Rebecca. A nightmare."

What were they talking about? I thought of putting my eye to the keyhole. But that would have been much worse than eavesdropping. I had to respect their privacy, though what I was doing really wasn't respectful at all. But like I've said, I just couldn't help myself because I was too frightened of their anger, this explosion of sharp bitter words I'd never heard from them before.

"Oh Bennett, why must you go on like this? Don't you believe the love I feel? Don't you trust me anymore? What happened in the past is a dead issue. The nightmares are over. They won't come back to haunt us."

"That's what you said the last time, and the time before that. I can't trust you, Rebecca, and that's the saddest part. Every time I do you disappoint me. Why couldn't you have just left well enough alone? Why must you toy with him so? Is it to get back at me, is that it? When have I ever done anything to hurt you that you'd treat me this way?"

Mother began to cry, and then Father was whispering to her in the right kind of voice, the voice that spoke of long years of caring, of a love that would burn in their hearts forever and ever.

"Promise me you'll be more careful," Father begged. "Their lives depend on it, Rebecca. They'd be lost without you. I'd be lost, too."

"But I don't see how a little—" Mother started to say.

Then all I heard were bits and pieces of words as their voices receded. They were getting undressed for bed. I heard a drawer being pulled open, a closet door slammed shut.

"Fires of hell," someone said, only I couldn't tell which of them had spoken.

What about the fires of hell? Who would burn in them, and why?

I wish I'd had the courage to knock on their door, to ask to come in. I wish I could have looked at each of them, seeing my parents as they really were. If only I'd done that, asking them what was wrong, and if there was anything I could do to help make things better. But I was ashamed of myself for spying on them. And then, when I heard footsteps on the stairs at the end of the hall, I just lost my head.

I turned and ran, tripping over my slippers, two fuzzy white rabbits that seemed determined to race on ahead of me. I barely made it to my room when I caught sight of Anna Darby. Her stiff arthritic steps made the stairs creak ominously. What was she doing down here, anyway? It was long past her bedtime, my bedtime too for that matter.

Quickly I closed the door before she could see me. But instead of hearing her walking down the hall, it sounded as if she paused for a moment, listening the way I had. Then she turned away, and once again I could hear her slow, measured steps as she mounted the stairs.

Fires of hell, burning forever not like an ageless love, but like an ageless hate.

I couldn't make sense of any of it. What was Father so afraid of? What was he trying to warn Mother about? He said that our Aunt Gwen remembered, but then he never said what. *The boy suspects.* What boy? Could he have meant Harry, Anna and Will Darby's son? But Harry hardly spent any time with us. It was only during the summers when he came to help his father with the groundskeeping that we ever saw him. Could Father have been talking about Jason? But what did Jason suspect?

All these questions kept circling round and round me,

like a merry-go-round gone out of control. I didn't want things to change. I wanted our lives to be just the way they always were. But now I was frightened, and with that fear came uncertainty. Something was very wrong. There were secrets my brother and I knew nothing about. And unless we found out what they were and tried to make things right again, those secrets might tear us all apart.

"Their lives depend on it," Father had said.

Maybe she was sick. Maybe she was dying and they didn't want us to know. He said we'd be lost without Mother, and it was true. Just thinking of what might happen if she left us brought hot, stinging tears to my eyes. I threw myself down on my bed, pressing my face into the pillows.

In just a few hours I was going to be twelve years old. But I felt like Peter Pan, because if I'd had my way I wouldn't have grown up. I would have remained a little girl, and nothing would change, and they would never shout angrily at each other, terrifying me with their secrets.

# 2

**C**all me Jason, everyone else does, though sometimes I call myself Lefland, like a tough-as-nails private eye in a detective story. My Dad has a whole shelf of them in his study, and I've read them all. I love books like that. I started reading the Hardy Boys when I was eight or nine, though our tutor said I'd be better off reading the classics. But I say give me a good rip-roaring action-adventure story every time. There's nothing that'll compare.

Call me Jason, or Lefland, or Quinnie's slightly older brother. She's my kid sister, and if there's anything I love better than a good mystery, it's her. I was thirteen and a half the day she turned twelve, the day our world started to come down on our heads. Even if I didn't like to think of myself as a kid anymore, she still was. That was a good thing too, because she kept me steady, gave me a center and place to hold onto.

Oh Quinnie, if only you weren't so trusting. You're an innocent, you know that, a real honest-to-God innocent. And maybe I'm just as innocent, too, and that's the problem. Maybe deep down inside where it counts I'm still a kid, too, even if I don't like to admit it.

But let me get back to the point. The story of our lives isn't a very happy one, and the older we got the worse it became. Sometimes if I don't watch myself, I feel the tears creeping into my eyes and nothing I can do will make them go away.

For a long time, we were a happy family. Not a big happy family, just an average-sized one with I guess, with more money than most. The Valley's the place where we lived, the "old Lefland homestead" as Dad jokingly called it. It had been in his family for over a hundred years. The house was much too large for the four of us. Even with the Darbys rooming on the top floor there were still dozens of rooms left empty.

Great-grandpa Lefland came out here to California in the 1870's. I don't know where he made his fortune, but when he bought land, this Valley I mean, he made sure to buy up enough so he never had to see a neighbor, not for miles and miles around. Dad once said that Great-grandpa Josiah had a thing about prying eyes, as if he were afraid of people spying on him. Whatever the reasons, he couldn't have picked a prettier spot. As isolated as the Valley is, it's just beautiful, a natural bowl with bottomlands and chapparal, low rounded hills and perfect privacy.

I've always loved it here. Even the privacy part never really bothered me, though sometimes I felt bad for Quinnie that she didn't have any little girls for playmates. But the house itself held enough surprises to keep her busy, at least most of the time. We once counted thirty-four rooms, not even including bathrooms and stuff like that. Thirty-four rooms all done up in every kind of style imaginable. The house was Victorian Gothic, with a high spiky roof and lots of gables, plus all sorts of strange decorations. I'm not big on architecture, but everyone who ever came out here to visit always commented about it, how the house was a real museum piece, and maybe even the state should declare it an historic monument.

But there I go again, forgetting the point I was trying to make. I was telling you about Quinnie's twelfth birthday, and the terrible things that started to happen right after. I remember that day as if it were yesterday, though years and years have passed since then, awful bloody-scary years if you want to know the truth. And you do want the truth, don't you, because that's what this is all about.

Well then, here's how it happened, or how it started at least.

Quinn was just brimming over with excitement that morning, so pretty she looked good enough to eat. And she didn't look like a flat-chested little kid, either. I mean she's cute, real cute in fact, but she was also starting to fill out, with bumps in places I'd never noticed before. The only part of her that looked the same as it always did was her nose. It's this funny little turned-up button Dad claimed she got from the milkman. I never figured out what he meant by that, because no one delivers anything to us except heating oil. Even the mail is put in a box in the Juniper City post office. And all that is is the back of the general store behind the garden tools and cans of Rustoleum. Her hair's the same color as mine, sort of blonde and brown all mixed together at the same time. It's cut almost the same way, too, as if someone put a bowl over our heads and went snip snip snip.

Mom used to say she liked us to look alike, even though I was taller and weighed more than my sister. When Mom saw us standing together she said it always made her think of porcelain figurines, or something else I think she said was called delft.

Well, anyway, there she was, trooping down the stairs the morning of her twelfth birthday, so excited and pleased-as-punch I had to give her a hug I thought she looked so cute. Birthday parties are supposed to start in the afternoon (I don't remember who told me that, but someone did). But that morning Mom said there were going to be changes around here, and even though she was joking when she said it, it kind of got to me because there was something in her voice that was real serious, too.

"Changes like what?" Quinn asked as she sat at the breakfast table. She sounded a little scared, or maybe just concerned. It was hard to tell.

Mom was trying to keep it all a big surprise but she couldn't hold it in much longer. The next thing we knew the door leading from the dining room to the kitchen flew open. There was Dad, with Will and Anna Darby standing right behind him. Dad had this huge platter of hotcakes he was doing a balancing act with, and there were twelve drippy wax candles stuck in the pancakes, just as if they were a cake.

The next thing I knew we were all singing "Happy Birthday," some of us in tune and some of us not. Quinnie sat there at the table like someone had cast a spell over her. She seemed entranced like a princess in one of those fairytales we used to read when we were kids—*little* kids, I mean.

"It's just . . . just . . . ." She was blushing and stumbling over her words she was so happy.

Dad kept laughing, thinking the pancake gag was a terrific joke which I guess it was. He set the platter down in front of Quinn, then stood behind her while she made a wish.

"I wish—"

"Don't tell us!" Mom interrupted.

"How come?" I asked.

"It won't come true that way."

Boy, I thought, grownups can be as weird as little kids sometimes.

So Quinnie closed her eyes tight as could be. She got up from her chair and just stood there, shaking and swaying from side to side. I bet if a good wind had come up she would've been carried halfway across the Valley.

When her eyes popped open you could've sworn she was a doll come to life. Then she bent low over the pancakes and blew out the candles, all in a single puff.

Everyone burst into applause. Mrs. Darby the house-keeper dabbed at her eyes with a dishtowel she happened to have in her hand. Her husband Will beamed as if Quinn were his own kid. Everyone was having such a good time, but for some reason I felt a little left out. Suddenly I remembered that I'd left Quinnie's present upstairs in my room. So right away I excused myself and rushed upstairs to get it, hoping she'd like it as much as I did.

By the time I got downstairs there was a whole pile of gifts on the table. "Which one do you want to open first?" I asked.

There were so many to choose from that Quinn couldn't make up her mind. "You pick for me," she said, and so I didn't think twice about thrusting my present right in her hand.

When she got the ribbons all undone—Mom had helped me tie it up—and then the gold-foil wrapping paper, she stared at the white cardboard box for the longest time. She was in a kind of trance again I guess, and I had to ask her if she was all right.

" 'Course," she whispered. "It's just that I'm . . . oh Jason, you're such a wonderful brother!" She threw her arms around my neck and gave me a kiss.

"Open it, sweetheart," Mom urged.

Everyone was still beaming like a bunch of sunflowers. I don't know to this day why I had this awful creepy feeling then, but I did. I started wondering if maybe I'd made a big mistake. Maybe there was still time to change it. In fact, I even reached out to take the box out of Quinn's hand. But by then it was too late. She'd already lifted off the top, and so I stepped back, watching from a distance as she pawed her way through the nest of tissue paper.

When she finally came to the present itself everyone was so quiet I couldn't tell if they were as pleased as I was, or if they all thought I was a big jerk or something.

At last Quinnie broke the silence. "Jason, it's the best present I ever got," she insisted.

I knew she was just saying that to make me feel good. You could see right on her face and the tip of her button nose that she really didn't like what I'd bought her at all. If I'd had my way I would've grabbed it out of her hand and thrown it away, bought her something else. But it was too late for that.

"What an . . . unusual knife," I heard Mrs. Darby mutter.

"It's an antique," I blurted out. "See, the handle is genuine bone. It's from a stag, part of the antlers I think. It's a ladies' dagger from the nineteen-hundreds the man said. He even showed me a picture of it in the 1908 Sears, Roebuck catalogue."

I wanted Quinnie to like the knife so bad I must've grabbed it out of her hand in my excitement.

"It's a real little beauty," I said, remembering the description I'd read in the catalogue. "With the very finest quality of steel in the blade. It has a German silver guard and fancy bolster, furnished with a fine leather sheath. It's the finest quality of a dirk knife . . . that's what the book said about it. Oh, and I forgot. The metal is warranted."

I wasn't sure what most of that stuff meant, but I hoped they'd be impressed.

"But why would your sister need a knife?" asked Dad.

"It's a ladies' dagger," I said again, and I finally handed it back to Quinn. "And now she's a lady and every lady has to have a dagger, like it says in the book. You have one, Mom, isn't that so?" Of course she did, because I'd seen it on her dressing table once or twice before.

"I have a letter opener, Jason, if that's what you mean."

"No," I insisted, "it's a dagger." I looked over at Quinn. She was holding the stag-handled dirk in the palm of her hand, turning it from side to side to admire the blade. I'd honed it for her, so it was nice and sharp.

"It's beautiful," she said. "I bet it's very rare, too. There probably isn't another one like it in the whole state, maybe even the country. Thank you, Jason."

"And it's a good, practical thing to have, besides," I added. "Now you'll always be protected, no matter what."

I returned to my place at the table. I was more concerned about what Quinnie thought than anyone else. She liked the knife and that's all that counted. It was an original kind of idea, anyway, wasn't it? If I'd bought her dollhouse furniture or silly junk like that, it would've only meant she was still a baby. And with the bumps and curves she was getting, I knew for sure she wasn't a little kid anymore.

As if to prove the point, the next present she opened was from Mom. One look at the shortie pajamas that were inside and Quinn gave a squeal of delight. She rushed over to Mom and nearly jumped into her arms, she was so thrilled.

"I love them," she kept saying, "I just love them." She held the pajamas in front of her, modeling them for us and prancing back and forth like she was in a fashion show. They had all sorts of ruffles, with little blue flowers sprinkled across the material just like the flowers on the wallpaper in her room.

"My, my," Mrs. Darby was saying. She clucked her tongue as if to imply no good would come of this, that it was a very inappropriate gift. "They are rather revealing, aren't they?"

"You can say that again," murmured Dad, only he murmured it loud enough so everyone in the room could hear. I caught him looking at Mom and there was something very dark in his eyes.

"She deserves them," Mom spoke up. "After all, she's a big girl now. And they're the latest fashion for big girls. Besides, you men don't know the first thing about what a woman likes. Isn't that so, Quinn?"

"Yes, and they're wonderful, Mother. They're the most wonderful grown-up clothes I've ever had." She gave me a quick, furtive look, almost as if she were apologizing for the knife.

"Personally, I think they're a very poor choice," Dad went on.

Everyone looked at him the way they'd looked at me when I explained about the dirk. Quinnie was crestfallen by his attitude. I got mad because it seemed that he was trying to make her cry on what was supposed to be her special day.

Right away, Mom tried to make things right again. "Your father is sad to see you growing up, Quinn. That's why he thinks it's a poor choice. He'd like you to always be his little girl, that's all it is."

"I think they're cheap looking, Rebecca. Surely you could have chosen something less . . . provocative."

Mom just glared at him. Her eyes which were ice-blue like the trapped fire of a diamond glinted and raged at him.

"Now that Quinn has something others might find provocative, what she decides to do with it is her business," Mom said in the firmest, most unwavering tone of voice I'd ever heard her use.

For a second I thought Dad was going to snatch the pajamas out of Quinn's hand. But then when he saw how he'd brought her to the verge of tears, he backed off. A moment later he tried patching things up by telling her she'd probably look very nice in them.

What was he so upset about, anyway? His present cost a lot but it was really the worst thing he could have chosen. He'd gotten her a pair of teenage-type dolls, Debbie and Donnie or something like that. They came in an enormous box, and inside it there were more changes of clothes than we had ourselves.

"Don't you like them, Quinn?" asked Dad.

It was obvious from Quinn's expression that she was trying hard to look pleased. But I knew she wasn't. Dad had gotten her the perfect present for a nine- or ten-year-old. But not for someone who prided herself on no longer being a little girl.

"I wonder if they're anatomically exact," I heard myself say. I don't know where the words came from, to tell you the truth. They just sort of popped into my head, then flew out of my mouth before I could stop them.

That really made Dad furious. I'd never seen him look so mad. "Why don't you watch your language for a change, Jason? I find nothing amusing about your smartass remarks," he yelled.

The minute he lost his temper the Darbys disappeared into the kitchen. The door closed behind them, and I looked down at my lap, staring at my fingers that were pretending to be two spiders doing pushups.

"No, please," he said a moment later, because everyone was just sitting there, not saying a word and not making a move. "Forgive me, Quinn. I guess I got up on the wrong side of bed this morning. I'll exchange the dolls for you tomorrow. You just tell me what you'd like instead."

"But I don't want them exchanged," protested Quinn.

33

"I think they're neat, the neatest most grown-up dolls anyone could ask for. I'm going to pretend they're you and Mother. Anna can help me make more clothes for them and everything." She reached into the box and took out the Donnie doll, holding it like it was a little baby, ever so gently in the crook of her arm. "Now don't look cross, Donnie," she cooed. "Everything's going to be fine."

It wasn't fine. It wasn't the least bit fine.

An hour later when I was coming out of my room I heard them slamming doors and drawers and maybe even throwing things at each other. I'm glad Quinn wasn't around to hear, because the things they were saying would have scared her worse than anything she'd ever heard before.

"You coward!" Mom was yelling. "What are you so afraid of, Benny? That she'll turn into me?"

"You're damn right," he said, and it came out like a snarl. "Her life's going to be perfect. No one's going to hurt her, not you or your family or anyone else."

"My family's dead. I don't need you to remind me of that."

"They may be dead, but their spirit's still alive. Besides, Rebecca, you saw what happened. You know what's wrong."

"Nothing's wrong except in your sick imagination," Mom cried out at the top of her lungs.

I think he must have slapped her then because she suddenly began to sob.

The sound tore me apart inside. "Don't you hurt her! Don't you hurt my mom!" I screamed. Only the strange thing is, the words were all in my head, as if they were trapped up there, unable to get out.

I raced down the hall to their room, but before I could throw myself against the door to force it open, I heard something else that made me freeze in my place.

"It's starting again, Rebecca, you know it is. You can't help yourself anymore. It's getting out of control, and you know what that means, don't you?"

"It means you're imagining things," Mom whimpered.

What was going on in there? What was he talking about? Getting out of control—who was? Did he mean Mom or Quinn or me or what?

"If you think I don't know what's been going on around here, especially when I'm out-of-town, then you must take me for a real fool, Rebecca."

"Don't threaten me with your accusations, Bennett! Just because you have a lurid imagination doesn't mean I have to stand here and take your abuse."

"Abuse!" Dad yelled. He began to laugh, only it was a sick, creepy kind of laugh, like there really wasn't anything funny going on at all. "Do you remember what your friend said the last time? Or shall I refresh your memory?"

What friend? Who was he talking about? Sometimes Mom went away on shopping trips and stuff like that. Once last year she wrote us from Paris and then London, and when she came home about six weeks later she looked so calm and happy I knew the trip had done her a whole lot of good. Did she have friends living over there, is that what Dad meant?

I wish I'd had the nerve to barge in and demand an explanation. But I was scared to death. There was something so naked and cruel about their voices, not just Dad's but Mom's too, that I wanted to slam my hands over my ears and pretend I'd never heard them yelling at each other.

Only I couldn't do it. It was more than just curiosity, too. I *needed* to know, just like a person needs food and maybe even kindness to survive.

Had Mom told him stuff she knew she shouldn't have? She'd made all sorts of promises to me and I believed her because she was my mom and moms weren't supposed to lie or go back on their word. But maybe she'd let some of it slip out by accident. If that's what had happened it was going to take a lot of explaining to make Dad understand.

"Do you remember the story of the little girl with blonde hair and cold blue eyes? Such a beautiful child, remember, Rebecca? But such a naughty child, too."

"She wasn't naughty, he was."

"Perhaps," Dad grudgingly conceded. "But of course he's not around, so we only have your word for it."

What little girl did he mean? Was Quinn keeping a secret from me, was that it?

"I don't want to hear anymore bad stories," Mom pleaded. "Because if you keep telling me things like that, I just won't be able to help myself."

"Help yourself do what?" Dad asked.

Mom began to giggle in a way that made my blood run cold.

"Becky says please no more bad stories. Becky says she'll be a good girl."

It was Mom's voice, only she was speaking in lisping baby talk, and it barely sounded like her.

"You've promised me that so many times already—"

"No, please, Becky mean it, Daddy-waddy. Becky-wecky's gonna be a goody-girl."

"Don't do that!" Dad said sharply.

But Mom ignored him. "I'll be a goody-girl. Daddy-waddy's best li'l goody-girl ever."

What kind of game was she playing? Why was she talking like that?

I crouched down in front of their door. I just had to see what was going on in there. When I put my eye up against the keyhole there was another eye staring right back at me. I started to get up but I was so scared I lost my balance and fell back on the floor.

The next thing I knew the door was thrown open and there was Dad. He was so angry his face looked on fire. His eyes were narrowed until they weren't much wider than slits. He just glared at me, and when I glanced at his hands they were knotted into fists and all the veins were raised up so you could see how thick and blue they were.

I started to pull myself back along the floor, even as I tried getting to my feet. I was stuttering and I didn't know what to say.

But before Dad could accuse me of spying on them, Mom came up behind him. She put her hand on his shoulder like they were the best of friends, then peered down at me with such a strange look in her eyes it was as if she'd never even seen me before.

"What in the world are you doing there on the floor, Jason?" She was speaking in her regular tone of voice. There was nothing about her expression or anything else to suggest that she and Dad had been arguing. In fact, the weird thing is that she seemed so calm.

Dad reached down and yanked me to my feet. He could have pulled my arm out its socket, he tugged so hard.

"I don't like being spied upon," he said. "Is this what you've raised him to be, Rebecca?" he went on, just as if I weren't even there.

"Jason, apologize to your father," Mom told me.

"I'm sorry, really I am," I stammered. Then, before he could say anything else, I did a quick about-face and rushed down the hall to my room. I was afraid to look back, because I had this awful sinking feeling I just might see him right behind me, reaching out to grab me. But by the time I made it to my room and locked myself in he wasn't pounding on the door, ordering me to come out.

37

In fact, I didn't hear anything, except the way I was taking deep breaths and trying to calm down.

"Burn for your sins!" a voice suddenly whispered in my ear.

I whirled around. But the only person there was my reflection, staring back at me and laughing from the mirror across the room.

# 3

The birthday party was like a turning point in our lives. For several weeks afterward Jason went out of his way to avoid me. Though I begged him to tell me what was wrong, he refused to talk about it. We'd meet on the stairs like strangers, passing each other without touching the way people do on a crowded street. I carried the stag-handled knife with me for the longest time, always taking it out and pretending to admire it whenever my brother was around. But he paid no attention to either me or the present he had chosen for my birthday.

The pajamas that for some reason had so incensed my father were put away. I knew it would have been foolish of me to wear them, even though they were Mother's special gift. But I didn't want to do anything to offend him.

Father often went away on business, mostly to Washington where he did consulting work for various government agencies. His background in the law served him well, though he never talked about his work much, preferring instead to speak of it in vague generalities. Although I knew he was attached to a law firm, I didn't really know exactly what he did for them. But instead of leaving for Washington as he'd planned, he decided for the time being to remain at home.

That year Jason and I were being tutored by a young man named Mr. Finney. There was a regular public school in Juniper City, but it took nearly an hour to get there. I guess that was why we'd never had anything but private teachers, because Mother always maintained that it was unfair to have children travel such a great distance every day.

"Besides," she would make a point of saying, especially when Father was around, "the quality of education you get at home is infinitely superior."

I don't think Father really approved. Not that he didn't like Mr. Finney. But it was just that he felt we weren't spending enough time with children our own age. And that was true. I didn't have any friends but Jason, and so in the weeks of unhappy silence that followed my twelfth birthday, I was probably lonelier than I had ever been in my life.

Days went by, and then weeks, and still Jason kept his distance, avoiding me as if I'd done something terrible to him. Even when Mr. Finney tutored us in the large, drafty room that had once been our nursery, Jason acted as if I weren't even there.

When Mr. Finney finally left during the latter part of June, and the long hot weeks of summer loomed before me like some kind of insurmountable barrier ("insurmountable" was one of the words I had added to my vocabulary list that year), I knew I couldn't let things go on like this much longer. I had no idea why Jason was punishing me, and one afternoon soon after we'd seen Mr. Finney off, I decided to demand an explanation for his coldness.

I found him in the garden, half-asleep on the grass.

"What's wrong?" I said. "What have I done to make you so mad at me?"

I'd asked him that before, but now I wasn't going to leave until he told me.

A hummingbird with a shimmering ruby throat darted this way and that among the oleanders. The air was thick and dry, dense with the smells of summer. Jason had taken off his shirt to enjoy the sun, and now he rolled over onto his back. His smooth chest was already darkening with a handsome tan, and little tufts of hair had sprouted like new shoots of grass under his arms. I thought of tickling him there to get him to laugh, or even just to smile because I hadn't seen him smile in so long.

"Nothing's wrong, Quinn," he said at last. "Everything's perfect, can't you tell? We're just one big happy family."

There was such bitterness in his voice, such rage and anger, that I didn't know how to respond. I sank down on the grass, pretending to ignore the way he made a point of edging away from me.

"Is this the way it's going to be from now on?" I asked. "We're just going to be strangers, is that it?"

"You sound so serious, Quinn."

"I am serious. I'm very serious."

"You shouldn't be. After all, you're only twelve. You're supposed to be happy, giggly and light-hearted like other girls your age."

" 'Supposed-to-be's' don't count," I told him. "Besides, I don't know any other girls my age. I don't have friends like that and neither do you. We just have each other, Jason. And if you keep acting like I'm not even alive I don't know what I'm going to do, I just don't."

I hadn't meant to cry. I thought that tears wouldn't solve anything except to prove I was still a child. But I couldn't help myself. All those weeks of silence, of getting the cold shoulder, were finally too much for me to bear.

When he sat up and put his arms around me I buried my head against him, holding onto him and not wanting to ever let go. Jason stroked my hair with the tips of his fingers, whispering that everything would be all right, that he wasn't the least bit angry with me. He said he loved me more than he loved anyone else, and I mustn't ever forget that, not for as long as I lived.

"Then what's wrong?" I said between sobs. "It's not just you, either. It's everyone. Father stays in his study all the time. He doesn't even sleep in his bedroom anymore. Mother always has headaches. She never comes downstairs, not even for dinner. Everyone walks around whispering and no one tells me what's wrong."

For a long time Jason just sat there, staring at me but staring right through me, too. At last he found his tongue, and his voice was cheerier and more optimistic than it had been in weeks. "We're going to have a new friend, Quinnie. That's why everyone seems to be acting so different."

A new friend? I didn't understand what he meant. I eased away, rubbing the tears aside with the backs of my hands. Jason had never lied to me before, and so there wasn't any reason why I shouldn't believe him now.

"Who do you mean?" I asked.

He smiled at me then, and it was a smile of old, full of infectious mischief and high spirits. "No sense keeping it a secret. We're going to have an addition."

I shook my head in confusion.

"A blessed event," he laughed.

"You mean—?" I was so surprised I couldn't even say it.

"Yep, that's what it is, all right," and he nodded vigorously. "A little brother or sister, won't that be great, Quinnie? Why, we can even pretend to be its parents, if you like. We can dress it and take care of it and you can get to change its diapers—''

"Why me?" I groaned, though by this time I was laughing as hard as he was, I was so excited.

"Lefland men never do stuff like that," he insisted, saying that women's lib hadn't come to the Valley, and if he had his way, never would. "Besides," he went on, "we guys have enough to do just bringing home the bacon."

"And what would you say if I told you I didn't like bacon?" I replied, pretending to be miffed.

"Well," he said, and he kept his voice real deep and low, "we can always try for shredded wheat."

The next thing I knew we were rolling around on the grass, tickling each other and laughing for the first time in weeks. I felt so good inside, and so thrilled about the baby, that I wanted to shout with joy. No wonder Mother hadn't been feeling well. No wonder Father stayed downstairs. She was pregnant, and I imagined that it was a difficult time for her and she needed all the rest she could get.

That was probably what they were talking about the night I'd overheard them arguing. I guess Mother said she was expecting and maybe Father didn't believe her and thought she was making it up. Or something like that. But old arguments suddenly seemed not the least bit important. What counted was the blessed event, the little bundle of joy that would soon be spending its life with us.

I wanted to rush upstairs to Mother's room and tell her how happy I was. But when I suggested that to Jason he shook his head.

"I heard Mrs. Darby telling her husband it was going to be a difficult pregnancy. Mom's not going to have it so easy this time, she said."

"But why? She didn't have any trouble with us, did she?"

"Not that I know of. But she's older now, don't forget. Maybe it gets harder the older you get."

Mother was only thirty-six, and most people thought she looked much younger. That wasn't so old to have babies, was it? But then, Anna wouldn't have said that to her husband if she didn't know it for a fact.

All the darkness that had been gathering around me began to break apart, like the sun coming out from behind a thick curtain of clouds. The frantic, whispering voices that followed me wherever I went were silent now. Father had once laughed and called me his dreamy-eyed little girl, the last of the great romantics. To this day I didn't really understand what he meant, though I knew it was a compliment. But now my dreams were filled with visions of gurgling, rosy-cheeked little babies, the five of us so happy and content we were the luckiest family in the world.

If only I'd known how wrong I was, maybe it would have been easier to accept what happened. But I didn't believe that anything could possibly get in the way of our happiness. I only believed our future was filled with joy, and that each day would be better than the day before.

What a baby I was. What a big, silly twelve-year-old baby.

I was dreaming the most wonderful dreams that night, imagining all the good times we would have with the baby. I guess the idea of having a little brother or sister appealed to the child in me more than the woman Mother had said I was well on my way to becoming.

A baby was like a doll, only a doll that could do all sorts of magical things. We would play together and I would get to feed it. I'd rock it to sleep in its cradle and take it for outings in its carriage. Not only would I be a sister to the baby, but if I had my way and Mother said I could, I knew I'd be like its second mother, too.

So I dreamed of all the fun things we'd do together, me and Jason and the baby. But then I heard a door slam, followed by the sound of bare feet running frantically down the hall. I woke with a start, listening to the way my heart was pounding.

A door closed and I knew the sound came from Jason's room, because a moment later his bedsprings creaked loudly. I sat up, rubbing the wonderful dreams from my eyes, wide-awake and unsure of what I'd heard.

What had he been doing out in the hall? I wondered.

We each had our own bathroom, so it couldn't have had anything to do with that. I glanced at the alarm clock. It was nearly three in the morning. If he'd gone downstairs for a glass of milk or something to eat, he certainly wouldn't have run all the way back. Then I remembered that the footsteps hadn't come from the direction of the stairs, but from the far end of the hall, nearest Mother and Father's room.

Perhaps I should have closed my eyes again and forgotten all about it. But I couldn't help thinking something wasn't quite right. I recalled what Jason had overheard Mrs. Darby saying, that Mother wasn't going to have such an easy time of it. Was she sick? Could that be what was wrong?

Something crashed to the floor and I was out of bed so fast I didn't have time to reach for my slippers. The day's warmth had long since vanished, and the floorboards felt icy-cold against my feet. I ran to the door and flung it open.

Father was just coming out of the bedroom, and as he started down the hall he caught sight of me.

"Is Mother all right? She isn't sick or anything, is she?" I called out.

"Go back to bed, Quinn. Everything's under control." His cheeks were flushed, and his words came out breathlessly, as if he'd just been running. His backless slippers slapped fitfully against the Oriental carpet.

"Where are you going?" I was standing there by the door, but now I stepped into the hallway, reaching out for him as he hurried past me.

"Go back to bed, do you hear!" he said again. This time it was definitely an order and not just a suggestion.

"But—"

"Do as I say, Quinton. It's merely indigestion, that's all. There's nothing to be concerned about."

If only I'd told him that I thought he was lying. But I didn't. I thought he was telling the truth. Only later did I discover that what he called "indigestion" was far more serious, and that complications had arisen which required swift medical attention.

Instead of going back to bed, I waited until Father had hurried downstairs, no doubt to make a phone call. Why he didn't use the extension in the bedroom was another mystery, though at the time it didn't seem all that important. But the moment he started down the stairs I rushed next-door to Jason's room, and began to knock frantically on the door.

"Jason!" I cried out. "It's me. Let me in. What's going on?"

"Go away and leave me alone. I'm asleep," I heard him call from inside the room.

"You're not asleep. You're as wide-awake as I am and Mother's not feeling well and let me in!" The words came out all at once, tumbling one right after the other I was so upset.

More steps sounded on the stairs, only this time they

came from the third floor of the house, where the Darbys lived in a kind of self-contained apartment.

"You heard your father. Back to bed, young lady." Anna Darby, her long quilted housecoat whipping about her bony ankles, hurried toward me.

"Just tell me what's wrong," I asked.

But she was in no mood to answer my questions. Will was right behind her, though he looked rather helpless and unsure of himself compared to his wife. Mrs. Darby took charge of the situation before I had a chance to say another word. She spun me around and marched me back to my room, refusing to take no for an answer.

The moment she closed the door behind me I heard an awful sound, but by then it was already too late to do anything about it. I grabbed for the knob, trying to wrestle the door open. But it was locked!

"Now stay there and behave yourself," Mrs. Darby said from the other side of the door. "This doesn't concern you, Quinton, so go back to bed."

"You can't lock me in like this!" I shouted. "It's not fair!"

But instead of answering, she called to her husband to come and help her, they had no time to waste arguing with a child.

Oh God! I thought. Is she going to lose the baby, is that what's happening? Or has she lost it already?

I tugged at the knob, jiggling it desperately from side to side. But the only way I could have gotten out was to break the door down, and I simply wasn't strong enough for that.

For a moment I just stood there, not knowing what else to do. Then I ran over to the wall adjoining Jason's bedroom and pounded my fist against it.

"Jason, can you hear me?" I called out.

At first he didn't answer, but then the bedsprings started

creaking again. I could just about hear his steps as he crossed the room.

"Jason, what's going on? What's the matter with Mother?"

"Do as they say, Quinn, and go back to sleep," he urged.

"But what's wrong?"

"We don't know yet."

He wouldn't say anything else, though I kept begging him to talk to me. But Jason can be stubborn like that. When he's set his mind on something, no one can ever get him to give it up. I went back to the door to give the knob a last futile try, then sank down on the floor, drawing my knees up against my chest.

More rushing footsteps followed. Doors opened and then slammed shut. I thought I heard Mother moaning but I couldn't be sure if it was her or Mrs. Darby.

Finally, Father returned from downstairs, adding his own anguished voice to all the confusion. "Go get the car," he ordered. "Everything's taken care of."

"They're expecting us?" Will Darby asked.

"Yes, yes, of course they are," Father said impatiently. "Just do as I say and bring the car around."

"But how will you—?"

"That's my concern, not yours. Just do your job and I'll do mine."

"Certainly, Mr. Lefland, certainly," Will murmured.

I could picture him shuffling down the hall, clinging to the banister as he started down the stairs.

"There now, everything's going to be fine, child." That was Mrs. Darby again, and she must have been speaking to Mother.

"They won't hurt the baby, will they? You can't let them hurt the baby."

I was crying without even knowing it. Mother was

weeping, too, and I started to pound against the door, screaming to them to let me out I wanted to see her before she left.

"You're going to be fine, dear. Everything's going to be fine." Mrs. Darby spoke in this drippy saccharine voice, and somehow I had the feeling she didn't mean a single word she said.

"How could you?" Father said then. "How could you do this to us, Rebecca?"

"Leave her be, for God's sake. Can't you see she's in no condition to argue?" Mrs. Darby told him.

"Mother!" I screamed. "Mother, where are they taking you?"

"Quinton—" she started to say. But then her voice was cut short, almost as if someone had pressed a hand over her mouth, muffling her cries. There was this terrible groan of pain and then silence, silence that cut right through me and left me trembling with fear.

It sounded as if they were dragging her down the hall. I put my eye to the keyhole, but by then they'd already passed my room, and all I could see was the empty hallway. There was something else though, and the moment I saw it the tears came rushing into my eyes.

There was blood on the carpet, a bright crimson patch that was already turning dark and muddy even as I stared at it, trying to convince myself my eyes were playing tricks on me.

A few minutes later I heard the car start up. As I stood by the window a pair of headlights played across the darkness, illuminating the long gravel drive that looped its way down to the main road. Half-hidden in shadows, the tall ghostlike figure of Mrs. Darby our housekeeper stood silhouetted against the trees. She raised her arm as if to wave good-bye. Then her hand fell limply to her side, and as the car gathered speed she turned away and started back to the house.

"Let me out! Unlock the door!" I shouted the moment I heard her coming back upstairs.

"Yes, yes, all in good time," she replied.

I held my breath as the key scraped in the lock, and then the doorknob slowly began to turn. When the door swung open she reached for my shoulders, grabbing onto me and holding me tight.

"Now listen to me, Quinton Lefland, and listen good," she said sternly, her expression as hard and unyielding as a piece of slate.

"I want Mother. I don't want to listen to you. I want Mother and I want to know where they've taken her and what happened and why there's blood on the carpet." I began rubbing the tears aside with one hand while I pointed to the floor with the other.

Mrs. Darby didn't even turn around to acknowledge the bloodstain that had spread out across the runner in the hall. Instead, she tightened her grip on my shoulders, digging her fingers into my skin as she forced me to listen to her.

"Your Mother isn't well. Whatever may happen, you have to be brave, Quinton. You can't be a little girl forever. Sometimes things take place that are beyond our control, and we have to grow up almost overnight."

"I don't know what that has to do with anything," I cried. "Where did they take her? What happened and why was she bleeding?"

"Your father will explain things to you, but all in good time. I'm sure by tomorrow morning we'll know more."

Mrs. Darby finally let go of me. Although I thought she was going to lean over and kiss me on the forehead, she stepped back and closed the door softly behind her.

I stood there for a long time, or at least it seemed a long time. The tears had dried on my cheeks, and my eyes felt raw and scratchy. When there was silence, and even Mrs. Darby had gone upstairs to bed, I crept back to the wall nearest my brother's bedroom.

"Jason, please," I whispered, "just tell me it's going to be all right. That's all, just tell me it'll be okay."

"Go to sleep, Quinn. It's out of our hands."

"What is?"

Jason didn't answer, and when I awoke the next morning I found myself on the floor, my head resting against the wall, my eyes caked with unremembered tears I must have shed while I slept.

I got shakily to my feet, trying to work the cramps out of my arms and legs. It was almost eight o'clock, but the house was absolutely still. Normally I would have heard Will Darby with his lawn mower, or Anna downstairs in the kitchen preparing breakfast. But there wasn't a sound.

After hurriedly pulling on my clothes I started downstairs, but not before I noticed that the bloodstain I'd seen on the carpet was nowhere to be found. Had Anna already cleaned it up, was that what had happened? For a moment I was ready to believe that everything that had taken place just a few hours before had been a dream, a kind of frighteningly vivid nightmare that neverth less wasn't real.

But when I reached the bottom of the stairs I heard voices. Jason was sobbing, and I began to cry even before Father looked up and saw me standing there.

"Oh Quinn," he said softly, and his voice was filled with an overwhelming sadness, "Quinn, I'm so sorry. I'm so terribly sorry."

He looked old and tired, and there were dark circles beneath his eyes. His hands shook as he reached out for me.

"Is it—?" I asked, unable to bring my voice above a whisper.

Father nodded, and a muscle began to throb nervously beneath his square, angular jaw.

"But . . . but how? Why?" I stammered.

"The Lord giveth and the Lord taketh away."

I glanced behind me. Mrs. Darby stood by the entrance to the kitchen, rubbing her hands together as if she couldn't get them warm.

"Shall I serve breakfast now, Mr. Bennett?" she asked.

"Whenever you're ready," he murmured.

Then he took me in his arms and held me close. I guess he wanted to comfort me, to make me feel safe and loved. But somehow all I could feel was a terrible dark emptiness, like a hole that goes down and down and never comes to an end.

I'd be like Alice, I thought. I'd tumble down that hole and they'd never find me again. I'd get smaller and smaller and then I'd pop like a soap bubble and there wouldn't be any Quinn. There wouldn't be anything, just the empty hole reaching down into nothing, nothing at all.

Jason was terribly fond of mysteries and detective novels, "addicted to them" was the way he used to describe it. Sometimes he'd make a game of it, too, sprinkling his speech with words and phrases private eyes liked to use, tough-guy stuff is one way of putting it. But the morning of the funeral he didn't sound tough at all. He sounded sad, and he looked defeated, as if he'd just come through a terrible beating.

As I finished getting dressed before going downstairs, I kept stealing glimpses of myself in the mirror, wondering who this unhappy girl was who stood before me. I think I was numb, and maybe that's why I barely recognized myself. I'd cried for so long that now there weren't any tears left. I felt as if I were sleepwalking. But no matter how hard I pinched myself, everything that had happened didn't turn into a dream. It was all for real. And what was worse, I knew it was going to stay that way.

I'd expected to find a great many people assembled for the funeral. But the only one who came was Mother's younger sister, Aunt Gwendolyn Howe. As for Mother's parents, I knew next to nothing about them. Mother never talked about her childhood, saying there was no point in living in the past.

There weren't any Leflands there, either, and that hurt me very much. Father's brothers and sisters hadn't bothered to come, and it made me wonder if any of my aunts and uncles had ever cared for Mother, or had any respect for her.

As for Aunt Gwen, she was all dressed up as if she were going to a birthday party. "I'm a Howe," I heard her saying to Father when I came downstairs, "and Howes have always managed to come through adversity with flying colors. After all, if I managed to survive the night—" But then she saw me standing there, and the rest of the sentence died on her lips.

Julia Ward Howe who wrote "The Battle Hymn of the Republic" was a fifth cousin twice removed (who they removed her from I never asked). Mother could trace her lineage all the way back to Roger of Howe, who supposedly did rotten things to Richard the Lion-Hearted during the time of the Crusades.

To tell you the truth, I was always very curious what those rotten things were. But when I'd asked Mother about it, she said, "There's no reason to worry about blood and gore . . . not at your age, anyway," and wouldn't tell me anything else. After she said that I made a point of looking up "gore" in Father's dictionary. Blood shed from a wound, especially clotted blood, is what it said.

Gore is what I'd seen on the carpet in the hall, though I don't know why I was thinking about this at the funeral.

The ropes were creaking when they lowered the coffin into the ground. I closed my eyes and I was on a ship somewhere with creaking ropes and sails like in a book I once read about a brother and sister traveling across the sea to seek their fortune. I kept my eyes closed as tight as I could, but try as I might I couldn't smell the ocean, even though it's less than an hour's drive from where we live.

"There, there," Aunt Gwen said when I finally opened my eyes and the casket was all the way down in the ground.

I could hear the Darbys sniffling through their tears, saying what a terrible tragedy it was, Mrs. Lefland was so young. Father seemed beside himself with grief, and fresh tears stung my eyes just seeing him cry. Aunt Gwen sobbed the loudest of all, and I couldn't help but wonder if she did it so everyone would hear. She had this little piece of lace hanky clutched between her polished fingernails. They were like ten sharp berries, glistening as if they were still wet with Revlon this or Estée Lauder that. Her pouty mouth was smeared with the same color lipstick, and as she looked down at me and brushed her hand against my cheek, it made me feel very dirty though I didn't know why.

How could any of this be happening? I asked myself.

Gone were all the dreams I'd had, all the plans I'd made. They were replaced by memories now, an image of Mother I held up in my mind's eye, studying it so I wouldn't ever forget. I could see her standing before me, her blonde hair cascading down her shoulders, a golden waterfall Father liked to call it. How beautiful she was, how absolutely perfect. I wondered if one day I would ever look like her, with a face and a figure and a golden waterfall that would make people sit up and stare.

Then I edged closer and looked down at the coffin as they pulled the ropes free. The polished wood caught my reflection, an image that wavered in the hot summer air, rubbery and distorted.

"Don't leave us!" I wanted to cry out. But Jason caught my eye, his expression telling me to be brave, for that's what Mother would have expected from me.

The worst part was when they started shoveling in the dirt. I heard it hit the top of the coffin, and I wondered if they all hated Mother who was so beautiful and perfect. Hated her because it sounded as if they were throwing stones, the dry clumps of earth striking the top of the wood casket with a vicious thumpety-thump that made my flesh crawl like the word gore.

I wanted to run, just turn and run for my life. Jason seemed to know exactly what I was thinking, because he reached out and grabbed my arm, stopping me before I did anything foolish.

Father dried his eyes with the back of his hand. "May she rest in peace," he murmured. He stepped closer, then held my face in his hands. He smelled of English toilet water, a familiar woodsy scent. But when he looked down at me, so tall I had to crane my neck just to meet his gaze, there was something other than grief and anguish in his eyes, something strangely distant that made me pull away.

"It's the strain, the terrible emotional strain," commented Aunt Gwen. She and Father exchanged glances, and it looked as if they were trying to keep something from us, a secret they had no intention of sharing.

I turned my eyes back to the grave. But I couldn't cry anymore. All the tears I'd shed had gone into the ground with Mother, and my eyes were so dry they felt on fire, like tinder that roars into flame at the slightest spark.

At last it was time to go. Father put his hand on my shoulder, murmuring how the tears would come later, they always did.

Hadn't he seen me cry? Hadn't he heard Jason sobbing

pitifully in his room, refusing to come out, even telling me to please go away, Quinn, I just want to be alone?

"Give yourself time, Jason," Father said patiently.

"Time for what?" Jason said with tears in his voice. He turned away and started marching back to the house, his shoulders all hunched in against each other.

"Terrible, just tragic," remarked Aunt Gwen. She wrung her fingers together, squeezing the gory juice out of her berry-colored nails, then stuffed the damp piece of lace hanky back into her purse.

I knew Jason wanted to be alone, but that still didn't stop me from chasing after him. The path leading away from the Lefland family plot made several broad loopy turns before reaching the house. On one side a tangle of uncleared scrub stretched all the way to the gently sloping hills that ringed the Valley. On the other side of the wide dusty trail was the Bottom, where cottonwoods, willows, and oaks grew thickest by the stream which cut a slender furrow across the Valley floor. Here in the Bottom was our secret place, and though I called to Jason, shouting at him to wait up for me, he kept on walking.

Only when I was right behind him, and the road was making the second of its four wide loopy turns, did he finally acknowledge me. I glanced back, but no one was following us. We'd come in two cars, and Father, Aunt Gwen, and the Darbys were no doubt already driving back to the house. They were probably using the paved road to avoid the dust which was always the worst this time of year, with spring rains well behind us.

"Hypocrites," Jason was muttering when I managed to catch up to him.

He kicked up the dust at his feet, sending a little ocher cloud spiraling into the still, motionless air. All around us insects were humming and droning like the chorus in a

Greek tragedy—we'd had our first taste of Oedipus when Mr. Finney made us read it aloud, earlier in the year. There wasn't a single breeze, even in the Bottom, which was usually the coolest spot in the Valley. A hawk soared overhead, its rusty-red tail glimmering like bronze caught in the glare of the sun. I felt so alone then, and reached for Jason's hand. He pulled me toward him, holding me close.

"It's just us, you know. Just the two of us," he said.

"But what about Father? He'll take care of us."

Jason laughed bitterly. "Oh, Quinnie, sometimes you're just too trusting for your own good. Haven't you guessed the truth by now?"

What truth was he talking about? He could have been speaking a foreign language, because I didn't understand a word he was saying.

"It's a lie, a big lie."

"What is?"

"This whole thing," he explained. "She's not dead, Quinn. She's not the least bit dead."

I stepped back, suddenly afraid for him. "You just don't want to accept the truth, Jason. I don't either, but we can't do anything about it."

My brother's green eyes flashed angrily. "Oh, but that's where you're wrong. We *can* do something about it. We can find her, and bring her back."

"Find her?" It came out like a squeak, I was so astounded by what he said. "Jason, Mother's dead. We can't bring her back to life."

"But she's not dead," he insisted. "They're making it all up, just to trick us."

"But why would they do such a thing?" I said helplessly. "Besides, doctors saw her at the hospital. They wouldn't lie."

Jason pursed his lips together, drawing a thin, tight line

57

across his mouth. "Haven't you ever heard of the word 'payoff'?" he asked. "Everyone knows that if you have enough money you can buy anything you want, people included."

Again I noticed the hawk riding the air currents, its bright beady eyes searching the ground for something tasty to eat. I watched it swoop down, disappearing into the high grass.

"You still don't believe me, do you?" Jason said.

I just shook my head because I didn't know what to say. "Why would Father do such a thing?" I asked again. "It doesn't make sense."

"It does if you knew what happened that night. But you were asleep. You didn't hear what they said to each other."

Everything that had taken place that night came back to me in a great, pain-filled rush. The terrible memories circled among my thoughts the way the hawk was once again circling in the cloudless sky. I'd awakened from a wonderful dream, only to hear Jason rushing back to his room. Then, when I'd stuck my head out to see what was going on, Father was just coming out of the bedroom, telling me to go back to sleep, there was nothing to worry about. Then they dragged Mother away and she was bleeding. And then, the next morning, we'd learned that she had died on the way to the hospital. Although the doctors had tried everything they could, they weren't able to revive her.

For Jason to now insist that none of this had actually taken place was just too much for me to accept. Father loved us the way we loved him. He wouldn't cause us pain, or tell us Mother was dead if he knew she wasn't.

"Maybe you'll be angry at me for saying this, Jason, but I don't think you want to deal with what's happened. I think it's too painful for you, and so you're trying to convince yourself none of it took place."

"None of it did," he said angrily. "I was there. I should know, Quinn, because I saw it."

"Saw what?"

"I was in her room that night," he blurted out.

I had the feeling he hadn't meant to tell me that, only now it was too late. But what was he doing there in the middle of the night?

"I'd heard them arguing," he explained. "I don't know why, but I was afraid Dad might do something he'd regret."

"Like what?"

"Hurt her," Jason said unhappily. He looked down at his feet, studying the aimless patterns he was drawing in the dust.

"Father would never hurt anyone, especially Mother," I exclaimed. "Besides, she was pregnant."

"Yes, and he didn't want her to have the baby. He was threatening to send her away. They yelled at each other, called each other awful names. Mom started throwing things at him, ashtrays and stuff I heard crashing against their bedroom wall."

I hadn't heard that at all. But then again, I hadn't heard anything out of the ordinary until Jason had run down the hall back to his room.

"First you say she isn't dead. Then you say Father didn't want the baby, that he was going to send her away somewhere. But they were in love, Jason. They were more in love than anyone else in the world!" I guess I was shouting at him by then, but I couldn't help myself. It was difficult enough just learning to live with my loss. But now, to have him say that it was all a big fake and we were being lied to, was too much for me to accept.

"Quinnie," he said softly, "there are lots of things you just don't know about."

"What things?" I demanded.

"Like . . . their relationship."

It was such a big grown-up word, a twenty-five-dollar word as Anna Darby might have called it, that I suddenly felt like a helpless child. I didn't know what to say to him, except to nod my head and pretend I understood what he meant.

"The only reason they stuck together was because of us, Quinn, not because they loved each other."

"That's a lie, Jason! That's a terrible lie! They loved each other more than . . . more than anyone. Anyone!" I wasn't going to stand there and listen to such horrible falsehoods. Mother and Father had an ageless timeless love, burning and passionate. Nothing Jason or anyone else could say would make me believe different.

I started to run down the road toward the house, but my brother's words were ringing in my ears.

"He hated her because she loved us more than she loved him!" he shouted after me. "She told me so herself, the night before they said she died. And before you run off, Quinn, think about this. They never let us see the body, did they?"

There were other voices ringing in my ears now, the whispering voices that were much too painful to remember. *The boy suspects . . . Gwen remembers . . . The nightmares are over. They won't come back to haunt us . . .*

But they had come back, like ghosts of the past claiming their due.

I stopped dead in my tracks, trembling all over, wanting to cry and yet somehow unable to remember how. Jason caught up to me and began to shake his head sadly. His hair was like bright shiny straw, swinging from one side of his face to the other.

"You see, there's a lot of stuff going on around here we

don't know about. If Mom really died the way they said she did, then why didn't we ever see her? The coffin was nailed shut from the very start, and Dad refused to open it."

"It's barbaric," Father had said, pronouncing the word like a curse. "Your mother wouldn't have wanted it. I want you to remember her as she was, alive and happy. But to see her lying there like someone in a waxworks—"

Jason had started to argue the point, but in the end I sided not with him, but with Father. After all, it was bad enough that she was gone, alive one day and . . . no, there weren't any tears left. It was Mother, Mother who was always so kind and loving and good to us. And then, to suddenly be without her . . .

Something wet began to trickle down my cheeks. Here I was, standing in the middle of the path and crying, unable to stop myself.

"Tears are good," Jason said solemnly. He reached out and touched his finger to my cheek, blotting up the salty tears. Then he put his finger to his mouth and licked it dry. Now our grief was complete, taken like food, shared between us. "You know why he wouldn't let us see her? Because there wasn't anyone to see, that's why."

"But they carried the coffin out. It was heavy. I saw them struggling to hold it up. It weighed a lot, Jason. It couldn't have been empty."

"They must've filled it with stones, or something like that. I'm telling you, it was empty, Quinn. It had to be. He wouldn't let us see her in the coffin because she wasn't in it to begin with."

The conspiracy I now saw in his eyes, heard in his voice, was suddenly becoming all too real. It made me think of a spider web, drawing us down into its very center where the spider who called himself Father sat on his throne, smiling his evil spiderish thoughts. But I still wasn't totally convinced, because how could Father have done such a thing when I knew how much he loved us?

"But if what you say is true, and she wasn't in the coffin, that means—"

"She's still alive." The way he said it was like a victory cry. I think if he had his way and he was sure no one could hear, Jason would have shouted it out at the top of his lungs.

"Then where is she?"

"That's what we're going to have to find out, Quinnie. And the sooner we start looking for her, the better."

# 4

I couldn't be angry at Mom, that was the important thing. She was in terrible trouble, the worst trouble any person could be in, in fact. So how could I be mad at her for anything, even for telling him stuff she knew she shouldn't? Granted, she'd made all sorts of promises . . . but maybe it just slipped out by accident. That's allowed, I guess, since I'm sure she didn't mean to do it.

But Dad must have gone crazy when she told him. Just thinking of that made my skin crawl. I figured he must've goaded her into telling him stuff he had no business knowing about, then threw a fit once he found out. If he'd made her lose the baby because of it— But no, I wasn't going to think about it. I was going to concentrate on finding Mom and taking care of her, helping her escape him for good.

Of course I couldn't let on that I knew. If I did, Dad would probably have tried to send me away, too, just like he did her. But Quinn knew, now that I'd told her. And pretty soon she'd start to understand what it was really all about. Then she wouldn't doubt me for a second.

Like I told my sister, you can pay a doctor to sign a death certificate. You can nail a coffin shut and say there's a body inside and get everyone to believe you. But I didn't believe it because I knew she was fine. There weren't any complications. Even if she lost the baby and I don't believe that either, it wouldn't have killed her.

Okay, I'm not a doctor, but she was fine, I'm sure of it. Healthy and full of life. Even though she and Dad quarreled, fighting and yelling at each other when they didn't think any of us could hear, bitter words don't bring on death. Not unless someone plunges a knife in your heart, then hides the evidence. But that didn't happen, either.

No, I'm sure he didn't hurt her that way. He might have wanted to, especially after she told him what should've remained a secret. But murder's just out of the question. Whatever else Dad may be, he's no killer. What probably happened is that he sent her away somewhere, where she's being kept under lock and key. That's why it's so important that Quinnie trust me. Without her help I don't think I can find Mom on my own, especially now that Aunt Gwen seems to have come to stay.

If there's one thing we *don't* need, it's for Aunt Gwen to take over around here. She's such a busybody, too. Honest, it's true. Mom warned me about her, and she was right. The only good thing is that she still thinks we're a pair of babies, so she probably won't take us seriously.

The important thing now is finding Mom. So I have to be as careful as possible not to let on how much I know. If Dad found out he'd have me locked up somewhere, too. And if Quinnie was left alone, I don't think she could take it. Not that she isn't strong, emotionally I mean. But all this time we've only had each other. There's no one else, no friends at all. And besides, don't forget we're Leflands, and Leflands have been in this Valley for over a hundred years. Leflands have always kept to themselves, too. Even my dad, whose work takes him to Washington and all over the country, still says he prefers the Valley. He says it's the only place where he can really find peace of mind.

Some peace, I thought. But the joke's on him now. He figured he could pull the wool over our eyes, get us to cry our hearts out and believe Mom was dead. She isn't. She's as alive as I am, just waiting for us to find her.

When Quinnie and I got back from the cemetery, Aunt Gwen came rushing over to us. She'd been crying (her mascara was all streaked, so it was easy to tell), and for a moment I felt sad to see her so upset. But then I thought again of what Mom had said, how Aunt Gwen couldn't be trusted. So when she started sobbing, saying how we shouldn't worry because she'd look after us, I just pretended not to hear.

"Now go into the kitchen," she said as she dried her eyes. "Mrs. Darby's made a lovely snack."

I knew Quinn so well that it was easy for me to tell what was going through her mind. She wasn't any more taken in by our aunt than I was. But for the time being I knew we had to be polite, and pretend to appreciate her concern. I didn't want Dad to start complaining we were fresh, or getting out of hand. It was important to keep them fooled. Then, when their guard was down, we'd be able to do what had to be done.

So we put up with all her fake babying, and trooped off to the kitchen. Anna Darby was just setting out two tall glasses of milk and a plate of oatmeal cookies. At the risk of sounding like I have a grudge against everyone—and honest, I really don't—I'd better tell you right off that I don't trust Anna, either. I'm not sure what it is, but every time I looked at her I felt uneasy. I guess maybe it's because there's something about her that's very mean looking. She's tall and sharp-edged like the blade of a knife, all skin and bones and with these big ugly liver spots on her temples and the tops of her hands. I just had this awful feeling I had to watch out for her, and I made a mental note to tell Quinnie to be on her guard whenever Mrs. Darby was around.

"Will says you can't buy oatmeal cookies good as mine for love or money," she said as she put the plate down on the table. Will sort of looks after things around here, does the gardening and groundskeeping. We used to be a lot closer than we are now, but I guess he's not so bad.

Anyway, we sat down at the table and started on the milk and cookies. Mrs. D. had been baking us treats for as long as I could remember. But today the cookies left a bad taste in my mouth, because all I could think of was Mom. I even started wondering if Anna had anything to do with Dad's plot, if she was in on it, I mean.

Quinn wasn't in a very talkative mood, which was just as well, because I didn't want her to start giving anything away. Mrs. D. was getting dinner ready, going on and on about a lot of stuff neither of us cared about—how Will was going to plant this and that, how the roof needed fixing, and if someone didn't come out and pump the cesspool there'd be hell to pay. She was probably just trying to keep her own spirits up, but who cares?

"Harry's coming," she said with her nose in a pot, and steam rising up from something she was cooking. She tried to sound casual about it, but I knew it was probably the most important thing on her mind.

Right away I had this real sinking feeling in the pit of my stomach, knowing things were getting a lot more complicated than I'd imagined. Harry's their son, their only child. I guess he's about eighteen now, but I'm not sure.

Every summer, Harry comes up from the city, L.A. that is, to spend July and August with us. He lives with his

aunt and uncle, Anna's sister I think, because there weren't
any schools around here for him to go to.

Since he was so much older than us, and since Mom
didn't especially care for him, no one ever suggested he
study with the tutor who stayed on at the house right after
Labor Day. The Darbys had to decide what to do, to board
him out with strangers in Juniper City where the school
was located, or ship him down to Los Angeles where he
could live with relatives. They decided on the relatives.
But every time Harry's come back to the Valley he's
gotten meaner and meaner, or at least that's the way it's
always seemed to me and Quinn.

He once told me how much he resented his parents for
sending him away. "You'd think I was a fucking orphan
the way they treat me." Harry's always been bitter and
angry like that, dropping dirty words just to impress you.
He's a real bully too, and that was another reason why I
wasn't looking forward to seeing him again.

Just as I was sitting there worrying about Harry being
around, Dad and Aunt Gwen came into the kitchen.

"It took a little convincing, but your aunt's agreed,"
Dad said with a grin. I think he was trying to put on his
best face, get us to forget what had happened. But it
wasn't all that believable. "She's going to be spending the
summer with us. Isn't that great?"

I knew enough not to say anything. But if looks could
kill, Gwendolyn Howe you better watch out!

"But what about your job?" Quinn piped up.

"Kindergarten doesn't start again till September," Gwen
replied. "I'll have all summer to be with you."

"Which works out just fine," Dad went on, "especially
since I have to be leaving in a couple of days. Conference
in Washington. You understand."

No, I didn't understand. If Mom was supposed to be
dead, if that's what he wanted us to believe, then why was

he already packing his bags? It seemed to me that if a person loses his wife, he doesn't rush back to work. And if he loved us the way he kept insisting, he should be spending time with us, helping us to get over Mom's death, instead of leaving it up to his sister-in-law.

See what I mean? As far as I was concerned that was added proof Mom couldn't possibly be dead. Dad was probably going to check up on her. Maybe he wanted to make sure she wasn't thinking of escaping and making her way back to the Valley from wherever it was that he'd stashed her away.

Anyway, I figured it was probably all for the best, because the plans I had would work out better if he wasn't around to check up on us. But Quinn wasn't half as silent about it as I was.

"Didn't you tell the people in Washington what happened?" she demanded.

I knew what she was trying to do. But if she hoped to make him feel guilty, she didn't succeed.

"Life has to go on, Quinn. That's only natural, and healthy. And don't forget, I still have to make a living for you guys."

"I know you care about us, Dad," I muttered, forcing myself to sound polite, even though I knew he was just piling the lies one on top of the other.

"That's what I was hoping you'd say, Jason. I'm sure you and your sister are going to make your aunt feel very much at home. Aren't you, Quinn?"

"You'll be bored," Quinn told her. "There's nothing to do all day. We don't even have a pool."

"Oh, I think I can keep myself busy. Your father says there are caves up in the hills that might be fun exploring. And I'd like to hike around and see the countryside," Gwen told her.

"The caves are full of rabid bats. You go up into the

68

hills during the day and mosquitoes and ticks eat you alive. That's why the people Grand-grandpa hired to build the house left the day it was finished. And I wouldn't start nosying around the shacks they left behind, either," I warned her. "Last year Quinn and I came face to face with a mountain lion. She was using it for a lair."

"My, what excitement," Gwen replied in a sugary voice that put my teeth on edge.

Dad jumped right in and started making excuses. The bats weren't rabid, he insisted. The only place where mosquitoes ever got bothersome was in the Bottom. As for mountain lions, there hadn't been one reported in the county in a good twenty years.

"Then it was a bobcat, but it sure was big," Quinn insisted.

"Maybe we'll be lucky enough to see it again," Gwen told us. "I'm sure there'll be plenty of things to keep us amused."

Out of nowhere, a voice started booming in my head. *A professional virgin. If cunts could talk, hers would have nothing to say.*

Where in the world did that come from? I wondered. I'd almost never heard language like that in my whole life. But I was sure I'd heard someone use those very words, and not that long ago, either. Maybe it was Dad. He must've said it to Mom when he thought no one was listening.

That's when I suddenly realized something I hadn't even considered. What if Dad and Aunt Gwen were in this together? What if they'd planned Mom's "death" from the very beginning? I could've kicked myself for not seeing it sooner. But now when I looked at them, Dad with his arm draped over Gwen's shoulders, the two of them standing so close together you could feel the bond between them, I started seeing what I hadn't ever suspected before.

I couldn't wait to tell Quinn what I was thinking. So right away I pushed my chair back, finishing what was left of the milk in a single gulp.

"We have to go," I said.

"What's the big hurry?" Dad asked.

"We promised to help Will do something."

If he found out later I was lying, so what. After all, I had the perfect excuse, because how could he get angry at a kid who'd just lost his mom? He couldn't, and that was just fine with me.

# 5

**S**o many things were going through my mind that I felt dizzy. I wanted to believe Jason, not just because I loved him and he was as much my friend as he was my brother, but also because it scared me to think he was making it all up. But I also wanted to believe Father, because I loved him, too. Yet one was telling the truth and the other was lying.

You see, I don't think I could have been more confused if I tried. And if what Jason said was true, that Father and Aunt Gwen were in this together because they were in love and wanted Mother out of the picture, then things were going to be a lot more complicated around here than I'd ever imagined. It was hard enough picturing the two of them together, kissing each other and whatever other stuff they did. But to picture them hurting Mother, sending her away from us, was so terrible I just wanted to scream and scream until they all swore on a stack of bibles it wasn't true.

But what if it was?

I was alone in my room, waiting to hear the whispery voices, probing my thoughts like needles. *The boy suspects . . . How could you do this to us, Rebecca?* Do what? What had she done? And if the boy was Jason, what had he suspected that made Father so upset? *Their lives depend on it . . .* Depend on what? Were we in danger now, too? But Father was looking out for us when he said that.

Oh God, why didn't it make sense? Why was it all so confusing? I wondered if maybe I should just go to Father, tell him what I'd overheard, ask him to explain what all the words meant and what the secrets were all about. But I was afraid to admit that I'd spied on them, because that would have proven to him that I could never be trusted.

Outside my window the sky was pitch-black. The great horned owls were sitting up on the television antenna on the roof of the house, making spooky noises at each other, wide-awake while everyone else was supposed to be sound asleep. Jason was in his room next to mine, and I was lying in bed thinking of all that had happened, wondering what we were going to do.

Two things were clear. Harry was coming and Aunt Gwen wasn't going. And it wasn't funny, either. Harry Darby's never been very nice to Jason, even though he's been okay to me. I guess we both knew he'd end up coming, because there hadn't been a summer when he wasn't around. But maybe Jason thought that because of what happened to Mother, Anna and Will would tell Harry to stay in the city.

So it didn't seem like we had anything to look forward to. If what Jason suspected was true, and for the time being I decided to keep an open mind, then I had no idea how we'd be able to find Mother, especially if she was being held miles away from here. Jason knew how to drive, because Father had let him try the car out around the house. But I didn't see how he could drive for miles without a license, and without even knowing where he was going, and where he'd finally end up.

There it was again, that confusion of loyalties. One part of me wanted to believe my brother, if only because I missed Mother terribly and wanted her back. But the other part didn't want to be disloyal to Father, either, because if Mother had really died, then I knew he was going through as difficult a time as I was just trying to cope with his grief.

When I heard someone knocking softly on the door, I scooted out of bed and went to answer it. Then I realized if it was Father he'd be angry, because I was wearing the shortie pajamas Mother had given me for my birthday. I'd put them on as a kind of remembrance, just so I could feel closer to her. But I knew Father didn't like them, even though I wasn't sure why. And if he saw me wearing them he might think I was being purposely disobedient.

When Jason and Father weren't around, Mother had told me they were very sexy, saying it was time I started wearing pretty, feminine things. I wanted to know what sexy meant—the explanation in the dictionary left more to the imagination that I thought was fair. But when I asked, Mother said there'd be time enough for that, my whole life in fact, and I shouldn't go rushing into anything until I was ready.

It all sounded very mysterious, but now I had other things to worry about. "Who is it?" I whispered.

"Guess."

I didn't have to since I recognized Jason's voice right away. As soon as I let him in, he closed the door behind him, taking care not to make a single sound. Then he put his finger to his lips, just in case I didn't get the message. I asked him what was wrong—which must've sounded stupid, considering what he'd already told me.

He had on pajamas too, the regular kind that Father always wore, with buttons down the front like a jacket, and loose, flapping pants. I thought they looked silly, especially when I remembered what Jason had once told me. Men didn't bother wearing P.J.'s, he'd insisted. But if they didn't wear pajamas, what did they wear?

"Their birthday suits," Jason had said, giggling and making a face like the explanation of gamine in Father's big dictionary.

"Are they all asleep?" I asked.

He nodded and started giving me this strange look, like he'd never seen me before and didn't even know my name. It gave me the funniest feeling. He was staring so hard that I crossed my arms over my chest like we were Indians at a powwow, though I wasn't even sure why I did it.

"You know," he said, "we just might be missing something. For all we know, they could be hiding her right here in the house."

"But they drove away. I saw them leave."

"But you didn't see them come back, did you?"

I had to admit that I hadn't.

Jason began rubbing his hands together like the solution to all our problems was right under our noses. After all, he went on, what better way was there to fool us? If they'd only pretended to leave and then come back, they wouldn't need strangers to look after her. They could do it themselves.

"But Will went with them," I protested.

"So? Who's to say he isn't being paid not to talk?"

"Then what should we do?" I whispered.

"Just follow me and keep your eyes open. They might be taking turns guarding her, Dad and Aunt Gwen and Mrs. D. We wouldn't want to surprise them, so we have to be very careful. Frank and Joe Hardy once had to search a

74

house for clues while the crooks were still there. If they could do it, so can we."

So we slipped out of my room and into the hall. Jason wasn't wearing slippers, and I left my fuzzy ones behind too, following him as he started down the hall in the direction of the stairs.

On either side of us were doors opening into bedrooms, and between each door hung a lit portrait of one Lefland ancestor after another. There was Great-grandfather Josiah, and right opposite him his wife Hepzibah. Then, further down the hall hung the portraits of their children; strange, moody Orin who left the Valley one summer's afternoon and was never seen or heard from again, and his sister Zenobia whom Jason used to call "the Chin," because hers stuck out so far that was the only thing you ever noticed about her.

Grandfather Ephraim watched us too, a little disapprovingly I thought. His picture was there along with both his wives, the beautiful Alethea about whose sudden death little was ever said, and the woman who later took her place, Father's mother, the stern and haughty Lavinia who had died just a few months before Jason was born.

Closest to the stairs hung Father's portrait, as well. Though he always insisted it wasn't a very good likeness, that he got mad at the painter and refused to smile because he had to stay in the house and pose for days on end, the eyes of the little boy in the painting belonged to Bennett Lefland and no one else. As for Mother's portrait, it hung over her bed, where anyone who opened the door could see it looking back at them from across the room.

As we passed by each picture I had the strangest feeling that we were being watched, and maybe even judged. All the Leflands were staring down at us from their places on the wall, and I began to wonder if they knew what had happened. Maybe if we'd had our portraits painted it wouldn't have been so bad. But Father said he wanted to wait until we were a little older, just so we wouldn't get mad at the artist the way he had.

"What do you suppose they're thinking?" I whispered as Jason gripped the smooth polished banister and started up toward the attic.

"That we don't find out their secrets."

"What secrets?" I kept right behind him, the soles of his bare feet looking white and ghostlike, rising and falling with each step he took.

"Lefland secrets. Skeletons in the closet and dirty deeds. Haven't you ever wondered why Alethea was murdered? And what do you suppose happened to Great-uncle Orin?"

"He got bored and left?"

Jason glanced back and made a face. "They killed him so he wouldn't spill the beans. He knew all their secrets, the evil things they'd done over the years."

"Whose secrets are you talking about?"

"Great-grandpa's and all the others. Lots of strange things have happened in this house, Quinn. Mom told me about some of them, and I know she wouldn't lie."

I was hoping he'd explain things a little more clearly, but by then we were on the third-floor landing and had to be as quiet as possible. The Darbys had two rooms up here, a bedroom with a view of the garden, and a sitting room where Will sometimes worked on balsa wood models of clipper ships and locomotives. I'd often heard Anna complain she was a light sleeper, and so now we had to take extra special care to avoid detection. If she came out of her room and caught us, we'd have to come up with a pretty good excuse to convince her we weren't up to any mischief.

From the third floor to the attic the stairs weren't half as wide, and there weren't any runners to absorb the sounds of our footfalls. Every time Jason took a step it was accompanied by a telltale creak. So it seemed to take forever before we reached the top of the stairs. There wasn't much of a landing, just a little pocket of a space and then the attic door.

I was getting so nervous I couldn't stop giggling. Even though Jason glared at me and shook his head, I had to put my hand over my mouth so I wouldn't make any noise.

He turned the knob and the door swung open, a musty smell like piles of old newspapers seeping into the air and down our lungs.

"There's a light here somewhere." He motioned at me to close the door.

I couldn't see much of anything, just shapes and shadows all jumbled together like the inside of the general store in Juniper City. But when I reached back and closed the door, the moment it clicked shut I had this awful feeling, like someone was holding my head underwater and I couldn't breathe. I grabbed hold of the knob, but before I could yank it open Jason pushed me away from the door and found the long dangling cord for the overhead light. It was a bare twenty-five-watt bulb, but as soon as he turned it on I began to feel a little better.

"What are you being so jumpy about?" he whispered.

"I don't like it up here, Jason. It gives me the creeps."

"Scared of Great-uncle Orin's ghost? Maybe he and Alethea are going to come back to punish the people who murdered them."

"They weren't murdered. You're just making it up."

"If you don't believe me, then ask Mom about it when she comes back. She was the one who told me about the curse in the first place, how the first wives of Leflands always died under mysterious circumstances."

"Orin certainly wasn't anyone's wife."

"I know. But I'm sure his murder had to do with the

curse. Maybe he found out what was happening and tried to put a stop to it.''

I realized what he was trying to do, scaring me for no other reason than he thought it was funny. So I kept taking deep breaths, and gradually I began to calm down. Now that the light was on I could see that the jumble of shapes were just things, not monsters about to rear up out of the darkness and devour us alive.

Suddenly I heard something scurrying through the shadows. I clutched Jason's arm so hard that he flinched.

''A rat, that's all,'' he said. ''Stop being such a sissy.''

I wasn't particularly afraid of rats, but cobwebs were something I definitely wanted to avoid. I didn't like the feel of them, all dusty and sticky, always getting in your hair. There were plenty of them, too, hanging down from the ceiling like dull, tarnished tinsel. The attic was much longer than it was wide, and it seemed to stretch on and on. At the farthest end I could see more shadowy shapes, cartons and old steamer trunks, packing cases and pieces of furniture, long discarded. There was a collection of three-legged chairs, and two lopsided chiffoniers made of wood that was so dark it looked like it was painted black.

With the door closed and the windows sealed shut, the stale, musty smell hung in the air, so thick you could almost see it. Each time I took a breath it felt like cobwebs were getting into my lungs. I had the hardest time just trying not to cough, because I kept thinking that right under our feet lay Anna Darby, the lightest sleeper in the Valley.

''How come they've never cleaned this place up?'' I asked.

''Mom said it gave the house charm. Besides, what would a Victorian house be without a dusty old attic?''

A lot less creepy, I thought.

But one look was enough to tell me that even if Orin

and Alethea's ghosts were watching us, Mother certainly wasn't. How could she be, when there wasn't any place to hide?

By then, Jason was already starting to poke around. He was doing something to the long wall opposite the windows, and as I watched he put his hands flat against the unfinished boards, touching them all over as if he were blind. I was sorry I hadn't put on slippers, because the floor was covered with all sorts of mucky dust, like ooze that gets between your toes when you stand in the middle of a stream.

"It's got to be here somewhere," Jason whispered.

I made my way toward him, sidestepping someone's big padlocked steamer trunk, covered with labels that had faded out so completely you couldn't tell where they'd gone. "What are you looking for?"

"I bet there's a hollow space behind the wall. There always is."

"Maybe on television, or in mystery books. But not in real life."

"Don't be so sure, Quinnie. A house as old as this one can have all sorts of secrets we don't know about. After all, Great-grandpa moved here for a reason."

Instead of telling me what that reason was, he started tapping his fist against the wall. But though I listened carefully, the sounds were all the same, and I didn't think he was going to have much luck.

"It stinks up here," I said. "How can you breathe?"

"Breathe through your mouth if it bothers you. It's just mildew or something."

"Something," I muttered, "and whatever it is it doesn't smell very nice."

"Instead of complaining so much, why don't you get to work?" He told me to check the wall at the far end of the attic, and so I picked my way through the jumble of broken furniture Leflands had been storing up here for over a century.

Even though I wasn't exactly sure what I was supposed to look for, I copied Jason, tapping my fist against the wall, from one board to the next. I guess if there was a room hidden away on the other side the sound would be different. But each time I tapped, there wasn't any change in the tone.

I was about to give up when Jason suddenly hissed at me between his teeth. He raised his hand, jabbing his finger in the direction of the door. I swear to God I thought I was about to come face to face with Alethea Lefland's ghost, all dressed in tattered rags and with the bones showing right through her skin.

I rushed back to Jason. Just as I reached him I must have stubbed my toe on something, because the pain shot through my foot and I cried out, unable to stop myself in time. At that moment I heard it.

A groaning, creaking sound drew near. It seemed to come from the other side of the attic door, and I grabbed hold of Jason, squeezing his arm for dear life.

"Don't be scared. It's probably just the house," he whispered.

Again we heard the creaking. When I saw a shadow pass below the threshold I knew it couldn't be the house, or the wind rustling through the trees in the garden.

"Remember, we were just up here exploring," he warned.

"In the middle of the night?"

"What's the difference? We couldn't sleep, and we thought it'd be fun."

I could think of a hundred other things I'd rather be doing. Before I had a chance to count them off the door-knob began to turn and the hair stood up along the nape of my neck, I was so frightened.

The door suddenly swung open. Although I gasped, it

wasn't Great-uncle Orin's ghost who'd been creeping up the stairs. Instead, Father stood in the doorway, looking so tall and imposing that his head nearly touched the lintel.

"What the hell is going on around here?" He sounded more annoyed than angry, and right away Jason and I started stammering, trying to come up with a likely excuse.

"We couldn't sleep," Jason said.

"We were overtired," I added quickly.

"We were wondering if we could turn this place into a playroom."

"And I was looking for Grandmother's collection of antique dolls."

"Your grandmother didn't collect dolls, antique or otherwise." Father motioned us to step forward. After hesitating a moment, Jason finally led the way.

I was hoping he'd tell us to go back to bed and that would be the end of it. And it would have been too, if Jason hadn't opened his mouth the moment Father turned away and started back downstairs.

"What exactly did Mom die of?" he asked.

Father stopped in midstep and looked back at him. An expression of either anger or confusion passed across his face. "Didn't I tell you, Jason?"

"No, not really."

"She was bleeding . . . internally I mean."

"Hemorrhaging?" he said.

"Yes. Exactly. They couldn't stop it in time."

"And the baby?"

Father jabbed his hands into the pockets of his robe. "The baby was too young. It was the miscarriage which caused the hemorrhaging." He sounded so sad that I couldn't help but feel sorry for him. "I know it's still difficult for you, son. Just give yourself time."

Jason gave him a halfhearted nod and followed Father down the stairs. But when I looked at my brother I could see how his hands were shaking. The hard, angry fists he made quivered as if they had a life of their own. I knew he didn't believe a word of what Father had said.

And as for me, I think I was beginning to have my doubts, too.

When I came downstairs the next morning, Jason and Father and Aunt Gwen were already halfway through breakfast.

"What took you so long, sleepyhead?" Father asked. He was buttering his toast, and there was nothing in his expression or tone of voice to indicate that he was annoyed at us for what had happened the night before.

I took my place at the table, and when Mrs. Darby came out of the kitchen to ask how I wanted my eggs I told her I wasn't very hungry, thank you.

"Suit yourself," she said. "Only don't come running to me an hour from now moaning how starved you are."

The door leading into the kitchen swung shut behind her. Jason looked up at me from across the dining table, toast crumbs caught in the corners of his mouth. He gave me a big smile, as if to say everything was going to work out fine, and I should just pretend nothing was wrong. But how could I pretend when I looked over at Mother's empty place? Mrs. Darby hadn't even set a plate there, the way she always did. I thought that was really mean and disrespectful. Why should we erase Mother's memory so quickly, putting her out of our minds when I wanted to remember her as clearly as possible.

I could even hear her laughing too, telling me that if I didn't watch myself I'd turn into a shredded wheat. (I had no taste for my favorite cereal this morning.) And speaking of shredded wheat, she would say, that's just what your hair looks like, Jason. What happened, dear, did you comb it with a rake? Nope, a pitchfork, he'd reply, and they'd start to giggle like two little kids sharing a secret.

But this morning Jason's hair was neatly combed, and the laughter and giggles that were as much a part of breakfast as shredded wheat were noticeably absent. In fact, it was probably the most depressing breakfast I'd ever had, the four of us sitting there and not even knowing what to say to each other.

"I've been thinking about school," Father announced when the silence became so heavy I could almost feel it like a weight pressing down against my shoulders. "After all, September isn't that far off."

Jason stiffened in his seat. He looked at me with anxious eyes, afraid of what Father was leading up to. "Isn't Mr. Finney coming back?" he asked. "You haven't fired him, have you?"

"No, of course not," Father replied. "But don't you think you're both too old for a tutor? After all, at boarding school you'd have a chance to make new friends."

We didn't have old friends, so what was the good of new ones? I was about to tell him that when Aunt Gwen interrupted me.

"It's very important to spend time with your peers," she said. "You know what 'peers' are, Quinn, don't you?"

Jason spoke up before I had a chance to say anything. "Sure she does. Quinnie's not dumb and she never was."

"There's no need for such hostility, Jason," said Father. He sounded like he couldn't wait to rush to Aunt Gwen's defense.

"I wasn't being hostile; I was being honest. And besides, we don't want to go to boarding school. Do we, Quinn?"

"No. We like things just the way they are."

"But there's a whole world out there." Father raised his

hand and made a broad, sweeping gesture, encompassing everything in sight. "You can't stay in the Valley forever."

"Why not?" Jason asked.

"It's not healthy, dear," said Aunt Gwen.

"It's not healthy to separate us, that's what's not healthy," I told them.

"Now don't raise your voice, Quinton," said Father. "I haven't decided one way or the other."

Jason suddenly pushed his chair back and sprang to his feet. "Yes you have!" he yelled. "Because the answer's no. We're not going. We're not going to let you separate us the way you did with—" He stopped short, afraid to speak his mind.

"Jason dear, your father's only trying to be helpful."

He looked over at our aunt, and for a second I thought he was going to hurl a big gob of spit at her, he was so furious. "Who asked for your opinion, anyway?" he shouted. "Why don't you go back to L.A. where you belong, and leave us alone? You'll never take our mother's place. Never!"

Aunt Gwen put her raspberry fingernails to her throat, where a little vein was pulsing like a heart. Her eyes got all wide and teary, but I was certain it was just a performance, one that was probably designed to arouse Father's sympathy.

"Apologize, Jason." Father leaned across the table and grabbed him by the hand.

Jason wrenched free and stumbled back. "I won't, and you can't make me, either. You can't make me do anything. And we're not going away to school, are we, Quinnie? We're not going to let you separate us."

Mrs. Darby poked her head out of the kitchen to see what the commotion was all about. By then, Jason had already taken off. I could hear his footsteps as he raced to the front door, flung it open, and hurried down the gravel path that snaked back and forth through the garden.

Then there was silence. Father stared at his empty coffee cup. Aunt Gwen stared at her long gory fingernails. And I just looked down at my plate and watched the butter melting on my toast.

"You mustn't be angry with him, Bennett. You know what a shock it's been," Gwen told my father. She reached over and patted him on the hand. Father returned the gesture by putting his hand on top of hers, and gradually his unhappy expression began to fade.

But why were they touching each other like that, and acting like I wasn't even there? Weren't they ashamed of what they were doing? Didn't they realize we knew what had happened? Jason said the coffin was empty and Mother was still alive. I missed her so much I wanted to believe him. And now, when I saw them holding hands or just about, I was more convinced than ever that they were lying to us.

"You hardly ate a thing," Gwen said when I got up and excused myself.

"It's the shock," I told her.

Before Father had a chance to tell me not to be sarcastic, I hurried from the dining room. I didn't stop running until I was outside, where the roses blooming in the garden brought a fresh surge of tears to my eyes.

But Jason wasn't anywhere to be found, though I called to him again and again. When he didn't answer I glanced back at the house, wondering if he'd snuck inside to continue his search. I was about to go back in when it suddenly occurred to me that now was a perfect opportunity to find out more about Mother's whereabouts.

So I crept around to the side of the house, taking care not to crush the flowers Mother had asked Will Darby to plant for her. Anna had thrown open the French doors that led into the dining room. As soon as I reached them I could hear their voices.

"—more difficult than I imagined," Father was saying. "But it just couldn't be helped, Gwen. I didn't have any choice."

I stayed out of sight, pressing my back to the wall nearest the open doors. I didn't have any trouble hearing them, and if it was wrong to spy I didn't care about that either, because I had to find out what was going on and if they were lying to us.

"Of course you didn't, Ben. I understand what you went through. It was a nightmare, but now it's over."

"It's not," Father said with a groan.

I couldn't tell if he was crying, but when I leaned over a little to peer inside, Gwen was standing behind his chair. She had her hands on his shoulders and her lips rested against the top of his head.

"Will they ever forgive me, Gwen?"

"Yes, in time. But now they're too young. They'd never understand."

"He would. He's too damn clever, that's his problem. He's beginning to think like an adult. He knows when you're talking down to him, and he resents it."

"But Quinn's a stabilizing influence. She'll help him," Aunt Gwen replied.

"Oh God," Father suddenly moaned, and he buried his face in his hands. "Why didn't I see it earlier? Why was I so blind to the truth? It's my fault, Gwen. If only I could have stopped her in time."

Stopped her from doing what? They were talking about Mother, but I couldn't make sense of what they were saying. Then I heard the most terrifying thing of all.

"Do you think he suspects?" Gwen asked. She even looked around as if she were afraid Jason might be listening.

"Probably not. But we'll have to be very careful and watch what we say. We can't let him know—"

"Know what!" I wanted to cry out.

But Mrs. Darby had come into the dining room to clear away the breakfast dishes. The moment she walked in, Aunt Gwen hurriedly stepped away from Father's chair. I couldn't help but wonder if Anna made her nervous. Maybe she didn't want Mrs. Darby to get the wrong idea about her and Father.

*Do you think he suspects?*

The words echoed in my ears, getting louder and louder until I couldn't even hear myself think. Do you think Jason suspects what we did to his mother? That's what Aunt Gwen meant to say, I was positive.

*We'll have to be very careful . . . We can't let him know . . .*

I ran through the garden, tripping over myself I was so desperate to find my brother. I knew then that Mother hadn't died a natural death the way we'd been told. Either they'd killed her or sent her away. But why? What had she done?

*If only I could have stopped her in time.*

Stopped her from doing what?

Jason will know, I kept telling myself. He'll know exactly what Father meant, and what to do about it, too.

# 6

I wasn't surprised, not in the least. When Dad announced he was thinking of sending us away to school come September, I knew it was just part of their plan to separate us now that they'd gotten rid of Mom. They'd probably try to keep us apart as long as they could. Then, by the time we got back together again they'd already be married, sleeping in Mom's bed and congratulating themselves on being so clever.

And all that baloney about peers . . . what did Gwen know about me, anyway? What did she know about what it was to be a Lefland? Mom never trusted her and now I didn't, either.

*Gwendolyn and her virgin ears. Call her a cunt and she'd probably have a heart attack.*

My skin started to crawl, but that didn't solve the problem, because there it was again, that awful nasty voice whispering in my ear, reminding me of things I didn't want to think about. I only wanted to concentrate on finding Mom, nothing else.

Not to worry, Lefland, not to worry, I kept telling myself. They weren't going to keep me away from Mom, and they weren't going to keep me away from Quinnie, either. We needed each other, all three of us. We were like a team, and that was something Dad never understood because he was always off somewhere on business, never able to find enough time for us. So it was just Mom and Quinnie and me, loving each other and making sure we were all safe.

But where was she? She wasn't in the coffin, and if I had to dig it up to prove that to Quinnie, then that's just what I'd do. You see, I needed my sister's help, and I needed her to believe in me the way Mom believed, saying Jason you're the smartest boy there ever was, and when you grow up you'll be the smartest, cleverest man.

The truth of it is I was well on my way to becoming a man. If Aunt Gwen knew that, I was sure she'd be surprised, especially since she thought we were babies, five-year-olds happy making choo-choo trains out of empty cookie boxes, just like they do in kindergarten.

I'd heard Quinnie calling to me earlier, but I didn't want to talk to her then. I just wanted to be alone for a little while. But now she came running, her arms and legs churning like windmills she was in that big a hurry. I was sitting by the koi pond that didn't have any fish. The last of them had been dinner for a family of raccoons, more than a year before.

"Didn't I tell you he wanted to separate us?" I said as soon as she came near. "Didn't I warn you this might happen?"

But Quinnie wasn't listening, or if she was it was only with half an ear. The moment she sat down beside me she started telling me what she'd overheard in the dining room. And just like everything else, I wasn't surprised.

"See? I wasn't making it up," I said when she was finished.

"But what does it mean, Jason? They think you suspect. But what?"

"What I've been telling you all along. We have to find Mom before it's too late."

"You mean they might kill her?"

She sounded terribly frightened, but it couldn't be helped.

"Of course they'll try to kill her. They don't want her getting in the way."

"So what do we do?"

"Elementary, my dear Quinton. The game is afoot."

I may not have been Sherlock Holmes, but I was still determined to give it my all. We had to be very organized, and so I suggested we finish checking out the attic before we went on to the cellar and every other room in the house. Then, when we'd exhausted those possibilities, we'd have to consider what to do next.

"You really think they haven't taken her somewhere?" Quinn asked.

I honestly didn't know. "Why don't we just play it by ear," I said. "Besides, we have thirty some-odd rooms to search. That should keep us busy for awhile."

I came to my feet and looked down at her. She seemed so delicate and cute as a button that I just wanted to protect her for the rest of her life. We were alike, Mom had said, two peas in the same Lefland pod. Quinnie wasn't just my sister, she was also my friend. That was another thing. Dad had said we needed friends, but then why hadn't he ever encouraged us to go out and make any? He could have sent us to summer camp, but he never did. He could have insisted we go to school in Juniper City even if it took an hour to get there, but he didn't do that, either. No, he just let us stay here in the Valley and never once complained about it. But now he was suddenly changing his tune. I think the only reason was because we were making him nervous. He was probably afraid we'd find out what he and Gwen had done to Mom.

I told Quinnie to wait a few minutes. Then, when the coast was clear, she'd meet me up in the attic. When I slipped past the dining room on my way to the stairs, I could hear the two of them at the table. Gwen said something about prep school and the need for role models. Dad agreed, saying, "They're too dependent on each other. It's stifling."

I didn't think it was stifling at all. If anything, I considered myself very lucky to have such a good friend in my sister.

When I heard him scrape his chair back I bolted up the stairs, not stopping until I reached the attic. I snuck inside, then leaned against the door and tried to catch my breath.

"Mom, can you hear me?" I called out in a whisper.

I felt very dumb not having thought of that before. If there was a room hidden away on the other side of one of the walls, maybe she could hear me. Chances were she was probably bound and gagged. But maybe she could tap out a message in Morse code, and I'd be able to hear it through the wall.

But Mom didn't answer, though I kept calling until I thought I'd lose my voice. Then I noticed something that made me realize I was getting pretty good at this detective business. One of the steamer trunks piled in the middle of the attic had been moved. There were footprints in the dust, and when I bent down to examine them I could tell right away that they weren't the prints Quinnie and I had made the night before.

Whoever had been up here hadn't gone barefoot. There were shoeprints, and then long marks like tracks where the trunk had been dragged across the floor. Someone had obviously snuck up here sometime between last night and this morning. But why?

I was still trying to figure that out when Quinnie arrived. "They were looking for something," she said when I showed her the footprints. "We'd better get the trunks open and see what's inside."

I was glad to see her starting to take charge of things, because it was just another way of proving that she trusted me.

"Thank God you're finally believing me," I whispered. "I really need that, too. I need it more than ever, because if we don't find Mom—" My voice cracked. I couldn't even bring myself to say it, that without Mom what good was living, what good was anything?

Quinnie reached out and cupped my face in her hands. Her skin was so smooth and soft, and her eyes were nearly as blue as Mom's. She had so much love for me that I wanted to cry. She wrinkled that little pug nose of hers, and I thought, She's so strong, she's so brave, probably a lot braver than I try to be.

"I love you, Jason. So you mustn't worry. We'll find Mother. It'll just take a little time, that's all."

Men weren't supposed to cry or show their emotions, but I couldn't help myself. I felt the tears welling up under my eyes. Before I could stop them they were rolling down my cheeks. If only I could get it all out, once and for all. If only I could cry until I'd used up every last tear, and all the dark places in my head were filled with light again.

Quinnie wiped my eyes dry with the tips of her fingers. I don't know what came over me, but I grabbed her hand and pressed it to my lips. "You're not going to ever leave me, are you? I like to think I'm strong and able to take care of myself. Only sometimes I feel like a baby, even though I don't want to be."

"You're not a baby, Jason. You're stronger than all of

them because you have faith, and you understand what love means."

Maybe she was just saying that to make me feel better. Love was so complicated that I couldn't even begin to figure it out. Although I knew what the obvious part was like, the pleasure I mean, I realized there was still a lot more to it than just trembles and stiffening. There was love that was like touching without fingers or bodies. And there was the other kind of love that was like thoughts snuggling up against each other. I wanted to tell Quinn about that, but by then she was already too busy trying to get the trunk open. Fortunately, it wasn't locked, and though it took a little doing, we managed to undo the rusty bolts.

Inside there was a big roll of yellowed paper tied up with string, so brittle it started to fall apart when we touched it. Next to it was an American flag with a lot less stars than the fifty we have now. And at the very bottom of the trunk there were piles of letters, some postmarked the turn of the century, and others much more recent.

When Quinn noticed that a bunch of them were addressed to Miss Rebecca Howe, 1049 Montgomery Street, she could barely contain her excitement.

"It's Father's handwriting," she said as she undid the faded black velvet ribbon that was tied around them. "When do you think they were written?"

Judging from the postmarks, most of them had been sent a few months before they got married. Quinn removed several sheets of thick gray paper from the topmost envelope. Then she hesitated, and suddenly thrust them into my hand.

"If a man wrote them, then a man should read them," she announced. She sounded real proud of herself, and when she smiled mischievously I couldn't help but smile too, because I felt much better now.

So I cleared my throat and got right down to business.

" 'Dearest Darling Girl,' " I began, warning Quinn not to giggle even if it sounded mushy. " 'It's only been three days since I held you in my arms, but it already feels like a hundred lifetimes, my darling.' "

Quinn sighed softly, and a dreamy look came into her eyes.

" 'I can picture you as if you were standing right beside me, your beautiful smooth breasts rubbing gently against my lips.' "

Again she sighed, as if this were just what she'd always imagined love was all about. "Go on, keep reading," she urged.

To tell you the truth, I really didn't want to. It was wrong to read about things like this. I wanted to forget the letter and go back to checking out the rest of the attic. But Quinn wouldn't hear of it.

"Come on, Jason, it's exciting," she said, impatient for me to continue. "Do you really think he did stuff like that?"

"Maybe. Once," I grudgingly conceded. I looked down at the letter, shaking so hard the piece of fancy paper was rattling in my hand. " '. . . against my lips. Never have I felt so sure of my love, my dearest darling Rebecca. I ache now just recalling what it was like when we were together, how I held you tightly, feeling the full warm length of your body.' "

"That's so romantic," whispered Quinn. "What do you think happened next?"

"They had sex together," I said angrily.

Maybe I shouldn't have said that, because Quinn didn't seem to understand. But instead of asking me to explain, she grabbed the letter out of my hand and began reading it aloud.

" '. . . touched you in all those secret places.' What's that supposed to mean?"

I didn't want to go into it, and so I told her it wasn't important.

"But it must be, Jason, or else he wouldn't have written it. And I bet you don't think I know what sex means, do you?"

I tried changing the subject. But sometimes Quinnie can be just as stubborn as me or Mom.

"It's intercourse, isn't it?" she said. "Mr. Finney explained all about zygotes and gametes and things, don't you remember? Intercourse makes babies. That's how the species survives. But it's more than just breeding, isn't it? I mean, people do it for other reasons, don't they, Jason?"

"I guess." I still didn't want to go into it, but she was so insistent she wouldn't leave me alone. Maybe it was wrong to tell her stuff Mom should have discussed with her first. But until Mom came back, Quinn was counting on me to take care of her. And if taking care of her meant explaining the facts of life, I guess I didn't have any other choice.

By the time I finished telling her what the whole thing was about she was shaking her head like she couldn't believe it really happened that way. "How did you find out about it?" she asked. "Did Father tell you?"

If she only knew how funny that sounded. "He never tells me anything, you know that."

"Mother then?"

"Maybe."

I think that confused her as much as my explanation of sex. She glanced down at the letter. "He touched her breasts and then he got on top of her and touched her secret places . . . what places, Jason?"

"Can't we go into this later? It's so hot up here I can't breathe."

"We should open those windows then," she suggested.

She motioned to the dormers across the room. "The smell's even worse than it was last night."

I started toward the windows. Only before I could get to them something very strange began to happen. I just stood there in the middle of the attic, listening and listening and so excited I was afraid to even breathe.

"What is it?" whispered Quinn.

There it was again, a voice or something very much like a voice, calling out to us. I looked all around, but I couldn't tell which direction the sound was coming from.

"It's Mom. It just has to be."

I ran to the window, tearing at the cobwebs that covered the moldy panes of glass. Something moved down below in the garden. I was sure someone had darted back into the shadows, but now I couldn't see anything.

By then, Quinn was standing right beside me. "What is it? Was someone there?"

"I'm not sure. You stay up here and keep looking. I'll go down and check."

I hurried downstairs, and by this time I didn't care if anyone saw me. Maybe Mom had managed to escape, and now she was trying to attract our attention. I'm sure I'd heard her, a cry or a whimper or something like that. But though I combed the garden, there weren't any clues like broken branches or footprints, scraps of torn cloth or anything to prove someone had been there.

"Looking for something, Jason?"

I whirled around, having been taken completely by surprise. Aunt Gwen peered at me from under the wide brim of her straw hat. I smiled as politely as I could. "Buried treasure," I said with a good-natured laugh. "Great-grandpa left a fortune in gold somewhere around here."

I think she knew I was pulling her leg, because she grinned and said, "And what will you do with it all when you find it?"

"I'll share it with you, fifty-fifty. Honest." Then I smiled again and nonchalantly strolled back to the house. Quinn was waiting for me on the second-floor landing, and I took her by the arm and led her down the hall to my room. "Don't worry, Quinnie, we'll find her."

"If they're hurting her, Jason—" She couldn't even bring herself to say it. Instead, she threw her arms around me, and when she began to cry it was enough to break my heart.

I held her in my arms, trying to comfort her. My lips nuzzled the top of her head, her blonde hair smelling of grass and wildflowers. It was good to feel her against me, to know that she needed me as much as I needed her. I held her even tighter, knowing I couldn't let go because if I did she wouldn't have the strength to face things on her own.

"Hey, what's with the tears," I said, trying to make a joke of it. "We haven't given up yet. We've only just started. Listen, we'll search every single room if we have to. If we heard her, then maybe she's already managed to escape. She obviously wants to find us as much as we want to find her."

Quinnie's whimpers slowly died away. She edged back until I could see her breasts moving under her polo shirt. They were like two little apples, and it made me realize she was already growing up into a woman. But I don't think she understood that yet. Mom hadn't had a chance to explain things to her, and Dad probably didn't care enough to even bother. It was all up to me now. I had to be everything for her, Mom and Dad and brother and friend, all rolled into one. But I loved her then more than I thought possible. And when you love someone like that, and care about them, it's a big responsibility, know what I mean?

"We'll find her, Quinn, I swear we will. As long as we don't give up, we'll find her before it's too late."

"Too late for what, Jason?"

The words tore at my throat, and I could feel my eyes beginning to fill up with tears again. "Before they kill her," I said, "and put her in her coffin for good."

# 7

I was too scared to tell Jason what I'd found. When he went out to search the garden, I stood by the window for a few minutes, hoping to catch a glimpse of Mother. The breezes turned the leaves from side to side like the rustling pages of a book. But I didn't see anything else, and when Jason disappeared among the trees, I turned my attention back to the trunk where we'd found the love letters.

There were so many letters to choose from that I didn't know where to begin. So the first thing I did was sort them out, because I was only interested in reading those that Father had sent to Mother when they were courting. I found two piles in all, the second tied up with the same black velvet ribbon as the first. But then, at the very bottom of the trunk lay a sheet of yellowed newsprint, and when I pulled it aside I found a beautiful little book, all bound in dark red morocco leather.

It was the prettiest book I'd ever seen. When I picked it up, there was something about just holding it in my hands that made me feel good, like it was some kind of link to

- my past. I wondered who it had belonged to, and so you can imagine my surprise when I opened the book and turned to the front page.

*PROPERTY OF REBECCA HOWE.*

The words were written in a painstaking script. Though at first glance it seemed to resemble Mother's handwriting, there was something about it that struck me as still unfinished, perhaps even childish. When I turned to the next page, my suspicions were confirmed by the date of the first entry.

*"October 25, 1956. Dear Diary . . . ."*

But that was Mother's birthday! And in 1956 she would have been ten years old. What a marvelous discovery, I thought. But then I began to read what Mother had written when she was a little girl, and all the joy I'd felt a moment before vanished under a cloud of fear and confusion.

> *"Your the only one I can talk to Diary. I'm afraid of Papa and Mama can't help me. Gwennie's too little and she can't help me either. I only have you Diary and so I'm going to be good and write everything down so I won't forget.*
>
> *"He tried to hurt me again Diary. Yesterday he took me down to the celler and said I was a bad girl playing with Mama's lipstiks and had to be punished cause bad was against GOD. But he didn't want to get the new dress dirty I wasn't supposed to wear till the birthday party. So he made me take it off and he hung it up and said now it was going to stay nice&neat. It was cold in the celler and I was scared Diary. I was real real scared.*
>
> *"Papa made me climb over his lap like when I was very little only I was going to be ten and a big girl.*

*Mama said so. But then he hurt me Diary. He hurt
me terrible. I cried and cried and begged Mama to
come & help me. But she didn't. She stayed away
cause she said Papa was right I was bad. And bad
girls had to be taught a lesson so they won't forget
GOD and the BABY JESUS are always watching even
when your sleeping.*

*"Papa said I'd burn in HELL for being a mean
girl. He said lipstiks were for the DEVIL. When I said
no please Mama wears lipstik too he said she is filled
with sin and just as evil as me. He called me a
daughter of SATAN and wouldn't stop hitting me with
his hand and his belt that he folded in two so it hurt
even more.*

*"And if you tell your Mama what we do down here
he said I'll find out and only make it worse Rebecca.
I said Becky will be a good girl Daddy I swear to
GOD. He said don't blast or some word like that and
pushed me off his lap so I fell on the floor near the
pile of coal. I was all dirty and crying it hurt so bad.
Then he made me*

*"I hear him coming to my room Diary. I better
hide you till tomorrow."*


I slammed the trunk shut, turned off the light, and
rushed downstairs. I meant to show Jason what I'd found,
but I suddenly remembered what I'd heard the night before
my birthday. It was like a puzzle, and now the first few
pieces were starting to fit together.

*What happened in the past is a dead issue. The night-
mare's are over.*

Was this the nightmare Mother had been referring to?
Father had said that Gwen remembered, and then Mother
shouted that she was much too young, that it was all a
dream for her. Could this be what they were arguing about

that night? Could something have happened when Mother was a little girl, something that Father was determined must never happen again?

I hurried down the hall to my room, and though I thought I'd sit there and read the rest of the diary from start to finish, I heard Jason talking to Aunt Gwen in the garden. The next thing I knew he was on his way upstairs, and I didn't even have time to think about what I was doing.

I hid the diary in my bookcase and went out into the hall to meet him. Maybe it was wrong of me not to tell him what I'd found. Maybe we should have read the diary together before we did anything else. But it was private, a secret. Mother had hidden it away in the attic for a reason, and that reason was because she didn't want anyone to know about it. I felt a little ashamed of myself, I guess, especially since Mother had often talked about the need for people to respect each other's privacy. Whenever I went to her room I always made sure to knock first, and never entered unless she gave me permission.

Perhaps I was afraid she'd find out what I'd done. Or maybe I was just afraid Jason would react very much the same way, angry at me for violating Mother's privacy. But they had their secrets too, things they never shared with me. So maybe it was jealousy, the feeling that I deserved to have a secret of my own. Whatever the reasons, and I suppose I can make endless excuses for myself, I didn't say anything about the slim leather-bound diary. But all I could think of was the little girl who had written it. She had grown into a beautiful woman, a woman whose past was still a great mystery to me. Yet it was that very mystery which I was now determined to solve.

We searched the attic from top to bottom, finishing what we'd started the night before. Even then we kept on looking, until the heat and the musty stench made us realize we weren't getting anywhere. Before we left, Jason pocketed Father's love letters. I didn't say anything about it because of the diary. But it made me feel a lot less guilty, knowing that now he had something he could call his own.

From the attic we proceeded to the cellar. I thought we might have better luck there, but Jason didn't seem nearly as confident. The stone walls were as solid as they looked, and when we finally went outside my eyes began to tear and I felt like a mole, blinking and squinting in the sunlight.

I was still trying to make sense of all that had happened, not only the way Jason was certain he'd heard Mother's voice, but also the diary and the letters, or the one in particular we'd read. It was strange to hear my brother explaining what sex was, and I wasn't so much confused as surprised by it all. I was beginning to understand why Mother had used the word "sexy" to describe the shortie pajamas she'd given me for my birthday. Perhaps that was why Father had disapproved of them so, saying he found them cheap looking. But I'm sure they must have cost a great deal of money because of all the hand-stitched ruffles and special material.

Still, it was all very strange, now that I knew what people meant when they spoke of the facts of life. Childhood was suddenly like a memory, like an album of old photos where you point and say, "Was that really me?" I was Quinton Lefland, twelve years and a couple of months old. Yet those twelve years seemed like decades, and the little girl in the old family album might very well have been my daughter, not myself.

Aunt Gwen was in the garden, wearing a big floppy straw hat that made her face look like it was peeking out at me from inside a wicker basket. "Why don't you put on a bathing suit," she suggested, "and come sit in the sun. You're getting awfully pale, Quinn."

Why was she trying to be so nice? After what I'd seen and heard in the dining room, the last thing I wanted to do was be her friend. But I guess I felt a little sorry for her, too, because she seemed to be trying so hard to be pleasant, instead of bossy like she usually was.

"I have enough freckles as it is," I told her. "But thanks anyway."

"We really should sit down and have a talk, you know. I bet we have a lot of things in common."

"Like what?" I asked, only I made sure to say it politely so she wouldn't go to Father and complain I was being fresh.

"You're going through a difficult time, Quinn. You're growing up in leaps and bounds. Now that your Mother's gone, wouldn't it be nice if you had someone to talk to?"

"About what?"

Aunt Gwen smiled nervously, and her fingers played with the brim of her hat. "Whatever you'd like," she said.

"Maybe later on." I was angry at myself for being taken in by her. She was going out of her way to be nice to me, but I knew she couldn't be trusted.

As I turned away she called after me. "There are things you just don't know about, Quinn."

I looked back, staring at her so hard she finally had to lower her eyes. "Like what?"

"I only want to do what's best, for you and Jason both."

"You sound like Father."

"He loves you, more than you can ever imagine," she replied.

But instead of answering I just kept walking. I wasn't going to let her trick me into liking her, not until I knew all the facts. Besides, Jason had told me to meet him in the Bottom, where no one could spy on us while we made plans. I didn't want to keep him waiting and so that's where I headed, still thinking about sex and the facts of life that were so much more than just breeding and making babies. If only Mother were here to explain things and tell me it would be all right, every girl becomes a woman, and it wasn't nearly as difficult or mysterious as I imagined.

Halfway down the cemetery road I found the overgrown trail that led through the Bottom, where the heat of the morning was caught in the boughs of the cottonwoods, and the ground was still cool and damp. Birdsong filled the air, and a moist earthy smell tickled my nose.

I waded across the creek, the water barely coming up to my ankles, just a slow lazy trickle lapping against the mossy stones. Up ahead was our secret place (I'd always called it that, so it had nothing to do with the secret places Father mentioned in his letter), a playhouse Father had made for us when we were little. Actually, Will Darby had built it, but an architect friend of Father's drew up the plans. The playhouse was a miniature cottage, perfect down to the last detail, with a picket fence and shutters that opened and closed on every window.

Now, the paint was faded, and what was once a bright glossy white was dull and gray, peeling in spots the way skin peels if you get a sunburn.

When we were little, Mother had planted dozens of flowers, all kinds of wonderful bulbs that came up in the spring. I remembered how excited I used to get when they finally began to bloom. There were rows of dark glossy maroon tulips (Jason always said they reminded him of dried blood) called Queen of the Night, and deep-red ones with fringed edges known as Burgundy Lace. Jason's favorite kind had long pointed petals of white and cherry red, a special wild strain called Peppermint Stick which Mother had to send away for, all the way to Connecticut I think. But now there wasn't a single tulip or hyacinth or daffodil. There was nothing but weeds and skunk cabbage covering the small plot of ground in front of the playhouse.

I had to crouch down a little when I went inside, and that too made me think of my brother's explanation of the facts of life. When I was a little girl the playhouse was just the right size, and I could always walk right in without having to bend over.

I started to close the door when I stopped short. Right away I knew someone had been here before me. Not that anything had been touched or disturbed. It was the smell that was different, a light, delicate scent of wild roses that meant only one thing. The air was filled with Mother's perfume. I hurried outside and began to call to her, thinking she might be hiding in the woods, might even be watching me without my knowing it.

Twigs snapped loudly, and suddenly all the birds stopped singing. Then, from behind a hedgelike row of old, overgrown raspberry bushes, I thought I caught a glimpse of someone.

"Mother, is that you?" I shouted. "Wait for me, please!"

I ran past the broken gate and the sagging picket fence. Why was she afraid of me, that's what I couldn't understand. But the raspberries were too dense and covered with thorns. I scratched my arms and legs in a dozen places trying to get through them.

You were imagining it, I told myself. There wasn't anything there except maybe a squirrel.

But when I returned to the playhouse, the scent of Mother's perfume still hung in the air, and I was certain she'd been here just a short while before.

"Why didn't you run back to the house and get me?" Jason asked when he finally arrived, maybe ten minutes later.

Before I could explain he rushed outside, shouting Mother's name at the top of his lungs. He didn't seem to care if anyone heard, he sounded so desperate. But Mother didn't answer. Jason kept shouting and begging her to come back. He tore through the raspberries when I told him that was where I thought I'd seen her. But all he got for his trouble were cuts and scratches.

When he gave up and came back inside, the first thing he did was open the windows to air out the playhouse. It made me wonder if it was too painful for him to sit there breathing in the fragrance of Mother's perfume. Then he squeezed himself into one of the child-sized chairs that were part of a set of four (two of which we'd broken years before) and paused to catch his breath.

"Why do you think she ran away?" I asked.

"I don't know. Maybe someone else was spying on us and she didn't want them to see her. Or maybe she's so confused and frightened she can't think straight."

"Like the sick headaches she used to get?"

"Maybe."

"But what if we can't find her, Jason? What do we do then?"

He took a long time before answering, and when he finally did his voice was grim. There was a look in his eyes, a kind of determination I guess is the best way to describe it, I'd rarely seen before. "We'll have to dig up the grave," he said somberly, "and open the coffin."

Just thinking of that gave me the creeps. It suddenly felt very cold, and I wrapped my arms around myself trying to get warm. "And if she's there?"

Jason's expression turned hard and cynical. "She won't be," he insisted.

"But if she is?"

"Then we'll know for sure that Father murdered her." He sounded absolutely convinced, and nothing I could say would make him change his mind. "Right now, what we have to do is keep looking. We can't let ourselves get discouraged, Quinnie. But we also have to keep an eye on Dad and Aunt Gwen. There's something going on beweeen them, and it makes me very suspicious.''

''Like touching each other in those places he wrote about?'' I asked.

''More than just touching,'' Jason confided. ''I have a feeling they're sleeping together, going to each other's rooms when no one's looking.''

I wasn't sure what he meant by ''sleeping together.'' When I asked, Jason smiled, explaining that it was just a polite way of saying sex.

''They really do that?''

''Everyone does it,'' he said. ''It's as natural as breathing.''

I felt the air going in and out of my lungs, and with it the last traces of Mother's rose perfume. But if everyone did it, then why didn't I? It was something I very much wanted to ask, but I felt too embarrassed and unsure of myself. After all, I didn't want my brother to think I was still a child, and not the woman I was supposed to be on the verge of becoming. So I just nodded my head, and pretended I knew exactly what he was talking about, even though I really didn't.

It wasn't until late that evening that I was able to dig the diary out from behind the back of my bookcase. All afternoon I'd wanted to read it, but Jason kept me busy with his plans. Certain now that Mother was hiding nearby, he suggested we continue our search of the house. So we spent much of the day going from one room to the next. There were over thirty in all, and we'd carefully gone over more than half of them on the upper floors when Anna called us down for dinner.

Although my brother insisted there was something going on between Father and Aunt Gwen, something which he referred to as "sleeping together . . . and not because they're tired, either," I saw nothing at dinner to indicate there was any truth to his suspicions. Certainly they were polite and friendly to each other. But there was none of the hand-holding I'd seen earlier, nor did their eyes linger on each other the way I'd often seen when Mother and Father were together.

While we waited for dessert—I wanted to excuse myself, but Father said, "What's the big hurry, Quinn? Isn't it nice now that we're all together?"—Father asked us what we intended to do while he was away. He planned to be gone for at least two weeks, and though I started to groan, Jason glared at me, and so I pretended not to be upset. I guess he was grateful for the time we'd have alone, for it would enable us to look for Mother without worrying that Father might interfere.

"Would you like to go up to San Francisco for a few days with your aunt?" he asked.

"What for?" Jason said. "There's nothing there."

"Then how about Yosemite?"

"It's too crowded. Besides, we like it here. Don't we, Quinn?"

The idea of going to San Francisco was wonderfully appealing. Mother had taken me there on a shopping trip, nearly a year before. It was the first time we had been alone for any length of time, and I felt closer to her that weekend than I'd ever felt before. But to share that experience with my aunt didn't seem quite the same. So when Jason vetoed the idea I wasn't all that upset.

Father obviously realized he wasn't making much headway. So instead of pressing the issue, he told us to think about it, the choice was ours.

"And if we just want to stay here?" asked Jason.

"If that's what you want, that's fine with me. I just thought a trip might do you good."

"I really don't feel up to it," Jason admitted. "Not so soon after . . . you know."

Yes, we all knew what he meant, and later, when I went upstairs, I could hear him sobbing in his room. But when I knocked on the door and asked if he was all right, he told me to please go away, he was fine.

I wasn't going to argue the point, not when I had Mother's diary to read. So I dug it out from behind the row of books where I'd hidden it, then got into bed and made myself comfortable.

The reading lamp cast a cheery glow on the closely written pages. When I closed my eyes I could picture Mother as a little girl, sitting in bed with the beautiful morocco diary propped against her knees, a stub of pencil clutched between her fingers.

I picked up the narrative where I had left off. But almost immediately the warm, tender feelings I had were replaced by emotions of despair and mounting terror. Yet even then I couldn't stop reading, for I found myself drawn deeper and deeper into a nightmare of cruelty and suffering, a tale of unrelenting horror that I could neither have dreamed of nor imagined on my own.

> *"October 27.*
>
> *"Dear Diary I'm sorry I didn't write down anything yesterday. I know I promised to but I couldn't cause of what happened on my birthday which was supposed to be fun but it wasn't. He was mean again to me Diary. He was meaner than ever but I still don't know what I did wrong. Mama says its my fault making him mad like that. But I didn't want to make him mad I wanted him to love me like I love the BABY JESUS. Only GOD doesn't watch me when I hurt. Do you GOD? I waited and listened real hard but he doesn't answer. He never answers.*

"It was going to be a nice party, Diary. Mama said so and she baked a cake and everything. Even Gwennie who is little got excited. Mama said I could ask my friends from school. Miss Blair my teacher helped me make a list and I gave the names to Mama. She said OK you can have six friends come to the party. Only don't tell your Papa I'll tell him. I asked Mama why cause it was my birthday and he knew that too. She said don't ask stupid questions child just be good & stay out of his hair.

"What did that mean, Diary? Papa has black hair real dark and mine is like the yellow color crayon. Mama says its blond and behave yourself or else you'll be in big trouble Rebecca. I didn't want to make trouble honest. I wanted to be good for Papa so he'd like me and wouldn't do things in the celler again.

"After school was over on my birthday which was Thursday I came home with the friends on the list for the party. Two girls named Rose Hotchkins and Aimee Trumble who is the tallest girl in class so she stands at the back of the line brought me presents. They were so beautiful, Diary. I never saw gold paper like that and the ribbons too. I thought I'd save them for later to put in my hair and make a bow. The other girls didn't have presents but I didn't care. They were my friends & were glad for me since it was my birthday and I was ten.

"When we got home Mama had the cake out on the kitchen table. Gwennie was there sucking her thumb and a bottle. Mama said you make in your diaper child you'll have HELL to pay. Rose Hotchkins giggled something nasty to Aimee and Beth too who didn't bring a present but I like her. She sits behind me in Miss Blair's room.

113

"I didn't want Gwennie to cry so I said to Mama its OK I'll change the diaper. Mama looked at me mean like I said a wrong thing. Then she told me to stand near the cake & blow out the candles.

"I did that and got them out all at the same time. Everyone clapped & Rose Hotchkins said open the present Becky you will like it a lot. My mother got it for you special.

"But Papa came home from work when I got the ribbon off. He came into the kitchen where the party was and the cake and everything. He said

"October 28.

"Last night I had to stop cause I heard him coming down the hall to my room. I don't want him to see the diary Miss Blair my teacher gave me. It is a secret. She didn't say so but I did. I have to have it cause no one else knows what happens here in this house which I hate hate hate. GOD knows and the BABY JESUS too. But they don't do anything about it so I must be a bad girl like Papa always says.

"Papa came home like I wrote yesterday. What's this?? He said it so loud everyone stopped talking all at once & looked at him funny. The kids ten years old Mama said to him. At ten you all ready had tits on you Mrs. He laughed but I was shamed in front of my friends cause that word he said is bad. Sinfull too.

"Mama said shut your face for a change. Papa slapped her in front of everyone & Gwennie dropped the bottle & started to cry. You shut your hole too Papa said to my sister who is very little she don't know better. I got to go now said Rose Hotchkins & she looked all around for her coat. Mama had put it somewhere in a closet I think. Me too said Beth and

Aimee & Gail who has yellow hair its blond like mine. But Papa didn't let them go right away. He said open the G*dam present first lets see what the kid got her.

"It was a red sweater so pretty I cried. It was so nice & special just for me. Then Diary he did the terrible thing. He took it out of my hand & grabbed it away & said to Rose Hotchkins my friend tell your kunt mother red is for the DEVIL no daughter of mine is going to wear the color of sin.

"I thought he would give it back to Rose but he didn't. He ripped it Diary. He ripped it up bad. He tore it & Rose and my friends ran out of the house without there coats on. Mama had to get them down from the closet & bring them into the St. where they were waiting & crying. It was cold but they were crying mostly cause he is a mean bad man Diary.

"Yes it is true. I hate him, Diary. I hate him I HATE HIM I'M GOING TO KILL HIM SOME DAY I HATE HIM!!!

"November 3.

"I couldn't write cause I was sick in bed. Miss Blair called on the telephone to ask when I was coming back to school. I heard Mama say she is OK it is just the flu you know how children are always catching one thing or another.

"It was a lie, Diary. I didn't go to school cause he used the belt on me after everyone ran out of the house cause of what he did with the red sweater. When they left I wanted to leave too only where would I go I'm only ten. I hid in my room but the door won't lock. He came in and found me hiding under the bed. He dragged me by the arm down the hall then down the stairs bumping myself all over to the celler.

*"You are going to learn the nature of sin he said. Mama I screamed & screamed only she didn't come. She never does. He ripped the new dress off like he ripped the sweater. I was real cold. He didn't care. Get over here he said. Then he pulled me over his lap like the last time. He took the belt off and hit me with it.*

*"How does it feel Becky-wecky? He giggled & I said please no more Daddy-waddy cause when I say that some times he stops. Only he didn't stop not this time. He kept hitting me over and over. When I woke up I was in bed, Diary, and hurting all over. Mama was yelling at him in the kitchen saying you want to get us into trouble with the cops??? Her teacher is a nosy kunt she'll come & take her away. You want that to happen you big prik???*

*"He slapped her hard then came into my room. I hid under the covers. You tell anyone what goes on round here Becky and I'll beat the living shit out of you. You hear?? I hate him, Diary. I think he did that mean thing to me again cause it hurts there when I touch. But when I looked under the covers I didn't see blood like last time so maybe not.*

*"November 6.*

*"Miss Blair I said. This was yesterday at school when I got there in the morning. I hurt but Mama said you go to school child. Your Papa don't mean nothing. Liars. Both of them telling big fat lies all the time and hurting us. Me & Gwennie both. Miss Blair I said please can I talk to you? How are you feeling Rebecca she asked? Not so good I said. I started to cry even if I'm ten and a big girl. What is wrong said Miss Blair? I told her what Papa did to me in the celler.*

*"Then Miss Blair took me by the hand and we*

*went to see the Nurse where you get the needles. She asked me real nice to take off my dress to show her. I was shamed but I did it anyway. Oh My GOD!!! That is what the Nurse and Miss Blair said. Did he do anything else to hurt you Rebecca they asked? I said yes. What???*

"*I pointed where Mama said I shouldn't not ever. Miss Blair made a face like she was going to be sick like when my stomach hurts. The Nurse who is very nice too said HEAVEN help us I wouldn't have believed it if I didn't see it with my own two eyes. Then they called someone on the telephone I don't know who.*

"*November 11.*

"*Diary, This place is nice only I miss Gwennie. A man came to school and told me he worked for the City. He said he was going to help me cause of the mean things Papa did. I stayed one night with Miss Blair she has a real nice apartment on a pretty St. with trees. She was so nice to me, Diary. I wish she was my Mama instead of the real one. The next day Miss Blair took me back to school. She held my hand in hers it felt real good. After we went by bus to this house where I'm staying till Mama & Papa are nice to me again.*

"*The lady here is sweet. She is old but nice. Her children are all grown up she says I can be her little girl. I like her but I miss my sister. Gwennie will come and stay just as soon as she can the lady says. Her name is Mrs. Stern. I like her she smells of cake & vanilla icecream.*

"*January 8.*

"*Dear Diary, I didn't write anything down because I was so happy. Miss Stern was my foster Mother. She was better than the real one. Just like she prom-*

*ised me Gwennie came here to live too. She didn't make in her diaper or anything but used the potty. She is getting big & talks all the time. Mama & Papa went away to a place for bad people. That is what Miss Blair who is still my teacher told me. But today they are good and they are coming to get us and take us home.*

*"But this is home now, Diary. This is the best home I ever had. Gwennie thinks so too even if she is little. I'm afraid, Diary. I'm real real afraid. Mrs. Stern cried when they came in a taxi for us. Papa had on a new suit. He looked nice and so did Mama. She had tears in her eyes when she saw us.*

*"Mrs. Stern took me into the kitchen and gave me a silver doller. She put it in a napkin and said it was mine I shouldn't tell anyone it was our secret. She made me say her telephone number. I memorized it like the multiplication tables. You call me if you have any problems. That is what she said, Diary. I think I know what problems she meant & I was scared.*

*"January 11.*

*"He did it again, Diary. He said he didn't want to but he did & if I told he'd kill me dead. He got into the bed with me when Mama was sleeping. I tried being asleep but he knew I wasn't. Becky-wecky. That is what he called me. Becky-wecky your Daddy-waddy is here honey. He touched me in that place. I was scared terrible. Miss Blair said it was wrong and evil. Also a big sin. He didn't care he did it. First with his finger like tickling. Then the other part he has. It hurt terrible . . ."*

I was going to be sick. I couldn't help myself. I felt nauseous and dizzy and I ran into the bathroom and leaned over the sink.

How could such horrible things have happened? How could people have allowed it, knowing what she had gone through? I kept asking myself those questions, but I didn't have an answer.

My stomach cramped and knotted. Beads of sweat stood out on my forehead. But I couldn't bring anything up. I guess it was fear that made me feel so ill, a kind of nameless dread for the anguish my Mother had suffered. When the dry heaves finally began to subside I washed my face with cold water, and when I glanced at myself in the mirror I looked green, I felt so sick.

So this was the nightmare Mother and Father had spoken of that night. This was the childhood of terror she'd forced to endure. But what kind of parent could do that to a child? I couldn't even think of them as my grandparents, but rather this monstrously evil couple who had willfully set out to destroy my mother's life. That she managed to survive their torment not only seemed a miracle, but testimony to her great strength. Yet she come through it, had grown into a woman, had fallen in love. And then . . . then something had happened, something that still remained a mystery.

Had my Howe grandparents come back, was that what it was? Had the grim nightmare of her past, my Aunt Gwen's past as well, returned to haunt her? Was that why she'd gone away, why Father had said she had died? Were the grandparents set on destroying what little happiness Jason and I had left?

Perhaps the answer could be found in the diary. So I dried my face and went back to my room, determined to finish reading Mother's story, no matter how painful it turned out to be.

But the slim leatherbound volume was gone!

I'd left it on my bed, but now it was nowhere to be found. Then I noticed that the door to my room was ajar, though I'd made sure to close it securely earlier in the evening.

I raced across the room, flung the door open, and rushed into the hall. Silence greeted me, not the silence of a tomb, but the bitter, loveless silence of a tortured childhood, of suffering beyond my imagination. I'd hoped to hear footsteps, quick and furtive, hoped that I might be able to chase after the person who had crept into my room to steal the evidence of my Mother's brutal past. But the only sound came from the grandfather clock in the downstairs entry, solemnly counting off the hours.

When I returned to my room and started to close the door, I caught sight of a scrap of paper lying on the floor. Written in a shaky hand I didn't recognize was a quotation I was certain I'd heard once before.

"For the sins of the fathers are visited upon the children."

I lay awake until dawn, too terrified of both the past and the present to close my eyes.

# 8

I wish I could have told Quinnie, instead of keeping it to myself. But I was scared of frightening her. If she really knew what sleeping together was all about, I don't think she could deal with it. And if she'd seen what I did, Dad and Aunt Gwen touching each other in the garden, that would probably make things so confusing for her she wouldn't be able to think straight.

But they were touching all right, because I saw it with my own two eyes. Dad kissed her and Gwen giggled and held onto his hands. They didn't think anyone was watching, but I saw what happened. And strange as it may sound, I don't even think I was all that surprised, especially since my sister had warned me they were acting a lot friendlier than just brother-in-law and sister-in-law.

After dinner, when Quinnie went up to her room, I started wondering if maybe I had the solution and didn't even realize it. After all, I'd read enough detective novels to know something very fishy was going on. Add to that the voice I'd heard coming from the garden, and the way we smelled Mom's perfume in the playhouse, and I knew all my fears and suspicions had a basis in fact. I thought maybe I'd sit at my desk, write everything down like a list of clues and suspects, try to put the pieces together.

I don't know what came over me then. I guess I was getting so frustrated and upset I couldn't control my feelings. All of a sudden I was crying, wondering if sadness wasn't a disease, like measles. Maybe some people were terminally ill—constantly sad, that is—and no one had figured out a way to vaccinate them against it. That's not to say that I'm infected . . . but I wonder. I wonder about a lot of things of late, but mostly I wonder about Mom, where she is, and if she's all right.

Quinnie knocked on the door. She must have heard me crying, I guess. She wanted to know if anything was wrong, and so I dried my eyes and tried to put as much conviction into my voice as I could, telling her not to worry, I was fine.

At least she didn't make a big deal about it, just went off and left me alone. But then the tears didn't matter, because I suddenly thought, Lefland you idiot, you're missing the dog in the night. I don't know if you know what that means or not. It's in one of the Sherlock Holmes stories. Holmes talks about the curious incident of the dog in the night. Dr. Watson or someone else, I forget, says that the dog didn't do anything in the night. "That was the curious incident," Holmes replies. Do you get the point now? It was the absolutely obvious that I was missing, and I could've kicked myself for not seeing it sooner.

Here we'd spent all day searching room after room, unable to find even a single clue. But we'd never thought to actually check out Mom's room. It would be so clever of them, too. I could picture her tied up in bed with a gag over her mouth, ropes around her wrists and ankles that were tied to each post of the bed. Boy, would she be glad to see me. And if the door was locked that wasn't going to stop me, either. I figured I could always get in through the window if I had to, though I'd probably have to wait until everyone was asleep.

I didn't know if Dad was sleeping in the room or not. He and Mom had one bedroom, but it was really her room much more than his. He didn't seem to care, so she did it up the way she liked, with lots of lace and frills and feminine touches like that.

Anyway, I tiptoed down the hall to her bedroom, waited a second to make sure no one was around, then tried the knob. I almost gave myself away by gasping when the door swung open. For some reason the nursery rhyme about the spider and the fly entered my thoughts. But then I quickly put it out of my mind, knowing that every second was precious.

One glance and I saw that Dad hadn't been sleeping here. The room looked as if it hadn't been touched, not since the night they dragged Mom away. The bed was made, the pillows plumped. Mom's portrait looked down at me the way it always had, her blonde hair so thick and shiny it seemed to be painted with gold leaf. Her blue eyes saw everything, understanding me so well I could never keep a secret from her.

It wasn't fair, that was the terrible part. How could he have dragged her away, saying she was sick and dying, about to lose the baby when I knew it was a lie? And what about everything I'd overheard after Quinnie's party? Some of it I'd already figured out, like the business about Dad knowing what was going on when he was out-of-town. But the other stuff, the Becky-wecky Daddy-waddy stuff. None of that made any sense.

I looked around, walking on tiptoes so I wouldn't make noise. At least no one had touched her things, or thrown them out with the trash. On the dressing table the bottles of perfume and hand lotion, all her creams and tubes of lipstick, were lined up like an army of tin soldiers. The silver-backed hairbrush and hand mirror waited to be put to use, lying there all shiny and polished just like always. I thought of how Mom would sit before the vanity mirror, how she sometimes let me brush her hair for her. The bristles would slide through all that thick, fragrant golden hair, hair that was so soft and shiny you just wanted to cover yourself with it, it felt so good.

"Slowly, slowly. Don't forget to count the strokes," Mom would caution. She'd always sit there watching us in the mirror, smiling as I brushed her hair for her.

All I could think of was how much I missed her. I sat down in her chair, but it was cold as ice. No one had sat here since that terrible night. I looked at myself in her mirror and I saw her standing behind me and I smiled, remembering all the special moments we'd shared together.

The big crystal bottle of perfume was right there where she left it. I pulled out the stopper and dabbed some on my wrist. Then I held the inside of my hand up to my nose. I kept breathing in her scent until I felt calmer and much more at peace with myself.

She was still alive, no matter what anyone said. I wasn't making it up to convince myself. I wasn't just saying it because it was difficult for me to contemplate a life without her. I knew she was alive because I was here, in this room, I mean. I saw them together. I knew what happened that night, and I knew for a fact she wasn't dying.

But who would believe me?

I couldn't tell Quinn, not yet anyway, not when she was having a hard enough time just coping with growing up and figuring out who Quinton Lefland was all about. I couldn't tell Aunt Gwen, not when she was probably in on the whole thing. And I certainly couldn't tell Dad, the man

Mom pretended to love when I know for a fact she couldn't even bear to be around him.

I got up and went over to the armoire that stood in a corner of the room. It was an antique that had come all the way from France. Owned by some king's mistress, Mom once said. That made me smile, because I recalled how I'd asked her what a mistress was, having never heard the word used before.

"Mistresses, my dear Jason, are young men's wives and old men's nurses."

"Then you must be Dad's mistress, right?"

"On the contrary," Mom had stonily replied. "I'm his whore."

I never liked hearing her use those kind of words. When she resorted to cursing it meant only one thing, that a sick headache was coming on and she'd be holed up in here for days on end until it went away. But I didn't want to think about that now. I didn't want to think about anything but finding her.

I opened the armoire. The dresses were lined up one after another, just like a rack in a department store. Each one brought back a different memory. I could picture how she looked when she wore them, so radiant and beautiful, so sure of herself and everything she did.

The bedroom was a shrine, a holy place, sacred to her name as well as her memory.

"I was good to you, Mom, wasn't I?" I whispered.

"And I was good to you," I heard her say. But the voice was only in my thoughts, something I couldn't ever forget.

Dead? Gone forever? No, that was impossible.

I climbed up onto her bed, thinking of how I used to do that when I was real little, knee-high to a grasshopper was the corny way Will Darby used to put it. Mom would tuck me under her arm, reach down and tickle me till it hurt, I was laughing so hard.

Lying there in her bed, I pressed my face into the soft down pillows. I wanted to shout or start screaming or something, just to get rid of all the hurt and anger that was building up inside me.

I lay on my stomach, pushing and pushing and finding nothing there but cool sheets and a memory of the past that refused to go away. Then someone touched me on the shoulder and I thought I'd go through the ceiling.

"You mustn't cry, Jason. She'd be unhappy to see you like this."

I didn't know what to say, because if my aunt had come in a moment later she would have seen me falling over the edge, unable to stop myself.

"I'm not crying, really I'm not." I sat up, but I couldn't bring myself to look at her. "I thought I heard something. That's why I came in. Then . . . it's not important, honest."

"Feeling better now?" She drew her lips back and smiled, but something told me not to be fooled, she was just putting on a performance to get on my good side.

"Yes," I said, "much better."

"Would you like to go now?"

I shook my head. "A few minutes. You understand."

"Yes, I think I do," she said, and she went back to the door. She seemed genuinely concerned for my welfare, my feelings, but I was afraid to allow myself to trust her.

When the door closed softly behind her, I glanced up at Mom's portrait. She seemed to be telling me to watch myself, I shouldn't let my anger get the better of me. Even though she was gone, taken away somewhere and maybe even left for dead, the secrets we shared had to be kept.

"Can't I tell Quinn?" I asked. "She'd understand, I'm sure of it."

But paintings only come to life for people suffering from insanity, and Mom's portrait wasn't the exception to the rule. I knew what she wanted from me though. Part of the secret was the memory, because when the memory died there wouldn't be anything left. So I took the big crystal bottle of perfume that was on the dressing table, the silver-backed brush and mirror and comb.

I hid everything in the top of my closet. I didn't think they'd be missed. If they were, well, that couldn't be helped because they were mine now, held in safekeeping until Mom returned. And she would return, much sooner than anyone expected.

\* \* \*

A few days after Aunt Gwen caught me in Mom's room, Harry Darby arrived from the city. He'd taken the bus up the coast to Morro Bay, then hitched a ride inland as far as Juniper City. Will drove his pickup into town, and though he asked me and Quinn if we wanted to come along for the ride, I made up a story about taking our aunt on a picnic, even though it was a lie.

Earlier in the day I'd found a scrap of cloth snagged on a branch in the woods. When I showed it to Quinn she recognized it immediately. It was the same material as a blouse Mom used to wear. So all that afternoon while Will was busy picking up Harry, and Mrs. D. was making a big dinner to celebrate her son's arrival, we combed the Bottom to the very edge of the Valley where the hills rise up and dozens of shallow caves provide shelter for bats and all sorts of animals.

But we didn't find a single clue. By the time I said we should head on back, I could tell how discouraged Quinn was just by the way her shoulders drooped.

"Doesn't she know we're looking for her?" she asked. "She's not afraid of us, is she, Jason?"

"Why would she be afraid of us when we're the only ones who can help her?"

"Maybe she has amnesia," suggested Quinn. "Maybe she's wandering around the Valley eating berries and stuff, not even knowing who she really is."

"You know how dumb that sounds? Why in the world would she get amnesia?"

"They could've hit her on the head. Or maybe she hurt herself trying to escape, threw herself out of the car or something."

She was grasping at straws but I didn't want to tell her that. Instead, I figured the best thing to do was change the subject. You know, get her mind on something else. So I reached over and tickled her under the arm which is her most sensitive spot.

Quinnie just about doubled over, she was laughing so hard. "No . . . don't . . . please," she begged.

But now that I'd started I had no intention of stopping. I kept tickling and tickling until her knees buckled and she collapsed right there in the middle of the road. It was beautiful too, watching her kick her legs in the air, squealing with laughter I hadn't heard in weeks.

"I thought you liked to be tickled," I told her.

"No, but it . . . no, Jason . . . oh God, please," she groaned. She tried to pull free but I got on top of her and pinned her down on her back, holding her there with my knees against her arms.

"Say uncle and I'll let go."

"I won't."

God, she's stubborn, just like me.

"It's not fair," she said. "You're bigger."

"And stronger. And older. And better at tickling." I got my fingers under her arms, and she started tossing and

128

turning like a bronco, just pleading with me to stop. "Kiss me first and I'll let you go."

"What?"

I'm sure she heard me and was just playing deaf. So I said it again. Then I bent over her until I could see my reflection in her eyes. But when she put her lips to my cheek I told her I didn't mean it that way, I wanted the real thing.

"On the lips?" she said, as if that were the most unlikely place of all.

"Yep, right on the ole smackeroo," I said with a laugh.

She was panting and trying to catch her breath. There was dust all over us, and by then she'd stopped struggling. So I loosened my hold, not wanting to hurt her.

"Why?" she asked.

"Because."

"Because why, Jason?"

"Because it feels nice. That's a good enough reason, isn't it?"

Quinnie closed her eyes the way an actress does on the screen. She put her lips together for a kiss, and though for a moment I thought of playing a joke on her and putting my tongue in her mouth, I behaved myself and didn't. I just kissed her very gently, hardly touching her at all. Then I helped her up and dusted her off, pretending not to notice the way she kept staring at me.

"Is that part of sex?" she blurted out.

I smiled patiently. "No, Quinnie. It's part of love."

We trooped back to the house, not another word said between us. Harry had just arrived, and he was busy taking his things out of the back of the truck.

"If it isn't His Royal Highness," he said the moment he saw me.

"Better a king than a peon," I replied.

I could tell he didn't understand what the word meant.

But before anything else was said, Will got between us like we were squaring off for a fight, one he had no intention of refereeing.

Will was as tough and leathery looking as his wife. I'd seen him work and knew how strong he was, wiry I guess was the word. Harry was much beefier, proud of the fact he played football in high school. He sort of looked like a heavier version of his father, except for his mother's gray eyes. They both had clefts in their chins and widow's peaks. Even though Will's hair was turning gray, you could tell it was once as dark as his son's.

I don't know what came over Harry then, but suddenly his whole attitude changed. He threw a hand over my shoulder and gave me a hug like we were buddies, the best of friends.

"So how's it going, kiddo?" he said.

I shrugged, knowing it was a very stupid thing for him to ask. He probably figured it was, because right after he gave Quinnie a big hello he told us he'd heard about our mom's death. He was real sorry, and if there was anything he could do—

"There isn't," I told him. "But thanks, anyway."

By then, his mother had come out of the house. Mrs. D. didn't rush up to Harry like she was overjoyed or anything like that. She just stood there by the door—they'd driven around to the back of the house—shaking her head and pretending she'd never seen him before.

"You been behaving yourself?" she finally said.

"Nope." Harry laughed and lifted her up in his arms, spinning her around until she started to protest and he set her down again. Soon as her feet touched ground she reached up and put her hands on his cheeks. She said she was real glad to see him, and she'd missed him and he was looking just fine.

Then they all went into the house together. When the

screen door slammed shut I turned to Quinn. She was standing there, just staring at the door with this strange, dreamy look in her eyes. Maybe she had a crush on Harry, but I wasn't going to let it get in the way of our plans. Even if we hadn't solved the mystery of Mom's disappearance, I told her she shouldn't be discouraged.

"But even if we find her and bring her back, Father's never going to let her live with us again."

"That'll be Mom's decision, not his. Besides, she wouldn't leave us here with him. That's why we should get everything ready for her, so when she comes back it'll all be taken care of."

Quinnie didn't understand what I was referring to. I didn't want to get into a big discussion out in the yard, so I took her upstairs to my room. As we passed the kitchen I could hear the Darbys arguing with each other, which didn't surprise me in the least. Harry and his mother were always getting into scraps. Even though he wasn't here but ten minutes, they were already at each other's throats.

I paused by the kitchen door, motioning at Quinnie to stay where she was, we might learn something valuable.

"Lower your voice, for God's sake," Mrs. D. was saying. "You seem to forget this isn't our home. We work here, Harry; we don't own the place."

"He owns you though, don't he?"

"Don't you dare say such a thing, young man. Mr. Bennett's been very good to you all your life. If you weren't such a damn fool you'd take advantage of his offer, go on to college and do something with your life."

"I'm not interested."

"What the hell are you interested in, anyway?" his mother yelled. "Every year you come back here with a chip on your shoulder, like me and your father's done you a world of disservice. How your aunt puts up with it's beyond me."

"She puts up with it because you send her money for my room and board, and she and Uncle Frank need the bucks, that's why. Hell, I wouldn't even have bothered coming up here if Pop hadn't offered to pay me for my time. Soon as September rolls around I'm going back to L.A. to get me a job. And after that I'm gonna get my own place, and I won't have to bother with anyone, especially those stuck-up Leflands you wait on hand and foot like you were their goddamn slave."

She must have slapped him then, because Harry gave a little cry, though he sounded more surprised than hurt. Will started to say something, only it was drowned out by Mrs. D.'s shouts. She kept calling Harry an ungrateful pup and other weird things like that.

"Don't matter none," Harry told her. "You don't like hearing the truth, Ma, do you?"

"The truth is more painful than you can possibly imagine, Harry Darby. We've got trouble here, and if you walk around mad at the world you're not going to help things any."

Harry asked her what trouble she was talking about. I gave Quinnie a nudge, just to make sure she was paying attention. I swear I could see her ears quivering like a rabbit's, she was listening so hard.

"What'd she die of, anyway?" Harry said. "I thought she was strong as a horse, the bitch."

"Harry!" Mrs. D.'s voice jumped an octave, she sounded so shocked.

"Come on, cool it with this self-righteous crap. You never liked her from day one."

"That's a lie."

Harry started laughing so hard I saw red. But when I made a move to go into the kitchen Quinnie held me back.

"He's laughing at our mom," I hissed.

132

"It's more important we let him finish. I want to know what this is all about."

"—and as for Mrs. Lefland," Anna was saying, "it's much more complicated than you realize."

"What's so complicated about someone kicking the bucket?"

Mrs. D. began to sigh, like she was at her wit's end or something. "You see things in black and white because you're eighteen years old and wet behind the ears. But the world's colored gray, Harry. And life and death ain't no simple matter. We have problems here, big problems. I didn't want you coming this summer, but Mr. Bennett wouldn't hear of it."

"Sure," Harry said with a snicker, "he knows he can get a good day's work out of me."

"That's not the reason and you know it. The boy's restless. Unhappy. He needs someone he can talk to."

"Jason?" said Harry in a tone of disbelief. "Shit, he don't wanna pal around with me. He's got his sister for that."

"That's not what your mother's referring to," Will Darby spoke up. "What she's trying to say is Mr. Lefland wants you to keep an eye on the boy, make sure he stays out of mischief."

I poked Quinnie in the ribs, so hard she had to put her hand over her mouth to stop from gasping.

"What kinda mischief?" Harry asked his mother.

Mrs. D. didn't answer, not right away. Will said, "Go on, Anna, might as well tell him and get it over with."

"He's acting peculiar, Harry. Flies off the handle. Breaks into tears. He and his sister's been poking around the house like they're looking for buried treasure. Only Mr. Bennett thinks they got other things on their mind."

"Such as what?" said Harry.

"Such as we don't know yet," answered Will.

"So Lefland wants me to spy on the little brat, is that it?"

"You just watch your words now," cautioned Mrs. D. "The boy's got a mess of trouble brewing in his head. He's confused and unhappy and I don't rightly blame him, considering what he's been through."

"So what am I supposed to do about it, hold his hand?"

"No use talking to him, Anna. He don't understand that when you're in service long as we are, you're family even if your name's different. We can talk about this some other time, Harry. Right now I got work to do."

Will started from the kitchen. I grabbed hold of Quinnie and just about had to drag her up the stairs.

"What were they talking about, keeping you out of mischief?" she asked as she followed me down the hall to my room.

"I bet Dad's scared we'll find out what he's done."

I wish I could have locked the door, but I didn't have a key. Besides, Dad didn't believe it was necessary, saying there wasn't any reason to worry about locked doors when everyone respected each other's privacy.

"We've got to be extra careful from now on in," I told my sister when we were alone. "And you'd better watch yourself when you're around him, Quinn. I don't want Harry trying any funny stuff."

Quinnie wanted to know what kind of funny stuff I was talking about. She sat down on my bed, crossing her legs, and looked up at me with such an eager expression it took me awhile to come up with an answer.

"I told you about the facts of life, remember? Well, I don't want you to let him touch you. Just make sure he keeps his hands to himself."

"Touch me where? Secret places?"

I nodded, embarrassed about discussing this with her. But I just didn't have any other choice. "They're not his to find out about. They're yours, and please make sure to keep them to yourself.''

I don't know if my answer satisfied her, but there were other things I wanted to talk about, namely what to do with Mom's things, the clothes and cosmetics and stuff. If we waited much longer, I had a feeling Dad would tell Mrs. D. to start cleaning out the bedroom. No doubt he'd make it sound as if it were just too painful for him, having to see all of Mom's things every day. But since we knew that she was still alive, though God only knew when we'd see her again, I wanted to make sure nothing was thrown away.

When Mom came back I wanted everything to be the same for her. So I told Quinnie what I had in mind. We'd have to start moving things out of her bedroom, taking them to the playhouse where we could re-create her room, and get it ready for when she returned. Even if we couldn't move the big pieces of furniture, we could still take the portrait that hung over her bed, that and all her clothes, the stuff on her dressing table, and whatever else we found in the armoire and the dresser drawers.

"Mom will live for us in her room," I explained. "That way, when she gets back she'll have a place to stay until we can figure out where to go."

"You mean we won't be living here anymore?"

"Not unless Dad goes to jail for what he did. And if that happens, I still wouldn't trust him. He's got lots of friends in Washington, people in the government who knows how to pull strings. It wouldn't be difficult for him to pay off a judge like he did with the doctor."

"Maybe someone else'll come here to live. Then we won't have to move."

"Who? Aunt Gwen?" and I made sure to laugh.

"I don't know. Maybe her or our—"

She didn't seem to want to say it. But I told her that if

we couldn't be open with each other we'd be in big trouble, especially since there wasn't anyone else we could turn to.

"Something happened the other night," she finally admitted. "I was scared of telling you, but—"

I knew she was trying very hard to be brave, but she just couldn't help herself. A tear began to slide down her cheek, and I got up on the bed and put my arms around her, trying to calm her down. She was trembling, and she pressed her face into my chest and started to cry.

"It's not fair, Jason, it's just not fair," she kept saying.

"I know it's not. But we're doing everything we can. We'll find her, I promise. We won't stop looking, no matter how long it takes. And we won't ever forget how good she was to us. We'll turn the playhouse into a place that's special. It'll be our secret, Quinnie, just between the two of us. Even if they want us to forget her, we won't let that happen. Her memory will live on and on, and the room will be like a shrine. And if anyone comes there and touches her things, they're going to be in big trouble."

"Because they tried to kill her, right?"

"Yes, and they think they got away with it too, which only makes it worse. And one day real soon she's going to come back for us. When she does, and she tells us what they did to her, then whoever's responsible is going to be punished."

Quinnie wiped her eyes dry. "Like Roger of Howe during the Crusades," she said. "It'll be just like that, a holy cause Mr. Finney said they called it."

"That's right. It'll be a holy of holies. Now what was it that you were going to tell me?"

She looked away, glancing at the bookcase crammed with tales of tough private eyes and women the writers always described as "reckless and full-breasted."

"It was nothing, honest." She looked back at me, her

eyes flickering uncomfortably. "I just get so upset at them. Sometimes I can't even think straight, it's all so confusing."

"But you said something happened the other night. What was it?"

She shook her head. "It was just a dream, that's all. A bad dream."

She was holding something back. I could hear it in her voice, see it in the way she kept avoiding my eyes. But I realized it wouldn't do any good to pressure her. So instead of making a big issue about it, I took down the toilet set from the top of the closet and put everything on the bed. Quinn reached down and picked up the silver-backed brush. When she noticed several strands of Mom's hair still caught in the bristles she suddenly dropped it as if it were on fire.

"I can't," she moaned. "I just can't."

Before I could stop her she rushed past me and out the door. What was really going on, anyway? It wasn't like her to keep anything a secret from me. I started to get very worried about it. Perhaps she'd found out where Mom was. Maybe they had talked things over and Mom had told her stuff she knew she shouldn't have.

No, I told myself, Mom would have come to you first. I tried convincing myself of that but it didn't do much good. My head started pounding like there was a sledge hammer in my skull, going boom boom boom and my brains were being smashed to smithereens.

"Burn for your sins, Jason Lefland!"

Voices were shrieking in my head. I clapped my hands over my ears but I still heard them, cackling and laughing hysterically. I knew they were making fun of me, but there wasn't anything I could do to stop them.

"I'm good, I'm good," I kept saying, over and over.

"You're not. You're evil, Jason. You must be punished

with hellfire. You must suffer an eternity of damnation for your sins.''

"It's not true, it's not," I groaned. I could feel the flames bursting out of my head, but my hands were over my mouth so they wouldn't hear me screaming from the pain.

"Sinner! Sinner!" the voices were shrieking. "You will be cursed forever, Jason Lefland. Even hell is too good a place for you."

I crouched down on the floor, holding my head in my hands, and trying to pretend they weren't there. But they kept whispering their filthy lies. They told me dirty things. They laughed and tore at my flesh, biting and scratching me. They wanted to cast me into the everlasting fire but I wouldn't let them because it wasn't my fault.

"I didn't do it!" I cried. "She made me!"

Don't let them hear! Oh God in heaven I'm good and don't let them hear! Silence then. Blood throbbing in my temples. The sun like candle wax dripping across the floor. The voices faded away, one by one. The flames were extinguished, the gates of Hell slammed shut. Silence, and the memory of a terrible secret that threatened to destroy me.

"I'm good," I whispered. "God and the baby Jesus know that I'm good. I'm very, very good."

# 9

I wanted to be honest with my brother, truly I did. And when I ran out of Jason's room I guess I was running away from the truth. He had been hurt so deeply by what had happened to Mother that I was afraid if I told him about the diary he'd go on a rampage, accusing everyone of stealing it. But for all I knew the person responsible could have crept in through a window or an open door while we were all asleep. After all, I didn't recognize the handwriting on that piece of paper, unless of course someone had purposely tried to conceal their identity by using a different hand.

But there was more to it than that. I was worried about Jason, especially after what Mrs. Darby had said. There were so many secrets in this house it was difficult separating one from the other. Anna said one thing and Jason said another. Father told his version and Aunt Gwen told hers. Who was lying and who was telling the truth, that's what I couldn't figure out.

Yet somehow I knew that if I could only find Mother,

she'd be able to tell me what I wanted to know. She would clear everything up for me, and perhaps we might even be able to start fresh, everyone forgiving each other for what they had done. I guess in the beginning I had a hard time believing Jason when he said she was still alive. But now I was positive, and I even wondered if maybe she was the one who'd snuck into my room to steal the diary.

It was hidden in the bottom of the trunk. But the trunk had been moved, and Jason had found footprints in the dust. Had Mother been searching for it, afraid we might discover the terrible truth about her past?

That night, when I came downstairs for dinner, Anna was ranting and raving her icebox had been raided. (She never referred to it as a refrigerator, even though that's what it really was.)

"Now what are you going on about, Mother?" said Will. He only called her "Mother" on rare occasions. It was a term of endearment, and now he used it to calm her down.

"There were six pieces of fried chicken in there, and now they're gone. If your son has gone sneaking into my kitchen—"

"He's your son too, Mother," said Will, and I could tell by his tone of voice he was trying to humor her.

"Then you call him in here so I can give him a piece of my mind," she said angrily. "He wants something extra to eat, let him come and ask. I have to know what's here and what isn't, Mr. Darby."

When Anna called her husband "Mr. Darby," it wasn't a sign of affection. Rather, it was a way of telling him she had a bee in her bonnet, and he wasn't doing anything to stop its buzzing.

I thought it was all very funny until I suddenly realized what was actually going on. If food had been stolen, and if Harry insisted he wasn't to blame, then perhaps Mother had taken it. Jason and I already suspected she was some-where nearby, and now the missing food only seemed to confirm that. Perhaps I should leave more food for her out on the porch, and maybe even blankets or my old sleeping bag that was up in the attic. And maybe, just maybe, that's why Jason wanted to move everything out of her room and install it in the playhouse, knowing that Mother needed a place to stay until she could come out of hiding.

I wondered if he'd seen Mother and wasn't telling me. And there it was again, everyone claiming they told the truth, yet everyone keeping things a secret.

When I came into the kitchen Harry was already there, and his mother was still going on about the chicken.

"If I'd wanted any I wouldn't have asked. And if I'd taken it, which I didn't, I sure as hell wouldn't lie to you about it," Harry told her.

He saw me come in and gave me a big wink. He had the darkest hair I'd ever seen, so shiny black it was like crow's feathers. I guess you could call him handsome, what with his smoky-gray eyes and dimples when he smiled. But even though he was trying to act nice and not teasing me like he used to, I remembered what Jason had said, how Harry was a bully and a troublemaker and I should keep out of his way.

"She's getting pretty big, isn't she?" Harry said to his mother, just like I wasn't even there.

"Filling out nicely," agreed Mrs. Darby. She looked at me and smiled. "Looks like her mother, don't she?"

"We both do," I murmured. I lowered my eyes, embarrassed at the way they were talking about me, and especially embarrassed because Harry was just staring and staring like he'd never seen me before.

"But as for the chicken, Harry," continued Anna.

I didn't give him a chance to answer. "I took it," I spoke up.

Mrs. Darby looked at me like she couldn't believe her ears. "You? Miss Picky Eater? Since when have you had such an appetite?"

"Since . . . since I took the chicken. And it was delicious. And I hope you'll make more." I turned and hurried out before she could say anything else.

\* \* \*

Halfway through dinner the telephone rang, and when Anna returned she said it was for Father. He put down his napkin and went to answer it, and though Jason made a point of asking Anna who had called, she pretended not to hear him.

Father took the call in his study, and it seemed to me that he was on the phone for the longest time. When he finally returned to the table he looked very agitated, and he and Aunt Gwen exchanged glances I could only think of as ominous.

Jason was watching them as closely as I was. "Anything the matter?" he said. He made it sound very innocent, but I could tell he was already getting suspicious.

"Problems in Washington," Father replied. "I'll have to leave sooner than I thought."

"How soon is that?" asked Jason.

"Tomorrow morning."

"Is it very serious?" said Aunt Gwen.

"Yes, but I think we can work it out. It'll take a little time, that's all."

"So you won't be back for awhile, will you?"

"I don't know yet, Quinn. I might have to be gone longer than I planned."

Jason was sitting next to me, and when he kicked me under the table I knew what he was trying to say. He didn't believe the call had anything to do with Father's work, and I was inclined to agree with him.

But we didn't have a chance to talk about it, because as soon as dinner was over Father asked if he could see me in his study. It had been a long time since we'd had a private talk, and when he closed the study doors I knew it was going to be a lot more serious than I'd first thought.

Father's study was lined with books, many of which had belonged to Grandfather Ephraim and Great-grandfather Josiah. The room smelled faintly of chocolate, and when I mentioned that, Father smiled and told me it was because of all the old books, a certain chemical the paper gave off as it aged.

I was a little nervous I guess, especially because I didn't know what Father wanted to talk about. He motioned me to a chair, and I chose the big leather wingchair near the fireplace. When I was a little girl it was always a major effort just to climb into it. But now I seated myself in the chair without any difficulty at all.

"Remember when you used to sit in that chair and your feet didn't even touch the floor?" Father asked.

I smiled because that's just what I'd been thinking about. "I thought it was the most important chair in the house, maybe because it was so big."

"It's still big," Father said with a grin, "only now you've grown into it, Quinn."

He sat down at his desk and cleared his throat self-consciously. "We haven't had a talk in a very long time," he began.

I sensed how difficult it was for him, though there wasn't anything I could do to make it easier. But just watching him like this, seeing him so nervous and ill-at-ease, made me feel very sad. Surely he had loved Mother as much as I'd always imagined. Surely the story he used to tell of their first meeting meant as much to him as it had to her. Then what had happened to destroy that happiness, that ageless love that used to give me such comfort and security?

Father's close-shaven cheeks looked blue in the dim light cast from his desk lamp. He couldn't seem to get comfortable, and first he crossed his legs and then uncrossed them, fidgeting in his chair.

"You're angry with me, I know," he said at last. "But you have no right to be, Quinn. If you only knew how much I loved you—"

"I know," I said, interrupting him before he could finish.

"Then what have I done to alienate you so?"

"Alienate" was such a big word, and I couldn't recall seeing it on my vocabulary list, that it took me awhile to figure out what he meant.

"Is it about your mother?" he went on.

I nodded and looked down at my lap.

"You miss her very much, don't you?"

"I miss her terribly," I replied, unable to bring my voice above a whisper. "I want her back."

"I see," Father said. He came to his feet and began to pace, holding his hands behind his back. "I wish you could have known your mother as I did. You see, Quinn, she was very unhappy. And the older she got, the more unhappy she became."

"You mean the sick headaches she used to get?"

"Those, and other things, too. People aren't always what they pretend to be, you know. Even parents can do things that . . . that aren't always right."

"I don't know what this has to do with anything," I blurted out.

I hadn't meant to get angry, but now I couldn't help myself. What was he trying to tell me, anyway? It seemed to me that he wasn't the least bit sorry about what had happened.

"It has to do with growing up, Quinn. You might as well know that your mother and I hadn't been very happy together. Oh, we tried, I swear to you we did. We tried very hard to make it work. But sometimes people outgrow each other. Maybe they stop needing each other the way they used to."

"Why are you telling me this? If she's dead then what's the point?"

"The point is that life goes on, Quinn, for all of us. I want you and your brother to have a chance. For happiness I guess is what I'm trying to say. I want you to have friends, Quinn. I want you to see something of the world, something other than this valley. I want you to experience the present, not live in the past wishing for what was. Because what was can't ever be again, no matter how painful that sounds. That's why I've made arrangements for you and Jason to go away to school."

"I see. Well thanks for telling me. It's nice to know I had something to say about it." I got up and walked stiffly to the door. I don't know if I was angry so much as disappointed. He was turning out to be everything Jason had said, trying to get rid of us so we wouldn't discover what he'd really done.

Oh, if only Mother were here she'd know what to say to him. And if she'd lied about caring for him, loving him the way she always claimed, I knew she had done it for us, for me and Jason, to protect us from things that were too unpleasant to even talk about.

"I suppose you'll get remarried, won't you?" I said while my fingers reached blindly for the doorknob. "And you'll have a big wedding, and all your brothers and sisters who hated Mother will make sure to come. They'll all throw rice and laugh and think it's wonderful 'cause it won't be a funeral this time, will it? Well don't expect me to be there, Father. I'll be too busy with my dolls and my new friends at school. I won't have any time for you at all.''

I opened the door and stepped outside. I thought he'd call me back, maybe even ask for my forgiveness. But he didn't. He just stood there with his hands behind his back, scared and guilty for the lies he had told, and the truths he couldn't bring himself to admit.

After Anna and Will had gone to bed, I crept downstairs and loaded a plate with leftovers, salad and cold roast beef, even a slice of the peach pie we'd had for dessert. I left the food out on the back porch, hoping Mother would come for it during the night. But the following morning it was still there, the slices of roast beef alive with flies, the soggy peach pie swarming with ants. I tossed everything into the bushes and tried to hide my disappointment as I went inside for breakfast.

Jason and I had had a long talk before going to bed. I'd told him what Father had said, and though it came as no surprise, he was still upset that he hadn't been consulted.

"At least he could've let us pick the school," he said. "For all we know, we can end up thousands of miles apart. But it doesn't matter, anyway."

I felt very hurt, but Jason told me to stop being so sensitive, I hadn't even given him a chance to finish. It didn't matter where Father wanted to send us, he explained, because as far as he was concerned we weren't going.

"Mother'll be back by then. We'll have a whole new life together, just the three of us."

"Or maybe the four," I said, because we still didn't know for sure if Mother had lost the baby.

The important thing however was not to add fuel to the

fire, by which Jason meant we mustn't let Father suspect
we were on to him. It was bad enough that he knew we'd
been sneaking around the house. It was even worse that
he'd asked Mrs. Darby to have Harry keep an eye on us.
So from now on we would have to be extremely careful—
"circumspect" was the twenty-five-dollar word Jason used—
exercising far more caution than we had in the past.

By the time we finished breakfast, Father was packed
and ready to leave. As soon as he came downstairs, freshly
shaved and in a suit and tie, I did exactly what Jason had
suggested. I ran right over to him like I didn't have a care
in the world. I threw my arms around his waist, hugging
him the way I used to when I was very little and dolls
interested me more than boys with dimples and smoky-
gray eyes.

I don't think he was prepared for my display of affection. But that was fine, because Jason said we had to catch
him off his guard whenever we could, surprising him in
ways he would never have expected. So I told Father how
much I was going to miss him, and that I was sorry if I'd
been rude the night before.

Father intended to drive down to Los Angeles, where
he'd leave his car at the airport and catch a plane to
Washington. He still wasn't sure how long he'd be gone,
though he said his business would probably take at least
two weeks to clear up. Then he leaned over and kissed me
and said he'd miss me too, and that he hoped I'd behave
myself and not get into trouble.

"I want you to listen to your Aunt Gwen just like you
used to listen to your mother," he said.

I could feel my cheeks reddening when he mentioned
Mother's name. But when I glanced at Jason, his eyes
warned me not to say anything, we didn't want Father to
think he had any cause for concern.

Jason carried Father's bags out to the car. Will had

some stops to make in Juniper City, and he was getting ready to leave in his pickup. Anna had given him a shopping list, and though he groaned it was women's work picking out toilet paper and furniture polish, he kept assuring her that he wouldn't forget anything.

Then there was another round of good-byes, with Aunt Gwen putting her arms over Father's shoulders and giving him a big hug and a kiss right in front of everyone.

"I'll call just as soon as I get there," Father told us.

You don't have to bother, I thought, because we're not going to miss you at all.

But of course I didn't say that. I just pretended to be real sad the way Jason and I rehearsed it earlier.

"I'm counting on you, Quinn," Father said as he got behind the wheel.

"For what?" I said, smiling innocently.

He motioned me to step closer, then stuck his head out the window and kissed me on the cheek. "Make your aunt feel at home. She very much wants to be your friend, Quinn."

"She's my friend. Honest."

I knew Father didn't believe me, but instead of arguing the point he just smiled and nodded his head. "That's all I wanted to hear. She cares about you and your brother very much. And if you want to go up to San Francisco or any place like that, all you have to do is ask, because she'd be delighted to take you."

"I'll keep that in mind." It seemed like an awfully formal thing to say, but I didn't know what else to tell him.

Then, when Father and Will both drove off, and all you could see was the dust they made going down the road toward Juniper City, we hurried back into the house to get started.

We had our work cut out for us, as Will would say,

what with moving the stuff out of Mother's bedroom and getting it set up in the playhouse. Jason suggested we use pillowcases, and so I stripped them off my bed while he stripped them off his. The two of us made our way down the hall, looking over our shoulders just to be certain no one was following us. I thought Mother's door would be locked and we'd have to find the key or figure out how to break in, but Jason said it was open and sure enough he was right.

As soon as we were alone in Mother's room I could feel her presence. It was almost as if she were actually there, or some part of her at least, watching over us to make sure we were safe. It was such a beautiful room too, with a lovely skirted dressing table just like the kind I'd always wanted when I got older and had permission to wear lipstick and eye shadow and stuff like that. Embroidered lace curtains hung over the windows, so sheer you could see right through them. The fourposter bed was very high off the floor, and there were six pillows on it, each one a different size, and all with matching ruffled shams.

Jason got right down to business and started emptying the bureau drawers, so anxious to get the job done you'd have thought the house was on fire and he was trying to save whatever he could.

If he wanted to rush around that was his business, but I wanted to take my time. I sat down at the dressing table, where a photograph of Mother smiled serenely from within its gleaming silver frame. At least Mrs. Darby hadn't forgotten to polish it, which made me wonder if she secretly knew that Mother was coming back. Perhaps by keeping her bedroom neat and clean she was somehow proving her loyalty.

Using an old madras skirt Mother hadn't worn in years, I carefully wrapped it around the photograph, then placed both in the bottom of my pillowcase. Jason found an empty plastic bag in Mother's bathroom, and I used it to put the cosmetics just in case they leaked. But I twisted every cap tight, thinking of the times when I used to watch her sitting here at her dressing table, making up her face.

"Never too much because you don't want to look like a painted woman," she would say.

When I was little I always wondered if she meant an Indian squaw because they wore war paint, or so I thought.

Mother would laugh and shake her head. "No, darling, the kind of painted ladies I mean don't live in teepees."

When the dressing table was cleared I opened the armoire and started taking down the dresses. It would have been much easier if we'd used a suitcase. But for some reason or other Jason said it would arouse too much suspicion. (I guess he didn't want them to think we were planning to run away.)

"I can't fit anything else in," I said, the pillowcase bulging at the seams like Santa's bag of toys.

Jason didn't answer me, and when I looked around I suddenly realized he wasn't even in the bedroom. I started to call his name when I noticed that the bathroom door was ajar. I pushed it all the way open and stepped inside, my footsteps echoing loudly on the cold tile floor.

Jason was staring at himself in the mirror above the double sinks, his fingers curled around the edge of the marble countertop as he gazed unblinkingly at his reflection.

"You all right?" I said after standing there for a couple of minutes, during which time he didn't say anything or even acknowledge my presence.

"No," he whispered.

He turned his head over his shoulder, and his eyes were so green that for a moment they didn't look human. Then he reached into his pocket and pulled out the knife he'd given me for my birthday. Before I could say anything, ask why he'd taken it from my room without permission, he slid the knife free of its leather sheath and held it aloft, spinning it in the air like a majorette twirling a baton.

"You'll cut yourself if you don't watch out," I warned.

"So? It's only blood." He gripped the bone handle more tightly, and before I could stop him he brought the sharp, gleaming edge of the blade right up to his neck.

"Jason!" I cried out in sudden panic.

"I'd do anything for Mother," he said in a dreamy faraway voice, as if he didn't know I was there. "I'd even kill myself if it would bring her back."

I couldn't bear to stand there and watch him and not know what he might do next. I was so frightened I couldn't stop shaking, and I rushed over and knocked the dagger out of his hand. It clattered to the floor, spinning round and round like a carousel slowly coming to a stop.

Jason stared at it and didn't seem to realize what it was. Then he bent down and picked it up, sliding the antique dirk back into its sheath. He handed it over as if I were the one who'd given it to him in the first place, then looked back at himself in the mirror.

"I wonder when it'll be time for me to shave," he said thoughtfully, like nothing out of the ordinary had happened. "Dad says the longer I can avoid it, the better." He stroked the down over his lip with the side of his finger, preening like a man with a thick, bushy mustache.

"Cute," I heard Harry Darby say. "Real cute."

Jason froze, and his hands clenched into fists that began to shake and tremble uncontrollably. I turned around and saw Harry standing by the bathroom door. He'd snuck into Mother's room without our knowing it, and now I was afraid of what Jason might do, especially since he knew I had the knife in my pocket.

"What are you doing here?" I said. "Don't you believe in knocking first?"

"What for? Since when do I have to worry what you

two think? And what the fuck are you doing in here, anyway? What's with the two bags of loot out there?'' He motioned with his cleft chin, and I could see the two bulging pillowcases where we'd left them alongside the bed.

"None of your goddamn business,'' Jason spoke up.

I tried to get between him and Harry, but my brother pushed his way past me.

"Pretty damn clever,'' Harry said as he bent over the pillowcases, peering into each one and even lifting out one of Mother's dresses.

"Don't you ever touch my mother's things!'' Jason shouted. He snatched the dress out of Harry's hand, tossed it on the bed and lunged at the boy.

Harry darted to the side, laughing and skipping back and forth. Every time Jason took a swing at him, Harry ducked and my brother's fist collided with nothing but air.

"You touch her stuff again and you're dead,'' Jason warned.

"Fuck you,'' Harry said with a sneer. He suddenly grabbed Jason by the shoulders and lifted him off the floor, holding him in midair while he shook him back and forth.

When he finally let go, Jason lost his footing and couldn't catch himself in time. He went sprawling onto the floor, where he managed to reach over and grab Harry around the ankle. He tugged with all his strength and then both of them were down, rolling over each other and trying to get to their feet.

"I don't want to have to hurt you, Jason, just remember that,'' Harry said. He had Jason's shoulders pinned to the floor, and I looked around for something to use to help my brother, something I could smash over the back of Harry Darby's head.

But then Harry let go and straightened up. He seemed

pretty winded, and even began to compliment Jason, telling him how strong he was for someone his age.

Jason didn't say anything, which I think was the smartest thing he could have done. He just got up and brushed himself off. But when he made a move to pick up one of the pillowcases, Harry stepped forward and shook his head.

"No way," he told my brother.

"No way what?" I said angrily.

Jason glared at me. "Keep out of this, Quinn."

Again my brother reached for the pillowcase. Only this time Harry shoved him aside with both hands. "I mean, come on, kiddo," said Harry. "You don't think I know what's going on around here, do you?"

"I don't care one way or the other," replied my brother, his voice cracking he was so livid. "So get out of my way."

"That a threat?"

"Call it what you like, but just get out of my way," repeated my brother. "You don't belong here, Harry. You never did."

"You take that stuff out of here and I'm gonna tell," Harry replied.

"Who?" I asked.

"Your aunt, for starters."

I turned to Jason, not knowing what to do.

" 'Course," Harry went on, "we might be able to work something out."

"Such as what?" demanded my brother.

"You know what they say. Money talks, and nobody walks."

"How much?" Jason said grimly.

"Your aunt mentioned how you were each getting fifteen bucks a week allowance. Come up with a tenner between you and we'll call it quits. Deal?"

Jason looked at me and didn't say anything, though I knew exactly what was going through his mind.

"What choice do we have?" I said.

"None," answered Harry. "Well? Yes or no?"

"How do we know you won't go back on your word?" asked Jason.

"You don't. So you're just gonna have to trust me."

Jason glanced at the two bulging pillowcases, then looked back at Harry Darby. "Deal," he said, speaking so softly I could barely hear him.

"That's what I thought." Harry tipped an imaginary hat at each of us in turn, then left the room as silently as he'd entered.

"One day I'm going to murder him," Jason said under his breath.

We hoisted the bags over our shoulders and tiptoed from the room, taking care to close the door behind us. If the person or persons who'd written that note to me were watching, we never saw them.

# 10

**H**arry Darby was a bastard, and he was going to pay for what he did. He tried to humiliate me in front of Quinn and he did it on purpose, too. That was something I wasn't ever going to forget. As for the business about giving him money, that was the least of it. Besides, Aunt Gwen hadn't gotten her figures straight. Dad was giving each of us twenty dollars a week allowance (hush money, if you ask me). And there wasn't any place to spend it, anyway. So if it kept Harry off our backs, then I guess it was worth it.

For now.

But later on—

He made me feel ashamed and that's what I won't ever forget. He made me look like a weakling, a sissy too, toying with me like I was a punching bag or something. I'm just glad I didn't cry even though he hurt me. If Quinnie had seen my tears it would've been awful. I have to be her hero, know what I mean? And I have to stay on top of things too, or else the voices will come back and then I'll really be in trouble.

Anyway, we left the house and headed straight to the Bottom. I was still smarting over Harry's treatment of us, but Quinn's mind was already on other things. All of a sudden she was playing Nancy Drew, trying to put together all the different pieces of the puzzle. What was that phone call all about last night? she wanted to know. Did I really think it had anything to do with Washington? And what had Father meant when he said he couldn't stop Mother in time and he wondered if I suspected? She was going over the conversation she'd overheard in the dining room. But as far as I was concerned, it was all old hat.

I knew what was going on, not where they'd hidden Mom, but what they thought they had gotten away with. And I was sure Dad wasn't going to Washington. He probably wasn't even leaving the state. Quinnie was asking so many questions though, that I decided it was time to ask some of my own.

"Why did you run out of my room last night?" I asked. "You were going to tell me something, and then you changed your mind."

Her face got so red it was a dead giveaway. "No I wasn't," she insisted.

"Come on, Quinn, you can't lie to me. I see right through you."

"It was nothing, Jason. I'm just having bad dreams, that's all. I keep thinking maybe there's more to it than we realize. Maybe there are people around that we don't even know about."

"Such as who?"

"Such as . . . I don't know, maybe Mother's parents or someone like that."

"But we've never even met them. I don't even think they're still living."

*My family's dead . . . but their spirit's still alive.*

Yes, I remembered. They'd had that awful argument

156

right after Quinn's party. But just because Mom said it to Dad didn't mean she was telling the truth. Not that she was a liar or anything like that, but in the heat of the moment she could have said all sorts of things she didn't mean.

"But what if they are alive?" Quinnie asked. "What then?"

"Then we have a new set of grandparents, what else? Who told you about them, anyway?"

She suddenly looked very guilty, the little faker. Something was going on that she wasn't telling me about. But if I tried to drag it out of her she'd never come clean because that's the stubborn streak all us Leflands share.

"And why did you sneak into my room?" she suddenly asked.

"What are you talking about?"

"You know exactly what I'm talking about, Jason. I'm talking about this." She dug into the pocket of her jeans and pulled out the stag-handled dirk I'd given her for her birthday. I was glad to see she hadn't thrown it away, though perhaps she just kept it around to try to convince me how much she liked it.

"What does the knife have to do with anything?"

She gave me one of her exasperated looks, like I was a big dummy or something. "You took it out of my room, Jason. You had it with you in Mother's bathroom."

"Mother's bathroom? What are you trying to say?"

"You mean you don't remember?"

I was about to lose my temper, I swear to God. "Don't remember what?" I just about shouted at her.

"Nothing," she said, and she stuffed the knife back into her pocket.

"You'd better watch yourself," I said with a laugh. "I don't want you losing your marbles on me."

As soon as we got to the playhouse her mood brightened, and so did mine. But I still wasn't about to forget what Harry had done. Not only had he embarrassed me in front of my sister, but he'd come into Mom's room which was a sacred, holy place. I guess Quinn knew I was still upset about it, because she did everything she could to cheer me up.

Anyway, we spent the day together, making trips to Mom's room, then taking the things back to the Bottom.

Anna Darby said, "My, my, aren't we two busy bees."

We smiled, and just pretended we weren't doing any-thing wrong. (Of course, she didn't see us carrying the stuff down the stairs, which was probably the reason why she never tried to stop us.)

We borrowed some of her cleansers and stuff, though we didn't tell her why we needed them. I guess she thought we were going to make a project of cleaning up our rooms, something I definitely wasn't interested in doing.

The fact is though, I wanted the playhouse to be abso-lutely spotless, sparklingly clean to receive the blessed instruments of our faith. That's what it was going to be, I told Quinnie, like a new religion, a way of preserving Mom's memory even though they'd already tried every-thing they could to make us forget her.

We scrubbed the floorboards down until the faded white paint glistened and almost looked brand-new. We polished the little round table where Quinnie used to hold tea parties for her dolls. The windows got the full treatment too, an entire childhood of dust and cobwebs disappearing under a haze of Windex with ammonia-D. It was nearly dinnertime when everything was done, Quinnie and I having worked so hard we both felt ready to drop. She turned on the lights that glowed down from the ceiling, and just stood there smiling, taking everything in and liking what she saw.

"It's perfect," she decided, though a moment later she

ran over to the portrait to make sure it was hanging exactly straight. "It even smells like her room now, doesn't it?"

"And it feels like her room too, and that's the important thing."

I got out the candles I'd snitched from the dining room sideboard, the box of matches I'd found there as well. We'd forgotten to look for proper candlesticks, so for the time being we used two dishes that were part of my sister's old tea set.

The floor at one end of the playhouse was raised up about a foot. When we were small we used it as a stage to put on puppet shows and skits for each other, and sometimes Mom would come down to the Bottom like it was a command performance.

We'd seat her right in front of the stage and draw the curtains back that were two old sheets strung up on a length of clothesline. Mom would applaud and stamp her feet, shouting, "On with the show!" and later, "Author! Author!" We'd take our bows and once Mom got up and gave Quinnie a rhinestone pin and said it was a present from the Queen. I wondered if Quinnie still had it. The pin was shaped like a heart and my sister used to wear it all the time. She even stuck it on her pajamas at night, she was so afraid of losing it.

But now we weren't small and it wasn't a command performance. We weren't actors on a stage either, playing out some kind of fantasy because we couldn't accept reality. No, we'd make our own reality, and that's what I told my sister. The stage would serve as an altar, and when we knelt before it we could look up and see Mom's portrait smiling down at us from where we'd hung it on the wall.

I'd worked everything out beforehand, what to call the things we'd use, how to go about the entire ceremony. I think when I started to tell Quinnie about it she must have thought I was the one who was losing his marbles, and not her. But who wouldn't start acting a little strange knowing their Mom had been dragged away in the middle of the night? Who wouldn't start feeling the pressure having to attend a mock funeral, with people crying and shedding crocodile tears. My God, he even bought a coffin for her and everything!

"You think I'm a little nuts, don't you?" I asked.

Quinnie responded like a born diplomat. "Why do you say that?"

"Because you're looking at me like you don't know what in the world is going on."

"It's weird, that's all."

"A new religion? If people hadn't started worshipping Christ he would have been forgotten and that would've been the end of it. But people remembered and they still remember. So what's wrong with remembering Mom?"

"But she's not a god, Jason."

"I never said she was. We're going to try to communicate with her, that's all. We're going to send our thoughts out into the universe and hope she'll hear them and answer us."

"Like telepathy, you mean?"

"Kind of. I read somewhere that if you want something bad enough, you can make it happen just by constantly wishing for it, and doing everything you can to see that it comes true."

It took her a little while to absorb that. Even when she nodded her head I had a feeling she might still be missing the point.

"If you don't want to—" I started to say.

She reached out and put her hand on my shoulder. Strange as it may sound, as soon as she touched me I got the chills. "Of course I want to, Jason. It'll be fun."

"It won't be fun. It'll be hard work, Quinn. There's nothing funny about what's going on around here."

"You can say that again," she whispered.

"So just remember, this is real serious business. Now, are you ready?"

"Ready," and she got into position, kneeling beside me.

"Here are the instruments of our faith," I announced, speaking slowly and solemnly and glancing at Quinn just to make sure she wasn't giggling. But she was as straight-faced as me, and I was grateful that she trusted my judgment.

I placed the silver-backed toilet set on the edge of the stage, arranging Mom's photograph between the comb and the brush. The mirror lay in front of it, the glass side down.

"And this?" asked Quinn. She handed me the bottle of rose-scented perfume, the faceted crystal cool against my skin.

"Here is the fragrance of remembrance," I told her. "Anoint thyself."

After carefully removing the glass stopper, I tipped the perfume bottle against the inside of Quinnie's narrow wrist. Blood rushed through the pale-blue veins along the under-side of her arm, blood that pulsed with life and vitality. Her eyes were closed, and it struck me that she was concentrating with all her strength, trying to remember Mom as she was and as she would always be.

"The blessed instruments of our faith. The fragrance of remembrance," Quinn repeated after me.

"And here is the flame of retribution," I went on. I lit the candles, placing one directly in front of me and the other in front of her.

"What's retribution?" she whispered.

"Punishment for evil deeds."

"The flame of retribution," Quinn recited, sounding very pleased with my explanation. "May it burn forever."

We knelt there with our foreheads touching the floor,

Mom's portrait watching over us, keeping us safe from all that was wicked and deceitful. The vicious tongues were stilled. The evil voices weren't whispering their filthy lies, obscenities I could never have dreamed of on my own.

I closed my eyes then, praying for Mom's return, and wondering if Quinnie had actually caught a glimpse of her the other day, when she thought she'd seen Mom near the playhouse.

"We'll wait for you," I whispered aloud. "We'll wait as long as it takes."

"Pray to the blessed Mother," whispered Quinnie in turn. "May the flame of retribution burn forever."

I looked up, and Mom smiled, beckoning to me with outstretched arms.

"You were always the smartest, cleverest boy," she said, speaking so softly that Quinnie couldn't hear. "You knew how to make me happy as no one else." She stepped clear of the confines of the painting, lifting her skirts so as not to trip over the bottom edge of the frame. The sight of her was so dazzling I had to look away else it would've blinded me.

Mother of radiance. Mother of perfection. They took you away but we'll bring you back, I swore to her.

The candle flame soared up, a blade of fire reaching halfway to the ceiling. Quinnie was praying silently beside me. I wanted to shake her, tell her Mom was standing right there in front of us. But I couldn't move a single muscle, as if the very sight of her had turned me into stone.

"When are you coming back for us? He wants to send us away, and there isn't much time."

"Soon, Jason, very soon."

"And we'll be happy then, won't we? It'll be just like it used to, and he won't ever interfere again, because this time we won't let him get away with it."

"Yes, we'll all be very happy, Jason. We won't let him hurt us again."

"But where are you, Mom? Why do you keep hiding from us when we want to help you?"

"Pray to the blessed Mother," Quinnie droned on and on, oblivious to what was really happening. "Here are the blessed instruments of our faith. Here is the blessed fragrance of remembrance and the blessed flame of retribution."

"It's time to look for me," whispered Mom. "It's time to test your sister's faith. She must believe in me as you believe. Only then will we be truly happy again."

"But she knows I'm telling the truth, Mom, I'm sure of it. She worships you!" I cried out, and yet I knew my sister couldn't hear me, though I didn't understand why.

"Then she must prove it to me as you have proven it, Jason. Make good your threats. Show her how she's been deceived, that she may finally believe. Then when she sees as you have seen, turn on the enemy, Jason! Bring them to their knees and make them feel the flame of retribution!"

"Yes, yes, I will, I promise," I groaned. I had to cover my eyes with my hands because she was golden fire, a blazing explosion of light that was so bright I couldn't bear to look at her.

Quinnie was shaking me again and again. When I opened my eyes I found myself huddled on the floor with my knees against my chest and one of the candles clutched in my hand.

"You burned yourself," she said with alarm.

She pried the stub of candle from my fingers. My palm was covered with dried wax, and when she peeled it away a perfect circular mark was branded into my skin. It was already blistering, and Quinnie removed the bottle of perfume from the altar, dabbing the fragrance of pain and remembrance onto my palm.

I kept telling her I was all right, it didn't hurt at all.

When I looked up at the portrait, nothing had changed. Mom smiled down at us, serenely confident of both her beauty and her strength of will.

"What happened?" Quinnie asked.

I still wasn't sure, but I knew that I had to be completely honest with her, especially since Mom wanted it that way. "I saw her. She came to me and told me what to do."

I pulled myself to my feet. My hand was throbbing but the pain was a reminder of the promise I'd made to her, and I was glad she'd left her holy mark on me.

Quinn leaned over and snuffed out the other candle. "Is she coming back for us? They haven't hurt her, have they?"

"We'll find out very soon," I promised.

"When?"

"Tomorrow night."

"At midnight?" Quinnie said excitedly.

If that's how she wanted it, that was fine with me. "Yes," I told her, "precisely at the stroke of twelve."

# 11

**J**ason didn't remember anything about the knife! He didn't even know what I was talking about. Had he been sleep-walking, was that it? Had he crept into my room without realizing what he was doing? And what exactly had been going through his mind as he stood before the mirror in Mother's bathroom? Why had he suddenly taken the knife and pressed it to his throat? Was he so unhappy that the only answer to his problems lay in a kind of eternal sleep we all knew was really death?

The more I thought about these things, the more upset I became. I began to wonder if it was Jason who had stolen Mother's diary, and the vague suspicions I had had about Mother's parents were pushed into the background. But how does a person do things and not know about them, that was the confusing part.

Then there was Harry to contend with. Lurking in corners, hiding in shadows, he seemed ready to spring out and surprise us when we least expected him. Why did

Father want Harry to keep an eye on Jason? He was afraid of something, but what?

Afraid he'll find Mother, of course, I answered myself.

Before we'd gone to bed, Jason had warned me to be on my guard, there was just no telling what might happen. I wondered if he might possibly be referring to Mother's parents, Grandmother Howe who had turned a deaf ear to her daughter's suffering, Grandfather Howe who had done unspeakable things in the cellar of their house. But what things exactly? He had beaten our poor mother so badly she hadn't been able to get out of bed. But he had done something else to her, too, something that had caused Miss Blair her teacher and the school nurse to look at her in shock and horror. If only I could find the diary, I was sure it would explain what had happened. But what if her father had continued to torture her? Had she suffered at his hands for years and years, was that the terrible secret she had never shared with us?

Mother was nearby, that was the only hope I had left. We'd find her soon and then there wouldn't be anymore questions to ponder or nightmares to scare us. Jason had had some kind of religious experience, but I didn't know if it was all wishful thinking, or if something supernatural or otherworldly had occurred. Lots of times I found myself anticipating things before they happened, knowing what my brother was about to say, or what he was thinking. But I'd always attributed that to the fact that we were very close, and not because I had a gift for telepathy or anything like that.

On top of everything else, I had no idea what Jason was planning. He'd sworn me to secrecy, promising that we'd soon have the answers to all our questions. Just thinking about it kept me awake half the night, and so when the telephone rang at two in the morning, a single ring that was instantly cut short, I was wide-awake and out of bed before I even realized what I was doing.

The only phones on the floor were in the guest room where Aunt Gwen was staying, and Mother's bedroom. It was there that I headed, knowing that the room was vacant and the door unlocked. Even before I got to the end of the hall I could hear Aunt Gwen speaking in hushed tones.

So the phone call was for her! I thought as I let myself into Mother's room.

It was dark and cold and empty, like a dead person's room. We had carted off everything that Mother had cherished, and now there was nothing but pieces of furniture, stripped of their contents. But the phone was still there beside her bed.

I wondered if they'd hear me when I lifted the receiver. Surely there had to be a way of breaking in on the connection without their knowing it. Ever so slowly I began to lift the receiver, knowing that when I raised it off the button there'd be a click and I'd be able to hear whomever was on the line. But since I wanted that click to be as noiseless as possible, I held the button down with the tip of my finger, not releasing it until I had the receiver against my ear.

If either of them heard me come on the line, they failed to mention it. And just as I'd suspected, it was Father who had called. Judging from his tone of voice, the problems in Washington were far from being solved.

"—Warren doesn't know when it happened," he was saying to my aunt.

Who was Warren? I wondered. I'd never heard anyone by that name spoken of before.

"And they call themselves professionals," Aunt Gwen replied with a sigh. "Sometimes I think you have to stand over people to make sure they do their job. Christ, now what do we do?"

"Alert them, for starters."

"I already have."

Alert who? If only I could have opened my mouth and come right out and asked.

"How are they bearing up, by the way?" Father asked.

"So far, so good."

"No sign of—?"

"None whatsoever," said Aunt Gwen.

"But what about—"

I never heard the rest of it, because suddenly there was a hand clamped over my mouth and the receiver was being wrenched away from me. Grandfather Howe! I thought in alarm. I twisted around, trying to escape and desperate to see who it was. But the man who had tormented my mother existed only in my imagination, for it was Jason who had his hand over my mouth. He grabbed the receiver and pressed it to his ear, letting go of me at the same time.

I fell back on the bed, and the terrible panic and sense of helplessness I'd felt just a moment before was now replaced by anger. Why hadn't he given me a chance to hear the rest of it? Why had he been so stubborn to get his way?

A moment later he swore under his breath and put down the receiver, letting it drop with a bang.

"They'll hear," I whispered.

"They already hung up."

"Thanks for scaring me half to death."

"I'm sorry, but it couldn't be helped. Next time come to me first, Quinn. I have more experience in these things. Now tell me what you heard."

I was still very angry, not so much that he'd frightened me, but that we hadn't been able to hear the rest of the conversation. Yet the damage had already been done, and now there was nothing we could do about it. So I told Jason exactly what I'd overheard, repeating everything that had been said almost word for word.

"Who in the world is Warren?" he asked when I was through.

"Whoever he is, he obviously wasn't doing his job."

"Did Dad say where he was calling from?"

I shook my head.

"If only he'd mentioned it."

"He could've been in Washington," I suggested.

"Don't be stupid, Quinn. That's the last place he was."

Oh, I was getting so mad but I knew I had to hold it in. Why did he have to call me stupid when I was the one who'd heard the phone ring and not him?

"I'm going back to bed," I announced, and I marched to the door. "If you want to keep picking on me, go right ahead. Only I'm not going to stand here and listen to it anymore."

I started to let myself out, but he raced across the room and grabbed me by the arm, spinning me around.

"Do you want to see her or don't you?" he whispered.

"Of course I do. You know that."

"Then please stop taking everything so personally. I'm trying to treat you like an adult, for Christ's sake."

I wanted to remind him that he wasn't an adult yet, either, even if he did have hair under his arms. But instead I said, "Adults don't call each other names."

"Don't be so sure," he replied. "Adults do rotten things to each other, and it's time you started realizing that. For God's sake, Quinn, it's just the two of us, don't you see? If we start fighting with each other we're the only ones who'll suffer for it, not them. Do you think Mom wants to come back to find us at each other's throats?"

"No," I said guiltily.

"Then stop being so sensitive. Save it for when things are better around here, all right?"

I nodded, and I felt pretty awful too, that here I was making a big deal about something that was really unimportant. But then he made everything better again, and he did it in the strangest way. He leaned over and kissed me, first on the forehead, then on one cheek and then the other. He put his hands on my shoulders and looked down into my eyes, staring at me with such honesty, such openness, I felt embarrassed.

"I love you," he said. "You forget that and I'll murder you, Quinnie."

I laughed shyly. "I love you too, Jason." I stood on tiptoes and kissed him on the lips. He closed his eyes as if he expected something else to happen, but I didn't know what he wanted and so I just stepped back and reached for the doorknob.

As I lay in bed I could hear him next-door. The bedsprings creaked rhythmically, a sad, doleful song. Gradually the springs quickened their raspy music, faster and faster as if he were trying to rock himself to sleep. Suddenly he gave a little cry, almost like a groan of pain and disappointment. Then all was still, and even the owls failed to call to each other in the darkness.

When Jason came down for breakfast the next morning there were dark purplish circles beneath his eyes, and it looked like he'd spent as sleepless a night as me. Aunt Gwen couldn't help but notice his sickly pallor, too. She came in from the garden where she was cutting flowers, and the moment she saw him she began to fuss. Insisting he didn't look at all well, that perhaps he was coming down with a cold, she tried to feel his temperature by putting her hand on his forehead. But the moment she touched him, Jason jumped back as if were afraid she was going to burn him. And speaking of burns, I noticed that he kept his hand in his lap, so I couldn't see if the burn he'd gotten was healing.

After breakfast I thought we'd head down to the

playhouse— which deserved a different name now, since it wasn't ever going to be used for play—and pray again for Mother's safe return. But Jason said he had things to do. When I asked what things, he said he'd tell me, but all in due time.

So I was stuck with Aunt Gwen, who thought she was doing me a big favor teaching me how to arrange flowers the way she'd learned from some course she'd taken. I thought it was boring, especially after the arrangement she made wasn't half as nice as any Mother had done, just sticking flowers in a vase and coming up with something a whole lot prettier. But I guess the flower business was just an excuse to get me alone, because my aunt seemed more interested in prying information out of me than improving my artistic skills.

"Wouldn't you like to sit and have a nice talk together?" she suggested when there weren't anymore flowers to arrange, and all the overflowing vases made it look as if we'd just had a big party, not a funeral.

I decided the best thing to do was play it by ear. That was one of Jason's phrases, by which he meant just take things as they come, figuring out what to do as you went along. So I said, "Sure, that sounds fine."

We were in the music room, which Mother had said was just a pretentious way of describing a living room with a piano. I took a seat on one of a pair of couches upholstered in a rich floral material. Aunt Gwen sat opposite me, and I had the strangest feeling that she was like a reporter, here to interview me for some magazine.

"By the way," I said, trying to sound casual, "have you heard from Father?"

Something very much like uncertainty passed across her eyes. "Not yet," she replied.

To be quite honest about it, I was glad she was lying. Perhaps if she'd told me the truth I might have been

171

inclined to start believing her. But now I knew she couldn't be trusted, just as Jason had insisted since the day she arrived.

"He promised to call when he got to Washington," I reminded her.

"I guess he's been very tied up. But what shall we talk about? How about some girl talk?" Gwen said brightly.

"What's that?" I asked, though I knew exactly what she was trying to say. But there was only one person with whom I could have a real girl-to-girl, and no one could ever take Mother's place.

"You know, the way you used to talk to your mom."

"If you're wondering if I know about the facts of life and puberty and menstruation, I know all about it because she told me already."

Gwen held herself very stiffly as if she were afraid of breaking. "Then you don't have any questions about it?" she asked.

"No, she took care of that before . . . you know."

Aunt Gwen frowned and looked away. "Can I ask you a question, Quinn?"

I shrugged. "If you'd like."

"Have I done something to offend you, is that why you're so angry with me?"

"I'm not angry," I lied.

"Come now, the least you can do is be honest. I'm only trying to be your friend. Wouldn't it be better if you had someone to talk to?"

I did until you took her away, I thought. "I have Jason. He talks to me all the time."

"But he can't talk to you about . . . well, you know what I'm saying."

"I told you already. I know all about it, sex and stuff like that. What's the big deal, anyway? It just means sleeping together like you've been doing with you-know-who.''

Aunt Gwen wasn't wearing the usual gobs of makeup she liked to put on, so I could see how red her cheeks got the moment I mentioned that. ''I don't think that's a very nice thing to say, Quinn, especially when I have no idea who you're talking about. And who told you such a thing, anyway?''

So Jason was right, they were sleeping together like he said, because if they weren't she wouldn't have gotten so upset.

''I don't even think you know what you said, do you?'' she went on.

''Probably not.''

I don't think she believed me, because she said, ''Who's you-know-who, Quinn?''

''Someone.'' Then I changed the subject before she had a chance to pin me down. ''Father told me that he and Mother weren't happy together. They probably would've gotten a divorce. Is that true?''

The question took her by surprise, and she seemed to have a hard time coming up with an answer. ''I'm afraid so,'' she finally said.

''He also said that people aren't always what they pretend to be. He was talking about Mother, and I was wondering if you knew what he meant.''

''My sister . . . your mother . . . well, Rebecca was a very troubled woman. I'm sure she always tried her best, Quinn, but sometimes one's best just isn't good enough.''

''Good enough for what?''

This was obviously making her terribly uncomfortable, because she kept looking around in every direction at once, unable to face me. ''She was ill, Quinn. She was very ill.''

173

"With what?" I demanded. "Was it a rare disease or something like that? Is that what she died of?"

Aunt Gwen shook her head nervously. "Do you recall the headaches she used to get?"

"The sick headaches she always called them, yes."

"Your mother went through periods of great depression. I don't know if you were aware of it, but in the last few years they only seemed to get worse."

What kind of terrible lies was she telling? Mother stayed in her room when she got the headaches, but they never lasted very long, just a couple of days at most. What did that have to do with her death?

"Are you trying to say my mother was crazy?" I said angrily, no longer able to hide my true feelings. "That's the meanest thing I ever heard. If she was crazy I'd know, I'd be the first to know 'cause we were very close and we still are. We still are!"

Aunt Gwen's voice rose up in alarm. "You don't mean that, Quinn, you know you don't."

"I mean every word of it." I got up and looked down at the big bouquet of flowers she'd set on the coffee table. "I don't think it's right to have so many flowers around until Mother comes back."

"Quinton, please," she begged, "you have to start dealing with reality."

"I know reality, Aunt Gwen, and it has nothing to do with Mother dying. And you can tell that to you-know-who or anyone else for that matter, because I don't care anymore!"

I hadn't meant to lose control, but now it was too late. Aunt Gwen tried to stop me but I was already halfway out the door.

"The truth is terribly painful, I know," she called after me.

"It's not the truth that's painful, it's the lies," I shouted.

I rushed outside. I wanted to get as far away from her as I could, but there were spies everywhere, just like my brother had warned. Harry Darby suddenly popped up out of nowhere, appearing like a ghost in the middle of the path. He gave me this big friendly hello, like he didn't even remember how mean he'd been the day before.

"Whatcha up to?" he said. He was wearing a handkerchief tied around his forehead to keep the sweat from dripping in his eyes. With his jet-black hair and prominent cheekbones, the sweatband and the deep suntan he'd already gotten, he looked just like an Indian.

"None of your business." I tried to walk past him, but he reached out and put his hands on my shoulders, blocking my way.

"You're awfully cute when you're mad," he said with a laugh.

You'd be mad too, I thought, if everyone lied to you the way they've been lying to me.

"Why are you bothering me, anyway?" I asked. "You already got paid, so why don't you just leave me alone."

"Still sore about that?"

"Sure I am. You're a bully and you like to take advantage."

"I'd sure like to take advantage of you," he said with a laugh.

No one had ever said that kind of thing to me before. I wasn't even sure what it meant. But I was afraid to ask in case it was a trick.

"Come on down to the orchard and I'll give you back the bread," Harry said.

"Why the orchard? Why not right here?"

"There's something I want to show you. A surprise."

"The only thing that surprises me, Harry Darby, is that you're trying to be nice for a change."

Harry grinned and grinned and showed off his dimples

which I had to admit were pretty cute. "I can be real nice. You just have to stay on my good side, that's all." He turned away and started down the path, only to pause a moment later and look back at me. "You coming or aren't you?"

I wasn't sure if it was such a good idea. But since I didn't have anything else to do, and I certainly didn't want Aunt Gwen to start asking me all sorts of questions, I followed after him, wondering what the big secret was all about.

Past the empty koi pond the gravel path widened, and a dozen or so yards beyond that a gate led into the orchard. All sorts of gnarled old fruit trees stretched out before us, rows and rows of them that Great-grandfather Josiah had planted when he first settled here.

Harry keep walking until there were trees behind us and in front of us and on every side. Finally, he stopped before an apple tree that looked about to topple over. A year or two before it had been struck by lightning, and now its trunk leaned crazily to one side. Even though Will had tried propping it up with a couple of stakes, the roots were half out of the ground, though surprisingly enough the tree was still bearing fruit.

"Look straight up there," Harry instructed. He pointed to the topmost part of the tree.

But I couldn't see anything but green apples hanging there like the balls you put on a Christmas tree.

"Here, lemme give you a hand."

Before I could stop him, he lifted me up in his arms. Both his hands were snug around my waist, and right then and there I realized what he was after. But there was something in the tree, after all. One of the great horned owls I often heard at night had taken over an old hawk's nest. As Harry held me in the air, I could just about see one of the owlets peering over the rim of the nest. The white ball of fluff was soon joined by another, and a moment later the mama owl herself came into view, her big feathered "horns" sticking straight up out of her head.

"Pretty neat, don't you think?" he said.

I wriggled free of Harry's grasp and jumped back down onto the ground. "For a city kid, maybe. But I see them all the time." I thought that was the end of it, but when I turned away, Harry called after me, reminding me about the money. I started to take the five-dollar bill he held in his hand, but he jerked his arm back and began to laugh.

"Indian giver," I said, getting more annoyed by the second.

"How's about giving this big strong brave a kiss first? After all, fair's fair."

He sounded just like Jason then, and I wondered why they both liked kissing a lot more than I did. Maybe it was because I hadn't had enough experience. And Harry was very nice looking, and he wasn't acting pushy or grabby or anything like that.

"Just one," I made him promise.

He stuffed the money into my back pocket. Then his arms came swooping down around me like an owl beating its wings, holding me tight in his embrace. Suddenly he closed his eyes, leaned even closer, and kissed me. Jason had said that kisses were love, not sex. But I didn't love Harry, not even a little bit. Yet when he kissed me it gave me the strangest sensation, and I didn't try to pull away.

I thought that was all there was to it, but before I could say anything he did it again. Only this time he opened his mouth a little and I could feel his tongue tickling my lips. That gave me goosebumps, it was all so new and strange.

"I could hold you all day," he whispered.

Even though it sounded romantic, I was sure it was just something he'd read in a book somewhere. "You'd get cramps," I said with a nervous laugh.

177

Harry looked down at me, grinning and showing off his dimples. Next thing I knew he put his hands under my polo shirt and started feeling around like he was looking for something. He was probably looking for my breasts (which weren't all that easy to find, I guess, since they weren't very big). The moment I figured out what he was up to, I realized it had to do with the secret places mentioned in Father's letter.

"I don't think you should do that," I told him.

"Why not? Don't it feel good?"

He moved his hands up until they were covering my breasts. Then he began to rub them against the nipples. The goosebumps started in all over again. But this time I couldn't stop shivering because not only did it feel very strange, but it was also very pleasant. It was sort of like tickling (which Jason was terribly fond of doing), but without the giggles that usually went along with it.

"You like that, don'tcha?" Harry said.

I did like it, but I wasn't sure if I should tell him or just keep it to myself. Then I got to wondering if Father had done this to Aunt Gwen, and if it was all part of what Jason had called "sleeping together." Were breasts and nipples what Father meant when he wrote about secret places? And if they were, what were the other places that gave you goosebumps if you touched them? Was it between the legs, was that it? I'd never been very curious about touching myself there, but now I wondered if I'd get the same kind of feeling rubbing myself the way Harry was rubbing his hands over my breasts.

I don't know if he read my mind, but the next thing I knew, that was exactly what he tried to do. As soon as I felt his hand going to that place between my legs I pulled away.

"Then how's about giving me a try?" Harry said. He

took hold of my hand and pressed it up against the front of his jeans.

Suddenly I was very scared because I knew he wanted me to touch his penis which I'd seen on Jason when we were little and we sometimes took baths together. Penises and vaginas were for breeding, unless you slept together which was sex. I wasn't so dumb as to think that if I touched Harry's penis I'd have to breed and get a baby. But I still didn't know what to expect. Maybe if I touched him he'd force me to do other things like in the letter, lying down on the ground on top of each other and weird stuff like that.

So I just pulled my hand away and told him I wasn't interested—I was only twelve and a half.

"Harry, can you be a dear and fix this hammock for me?" It was Aunt Gwen, calling to him from the garden.

There wasn't any way she could have seen us, but I didn't want to take a chance. So before Harry could say anything I ran back the way we'd come.

"Hey, come on, don't be such a baby, Quinn," he called after me.

When I looked back he was still standing there by the crooked apple tree. Only now he was doing something to himself that I knew wasn't nice. He was starting to unbutton his fly—and making a big show of it, too. If he thought that would scare me, he had another guess coming because I wasn't about to stand around and watch him act dirty.

But was it dirty, or was it just part of sex?

If only Mother hadn't left, I could have gone to her and asked. If it were wrong she would have told me. And if it were right she would have told me that, too. But Mother was nowhere to be found, though tonight at the stroke of twelve Jason had promised that we'd finally find out what had happened to her.

She'd gone away before, I recalled, though of course in the past she hadn't been forced to leave, dragged down the stairs and hustled into a car. Once she went to visit a friend of hers, someone she'd known in school. Maybe it was even Rose Hotchkins or Aimee Trumble, whom she'd mentioned in her diary. Now that I thought of it, it seemed very odd that we'd never met Mother's friend, nor had Father said anything about inviting her when it came time to plan the funeral. Another time Mother went off to Europe on a shopping spree, and several months before that she'd gone to a resort in the desert where ladies stayed until they got their figures back. Mother hadn't lost hers, but she still went anyway. Those last two trips, I remembered, were kind of strange because she'd gone away very suddenly, and she hadn't even said good-bye to us, either. She just went off in the middle of the night, and when she came back she always had wonderful presents for us and she was always very sorry for having left so quickly, "on short notice" she used to call it.

So it wasn't as if this last disappearance of hers didn't have any . . . what was the word? Precedence or precedents. Something like that. If it had happened before, her leaving us without bothering to say good-bye or tell us where she was going, then maybe this fake death they'd cooked up was just like the other times.

"Did you happen to see Harry, by any chance?" Aunt Gwen asked when I got back to the garden. She was trying to hang the hammock between two trees, and not having the easiest time of it.

I was afraid of what she might think. Since I didn't want her to be even more suspicious of me than she already was, I said, "Why would I want to see him for?" making it sound like he was the last person on earth I cared to spend time with.

But no sooner did I get the words out when there he

was, just as out of breath as me, only with something in his pants nice people kept buttoned up and out of sight.

"How ya doin', Quinn," he said, like we hadn't seen each other all morning. "Keeping yourself busy, kiddo?"

"Very."

I thought he'd continue to make conversation, which would have been the polite thing to do. But by then he was already giving Aunt Gwen the eye, pretending to be helpful and considerate when what he really wanted was to touch her the way he'd tried touching me. Well, as far as I was concerned he could do whatever he felt like, because that's what she deserved.

But instead of going back to the house, I tried to put myself in Jason's place, wondering what he might do— right that moment, I mean. He'd probably double back if that's the word, and see what information he could gather. Harry wasn't rushing off to help his father, and I figured that if I stuck around I might learn something valuable.

So I strolled back to the house, trying to act as nonchalant as possible. But the moment I was out of sight I ducked between the oleander bushes that bordered the garden path.

When Jason and I were little we'd made tunnels through the shrubbery like mice do in a field. You couldn't see them unless you got down on your hands and knees and crawled into the bushes. Jason used to play jungle warfare— that was the name he'd given the game, while I played Alice in search of the White Rabbit.

The hidden paths were still there, though they were much narrower than I remembered. But it was cool and shady, and despite the occasional fly that buzzed around my face, it wasn't very uncomfortable at all. I did have to inch my way along, however, because the shrubs were so densely overgrown it was impossible to straighten up, or even get into a crouch.

Oleander blossoms were poisonous, and the trail was strewn with them. But I wasn't afraid to touch them because Jason had once told me that you had to eat them, or boil them in water like tea, to really get sick and die. From the few piles of droppings I saw I knew that animals were still using the tunnels, though I didn't see any, not even a squirrel.

It was hard to tell which way I was going, because it was very difficult to see through the bushes. But fortunately I was soon able to hear their voices. So I headed in that direction, forced to make a new tunnel as I crawled along.

When I could go no further, I sat back and tried to get comfortable, wondering how long I'd have to stay here before I heard anything of importance. I still couldn't see them, though I could tell where they were because dark, shadowy shapes occasionally passed before the bushes. The shadows were fairly large, so I guess I must have been just a few feet from the clearing where they were still trying to hang the hammock.

"There used to be a hook here somewhere," I heard Harry remark.

"I couldn't find it," replied Aunt Gwen. "I'm usually much handier. Guess I'm out of practice."

"There, that should do it," Harry said a moment later. "You want to try it out? Don't want you falling on your . . . they seem to be in pretty solid, don't they?"

I guess he was still talking about the hammock, because Aunt Gwen said it seemed perfect, the hooks weren't about to pull free.

"You hear from their old man?" Harry suddenly asked.

"My brother-in-law? Yes. As a matter of fact he asked me to tell you how much he appreciates what you're doing."

"All in a day's work," Harry said with a laugh. "What's

he so worried about, anyway? The kid cracking up or something?''

''He's having a difficult time adjusting to what happened. I don't think it's all that unusual for someone his age, but Mr. Lefland doesn't want to take any chances.''

''And you?'' asked Harry.

''Pardon?''

''Do you take chances, Gwen?''

Was he snickering or was it just my imagination?

''You're a very attractive young man, Harry. And I'm also ten years older than you.''

''It don't bother me none, Gwen. Don't forget now, it gets pretty lonely here, this place is so isolated.''

''Mr. Lefland's grandfather wanted it that way.''

''So my old lady always told me. How come?''

''I really have no idea. He liked his privacy, I suppose.''

''And you?''

''I like mine as well, Harry,'' my aunt replied when suddenly I heard something like heavy breathing, only I couldn't tell exactly what it was. The two shadowy shapes beyond the shrubs now became one, and just as I realized what was going on they broke apart again.

''I don't appreciate that, Harry,'' Aunt Gwen said sternly.

''Can't blame me for trying.''

''But I will blame you if you try it again.''

''Saving yourself?''

''Excuse me?''

''Just wondering if there was a man in your life, that's all.''

''Not that it's any business of yours, Harry, but it just so happens there is.''

''That's cool,'' Harry told her, only he didn't sound very cool at all. If anything, he sounded annoyed, probably because she'd just told him she had a boyfriend, and it wasn't him. "Guess I better go look for the kid. Don't want him getting into mischief now, do we?"

"No, Harry, we don't, especially since that's what you're being paid for."

"You seen him around?"

"Not since breakfast."

Something creaked. It must have been the ropes attached to the hammock. Aunt Gwen didn't say anything after that, and Harry finally got the message and walked off. At least he hadn't told her about finding us in Mother's room. Not that I trusted Harry, especially after what he had tried to do in the orchard, but it was nice to know that he kept his word. As for the other business, Aunt Gwen saying there was a man in her life, I had no doubts she was talking about Father.

I was beginning to realize that everything my brother had been telling me was true. And tonight, at midnight, I knew I would learn the most frightening truth of all.

# 12

got a burn on my hand and everything. Proof, that's what it was. The spirit's still around, even if we can't find the flesh. Why does that make me giggle? Lefland, you're getting weirder by the minute. So cool it.

COOL IT!!!

That's better, calmer. I have to take things one step at a time, nice and slow. But it's hard to think straight, knowing that Dad called that cunt in the middle of the night. I don't care if it's a dirty word, because it's true, that's just what Gwen is.

Of course Warren didn't know when it happened. Mom was much too clever for that. She escaped his wiry clutches and flew the coop. "No sign of that sick bitch?" Dad must have said. "None whatsoever," said cutesie-pie Gwen, the rotten phony. "But what about that pain-in-the-ass son of mine?" "We'll put him away soon, too, don't you worry, Benny dear." "Alert the Darbys. Tell them to call out the National Guard." "They have too much firepower, sweetheart. Let's trust Harry's judgment. He's such an eager young man."

Sure, that's how the conversation must have gone whether Quinnie heard it that way or not. The voices were right upstairs between my ears, just where they were supposed to be. Only problem, I had to start proving to Quinn that I wasn't losing my marbles, and that everything I'd told her was the truth.

There, feeling better now, Lefland?

Yes, much.

Can't let yourself get too excited.

I know.

I wasn't a kid anymore, and I knew what my mom expected from me. Demanded of me, I guess. She'd spoken to me, if not in real life then at least in a vision, which was kind of like a waking dream. I had a blister in the middle of my hand to prove it. Maybe when it healed there'd be a scar, permanent reminder of how much I cared.

But before I could find her there was lots to take care of, and I only had until midnight to do it. So right after breakfast, I went into the kitchen and had Mrs. Darby pack me a picnic lunch. I told her I was going up into the hills to look for rocks. She'd seen the collection I had in my room, so she wasn't the least bit suspicious. But it was important to have a good alibi so that no one would wonder where I was when I didn't show up for lunch.

Of course, I had no intention of hiking up into the hills. The fact is, I never even got near them, because whatever needed to be done was a lot closer to home. Lucky for me, Will wasn't around to see what I was up. He had stuff I needed, tools and such. I couldn't very well come right out and ask if I could borrow them, so I had to sneak into the shed when he wasn't looking.

As soon as I got everything together, hiding it so no one could possibly guess what I was up to, I went down to the Bottom, keeping clear of the cemetery road just in case I bumped into Harry. I'd take care of him too, but all in good time. The first order of business was Quinnie, because in the vision Mom had told me it was time to test my sister's faith.

The only way to do that was prove to her that Mom was still alive, desperate to be with us again. But Mom had also spoken of retribution. To tell you the truth, I wasn't quite sure how to go about avenging the wrongs that had been committed if she wasn't actually there to give me a hand. That's why I needed to be alone, to pray to her and ask for guidance. Maybe it was the strength of our love that made it easy for her to speak to me, in the vision I mean. And maybe if I prayed hard enough, she'd come back and speak to me again.

Down in the Bottom it was cool and secluded, so different from the rest of the Valley I could easily have been miles from home. Great-grandpa Josiah didn't like prying eyes and neither did I. Besides, who could blame him? The events surrounding his first wife's death were shrouded in mystery, and even the source of his fortune had never been explained to my satisfaction. There were skeletons in the Lefland closet, all right. Take his son Ephraim, for example. His first wife, Alethea, had also died under mysterious circumstances, circumstances that Mom had told me constituted a family curse. But who had cursed the Leflands, to begin with? And were Quinn and I doomed to suffer because of events that had taken place years and years before?

If only I knew more about the curse, I might be able to do something to stop it. But I certainly couldn't talk to Dad about it, and at this point I couldn't go to Mom, either. So the best thing to do was put it out of my mind, at least for the time being. One thing about Great-grandpa though. When it came to privacy, he had the right idea. People never seemed to mind their business, did they? No, they just interfered and took advantage whenever they could.

But things were going to change. As soon as Mom came back she'd confront them with their lies and their treachery. Then everything would be different, the way it was supposed to be.

At least here in the Bottom a person could be alone with his thoughts. And of course the Bottom meant the playhouse, only we wouldn't call it that anymore. No, it was a holy of holies, a temple and a shrine.

I'd brought along two silver candlesticks I'd found in the same sideboard where I took the candles. They were black with tarnish, but before I'd left that morning I'd managed to get a tin of silver polish from the pantry. Now, they gleamed just as brightly as the blessed instruments of our faith, the comb and brush and hand mirror, each of which were engraved with Mom's initials.

You're feeling better now, Lefland, aren't you? You're your old self again, right?

Yes, I'm fine now. I'm totally in control, and I'm going to stay that way, too.

The temple door didn't have a lock, so I wedged a chair up against the doorknob, just in case someone decided to come barging in. Not that I expected anyone, Quinn included. But it couldn't hurt to take the necessary precautions.

Then I knelt before the altar, the candles flickering dimly and sending sparks of fiery light shooting up toward the portrait of our blessed Mom. The artist had done an excellent job, and Mom had always loved the painting. She used to say it was like having two sets of eyes, or being in two different places at the same time.

I could hear her voice so clearly then, her laughter as well. Tears stung my eyes but I couldn't help myself. I guess it was all right to cry in front of her. Even if it meant

I was still a baby, I just didn't care, because I missed her so.

"Please," I begged. "Can't you come back? We need you, Mom. And I'll be good, I swear. I'll do anything you say."

Mom watched me in silence. I tried to look away, but her eyes held me. I began to drag myself along the floor, pulling myself up over the altar.

"He wants to separate us," I told her, "send us off to different schools. He wants to keep us apart for the rest of our lives. I bet he'd like to kill us too if he got the chance. He doesn't want anything to stand in his way, Mom. He'll marry Aunt Gwen and then they'll kill us and say it was an accident. That's why you've got to help us before it's too late!"

Mom reached out, and though I wanted to run to her, wanted to press my cheek to hers and feel her arms around me making everything right again, I was afraid.

The candles sputtered, hissing like an army of cats. A searing wind rushed through the Bottom. The shutters clattered angrily, and a brooding presence hovered just outside the door. It wanted to get in, stop us before we'd made our plans. But there were roses in the air, the blessed fragrance of remembrance. I looked up at Mom, shielding my eyes from her stern, uncompromising expression.

They had to be punished. Sure, that was what she was trying to say. There had to be retribution before she would consent to return. Only when they'd suffered for their treachery, their cruelty and evil deeds, would she come back for us.

"Do you still love me, or have they taken that away from us, too?" I whispered.

Mom showed me her hands with their beautiful tapered nails. Her fingers were slim and delicate, her hands as perfect as any that had ever been created. But now the

189

fingers trembled, and the hands stiffened and clenched into fists.

"What is it?" I asked. "What are you trying to tell me?"

From beneath her tightly clenched fingers blood began to trickle, dripping onto the altar like a thick, sluggish rain.

"No, don't!" I pleaded. "Don't hurt yourself like that!"

But Mom didn't answer, and the blood kept dripping. As painful as it was to watch, I couldn't tear my eyes away, almost as if I were being hynotized. Each drop hit the painted floorboards in slow motion, like rose petals strewn adoringly before her. Mom looked beyond me then, her eyes focused on the opposite end of the room. She raised her arm and pointed, and though I was scared to death of what I might see, I knew I didn't have any choice but to obey.

And the blood kept trickling down her fingers, hot and steaming.

And each drop of her life that was so good and giving fell onto the altar making a sound like thunder.

And painted on the far wall of her temple, her shrine, was the word QUINN, and the word was written in letters of blood.

But what did it mean?

Maybe Mom wanted Quinnie to share in the pain of her betrayal, so that my sister would finally understand what they had really done to her.

But Mom shook her head, and as she stepped back, she motioned to the blessed instruments of our faith. Suddenly I understood what was expected of me. Hurrying now, anxious to demonstrate my obedience, I pulled my shirt over my head and flung it to the floor. Mom watched approvingly. She smiled full of laughter full of life when I picked up the hairbrush, holding it tightly in my hand.

"Count the strokes, Jason. Don't forget to count the strokes."

I bent forward, pressing my forehead to the floor. I felt more in control of myself than ever, more certain of the unique bond that still existed between us. Then I reached back, hesitating no longer as I brought the bristle side of the brush down across my shoulders.

"Harder," whispered Mom. "Don't forget to count the strokes, my dearest son, my beautiful boy."

"Two," I said.

The bristles tore into my skin and it was good and the pain was a reminder of how they'd made her suffer, her and the baby both.

"Three," I said.

I would draw blood. I would give my life in return for hers.

"Four."

It was good, it was very, very good.

"Five . . . six . . . seven," the stiff bristles digging into my flesh, again and again and again.

"Don't forget to count the strokes. Don't ever forget."

". . . nine . . . ten . . . eleven."

Now I knew what she wanted me to do, knew it as surely as I knew my name. But the moment I realized what it was, the feeling-good suddenly came over me. I hadn't meant for it to happen. I was ashamed that she'd see, but I couldn't help myself. I began to tremble and there was no stopping it after that. It was the shuddering and the falling over the edge, biting into the pillows because the Lefland secret had to be preserved. No one could know and no one could hear and no one could guess and—

"Quinn!" I cried out.

Yes, that was the meaning of the sign, the purpose of the letters drawn in lifeblood. Mom would never let them separate us. Mom would make sure we were together because that was what she wanted, and that was what I wanted, too.

"Quinnie, Quinnie," I groaned when I felt it happening.

It was the feeling-good and I didn't try to stop it or make it go away. My arm rose and fell. The bristles were slippery with blood. But I wanted it to go on and on and on, and Mom said it was okay, and so I let it begin.

"Quinnie, how I love you, how I love you so!"

Mom smiled and held me in her arms. She rocked me back and forth, saying what a good boy I was, and I was glad. Then, as the strokes began anew, she told me what to do, and how to go about punishing them for trying to keep us apart.

# 13

When dinner was over and Anna started clearing away the dishes, Jason and I excused ourselves and left the table. I wanted to tell him what had happened with Harry, but he seemed very preoccupied and withdrawn. When I put my hand on his shoulder to ask him what was wrong, he winced in pain even though I was barely touching him.

"Sunburn," he said.

"Where have you been all day?" I whispered. I knew enough to keep my voice down, but he still didn't want to talk about it until we were out on the porch, and no one else was around.

"The temple," he explained as soon as we were alone.

For a second I wasn't sure what he meant. Then I realized he was referring to the playhouse. I thought Temple was an excellent word for it, but even when I complimented him on his choice, Jason didn't seem very interested in what I had to say. Right then and there I wondered if Harry had already spoken to him, bragging about feeling me up and kissing me. If that had happened, perhaps Jason was angry with me, or jealous even, though I couldn't understand why since he was my brother, not my boyfriend.

"Is everything all right? You seem awfully strange to-night," I told him.

"How can everything be all right?" he said accusingly. Something glinted in his eyes like fire, only I knew it was rage. "Do you want to find out what happened to Mother or don't you?"

"Of course I do, Jason. More than anything. In fact, that's what I've been doing all day, too."

He looked at me nervously. "Doing what?"

I glanced behind me to make sure no one was eaves-dropping. Then I hurriedly told him about the conversation Harry had had with Aunt Gwen, and how she'd admitted to him that Father had called.

"She said he was being paid extra to spy on you," I added. "And then he did something else."

"What?"

I put my arm under his and walked him down the porch steps. Fireflies sent their winking signals into the darkness. A sharp green smell filled the air, and there were so many sentinel-like shadows cast by the trees that I was afraid one of them belonged to Harry. But as soon as I told Jason how Harry had made a pass at our aunt, my brother threw his head back and burst out laughing.

Frankly, I didn't see why he thought it was so funny.

"They all cheat on each other, every one of them. They're all rotten, and corrupt, and evil. It's the Lefland curse. It's in the blood, Quinn, and we have it too, whether we want it or not."

The words on that slip of paper came back to me then, and they seemed more ominous than ever.

*For the sins of the fathers are visited upon the children.*

But what were the sins that had been committed in the past, and why were we being made to suffer for them? If

194

only I knew the answer, Mother's disappearance would probably begin to make a lot more sense.

"It was just a kiss, Jason, that's all," I said, trying to make light of it. But now I was terrified that Harry might tell him what we did in the orchard. If Jason found out that I'd let Harry touch me, he'd think I was as evil and corrupt as everyone else. So I hurried to change the subject, telling him that Anna had been complaining again that food was missing.

"I'm not surprised," he admitted. "I've been able to feel her presence, and today it was even stronger than ever."

"Aunt Gwen just about called me crazy when I told her I knew Mother was still alive."

"You did what?" He looked at me angrily and I shrank back, afraid to meet his hostile gaze.

"She just got me so mad and I didn't mean anything but I couldn't—"

"Quinn, how could you be so stupid?" He started to shake me, and I was never more afraid of him than at that moment.

"You're hurting me," I whimpered. "She said Mother was ill, depressed all the time. She called her crazy and I said it wasn't so and you're hurting me. You're hurting me, Jason!"

I must have screamed it out, because my brother suddenly released me and stumbled back, tripping over his feet he seemed in such a hurry to get away from me. He looked at his hands as if they didn't even belong to him, and I thought of the knife he had taken from my room, and how he had come so close to using it on himself.

"You know who's crazy, Quinn? They are, because they think they can twist our minds, get us to believe whatever they say. But we're going to surprise them. We're going to learn the truth, even if it kills us."

195

I could still feel his hands gripping my shoulders like pincers, shaking me back and forth as if he were powerless to stop himself. "It's tonight, isn't it? I mean, you haven't changed your mind, have you?"

"No, it's tonight, all right," he said, and as he nodded his hair fell over his eyes and I reached out and brushed it back for him. "Do you know how much I love you, Quinnie? Do you have any idea?"

He sounded so serious that I was suddenly at a loss for words.

"I just want you to remember that," he went on. "No matter what happens, you mustn't forget. I'm sorry I hurt you. It's just that . . . don't talk to them, Quinnie, not if you can help it. They're gathering information on us all the time. They want to know where we are and what we do and even what we think. And if they know so much about us, we'll never be able to trap them in their lies."

I promised that I'd be more careful in the future.

"I'll come to your room when it's time. We'll have to make sure they're all asleep first."

Aunt Gwen came out onto the veranda with three dishes of fresh peach ice cream. Jason smiled and thanked her and acted like a perfect gentleman. I got the hint and did the same, despite the fact we'd argued so bitterly that morning.

"Your father called," she announced. "He was very anxious to speak to you, but neither of you were around."

"When did you hear from him?" Jason asked.

"This afternoon. He's working day and night to clear up that business in Washington. When he comes back, he said he'd like to take you on a trip."

"Where?" said my brother.

"You know he has two wonderful schools picked out, and he wants you to see them before classes start."

"So if we hate them, we can tell him, is that it?"

"Oh, I don't think you'll hate them, Jason. They're only a few hours away from each other, and they're considered two of the finest boarding schools in the West."

"That sounds like a wonderful idea," I spoke up, and when Jason started glaring at me, I made sure he saw me wink. "Won't that be fun, Jason, just the three of us?"

"Terrific. I can't wait."

"You don't sound very enthusiastic, Jason," said our aunt.

"Oh I am, honest. I'm just tired, that's all. I guess I must've taken too much sun today."

"Really?" said Aunt Gwen, and she peered at him inquisitively. "You don't look very burned."

"It's the light," he replied, and he got up and excused himself.

So the two of us sat there, eating our ice cream and trying to figure out what to say to each other. After several false starts we each gave up and lapsed into silence. As soon as my spoon scraped the bottom of the dish, I came to my feet and told Aunt Gwen I was going to turn in, too.

"So early?" She actually sounded disappointed. But since we didn't have anything to talk about, I didn't see what good it would do to sit around and pretend we were enjoying ourselves.

"I'm reading a wonderful book," I told her. "It's a diary. It's just fascinating."

I looked at her searchingly, trying to read her mind. But all she did was smile blankly, so I couldn't tell if she knew about *the* Diary or not.

Although I thought I'd lie down and take a nap, I was too excited and couldn't even close my eyes. The grandfather clock in the front hall was still striking twelve when I finally heard my brother's knock. He was dressed in jeans and a dark sweater, and he told me to put on a sweater too, it was chilly out. I was glad to see he'd come prepared, because he was carrying a flashlight, though he still hadn't told me where we were going.

As soon as I pulled the sweater on, I motioned to the bed, where I'd arranged the pillows under the blanket. If anyone decided to check up on me in the middle of the night it would look like I was sleeping. Then I closed the door behind us and followed Jason down the hall.

But no sooner did we get downstairs when I heard a door opening. I froze in my place, not knowing what to do. Jason grabbed me by the arm, pulling me along with him until we were safe behind the stairwell.

We heard footsteps, and then someone coughing loudly and trying to clear his throat.

"Who is it?" I whispered.

Jason clapped a hand over my mouth and shook his head. Only when the person in the hall started up the stairs did he tell me it must have been Will because he recognized his shuffling walk.

Anna had put the chain across the front door (perhaps she was afraid of a ghost named Rebecca, I couldn't help but think), and I guess Jason was worried that if we left that way someone might notice it was undone before we had a chance to return. So instead of going out by the front, he led me through the dining room and on into the pantry, and from there we made our way to the servants dining room. Here, there were two doors, one that opened onto a back porch, and another that led directly outside.

Neither door was furnished with a chain and bolt, and as soon as we slipped out of the house, Jason started off in the direction of the Bottom. A few minutes later he turned on the flashlight, keeping the beam aimed low at the ground. He was walking so quickly I had trouble keeping up. But when I called to him to please slow down, he told me to be quiet and not make a sound, else everything would be ruined.

When I glanced over my shoulder I couldn't see anything at all, neither the house with its tall craggy facade and dozens of rooms, nor the lush greenery of the garden. Even the road itself was difficult to make out, just the faintest track etched in the darkness. Off in the distance one of the owls was hooting, and then a falling star streaked across the sky, a trail of reddish sparks vanishing beyond the hills.

"Jason, can you please slow down a bit? There's something in my shoe and I can't walk." That was a fib to get him to stop rushing along like we were in a race or something.

He paused in the middle of the road while I yanked off my tennis shoe and pretended to shake a pebble out.

"I have something to tell you," I said.

"What?"

"Just hold on a sec." I grabbed him by the elbow, but that didn't stop him. I think he was afraid of being followed, but I hadn't heard anyone behind us and so I didn't know what he was getting so worried about.

I thought we might be going to the Temple. Though I didn't relish the idea of trooping through the Bottom in the middle of the night, I knew my brother wasn't in any mood to listen to my complaints.

"It's about Harry," I said.

Despite my initial fears, I'd resolved to tell the truth. More than ever, we needed to be honest with each other. But before I had a chance to explain he suddenly veered off the road. If I hadn't been clinging to his arm I would have lost my footing because the ground was wet and spongy, and with every step I took it felt like something was pulling at my ankles and trying to drag me down. The beam of the flashlight wavered before me, then alighted like a moth on a lichen-covered rock near a stand of alders.

"Where did all that come from?" I asked.

"Will's toolshed." He reached down and picked up the shovel that was leaning against the rock, then took the length of rope that lay alongside it and coiled it over his shoulder. "Here, you carry the hammer. I couldn't find a crowbar so it'll have to do."

"A crowbar for what?"

Jason held the flashlight under his chin. It made his face look like a jack-o'-lantern, and I was suddenly very nervous about being out in the dark like this, creeping around and not knowing where we were going or what to expect.

"Please don't do that, Jason."

"Scared of big bad me?" he said with a laugh. Then he started making these awful creepy sounds like you hear in horror movies.

"You do that again and I'm going back," I warned him.

He didn't seem very impressed by my threat. "Suit yourself," he said smugly. "But if you do, you'll have to go back all by yourself. There's no telling who's lurking in the woods, Quinnie."

"Stop it!"

"And besides, if you chicken out now you'll never find out about Mom, will you?"

"Then what's the shovel for, and the hammer and the rope?"

Jason eyed me impatiently. "I told you the coffin was empty. Now I'm going to prove it."

He'd spoken of doing that before, but I guess I hadn't taken him all that seriously. Only now he wasn't just saying it for effect. He meant every word of it, and before I had a chance to offer my opinion, he started back to the road.

To talk about it was one thing. But to actually go through with it was an entirely different matter. I rushed after him, asking all sorts of questions I'm sure he thought were dumb. But for everything I said he had an answer. What it came down to was that he knew I still had my doubts. So the only way to resolve them was to show me the empty coffin.

"But I do believe you," I kept insisting. "I thought I saw her myself, by the Temple. You know that. And you heard her up in the attic. And we both smelled the perfume, the fragrance of remembrance I mean."

Jason reached out and put his hand on my cheek. He was smiling, but it was such a sad, forlorn little grin that I wasn't sure what it meant. Was he sad for me or him or the both of us?

"Mom wants it this way, don't you see? She came to me again, like the last time. The vision was stronger than ever, Quinnie. She told me what to do, and now we have to obey her. We can't let her down, not after all she's been through."

"She wants you to . . . you know, with the coffin?"

"Afraid to say it?" he laughed. "Come on, Quinnie, you can be honest with me. You still have your doubts. Mabye I do, too. Who can say?"

He gave me a hug, and I leaned my hand against his shoulder, only he winced like he had earlier in the evening. He'd said it was sunburn, but his face wasn't the least bit red.

By then we were nearing the cemetery, and I could just about make out the wrought-iron fence that encircled the Lefland family plot. The dark, upright shapes of the tombstones rose out of the ground like witnesses to the sins of past generations. Was it just my imagination, or could I actually hear their voices, calling out to me in the darkness? Was that Alethea, Grandfather Ephraim's first wife, whimpering in pain and begging for mercy? Had she really been murdered, as Jason had said, or was that merely a story he'd concocted to explain her sudden and unexpected death so many years before? And the maniac laughter from the far end of the cemetery, could that be the ghost of Orin Lefland, a young man whose past was also shrouded in mystery?

I was letting my imagination get the best of me, I realize that. But I couldn't help but wonder about these things, knowing that Jason and I were Leflands just like all the others, and perhaps we too would face truths beyond our comprehension. The last person I had on my mind was Harry Darby, but Jason brought his name up, reminding me of what I'd started to say. It didn't seem important now, but he was very persistent.

So I told him what had happened in the orchard, and how I'd let Harry kiss me. I didn't intend to mention the business of his feeling me up, but Jason made a point of asking if he'd touched me. Although I was going to lie about it because I thought it would be easier that way, I couldn't bring myself to do it. After all, we'd been hearing enough lies to last a lifetime. I didn't want to add mine to the pile.

"Yes," I admitted, "but just a little."

"What does that mean, 'just a little'?"

I heard something in his voice that was like anger, only it wasn't quite the same. Was it jealousy, was that it? The idea of Jason being jealous over me was somehow very pleasing, because it sort of made me more like a woman, more attractive too, I guess.

"Just a little means just a little." I was about to make a joke about having just-a-little breasts, but he stopped me before I could get the words out.

"Did he do this?" He reached down and put his hand below my belly, holding it there like he was feeling my temperature in the wrong place. That made me smile to myself, but Jason didn't think there was anything humorous about it. "Well, did he or didn't he?" he asked again.

I shook my head. "No, but he tried. He wanted me to touch him there, too." No sooner had the words popped out when I realized I should never have said them.

Jason stared at me as if he couldn't even recognize who I was. His eyes began to blink uncontrollably like a twitch, and I was scared to glance down at his hands, certain they were beginning to clench into fists.

"And did you?" he finally got the words out.

"No, I was afraid," I said hurriedly, hoping that would calm him down.

"Of what?" he demanded.

"I don't know, Jason. I didn't feel like experimenting, I guess."

"You *guess*?"

"I'm not guessing. I didn't do anything. I didn't want to with Harry."

"But you'd experiment with someone else, is that it?"

"What is this, Jason, the third degree? What's the big deal, anyway? So he touched me. There isn't all that much there to touch, anyway. And if you want to know the truth, I thought it was interesting."

Jason peeled his lips back and began to snicker. But I could tell from the hollow sounds that came out of his throat that he was laughing *at* me, not *with* me. "Interesting," he repeated, trying to imitate my tone of voice. "Now that is one weird way of putting it, Quinton."

Why was he calling me "Quinton" when he'd never called me that before? And why was he getting so upset? I couldn't help myself, and I nearly shouted as I said, "Next time you'll do it instead, okay?"

But the strange thing was, my answer seemed to please him. He opened the gate for me and stepped back, slapping me playfully across the bottom when I walked past him.

"Fresh," I heard myself say.

Only right then and there the smile died on my lips. I wrapped my arms around myself and didn't take another step. It didn't matter that we were alone and this was our Valley, or even that we were among our own kind, Leflands I mean. A cemetery in the middle of the night was definitely a place to be avoided.

The gate creaked shut behind us. The moment Jason turned off the flashlight I wanted to throw myself into his arms and never let go.

"I thought I could hear them," I whispered.

"Who?"

"All of them." I motioned before me, where the weathered stone monuments pressed against the blackness of the night, demanding to be noticed.

"They're waiting for us, Quinn. They know all our secrets. They've been expecting us, too."

I think he really believed that, which only frightened me all the more. "What if they find out?"

"Dad and his sweetie-pie, Aunt Gwen? They won't. As soon as we get it open, we'll close it up again. Here, you hold this." He handed me the flashlight and started down the nearest row of markers.

This was where Josiah and Hepzibah lay, side by side under slabs of pitted black marble. Here their children had been buried, and their children's children. I played the beam of the flashlight over the tombstones, catching glimpses of old-fashioned Biblical names and dates consigned to history books.

The voices I thought I'd heard earlier were stilled, and the sounds that came back to me were the ordinary ones of a summer night. A poor-will uttered its melancholy song. Cicadas clicked endlessly, and crickets added their raspy music until the air was alive with an unseen chorus. The yapping of a coyote tumbled down from the hills, and once again the owls began to call as they hunted through the darkness.

Jason walked on ahead, the rubber soles of his shoes squeaking like tires along the gravel. He paused before Mother's grave, and though I half-expected him to kneel down and pray, he suddenly set to work with a vengeance.

"There's nothing to be scared of, Quinn. Just remember, we're doing this because Mom asked us to. She's watching over us, so nothing can possibly go wrong."

Unless the coffin isn't empty, I thought. In which case how will we ever prove it was murder?

I didn't want to think about that, or even think about finding myself staring at Mother's withered, decomposing remains. That wasn't how I remembered her, and as Father himself had said, it wasn't the way to remember her now, like a mummy, or someone in a wax museum.

Jason instructed me to keep the flashlight aimed on the shovel. Instead of heaving the dirt over his shoulder, he was piling it up neatly alongside the grave. At the rate he was going we'd be here all night. I asked him why he hadn't thought of getting another shovel for me. But either he didn't hear or he was too preoccupied with what he was doing, because he never bothered to answer.

So I sat down on the ground, feeling the dampness of the earth against the seat of my pants. As long as I concentrated on watching Jason and holding the flashlight steady, I was all right. But the moment I let my mind wander (my imagination too, I suppose) I began to get frightened.

Maybe this was all a big mistake. Maybe Mother had died after all, the way we'd been told. I still didn't want to believe that, especially after all that had happened since the night they'd taken her away. But the longer I sat there, and the deeper Jason dug, the greater were my doubts.

He'd shoveled away more than a foot of earth and still he kept going, not even stopping to catch his breath or wipe the sweat from his eyes. The flashlight batteries were beginning to give out, but luckily for us the moon finally came out from behind the clouds, and there was just enough light to work by.

I'd forgotten to put on my watch, so I had no idea how much time had already gone by. But judging from the color of the sky, a deep indigo-blue like Aunt Gwen's eye shadow, dawn was still a long ways off.

"Do you want me to take over for awhile?" I asked.

By now, my brother was standing in a rectangular pit that was probably at least three feet deep, because all I could see of him was from the waist up. His pace had slowed considerably, probably because it was getting harder to raise the shovel high enough in order to clear the rim of the grave.

Jason nodded, and he pulled himself out while I hurriedly took his place, afraid of what might happen if we weren't done by the time the sun came up. Then we'd have to cover the hole up all over again, and we wouldn't have accomplished anything except a lot of sore, aching muscles.

So I kept digging while he took a breather. When I was ready for a break he took over, and then when he got tired, he lowered me down into the hole and I resumed the work. We dug in shifts like that for at least another hour, though it was hard to tell how much time went by because we never stopped.

It was Jason though who finally reached the coffin itself. The moment we heard the blade of the shovel striking wood, everything we'd worked so hard for seemed to take on new meaning. I peered over the edge of the grave that was now as deep as my brother was tall.

He looked up at me, reminding me of a coal miner with dirt smeared over his face and clothes. "Hand me the hammer, will you."

I tossed it down to him, then stepped back, not wanting to watch while he tried to get the top off. I could hear the wood splintering, and from the direction of the Bottom the poor-will sent its sad, lonely song drifting across the Valley, searching for an answer that never came. A wind suddenly sprang up, and when I glanced at the sky it was almost as if the breeze were blowing the night aside, peeling away the darkness to expose the faint ruby heart of dawn.

The brittle sound of cracking wood was now replaced by dull, muffled hammer blows. I thought I heard something else then, but when I jerked my head over my shoulder there wasn't anything there but the graves of our ancestors, a hundred years of Leflands buried in a place they'd never thought to leave. But perhaps they couldn't leave. And maybe that in itself was the curse my brother had spoken of earlier. We were all bound to stay here, rooted to the Valley like the great gnarled trees that grew undisturbed in the Bottom, unable to escape our destiny even in death.

I crouched alongside the grave, watching Jason use the hammer to pound a big rusty eye hook into the splintered edge of the coffin lid. He gave it a few tugs to make sure it was in securely, then told me to throw down the length of rope. Drawing one end through the eye, he knotted it as tightly as he could.

By now I'd already guessed what he was going to use it for, though I was still having second thoughts about the entire business. Jason flung the rope into the air like a cowboy performing tricks with a lariat. I leaned over and tried to catch it. But each time I thought I had it, I ended up with nothing but air between my fingers.

Rather than spend another hour trying to toss me the rope, my brother tied it around his waist and started to climb out. But the hole was so deep, and the earth so dry and crumbly, that even when he jumped he couldn't make it over the edge.

"Try standing on the shovel," I suggested.

He wedged it into a corner and managed to balance himself along the top of the blade, the point of which was digging into the coffin. I tried to help him but he told me not to, he was afraid I might lose my footing and fall in after him. It took a little doing, but finally he managed to haul himself out.

Breathing a sigh of relief as he stood beside Mother's grave, Jason flexed his knees and tried to work the cramps out. He untied the rope from around his waist, glanced down into the hole to make sure the other end was still knotted around the eye, and began to slowly pull the lid up.

I'd known all along that if we ever got this far I'd probably chicken out. So the moment I heard the hinges creaking, I thought of all the scary movies I'd ever seen, and slammed my eyes shut as tight as I could.

That's when I felt the hands touching me. Then something hot and sweaty was covering my mouth so I couldn't breathe.

I wrenched free, kicking back with my foot as hard as I could. In my mind's eye I saw Grandfather Howe, grinning evilly in the darkness. But in actuality it was none other than Father's personal spy, Harry Darby. I shouted at Jason to watch out, but it was already too late.

The lid was open now, and the three of us stood there as if we were all frozen solid, just staring down into the coffin. The empty coffin. The coffin that didn't have anything in it but a bunch of heavy stones.

"Jesus Christ, what the fuck did you do with the body?" whispered Harry, shaking his head in astonishment.

The moment he broke the silence, Jason started to tremble so violently I didn't know what to do. It wasn't even first light yet, but I could see him getting redder and redder as the blood rushed into his face. He swung his arm out, knocking Harry aside with a blow that was so powerful I don't think Harry even knew what hit him.

But the coffin was empty. Empty! Everything Jason had told me was turning out to be true. We'd been lied to, right from the start. Mother hadn't died the way they kept insisting. The funeral was a fake, a mockery, a big charade to convince us of a death that had never taken place!

Harry was clutching at his stomach, but I think he was groaning more out of fear than pain. "What the fuck did you do with the body?" he kept muttering, like those were the only words he knew how to say.

"We didn't do anything," I started to tell him, when Jason glared at me with such incredible fury that the rest of the things I was going to say faded away into nothingness.

But the coffin was empty. As empty as all of Father's promises.

That's all I could think of. Even if Harry was there to see it, how could we possibly be afraid of the truth? What did it matter if he told everyone? Wouldn't we have to go to the police and tell them ourselves?

"You did it once before, Harry, spying on us, and you got away with it. Then you tried to molest my sister—"

Harry cut him off before he had a chance to finish. "What the fuck are you saying, Jason? Molest?" He looked at me quizzically and shook his head. "Is that what you told him, Quinn?"

"No, but I—"

"Shut up, Quinn. This doesn't concern you," my brother said sharply. He held himself stiffly erect so that he almost looked as tall as Harry. "You didn't learn your lesson, Darby, did you? You're a spy, a fucking nosy interfering spy."

"And I couldn't be happier about it, too," Harry replied, sounding so smug I even wished that Jason would hit him again, because that's what he deserved. He glanced down at the empty silk-lined coffin, and all he could do was shake his head. "You're sick, you know that, Jason? The two of you, creeping around in the middle of the night, digging up your own mother's grave. Where the hell did you put the body, anyway?"

"There was never a body there to begin with," I insisted, even though Jason didn't want me to talk to him. But I was as much a part of this as he, and if Harry ran back to the house and started telling everyone that we were graverobbers and we'd stolen Mother's corpse, then the police would never believe the coffin was empty in the first place.

And that's just what Harry started threatening, too. He took another look at the empty coffin, and nervously stepped back. Any second I had a feeling he was going to break into a run, and then we'd never be able to stop him. But while I watched him, I caught sight of Jason out of the corner of my eye. He was leaning over the freshly dug grave, reaching for the handle of the shovel he'd left there when he climbed out.

"I gotta them tell, I just gotta," Harry muttered. There was something in his voice that reminded me of pity, as if he really believed we had done something terrible. "You just can't go around stealing bodies. What did you think you were going to do with it, anyway?" He made a sound like a nervous laugh, only it seemed to get stuck in his throat and he. began to cough.

It was at that moment I saw Jason take aim with the shovel, holding it in both hands like a baseball bat.

"Harry, look out!" I screamed.

But I was too late. The shovel went slicing through the air with such amazing force I could hear the hum of the metal blade. A high-pitched whine echoed in my ears, followed by an explosive outpouring of breath as the shovel slammed into Harry's stomach.

A look came into his eyes that was as much surprise as pain. Then his knees buckled and he slumped forward, gagging as he tried to get air into his lungs.

Jason looked down at him, and when he spoke his voice was filled with utter contempt. "We warned you, Harry. You took advantage of us. You touched my sister and that wasn't very nice. You were going to do other things to her too, weren't you? Nasty things. And tell them about our mom. Only you got it all wrong, Harry. She told me about you. She told me you had to be punished."

Jason raised the shovel above his head. The dirt-encrusted blade swung lazily from side to side. I knew what he intended to do, but I couldn't allow him to go through with it. We hadn't done anything wrong, but if he hurt Harry we'd end up being the guilty ones, and everyone responsible for lying about Mother's death would get off scot-free.

So before Jason could make good his threats, I wrenched the shovel out of his hands and threw it to the ground.

"He deserves it, Quinn. Don't you see, he'll tell them and then it'll be all over for us," my brother cried.

"We can't behave the way they have, Jason. We haven't committed a crime. We've done nothing wrong."

"But he'll tell!" Jason insisted.

By this time Harry had managed to pull himself back to his feet. He kept shaking his head as if he couldn't think straight. "You did right, Quinn. He's sick. He needs help," Harry told me.

"You're the sick one, you filthy pig!" Jason shouted. Suddenly losing all control, he lunged forward, wrestling Harry to the ground.

I tried to separate them, but it didn't do any good. Harry managed to get on top of my brother and began punching him in the face. Though I grabbed him by the back of his shirt, he wouldn't let go.

With a convulsive effort my brother tore free, and as they rolled over onto the ground they got closer and closer to the edge of the grave.

I couldn't stop them; I didn't know how. I shouted at them, I pleaded, but it didn't do any good.

Jason staggered back, trying to get to his feet. Harry rose up in a crouch, but the heel of his shoe was caught on the edge of the grave. The earth began to give way beneath him and his hands flailed wildly at the air as he tried to regain his balance. I reached out to grab him, but I couldn't get to him in time. Even Jason tried to catch him before it was too late, but Harry teetered back and fell into the open grave.

There was this awful crunching sound and then silence that was as thick as the blood dripping down my brother's battered face. Harry lay across the stones that filled Mother's coffin. He was like a broken marionette, and though his eyes were open, they were no longer capable of seeing my anguish.

"Oh my God," I whispered. "It's all right, Harry, don't worry. We'll get help. They'll take you to the hospital and everything'll be all right again, I swear!"

"He can't hear you, Quinn. He can't hear anything."

I refused to believe him, and got down on my stomach, telling my brother to hold onto my legs while I tried reaching down into the grave.

"His neck is broken. It won't do any good," Jason said.

"It isn't. It's just the wind knocked out of him," I said desperately. If Jason wouldn't help me then I knew I'd just have to do it on my own. I started to climb over the side to get to Harry, pushing my brother back when he tried to stop me. "We'll tie the rope around his waist, haul him back up," I said.

"It's too late," Jason whispered. "He's dead."

"He's not, he's still alive, he has to be," I cried.

I lowered myself down, holding onto the loose soil as best I could. Jason finally agreed to help, and a moment later I landed on one of the stones that lined the bottom of the coffin.

"Harry, we're going to get help for you, I promise," I said as I inched forward, taking care not to step on him. I put my hand under his head, but there was something there that was wet and sticky. He wasn't even moaning, and his eyes continued to stare up at the sky, looking for the first faint hint of dawn. As gently as I could I began to turn him over onto his side.

It was then that I realized my fingers were covered with blood. The back of Harry's head wasn't round anymore. It was crushed and flat looking, and there was blood dripping everywhere and getting caught in his beautiful jet-black hair the color of crow's feathers. Only the crow wouldn't fly, not ever again, and I was crying and Jason was trying to help me out and telling me to be quiet, I had to be quiet, a good little girl.

I couldn't say anything. I wanted to be sick but I couldn't feel anything, either. I don't even remember how I managed to climb out of the grave, but the next thing I knew I was looking down into the open casket, unable to believe that any of this had really happened.

"He shouldn't have come here," Jason told me. "He had no business interfering. God punished him, Quinnie. I didn't kill him, he killed himself. If God and the baby

213

Jesus didn't want him to die he wouldn't have tripped like that.''

"God and who?" I said, trying to remember where I'd heard those words before.

But instead of answering, Jason reached down and pushed the coffin lid back into place. Hurrying now, he began to shovel in the dirt. I thought of Mother's funeral, and how a monstrous lie had been perpetrated against us.

Mother wasn't dead. I'd seen her near the Temple. She was hiding out from them. They'd kill her for sure if they found out what we had done. We couldn't tell anyone. It was just the three of us now and we had to protect each other or else . . . or else they might even send us to reform school or prison, accuse us of murder, maybe even Mother's "murder" too.

"Don't you see, Quinnie, we're the only ones who can help her now. There wasn't anyone in the coffin, just as I thought. She never died. They took her away somewhere, and maybe she escaped or maybe she didn't. But whatever it is, we have to find her, and help her. Save her, Quinnie."

Save us, I thought, and I didn't want to look anymore. Not at Harry, not at Jason, not at anything. But as I turned away I heard something I hadn't wanted to ever hear again. I had to put my hands over my ears because if I didn't I knew I would have started to scream and I wouldn't have been able to stop.

It was the sound of dirt hitting the top of the coffin. It was Jason and I who were throwing the stones this time, the dry clumps of earth striking the top of the wooden casket with a vicious thumpety-thump that made my flesh crawl.

"Help me, for God's sake," Jason called out, pleading with his eyes as well as his voice.

I didn't have any feeling left. I knelt beside the grave, glad of only one thing—that the coffin lid was back in place and I couldn't see Harry with his dimples and his cleft chin, his mouth that had felt so nice when he kissed me.

I began to push the dirt in with my hands, pushing more and more of it in like a little kid playing in a sandbox, burying hidden treasure. Only it wasn't pretend. Whatever game of make-believe we had been playing was over. We were burying someone, and it was all for real.

# 14

It wasn't my fault, I didn't trip him up. He did it to himself. God punished him, just like I said, God and the baby Jesus both who looked down from heaven, picking out sinners and casting them into the everlasting fire. He'd burn for his treachery, just as all of them would burn.

It wasn't my fault I tell you. He deserved it, getting in our way when he should have stayed in bed instead of following us. And I wasn't sorry about what had happened to him, either. In fact, I was glad. He got in the way, spied on us, touched Quinnie. He was going to spread terrible lies about me and get me into trouble. So God punished him, made him break his neck.

Besides, who the hell would miss him, anyway? His folks didn't care about him or else they wouldn't have sent him off to live with relatives. Dad wouldn't miss him and Gwen wouldn't either. As for my sister—if she liked to be kissed like that, there were other people who could do it just as good as Harry. Probably a whole lot better, too.

But she was so quiet for such a long time that it scared

me. I didn't want her to suddenly give in to her feelings and start blabbing, telling everyone about the accident. So after we filled in the grave, and it looked as good as new, I took her hand in mind and led her home.

Suddenly she pulled away from me and stood there in the middle of the road. She had this real weird expression on her face, and the tears she'd already shed for that nobody, that nosy interfering pig, made tracks down her dusty cheeks.

"Won't they start a search or something when they find out he's missing? What if they call in the sheriff or the state police?"

"They won't," I said, "because I've got everything worked out."

"But he's dead, Jason."

"And we didn't do it," I reminded her. "Besides, you should be glad it happened, because if he told on us then they wouldn't have any choice left, would they? They'd have to kill her, just to prove to everyone the coffin wasn't empty. But now they won't find out. So at least we know she's safe."

I told her my plan, one I'd thought up entirely on my own.

"Soon as you get to your room, hide your dirty clothes so Mrs. D. won't find them. Later we'll stick them in the washing machine when she's not looking. Then make sure to wash up before you get into bed. If she sees any dirt on the pillow or the sheets she's bound to get suspicious. And don't say anthing to anyone, Quinnie. As far as you know, Harry's still around. When Mrs. D. tells you he left, you can pretend to be surprised. But not before."

Quinnie looked at me with these big sad waif eyes of hers. God I loved her so. I'd take care of her, no matter what. She didn't have anything to worry about. Only I did.

Calm, Lefland. One step at a time.

She repeated my instructions, and when I felt certain she wouldn't screw things up, I led her around to the back of the house, where we slipped inside the way we'd come.

I heard the ticking of the grandfather clock, a fly buzzing overhead. The downstairs smelled of lemon wax and fresh-cut flowers. I started up the stairs with Quinnie right behind me. Then, as soon as I saw her safely to her room, I went on up to the third floor. Harry's room was across the hall from his parents. The door was ajar, and for a moment I thought someone had gotten there before me.

You're getting good at this, Lefland. Real professional.

Only I didn't like calling myself that anymore. I had to think of another name, something more appropriate to the new identity I was going to give myself to keep them off the scent. And talking about scents, the minute I stepped inside Harry's room I smelled Mom's perfume.

Was it possible she'd already been here? Maybe she had been watching us all along, even when we were at the cemetery. But then again, it could have been my imagination working overtime, because the room didn't look as if it had been searched.

The alarm clock read five-thirty on the button. By the time I'd packed all of Harry's things in his suitcases, it was getting close to six. I'd even made sure to check the hamper in the bathroom, stuffing his dirty clothes into the suitcases along with everything else.

That was real smart, Lefland. That's what I call good thinking.

It's not Lefland anymore. The name stinks, especially since it belongs to Bennett. I'm going to call myself something else, maybe Warren whoever he is.

Why Warren?

He knows where Mom is. If I'm Warren I'll know too.

Along with his clothes, his toiletries, and everything else, I even found a bunch of dirty magazines Harry had hidden under the mattress. I'd never seen anything like them, just page after page of women with legs spread wide as an embrace, like they were saying, "Come into my parlor," said the spider to the fly. There were photos of women stroking their nipples, poking their fingers inside themselves, doing all sorts of things that were just too filthy to mention. But the truth is, I really liked looking at them, and so I rolled one up and stuck it in my back pocket before throwing the rest of them in the suitcase.

I wanted the Darbys to think their son had taken off in the middle of the night, no good-byes and no questions asked. It wouldn't be unlike Harry to do something mean like that, anyway. By the time they started wondering why they hadn't heard from him, no one would ever suspect he was still here, in a dark, maggoty place where they'd never think to look.

When I'd gotten everything together, I opened the door just a crack and took a peek outside. Neither Anna nor her husband were stirring, and so I dragged the suitcases out into the hall, trying to make as little noise as possible. By the time I got them downstairs to my room my arms were about to fall off, they were so heavy. But I still couldn't take any chances. So before I did anything else I got up on a chair and managed to hide them in the top of my closet. Then I had to wash, and get the dirt off my face and hands. My nose didn't look so hot, and neither did my face. It was pulpy and swollen like the inside of a piece of fruit. Harry had really laid into me, and I wondered how I was going to explain why I looked like a punching bag.

Tripped and fell down the stairs, Warren.

When?

Last night on the way to bed.

Why didn't you tell anyone? That's a nasty looking cut there under your chin.

Caught it on the edge of the stairs. Didn't want to make

a fuss. I'm all right now, anyway. I should've put ice on it, but I'm okay, honest.

I would have showered too, but I figured I might make too much noise. I didn't want Gwen who was down the hall to suddenly wake up and wonder what I was doing up so early in the morning. So I just washed up as best I could, then dragged me and Warren into bed and pulled the covers over our heads.

It was dark as the inside of the caves up in the hills, warm as the blood that trickled down the back of the spy's broken skull. Warren and I closed our eyes, pulled our legs up to our chest, and tried to get comfortable.

"We did good, didn't we?"

"Very good," Mom said, whispering her secrets in my ear.

"He got what he deserved, didn't he? Couldn't have happened to a nicer guy." Warren and I were giggling so hard we had to put our hand over our mouth so no one else would hear. Mom was tucking us in, saying that accidents happen, boys, because that's God's plan.

"But aren't you glad he slipped and fell?"

"Shh, go to sleep now. You've been up all night and you must be exhausted, sweetheart."

Yes, it was true, we were really bushed and our arms hurt and our legs and our poor swollen punching-bag faces. But Quinnie had her proof now and that was the important thing. She knew that we hadn't lied to her, and now she would trust us no matter what.

So we slept and we dreamed good things until someone came creeping by our door and Warren woke me first, shaking me out of my dreams.

Someone's out there!

I glanced at the clock near my bed. It was six-forty and counting. The sun was already splashing across the floor, and the birds were singing in the garden. But there was someone stalking us, creeping not so silently on the other side of the door.

"Mom, is that you?" I whispered. But Warren barely let me get the words out before he slammed his hand over my mouth.

You want to ruin everything, you idiot? he hissed in my ear. Mom's supposed to be dead, moron. They hear you talking to her, they'll know the game is up.

So we got out of bed, grabbed a robe, and tiptoed to the door. I wanted to throw it open and scare the bejesus out of whoever was there. But Warren warned me not to, saying that it could be Mom and it wouldn't be fair to surprise her that way. He was right and I agreed. I touched the doorknob, caressing it like a cheek. Then I turned it slowly, opening the door as soundlessly as possible.

Something's moving over there by the stairs.

What is it, Warren?

Ivory. Satin. Something. Can't see clearly.

We rubbed the sleep from our eyes and looked again. Mom's nightgown! But even before we had a chance to call out to her, she ducked out of sight and started up to the third floor.

What's that? Warren asked. Over there, under Alethea's portrait.

We crept down the hall. It was a slip of paper, folded neatly in two.

What's it say? Warren asked.

I bent down to pick it up, wishing I could be as quiet as Warren. You couldn't even see him, he was so silent.

"For the sins of your fathers you, though guiltless, must suffer."

It was neatly typed, probably with Dad's typewriter because that was the only one in the house. But why did she want me to suffer, especially if she knew I was guiltless?

Ask her, Warren whispered.

Yes, of course, why the hell was I just standing here like an idiot when she was waiting for me upstairs. Could she be using the attic as a hiding place? It got awfully hot and stuffy up there. Besides, how could she survive without food and water and stuff like that?

*Anna's been complaining again that food is missing.*

Quinnie told us that last night, Warren, remember?

Sure he remembered, because we were always together, just like a team. I stuffed the slip of paper into the pocket of my robe and started down the hall after Mom.

The stairs seemed steeper than usual. We had to hold onto the banister and drag ourselves up, not stopping until we reached the attic. The door was open, and sunlight trickled through the dusty windowpanes, scattering gold coins across the floor. She was up here, I was sure of it.

"Mom, it's me," I called out in a whisper. "You don't have to hide anymore."

The big steamer trunk in the middle of the floor began to creak. I thought of the love letters and how he shouldn't ever have touched her, the big roll of yellowed paper that were the blueprints to the house. Quinnie didn't know about them, but I couldn't tell her yet. The lid started to rattle as if something were trying to get out. I thought of the coffin and I got very scared. The lid creaked and creaked, then suddenly flew open like an explosion.

It was Quinnie, dressed in Mom's favorite nightgown, the long ivory one she liked best of all. But she didn't look right. Her face was made up worse than any of the whores in Harry's magazines. She had on lipstick and mascara, eye shadow like Aunt Gwen's, false lashes, even a long blonde wig that was the same color as Mom's hair.

"Look what we've got for you, Jason, a surprise," she said.

223

I was gasping, unable to catch my breath. "Quinnie, what's going on? What are you doing here?"

"Only what you want me to do, Warren." She stepped out of the trunk, bent down and reached inside. "This is for you, darling, just for you."

She held it up in the air and I started to scream.

"Don't you like it?" she said.

It was an arm, severed at the elbow. Rings flashed on every finger. Bracelets clattered about the bony wrist. It was Mom's jewelry, every single piece. But the flesh was rank and putrid, the skin a gangrenous shade of green.

"But there's more," she said. "Here's something just for you, Warren. Just for you, Jason." She reached down and brought out a hand, the blood still oozing from where it had been hacked off at the wrist. "Just for you," she said. "A matching set."

She put the hand up to her cheek, caressed herself with it, licked the dead rigid fingers and I couldn't stop gasping.

Gotta get air! Can't breathe, suffocating! Gotta get air!

I sat up, choking and unable to catch my breath. I was in bed, the covers a tangled ball at my feet.

It was just a dream, a horrible dream, I told myself. Just take deep breaths. That's it. Calm, calm, Jason. Count to ten. Look around. See, it's your room, your very own room and everything's okay, everything's fine. Just a dream, a nightmare.

I fell back against the pillows. I was soaking wet and the sheets were damp and clammy.

"Warren made it happen," a voice whispered in my ear. "He's trying to take advantage of you, Jason. You mustn't let him."

"No, of course not. I won't," I said aloud.

But what was my robe doing on the floor? It was hanging behind the door when I went to bed. Had it slipped off the hook? I got to my feet, still woozy. My knees started to buckle and I had to grab onto the night-stand for support. The clock said six-fifty-one, but it felt like I'd been asleep for days on end.

I stooped down and picked up my robe, remembering something from the dream. A message, was that it? A note of some kind? I reached into the righthand pocket. Empty. I tried the lefthand pocket. There was a slip of paper there, crackling like fire the moment I touched it. I pulled it out, read the typewritten words and wanted to scream all over again.

"For the sins of your fathers you, though guiltless, must suffer."

Warren, that's who it was. Warren did it, not Mom. He must have planted it there while I was asleep, then made me dream of it so I wouldn't forget to look when I woke up. Something like that. Something.

"Warren," I whispered, "can you still hear me?"

Dead silence. Nothing up there between my ears but good old reliable Jason Lefland.

God, I was so confused. I was so mixed up I didn't know what was real anymore and what wasn't. Go back to bed, I told myself. Go back to bed and sleep it off.

But when I got between the covers I couldn't sleep. Every time I tried to close my eyes they refused to stay shut, flying open like the startled looking dolls Quinnie used to play with when she was little. Only we weren't little anymore. We couldn't act like children, not after what they'd done. They'd taken Mom away, and now they were using Warren to get back at me. Only I wouldn't let them. I'd be strong, so strong and brave that Mom would be real proud of me. Yes, and God would be proud of me too, God and the baby Jesus both. And I'd sit on Grandpa Howe's lap and the angels would sing and he'd tell me funny stories. We'd laugh so hard we wouldn't be able to stop, me and Grandpa and Quinnie, too. But not Harry. No, Harry could never go to heaven because he was bad. He was a bad, bad boy and that's why he got what he deserved.

# 15

Even though I wanted to pull the covers over my head and never get out of bed, I was afraid of doing anything that might make me look suspicious. If I started acting guilty, the Darbys would sooner or later put two and two together and come up with Quinn. I was so nervous that I thought if Anna so much as looked at me I'd end up giving myself away. But when I came downstairs for breakfast, she was too busy yelling at her husband to even notice me.

"That good-for-nothing!" she was shouting. "After all we've done for him, and he just up and leaves without so much as a how-de-do. You searched his room, didn't you, Mr. Darby? Didn't he leave a note for us at least?"

"Nothing," Will replied. "The boy's lazy, Mother, always was. Nothing we can do about it now."

But I was so scared I couldn't stop shaking. Even if Jason's plan was working out the way he said it would, it still didn't make me feel any better. Oddly enough, he looked fine, and when I joined him at the table he smiled and nodded his head, as if to say everything was okay, and

I should just quit worrying. But how could I not worry? How could I not forget what had happened, Harry tripping and falling over the edge of the grave, that awful crunch when he landed, the eyes that stared and stared yet couldn't see anything, not even the faintest glimmer of light.

I looked at the bacon and eggs Anna had set before me and I thought I'd be sick. But Jason kept shoveling the food into his mouth like he hadn't had a decent meal in days.

I heard Aunt Gwen on the stairs, and when she came into the dining room the first thing she mentioned were the Darbys. "My, but they're at each other's throats this morning, aren't they?" she remarked.

Right on cue, Anna came out of the kitchen to mumble something about that ungrateful son of hers. "Lucky thing he didn't try to steal Will's pickup. And what'll you have this morning, Miss Howe?"

Instead of breakfast, Aunt Gwen wanted an explanation, wondering why everyone was suddenly so concerned about Harry. Anna told her what had happened, how her son had cleared out in the middle of the night, leaving nothing behind.

"What did he take, do you know?" Gwen asked.

" 'Scuse me?" said Anna.

It was then that Aunt Gwen told her what she had discovered just a few minutes before. She had gone into Mother's room to borrow a lipstick, only to find that everything was gone.

"Even that lovely painting she had over her bed is missing."

I don't know why Anna looked at me, but she did. She didn't come right out and ask if I knew where everything was, but that's what her expression was all about. I pretended not to notice, and opened the box of cereal and poured out enough shredded wheat to choke a horse.

"Did Mr. Lefland ask you to clean out my sister's room?" Aunt Gwen went on.

Anna got all bristly with indignation, and her little gray eyes opened so wide I thought they'd pop right out. "He said nothing of the kind, Miss Howe. In fact, I haven't been in that room since . . . well, not since quite awhile now."

"I think Dad must have gotten rid of all that stuff on his own," Jason spoke up. "He said . . . what were the words he used, Quinnie? Painful, that's right. He said it was much too painful to have Mom's things around."

"So he just threw everything away?" asked Aunt Gwen.

Jason shrugged. "I guess people do strange things when they're in mourning."

I don't know if she believed him or not, but she didn't say anything else about it. Instead, she sat down at the table and unfolded her napkin, only to suddenly stare at my brother as if she hadn't noticed him until now.

"My God, what did you do to yourself?" she burst out.

"I fell down the stairs," my brother replied. "Clumsiest thing I ever did."

"But when?"

"Last night, on the way to my room. I felt like such an idiot I just put some ice on it and went to bed."

Aunt Gwen clucked her tongue in sympathy. "Such an ugly bruise, too. How does it feel?"

"Not too bad," he said. "Little sore, but I'll survive."

"You should try to be more careful, Jason. The way you run up and down those stairs it's no wonder you tripped."

Soon as we were able to excuse ourselves, Jason took me aside and told me what to do. I was to wait in the garden while he went upstairs to his room. When the coast was clear, he'd throw down the suitcases he'd hidden in his closet.

229

"Then we'll take them down to the Bottom and bury them," he explained.

"But what if someone sees?"

He looked at me with annoyance. "Would you rather I just walked downstairs with them, one in each arm?"

I shook my head.

"Then stop making such a big deal about it."

"I'm not making a big deal, Jason. I'm just being cautious, that's all."

I stood below his window, praying that no one would see us. As awful as it sounded, at least we didn't have Harry to worry about anymore, though that really didn't comfort me very much. I kept seeing him standing before me, and even when I looked away he was still there, showing his dimples as he smiled mischievously and asked me for a kiss.

Finally Jason stuck his head out, and I double-checked to make sure there wasn't anyone around before giving him the go-ahead. The suitcases came tumbling out the window, and I had visions of the locks breaking and all of Harry's things scattering across the yard. But the clasps held, and as soon as I dragged both pieces of luggage into the bushes I waited for Jason to come downstairs and help me.

"Have you seen Will around?" he asked when he joined me.

"They're still arguing in the kitchen."

"Good, then let's get a move on." He grabbed hold of one of the suitcases, told me to take the other, and hurried down the road to the Bottom, stopping every few feet to look over his shoulder and see if we were being followed.

Halfway to the cemetery he turned off the road and started poking around in the underbrush. I had no idea what he was looking for until he pulled out the shovel from where he'd hidden it the night before.

"What if Will misses it?" I asked.

"He's got so many different ones in the toolshed he'll never notice it's gone. So stop worrying about everything, Quinnie."

"But Harry's dead," I reminded him. "How can you act like nothing's happened?"

Jason glared at me as if I'd just called him a dirty name. "Did we ask him to spy on us?"

"No."

"Did we tell him to trip and fall and break his neck?"

"Of course not."

"Then start getting rid of all this guilt you're carrying around, because it's not going to do us any good."

I knew Jason was in one of his moods, and so I didn't say anything after that. He led the way through the Bottom and I followed dutifully behind him. The trees soon closed in around us and the air that had felt so warm a few minutes before was now cool and damp against my cheek. All sorts of little animals and birds moved in the dense undergrowth, scurrying out of sight before I could catch a glimpse of them.

"This should do just fine," Jason said at last, and he put down the suitcase and immediately started to dig.

"We have to have a talk, you know," I said as I watched him, shoveling the dirt with the same sense of purpose and commitment he'd shown the night before.

"About what?"

"Everything."

"What's that supposed to mean, Quinn?"

"It's supposed to mean it's time we were honest with each other, Jason, totally honest."

"I've been honest," he replied. "Maybe you haven't though."

I hadn't told him about the diary, or the strange note I'd found under my door. But he hadn't told me what had happened the night they'd taken Mother away. Yet I was certain he'd mentioned having been there, in Mother's room that is. When I asked him about it, he pretended not to hear me, and kept right on digging.

"But you said you were there that night. That's why you were so sure Mother hadn't taken sick, because you were with her."

"Did I? I forget."

"Just the way you forgot about the knife?"

He looked at me with a blank expression. "What knife?"

I was so exasperated I could barely keep my voice down. "The one you gave me for my birthday. The one you stole from my room. And don't pretend you don't know what I'm talking about, either. If you wanted the knife so bad why didn't you just come right out and ask me for it?"

Jason put down the shovel and fixed me with a penetrating glance. "I swear to God I don't know what you're talking about, Quinnie. I haven't seen that dagger since the day I gave it to you."

"I'm sorry, but I don't believe you, Jason."

It was clear that my accusations were beginning to upset him. "I'm telling the truth, Quinn," he insisted. "Even if I did take the knife from your room, I swear I don't remember."

"But how can you do something and not know about it?"

"Maybe Warren did it," my brother blurted out.

Warren? I thought. But he was the person Father mentioned on the phone. What did he have to do with it?

"You mean you know who Warren is?" I asked.

"In a way," Jason said hesitantly.

By now the hole was large enough to accommodate both of the suitcases. Jason laid them one on top of the other, then began to pack in the dirt around the sides before shoveling the rest of it over the top.

"Well, who is he?" I asked again.

My brother began to giggle, but I had no idea what he was laughing at. "Warren's a very bad boy, Quinnie. He wants to get me into trouble. He does things he shouldn't."

"What things?" I was suddenly so cold my teeth began to chatter.

"Dirty things," Jason snickered. "But don't you worry, I took care of him. I sent him away. He won't ever come back."

"Jason, I don't know what you're talking about, but you're scaring me and it's not funny."

"But I wouldn't scare you, Quinnie. I wouldn't do anything to hurt you." He stamped the last of the dirt into place, packing it down before scattering twigs and leaves over it so that the forest floor showed no sign of ever having been disturbed. "Come," he said when he was done, and he reached for my hand.

I was too frightened and I pulled away. What was happening to my brother? Aunt Gwen had implied that Mother was crazy, and now Jason was acting just as disturbed.

"Jason, is Mother really alive, or are you making it all up? Please, we can't lie to each other. If there isn't trust between us then there's nothing. We might as well be strangers then."

My brother stood stock-still, so shocked by what I'd said he didn't know how to react. "The coffin was empty, Quinn. You saw it yourself. If she was dead, then why didn't they bury her?"

"I don't know!" I cried out. "I don't know anything. It's all so confusing. You say one thing and then you do another. You take the knife, you almost cut yourself with it, then you don't remember where you got it. You talk about this person named Warren like the two of you know each other for years, and yet you've never even met him. You don't even know who he really is.''

"He's a doctor. A psychiatrist."

An agonizing chill went through me as yet another piece of the puzzle slipped into place. "My God, Jason, do you realize what you're saying?" I exclaimed.

He looked away, and when he spoke he sounded like a little boy, not the Jason who was so proud of the fact he was well on his way to becoming a man. "I'm so mixed up, Quinnie. Nothing makes sense anymore."

"Who told you about him?"

"I can't remember," he whimpered. "Quinnie, I just don't know. It just came to me like . . . like a voice was speaking or something."

"But you must've heard someone talking about him. Was it Aunt Gwen? Did she tell you about Dr. Warren?"

"I just can't remember," he insisted. "But I thought . . . I don't know. Maybe I thought he was someone else, someone who came alive in my dreams. But no, Dad called him her friend, yet he didn't mean it that way. He was making a terrible joke about it because Warren wasn't her friend at all. He was the one who treated her when she went away. He told Dad she was sick, she needed help or else she'd—" He kept shaking his head, almost as if he couldn't believe what he was saying.

"She'd what?" I shouted. "Jason, tell me before you forget it again. What was Father so afraid of?"

"That Mom would kill herself," he whispered.

At that moment my head felt like a balloon swollen to the bursting point. Words and images collided frantically with each other, for there just wasn't enough room for all of them. *How could you do this to us, Rebecca?* Those were Father's words, the night they'd taken her away. Was he angry at her because she'd tried to commit suicide, was that the horrible secret they were trying to protect us from? There was blood on the carpet, I recalled, a bright crimson patch the sight of which had brought tears to my eyes. *Your mother isn't well. Whatever may happen, you have to be brave, Quinton. You can't be a little girl forever.*

But I didn't want to grow up, not now when there were so many unanswered questions, and Jason just standing there shaking his head, unable to comprehend what was happening to him.

*I can't trust you, Rebecca, and that's the saddest part.* Had Father meant he couldn't trust her not to harm herself? *Their lives depend on it. They'd be lost without you.* Was he trying to convince her that if she took her life Jason and I would be shattered by the loss? Was that what their argument had been about, the night I'd crept from my room to hear them shouting at each other behind their bedroom door?

*Why didn't I see it earlier? Why was I so blind to the truth? It's my fault, Gwen. If only I could have stopped her in time.*

Stopped Mother from killing herself? Could that be what Father had been referring to when I'd overheard him talking to Aunt Gwen? But then, as if a curtain were being drawn aside, I realized that I wasn't allowing myself to see the entire picture. If Mother had committed suicide, if that was what Father was trying to conceal from us, then why had he staged a mock funeral?

I grabbed my brother by the shoulders and began to shake him, begging him to tell me the truth, no matter how painful it might be. "You've got to remember what happened that night! Did she try to kill herself, was that it? Was that why she was bleeding? Was that why you took the knife, because you remembered what Mother had done?"

A bubble of saliva burst across his lips. Yet when he tried to speak, no words came out of his mouth.

"Answer me, Jason! You were there. What did she do that night?"

"I . . . I can't . . . remember," he stammered. "It's . . . it's not there anymore, Quinn. It's . . . not in my head, like . . . someone took it out. Empty . . . Warren . . . he did it. He took it away. Doesn't . . . doesn't . . . want us . . . to know."

He collapsed in my arms, his entire body convulsed with sobs. He couldn't control the tears that surged down his cheeks, and I held him as Mother used to hold him, trying to help him through his pain.

"No, you mustn't, you mustn't," I whispered. "The coffin was empty, Jason. She's alive, as alive as we are. We'll go to the Temple and pray to her and maybe she'll hear us and come back. And there are other places to look, lots of places . . . oh Jason, please don't cry, please. We'll go up into the hills. Yes, that's what we'll do. We'll search those caves up there. And the shacks, remember those, where we saw the bobcat last year? Maybe she's there, Jason, maybe that's where she's hiding. But please don't cry, dear. Please, because we haven't given up. We'll never give up, I swear, not until we find her."

Seconds passed, then minutes, and still he sobbed, trembling pitifully in my arms. I murmured whatever words of encouragement I could think of, even as I tried to put the pieces together and make some sense of the terrible puzzle that confronted us. At least we now knew who Warren was, though why my brother had said Dr. Warren had caused him to lose all memory of that fateful night was something I was yet to understand.

Perhaps tears were like a well, capable of running dry, for gradually Jason's plaintive cries subsided. At last he edged away, slipping free of my embrace.

"I . . . I didn't mean it," he said as he dried his eyes. "I shouldn't have lost control. It's wrong."

"It's not wrong. It's healthy, Jason. It's good to get things off your chest." I reached out, cupping his face in my hands. "You're so much handsomer when you smile. It breaks my heart to see you cry."

"I won't anymore," he said. "I have to be strong, strong enough for the both of us, Quinn. But certain things make a lot more sense now, don't they? All those times she went away, always leaving on such short notice. That's what she called it, remember?"

"Like the time she went to that health spa," I recalled. "And when she said she was going to visit a friend from school. Do you think that friend was really Dr. Warren?"

"I'm sure of it," Jason replied.

"Then what Aunt Gwen told me must've been true. Mother was very depressed and it was only getting worse. But why couldn't Dr. Warren help her, that's what I can't figure out."

"We'll ask her. Yes, we'll ask her all these questions, Quinnie, every last one of them."

"But we don't know where she is," I reminded him.

"I know, but we can still pray, just like you said. And maybe if we pray hard enough she'll come back to us like she did the last time."

"You mean the vision you had?"

"Yes, and I've had others since," he admitted. "And each one gets stronger than the one before, so I'm sure she's getting closer to us."

"And the missing food," I said hopefully.

"And the—" The words trickled away, and once again he began to shake his head, trying to jar the memory out of hiding.

"Tell me, Jason," I urged. "Get it out before you lose it again. The more we know, the easier it'll be for us to find her."

"Someone left a note for me," he said. He spoke so

faintly it was as if he were afraid the trees themselves were capable of hearing him, each leaf like an ear trained on his every word.

"But that's what happened to me, too!"

"When? You never told me; you should have, Quinn. You should've told me everything. What did it say? Who wrote it, do you know? When did it happen?" He couldn't get his questions out fast enough, and now he was smiling, and his face was animated like I remembered from the days when Mother was still with us, and the frightening Lefland secrets were yet to make themselves known.

Hurriedly I explained what had happened. When I told him about finding Mother's diary, and the dreadful torments she had suffered as a child, his eyes filled up with tears all over again, that our poor mother had been forced to endure such agony.

Even as we spoke he was leading me in the direction of the playhouse. There was a buoyancy to his step, a renewed sense of purpose and resolve. Somehow the very air we breathed was sweetened by this new honesty we shared between us. I was more certain than ever that very soon, perhaps even in the next few days, we would at last learn of Mother's whereabouts.

Having told him as much as I could recall—which was quite a bit, I guess, since so much of the diary remained painfully etched in my memory—I finally confessed to having suspected him of sneaking into my room and making off with it.

"But why would I do such a thing?" he exclaimed. He sounded so injured by my suspicions I was sorry to have brought them up.

"I don't know," I admitted. "Maybe you were trying to protect me from the truth. So many of the things she wrote about still don't make sense. And now, of course, we won't know how it all turned out until we find the diary, and read it to the very end.''

"I can understand why someone stole it though," Jason said thoughtfully, "especially when we know she'd hidden it away. So it wasn't as if she ever intended for us to find it. But why would someone leave a note like that? 'The sins of the fathers . . .' What sins, that's the question.''

"And what fathers, too," I reminded him.

By then we were within sight of the Temple, this weathered little cottage stuck away in the middle of the Bottom. The area surrounding it had been cleared in a rough circle, perhaps forty feet across at its widest. As we emerged from the woods Jason paused, once again reaching for my hand, then signaling me to silence with a cautious glance.

He sniffed at the air the way a rabbit does, wary of the coyote and the fox, the bobcat padding silently in search of prey.

"What's wrong?" I whispered.

"Just checking.''

"For what?''

"No one knows about this place, and that's the way I want it to stay." He crept forward, shoulders hunched, eyes darting every which way at once. I followed right behind, but when he threw open the Temple door and burst inside, he failed to surprise anybody, for the playhouse was just as we had left it.

"What's that?" I pointed to the wall opposite the altar where, between two shuttered windows, a faint reddish stain was visible.

"Looks like someone was trying to scrub away some dirt or something.''

"But dirt isn't red. The playhouse wasn't ever painted that color, was it?''

"Not that I recall," Jason replied. He went up to the wall and closely examined the stain. "Mildew," he decided.

239

"Since when is there such a thing as pink mildew?"

Jason shrugged. "Beats me," he said, and he turned away, his mind on other things.

As I watched him prepare for the ceremony, I couldn't help but think how odd it was that the stain had appeared almost overnight, for I was sure it hadn't been there the last time we had prayed together. But though I continued to remark about it, Jason was too preoccupied arranging the blessed instruments to pay much attention to what I had to say.

Finally, when everything was laid out to his satisfaction, he motioned me to kneel beside him. After anointing each of us with the fragrance of remembrance, Jason solemnly lit the candles.

"To the flame of retribution," I said aloud.

"May it burn forever," added my brother.

We bent forward, our foreheads touching the floor. Jason instructed me to close my eyes and pray to the blessed Mother, that through our love and devotion she might appear before us.

"Touch the blessed instruments of our faith," he whispered. His voice gradually grew louder and more insistent, pleading with Mother to come forward and reveal herself to us. "Pray to the blessed Mother," he called out, groaning now and shuddering as he knelt beside me.

I squeezed my eyes shut, trying to draw her image out of my memory, to see her in my mind's eye as if she were standing right before me. And still Jason continued to pray, his voice a kind of guttural wail as he swore his undying loyalty to Mother.

The fragrance of remembrance filled the air with its wild rose scent. The twin flames of retribution flickered fiercely, propelled by the strength of our faith. The blood rushed to my forehead, and though I felt dizzy, and even drained of physical energy, I continued to murmur the words that might somehow bring us closer to Mother.

"Yes," Jason suddenly whispered. "Yes, I can feel you now. Yes, I can see you, too!" He stiffened and threw his head back. A spasm clutched at his throat, and when he spoke his voice was thin and high-pitched, barely sounding like him at all.

"Is she there? Can you see her?" I asked excitedly, wishing that I too could share in his vision.

"Quinton my dearest, how I've missed you," Jason said. But somehow it wasn't my brother who was talking. It was Mother, her spirit at least, using him to make her presence known to us. Jason's eyes were closed, and the veins in his neck stood out in sharp relief. "Do not forget . . . my love . . . it will . . . save . . . us yet," Jason managed to say, though it was a great effort for him to even get the words out.

"Yes, I hear you, Mother, and I love you, too!" I cried. I raised my head and gazed at her portrait, trying to will her into existence that she might hold me in her arms again, and comfort me in my pain.

How serene she looked, how peaceful. There was a regal quality to her expression I had never noticed before, a strength of will that would surely see her through every adversity.

"My dear . . . children," Jason said with a gasp. Beads of sweat collected on his forehead and began to drip down the sides of his face. His knees thumped violently against the floor, and he started to shiver as if he were standing in a draft. It made me think that someone was shaking him, grabbing him by the back of the neck and jerking him this way and that. "Remember . . . my love . . . I know . . . how difficult . . . this must be . . . for you . . . You must . . . listen . . . to your brother . . . do . . . as he asks . . . he knows . . . what is best."

The strain of communicating with her was too much for him. Jason let out a desperate cry as the link to Mother's spirit was severed. He fell forward, striking his head on the altar and moaning softly to himself. When he finally managed to pull himself back into a sitting position, his eyes looked dull and glassy, and his face seemed prematurely aged. A drawn, haggard mask had slipped over his features. The moment he turned to me it was as if I were looking into our future, and seeing him as he would be many years from now.

"Did she tell you where she is?" I asked.

Jason shook his head sadly. "It was dark, so terribly dark, Quinn. I could barely see her."

"And the baby?"

"She didn't say."

"But she's alive," I told him, "and that's the most important thing." I started to get up, for I thought the ritual had come to an end. But my brother motioned me to stay where I was.

"We have to try to reach her," he said.

"But how? You can't put yourself through this again, Jason. You might not come out of it."

My brother looked around the room, his eyes alighting on the clothing we had taken from Mother's bedroom, neatly stacked along one wall. "I can't do it on my own," he said. "It has to be the two of us, working in unison."

"Doing what?"

"A ceremony to bind us together, Quinnie."

"But we are together, you know that."

"Yes, but Mother wants us to be even closer to each other. She doesn't want us to lie anymore, or keep things a secret. She wants us to share in everything, Quinnie. Everything."

Jason got slowly to his feet, and with a loving glance at Mother's portrait, another at the photograph smiling in its silver frame, he crossed the room and began to rummage among the piles of clothing. Having found what he was looking for, he turned and held it up for my inspection. It was Mother's satin nightgown, the long ivory one that was her very favorite.

"It's yours now," he said. "Mom told me she wanted you to have it."

"But she's coming back. She'll wear it again."

"Yes, but she still wants you to have it. She says you're a woman now. You have to put childhood aside." He rubbed his cheek against the hem of the nightgown, smiling dreamily to himself. "Put it on, Quinnie."

I looked at him in disbelief. "Now?"

"Yes, right now, right this very minute. It's important."

To whom, you or Mother? I thought. But I kept that to myself, feeling the same nameless dread I'd experienced earlier, when Jason had first mentioned Dr. Warren. He was grinning at me, nodding his head, motioning me to get to my feet. Yet somehow he was like a puppet, like someone else— Mother perhaps—was standing overhead, pulling the strings and manipulating his arms and legs, telling him what to do and what to say.

Why was it so important that I put on the nightgown? What purpose did it serve? I asked him that, but Jason insisted it was Mother's wish. He said that if we disobeyed her we would never find out where she was, for she would want nothing to do with us if we failed to trust her judgment.

Reluctantly, humoring him too I guess, I took the nightgown and began to pull it over my head.

"You're not doing it right!" he said sharply. "No one wears a nightgown over their clothes. Do you think Mom would accept such a thing? Take everything off first, then put it on. You'll feel her against your skin that way."

I could see there was no point in arguing with him. His

mind was made up, and nothing I might say would convince him otherwise. Although I expected him to at least leave the Temple for a few minutes so I could have some privacy while I undressed, my brother made no move to go outside. Rather, he returned to his place at the altar, and though he bowed his head and his lips moved in prayer, I was certain he kept sneaking glances at me as I turned away and began to remove my clothes.

"Everything!" he insisted when I stood there in my panties, keeping my back turned and my hands across my breasts.

"But why?"

"Because she wants it that way, and that's reason enough."

"She told you that?"

Jason caught my note of skepticism. "She told me everything we have to know," he replied, sounding annoyed at all my questions. "She said you're a woman and it's time you started acting like one, Quinton."

"Quinnie," I corrected.

"You're a woman now, Quinton Lefland. Quinnie is the child you're about to leave behind."

Although he was still frightening me with his adamant tone, I had to admit I was beginning to feel flattered by all the attention he was giving me. If Mother was convinced I was no longer a child, then who was I to question her? Realizing that, I slipped out of my panties and hurriedly pulled the ivory nightgown over my head. The low-cut bodice accentuated my breasts, making them look larger than they actually were.

I turned to Jason, modeling the gown for him. The long clinging skirt trailed across the floor. I spun around, letting it balloon about my ankles.

"What do you think?" I asked.

"Mom would be pleased. She'd be very, very pleased," he murmured.

He found the plastic bag where I'd put Mother's cosmetics, and brought it back with him to the altar. After laying out the lipsticks and face powders, the eye makeup and whatever else was there, he lined them up alongside the hand mirror that was one of the blessed instruments of our faith.

I sat beside him, arranging the skirt of the nightgown in a circle around me. When I looked up at Mother's portrait I was certain she was smiling her approval, and so I no longer questioned my brother when he told me to make up my face.

Mother had shown me how to apply makeup, though she had never given me permission to buy any of my own. I didn't really care to use it, to tell you the truth, but now I did as I was told, putting it on as best I could.

By the time I finished, I could barely recognize myself. "Does it look all right?" I asked.

Jason studied my face like an artist contemplating a canvas. He suggested I use a little more of the eye liner, then nodded approvingly. Once again he anointed me with the fragrance of remembrance, and as the scent of wild roses swirled around us, he moved behind me and put his hands over my shoulders. He bent forward, gently kissing the back of my neck.

"It tickles," I said with a shiver.

"It's supposed to. Does this tickle, too?" His hands moved down, his fingers lightly caressing the base of my throat. "Look in the mirror, Quinton, and tell me what you see."

His voice was thick and husky now. When I swiveled around to face him his eyes were far away, gazing into a dreamlike world of his own devising. He leaned toward me, and before I could pull away his lips were against mine, and his tongue had slipped between them to coax mine out of hiding.

I was afraid then, terribly, terribly afraid. He wasn't acting like Jason anymore, but someone older and wiser and infinitely more sophisticated. I couldn't help but think of Harry, so sure of the power he had over me that he hadn't thought twice about taking me in his arms, kissing me the same way my brother was now doing.

I broke away, feeling the color rise in my cheeks. "You shouldn't," I said.

"Why?"

I hadn't thought of that, and though I tried to come up with an answer, certain I knew the reason, I couldn't think of one.

"Mom wants it this way, don't you see?" he told me. He reached down and put his hand under the hem of the nightgown, ever so gently stroking my leg, then moving higher still to tickle the inside of my thigh.

I edged back, but my fear only served to goad him on.

"Mom wants me to show you what it is to be a woman," he whispered. He captured me in his arms, smashing his lips against mine.

I struggled to free myself, but the more I fought, the more determined he became. He was lowering me down onto the floor and I was beating my fists against his chest, begging him to let me go.

"It's wrong!" I cried. "You're my brother, Jason. My brother! You're not my—" But I couldn't even say it I was so ashamed.

"Not your lover?"

The word was too adult. It didn't even sound right when he said it. "Yes, and it's not . . . it's not natural," I blurted out.

"Who told you that?"

He was staring at me so hard I got embarrassed and had to look away.

"No one. I just know it, that's all."

"Do you think it's wrong because of Grandpa Howe?" he asked.

I wasn't sure what he meant, and when he began to explain I was so horrified I didn't know what to say.

"How do you know about that?" I demanded. "You didn't read the diary, I did."

"But you told me about it, remember? Why do you think her teacher was so shocked? Not because of the beating he'd given her, or the bruises she had, though those were awful enough. But because he raped her. Violated her, Quinton. Used her the way he should have used his wife, not his daughter."

I was so shaken I couldn't even catch my breath. "But . . . but she . . . she was just a little girl. How could he be so cruel, Jason? How could any father hurt his child like that?"

"He didn't love her," my brother said simply. "He cared nothing for what happened to her. But I'm not like that, Quinton. I'd never do anything to hurt you because I love you too much. Yes, it's true," he insisted. "I love you so, and I want to give you pleasure more than anything else in the world. Harry tried, but he didn't care about you; he only cared about himself. But I'm not like Harry, and I never will be. You do believe me, don't you?"

"But you're my brother," I said again.

"And who but your brother could love you as I do? Trust me, Quinn. Trust Mom. She knows what's best for us, she always has."

I lay there on the floor, eyes on the ceiling, tears trickling down my cheeks. I had wanted to be a woman, claimed to be one, too. But now I longed for childhood again, longed for it with a fervor I would never have thought possible.

Yet Jason could not be dissuaded. Reminding me of the secret places Father had written about, he began to show me where they were. I held myself rigid and unmoving, refusing to be a part of what he began to call the ritual of the undivided spirit. I did nothing to encourage him, and when he touched me, using his fingers and then his lips and probing tongue, I felt as Mother must have, when her father had taken her down to the cellar, there to inflict upon her the most sadistic punishment of them all.

Incest.

Rape.

Those were words from Father's dictionary, not words that I cared to make a part of my own experience.

But slowly, almost imperceptively, my body rebelled against me. I struggled to control myself and yet I couldn't. Something was opening up inside me, like a flower perhaps, or a mysterious hidden room, the door to which Jason had now unlocked. I wanted to slam that door shut, lock that room forever. I wanted to race back to the safety of my girlhood, when dolls were more important than boys with cleft chins and smoky gray eyes, or boys with palomino hair and mischievous grins. But there was no turning back.

"No one will ever love you as I do," Jason promised. "We share the same soul, Quinn, the same spirit. We're part of each other, and always will be."

I reached up, tracing the outline of his face with the tips of my fingers, learning his features as if I had never known them before. His green eyes opened wide, reflecting neither my fear nor uncertainty, but rather my gradual awakening to his touch. He did love me, I knew that. He would always love me, no matter what I did. He would be there for me, constant and unswerving, as devoted to me as he was to Mother.

"I love you, too," I whispered.

And so it began. And when it was over, I had left Quinnie to play with her dolls and race across lawns as green as Jason's eyes. I wept for her too, for I suppose there is a pain attached to leaving one's childhood behind, knowing that it will only live again in memory. And when that memory fades, another door is locked, and we are all grown up, ready to have children of our own.

# 16

I had to do it, don't you understand? I loved her, and that was the only way to prove it. We were Leflands, and Leflands were special, different from other people. Besides, how could Quinn love anyone but me? She couldn't, and that's the God's honest truth.

Only now I have to very careful. I can't let Aunt Gwen guess what's going on, especially since there isn't much time left, either. You see, the day after it happened (I wanted to do the ritual of the undivided spirit again that night, but Quinn said, "Jason, please, just give me a little time. It's all so new and I want to be alone for a while to think things over") Dad phoned and asked to speak to me.

"That you, son?"

How I wished I could trust the tone of concern he was trying to put into his voice. But he was responsible for all the evil and wickedness that had happened here, and I knew for Mom's sake I could never allow myself to forgive him. But I still had to pretend, had to act friendly, the true and devoted son, or else he might have gotten suspicious.

"Yes, Dad, it's me, Jason. How have you been? We miss you," I replied, trying to sound as if nothing were wrong.

"I'll be coming home sooner than I thought."

"Oh?"

"You sound disappointed."

"Not at all, Dad. Not at all. Can't wait. Honest. When do you think you'll get here?"

"Week from today. Do you guys want to drive down to L.A., meet me at the airport? We could take a little side trip if you like, go down to San Diego to the zoo. Or maybe you and Quinn would like to go to Disneyland."

"Too crowded," I said. I knew what he was up to, all right. He wanted to get us out of the Valley so he could bring his people in to look for Mom. But I couldn't let that happen.

"Sure now? Why don't you ask your sister, see what she says?"

"Okay, hold on a sec." Quinn and Aunt Gwen were standing right near the phone. I made sure to smile, just so Gwen would think everything was okay. Then I told Quinn what Dad had said. "I'd rather go up to Yosemite or maybe even Yellowstone, wouldn't you?"

I don't think Quinn understood what I was getting at until I added that I just didn't feel like leaving the Valley, especially now when the weather was so nice.

She finally got the message and said, "Sure, whatever you want is fine with me."

So I got back on the phone and told him we'd rather go up north to one of the national parks. I thought he'd bring up the subject of private school, but he didn't say a word about it. "Would you like to speak to Aunt Gwen? She's standing right here." I handed her the receiver and didn't even stick around to hear what she had to say. She wouldn't tell him anything important, anyway, not if Quinn and I were within earshot.

Quinn hurried after me. No more Quinnie, remember? It was Quinn now, and she was so pretty, so full of life, blossoming just like Mom said she would.

"What was that all about?" she whispered.

"He wants to get rid of us, what else."

"But when he comes back—"

"We'll have everything taken care of by then. I'm working on a couple of things. As soon as I set them in motion we'll get some answers for a change."

But it was hard. Boy, it was so hard trying to keep Warren from popping out of my head and spoiling everything. He was back from his little vacation, and now he was sitting up there between my ears, listening to what was going on and being just as mean and nasty as he could be.

The first thing he started in about was Quinn. He called it rape, and said it was an unnatural act that even animals in the wild didn't do. You've scarred her for life, he said. I told him he was all wrong, that he couldn't possibly understand the bond that Quinn and I had between us. The ritual of the undivided spirit was the purest expression of love there was. If he couldn't see it that way, that was his problem, not mine.

She loves you, Lefland, that's why she went along with it. And she's afraid of saying no to you, too. That's another reason.

Not true, I told him. Not the least bit true.

You're a sick boy, Lefland. You'd better get Dr. Warren on the phone, tell him to send the guys in white coats for you.

You're the sick one, Warren, not me. You're trying to mix me up, putting things in my head that don't belong there. But I'm not going to listen to you anymore.

That's what you think, Lefland. Just try ignoring me and see what happens.

I did try. I tried real hard. I went upstairs to my room, whistling all the way and pretending I didn't have a care in the world. But Warren followed after me. He started calling me dirty names, saying I was a psycho who should be locked up for the rest of my life.

I'm not listening, Warren. As far as I'm concerned you're not even there. Besides, I'm the one who made you up in the first place. So I can get rid of you just as easily.

Afraid it doesn't work that way, he said. I've always been a part of you, Jason. You and me are pals. We're like Siamese twins, can't separate us no matter how hard you try. So you'd better start getting used to me, because I'm going to be here for as long as you live.

But I loved Quinn, so how could what had happened between us be bad? I didn't do it just for the feeling-good, the shudders and the falling over the edge. I did it to bring us closer together.

Go on, Lefland, tell me about it. I'm real interested, you weirdo. Look in the mirror if you don't believe me. Anyone can tell to look at you how sick you are.

No, it wasn't so. Quinn needed me just as much as I needed her. Didn't Warren realize it was the two of us against all of them? Didn't he understand what had happened? No, I guess he didn't. He was too busy trying to trip me up and get me into trouble.

"Why don't you just shut up for a change and leave me alone?" I whispered aloud when I was alone in my room.

And spoil all my fun? Warren laughed. No, that would be too easy, Lefland, too kind for someone as sick as you.

I tried to ignore him. I did the best I could. The letter I'd written the night before, just hours after Quinn and I had shared each other's spirits in a way Warren could never understand, was still where I'd left it, hidden in a desk drawer. I took it out, folded it neatly, and put it in my back pocket. Then I slipped out of my room and headed upstairs to the attic.

But the moment I snuck inside, taking care to close the door softly behind me, there was something in my head, something that had nothing to do with Warren. It was kind of like a memory, or maybe it was a dream. I tried to recall what it was all about, but Warren kept blabbing away, and I couldn't even hear myself think.

You blocked it out, he said. He was laughing so hard it made my head hurt. Don't you remember what happened, Lefland? We came up here the other night. Early morning it was. The trunk flew open and guess who popped out?

That was a dream, I recalled. A nightmare. It didn't really happen.

But you're not sure, are you? No, of course not. You get things mixed up all the time now. You don't even know what's real and what isn't. So if I were you which I am, Lefland, I wouldn't go opening that steamer trunk over there. You might find something inside, something that'll scare the shit out of you.

Such as what?

Warren wouldn't tell me, and though I tried to remember, I just couldn't. But I had to open the trunk because that's where the blueprints were. Mom might be hiding in the house, and without the blueprints I'd have no way of knowing where to look. There might be secret rooms or passages Quinn and I had never discovered. And chances were, the blueprints would show me where to find them.

You promised her you'd never lie again, Warren reminded me. You swore you'd be honest. But you didn't tell her about the blueprints, did you?

I will.

When?

Soon, I told him.

Maybe you don't want her to ever know about it. Maybe you're going to keep it a secret, like everything else.

There aren't any secrets! They're all used up!

Liar, filthy disgusting liar does the feeling-good to his little sister and thinks he can get away with it. They're going to come and get you, Jason. They're going to put you away and never let you out again.

"They won't, and you can't make them, either," I whispered.

I took a deep breath and threw open the lid of the trunk.

Warren started to laugh, he thought it was so funny. There was nothing there, anyway, just the dirty letters he sent her and the big roll of yellowed blueprints. I spread them out on top of the trunk, then went through them until I found the plans for the attic. Great-grandpa Josiah was the one who'd built this house, and he always struck me as someone who had a great deal to hide. Sure enough, it was there all right, just as I'd long suspected.

I rolled up the blueprints and put them back in the trunk, then crossed the attic to where the two lopsided chiffoniers were crouched against the wall. I had to be very careful. I couldn't let anyone hear me, Warren included.

Nice and slow, I told myself. Just take your time.

I started pushing the chiffoniers away from the wall, moving them inch by inch and praying they wouldn't topple over. Great-grandpa was real crafty, storing them up here so no one would ever suspect what he'd hidden behind them. But I was Mom's son, determined to beat them at their own game. You see, I'd read the blueprints and discovered Josiah Lefland's secret, and now everything was as plain as daylight.

Having managed to move the two broken wardrobes out of the way, I began to tap along the wall, looking for the panel the architect had drawn into the plans. It took time, but I finally found what I was looking for—a specific panel that was designed to look like the rest of the wall. When I tapped my fist against the wall (just like Quinn and I had tried when we first came up here) a hollow sound told me that success was close at hand. Now I had to figure out how to slide the panel open and I'd be home free.

Warren was keeping his trap shut for a change, though I knew he was still around, spying on me and ready to say mean things first chance he got. I tried pulling at the wood along the wall, twisting the molding this way and that.

There was a whoosh of trapped air and suddenly I was staring into darkness, so thick you could almost touch it with your fingers.

I wouldn't go in there if I were you, Warren said. He started giggling like he thought it was the funniest thing in the world.

I'm not listening to you, not ever again, I told him.

But the moment I bent down and stepped into the passageway hidden behind the wall, I started to gag. I had to duck back out again, because the smell was so bad that I couldn't even breathe. There was something awful in there, something that wasn't meant to be found, its hideous stench filling the attic like a poison gas.

Please, Jason, don't go back in there, Warren pleaded. Even if you don't listen to me ever again, listen to me now.

"Why should I, when all you do is tell me lies?"

Not this time, I swear. Please, there are things you shouldn't know about, Jason, things that are best left undisturbed.

"Shove it, Warren. You seem to forget that I'm in charge around here, not you."

I hurried downstairs to my room, grabbed my flashlight, and rushed back to the attic. But just as I reached the third-floor landing a voice cried out and I froze in midstep.

Don't answer, I thought. Don't say a word or you'll give yourself away.

"Jason, are you up there?"

No, Warren said. Jason isn't here anymore. I'm taking his place for him.

He tried to get me to open my mouth. It felt like a pair of hands were ripping my jaws apart. I pushed him away but he was just as strong as me.

Because I am you, Warren said.

"Jason?" my sister called again.

Answer her or I'll do it for you! Warren threatened.

You bastard, I told him, always making trouble for me.

No, Lefland, you've got it all wrong. You're the one who makes trouble for himself, not the other way around.

"Up here," I hissed.

Quinn moved silently up the stairs, never once taking her eyes off me.

That's because she cares about me, and she's my only friend, I thought.

That's because she's scared to death of you, Warren replied.

"What are you doing up here?" she whispered.

At least she knew enough to keep her voice down. She stood there on the stair, looking up at me with her sad blue eyes. The little line of freckles on her cheekbones visibly darkened, and I wondered if that meant she was blushing.

It means she's scared, Warren said with another nasty laugh.

"He says you're scared of me," I blurted out, unable to stop myself in time.

"Who does?"

You creep, I told him, tricking me like that. Do you want her to think I'm crazy or something?

But you are crazy, Lefland. You're as crazy as a loon.

"My alter ego," I said, and I tried to smile.

"Is that the same thing as your conscience?"

"Kind of. And I wish you wouldn't come sneaking around like this. Anyone see you?"

She shook her head, wanting to know what I was being so secretive about.

I motioned her to follow me and started back up the stairs. As soon as we were alone in the attic she looked at me excitedly and asked if I'd found the diary.

But instead of answering her question, I asked her if she still loved me.

Quinn cocked her head to one side and looked at me quizzically.

"I mean, you're not upset or anything, are you?" I asked. "Because I couldn't stand it if you hated me, Quinn. I wouldn't even want to live if you didn't love me."

"Of course I love you, Jason. I always have and I always will."

"Then you're not angry?"

"Because you taught me about love?" She shook her head. "No, anger has nothing to do with it. I'm confused I guess, but I'm not angry, not the least bit, I swear."

"Can I kiss you then?"

When she smiled it lit up her face. Her eyes shone brightly, and the flush in her cheeks gave her a radiant glow. She threw her arms over my shoulders and pressed herself against me. I felt more certain of my love for her than ever before. When she kissed me even Warren stopped laughing, and for that I was grateful.

But the moment I released her she wrinkled her nose and looked in the direction of the passageway I'd uncovered just a few minutes before. "What's that awful smell?" she asked.

"I don't know yet." Reluctantly I told her about finding

the original set of blueprints to the house, and how I had located a hidden passage behind one of the walls.

She started toward it, but the stench was already making her sick to her stomach, and she was forced to turn away. "What's in there, Jason? It's like something crawled in and died."

That was just what I was afraid of. No, not afraid. Terrified. Quinn must have read my mind, because a moment later she let out a gasp and her eyes flew open in horror.

"Oh no," she said. "It can't be, it just can't. Have you gone in there yet? Have you seen who it is?"

"Who?" I said.

"You know what I mean, Jason. Do you think it's—?" She couldn't even bring herself to utter Mom's name, but I knew that was the only person on her mind.

Close the panel. Forget you ever found out about it. Push the wardrobes back in place and leave well enough alone. Jason, please, I beg of you. Don't go in there.

Why are you being so friendly all of a sudden, Warren? Since when have you started looking out for me?

Since now, he said. Go up into the hills, look for Mom there. But don't crawl down that passage. Don't!

"I'm going to go in and see what's there," I told my sister, even though Warren was still begging me to reconsider, screaming at me now and saying I was making a terrible mistake.

"I'm going with you," Quinn announced.

I didn't want her to, but one thing Warren had said was right. The less we kept from each other, the better. So I took off my shirt and tied it over my mouth and nose. The smell didn't go away, but at least I was able to breathe without getting sick. Then, armed with the flashlight, I bent down and slipped into the narrow opening. Quinn was right behind me, having tied a handkerchief around the lower part of her face.

I crept forward, shining the beam of the flashlight on the unfinished walls. It was less a passageway than a crawlspace, the ceiling so low it was impossible to straighten up without hitting our heads. We inched our way along, and with each shuffling step the smell intensified. It was rank and putrid, a stench of something dead and decomposing.

"Jason, if it's what we think it is—"

I was afraid to answer. If they had done this to our mother, if they had walled her up in here and left her to die, I knew I would never rest until they too had been sealed up behind this wall, never to see daylight again.

But how could it be Mom when I had spoken to her, seeing her before me as clearly as I saw Quinn? No, it's something else, I kept telling myself. It just has to be.

Some twenty or so feet up ahead the crawlspace made a right-angle turn. As soon as she noticed it, Quinn reached out and grabbed my arm.

"I don't want to look," she said. "If it's what . . . what we're afraid of, I don't want to ever know her that way."

"You wait here then," I instructed.

I blamed them for the terror and despair I saw in her eyes, blamed them for all they had put us through since the night they had taken Mom away. If only I could remember what had happened. But Warren had stolen the memory and swallowed it whole, feasting on it the way maggots feast on a corpse.

Whatever was causing the smell was just ahead. I reached the bend in the passage, held my breath, and shone the flashlight into the darkness. There was a door there, so narrow a man could barely pass through it. I hurried forward, my fingers scrabbling at the doorknob. The rusty hinges creaked in protest, but the lock held. Again and again I tugged at the knob, finally smashing the side of the flashlight against it.

"Jason, what's happening?" Quinn called out.

"It's all right," I said, my voice echoing through the darkness. "There's a door here. I'm trying to get it open."

"A door?" she said in disbelief, and I could hear her moving along the passage.

I shone the flashlight behind me, and she put her hand over her eyes and looked away.

"It's locked," I said. "And needless to say we don't have the key."

"Should I go back and find a hammer?"

"No, the lock's pretty well rusted through. And I think termites have been here before us, anyway."

I stepped back, straightening up as best I could before I slammed my foot into the door. I just hoped they wouldn't hear me downstairs. But there were four floors between us, so I didn't think there was that much to worry about.

The doorjamb began to splinter, and with the third kick the lock gave way and the door swung back. By then, Quinn had overcome her fear. She was right behind me, and as I played the beam of the flashlight across the dusty floor, she suddenly gave a little cry and stumbled back. I could hear her being sick, and yet it didn't matter, it didn't matter at all.

"A possum, a dumb opossum!" I said, and I even started to laugh I felt so relieved.

It lay there on its side, its matted gray fur alive with ants and maggots. But how had it managed to get in here? And once inside, why hadn't it been able to get out again?

Cautiously I moved forward, the flashlight illuminating a bare, windowless room not much larger than a closet. Several feet beyond the swollen and decomposing carcass I made out the legs of a straight-back chair. I aimed the light a little higher, and goosebumps erupted along my arms and the back of my neck. With a groan of desperation I rushed forward, screaming out Mom's name.

It sat in the chair, face turned to the wall.

"How could they?" I cried, and tears were already flooding my eyes. "How could they have done such a thing?"

Quinn was weeping as she crouched near the doorway. I wanted to go back and comfort her, have her comfort me as well. Instead, I reached out and grabbed hold of the back of the chair, forcing it around.

My God, it wasn't Mom, it couldn't have been!

It was a skeleton, clothed in tattered shreds, a few wisps of dun-colored hair still clinging to its skull. It was tied to the chair with leather straps securing its arms and legs. But it wasn't Mom. It was someone else, someone whom Great-grandfather Josiah must have locked in this room nearly a hundred years before.

When Quinn finally raised her eyes and saw the skeleton, she didn't scream, or gasp, or run away in terror. She just stood there in the doorway, shaking her head and whispering, "Thank God, thank God," over and over again.

I shone the flashlight down along its legs. Judging from the high-buttoned shoes the figure wore, these and what little remained of its clothing, I could tell it had once been a man, perhaps even a Lefland like myself.

A scrap of yellowed cloth was pinned to what must have been the lapel of a jacket. But when I started to unpin it, I realized it wasn't cloth, but a thick parchmentlike paper that had gone yellow and brittle with age.

Part of it crumbled in my hand as I pulled the rusty pin free. I held it under the beam of the flashlight, trying to read the faint letters that had been written so long ago.

"What does it say?" Quinn whispered.

It was very hard to make out, for the ink had faded and the writing was barely legible.

"E-X something," I said. "Let's take it out into the light."

"Who do you think it was?" she asked as I led her from the room, taking care to avoid the bloated remains of the opossum lying stiffly near the threshold.

I closed the broken door as best I could, then hurried back the way we'd come. Only when the sliding panel was once again secured, did we turn our attention to the yellowed and brittle scrap of paper. I took it over to one of the dormer windows where the light was strongest. Quinn peered over my shoulder, trying to make out the message— or maybe even the warning—someone had clearly meant to be preserved.

"E, X . . . I can't read the next letter. Then there's a D, and a bunch of numbers."

"E, X, space, D," Quinn repeated, trying to figure out what it meant. "What do you suppose the numbers are for?"

"Two something," I read. "Is the next one a number or a letter? It looks like a U."

"No, I think it's a zero. Two, zero, five."

There was another set of letters and numbers right below. These were no less clearer than the others, though Quinn and I were fairly certain they spelled out LLV 2011.

"Do you think it's a kind of secret code?" my sister asked. "LLV is fifty-fifty-five in Roman numerals."

"Ex something," I said, thinking aloud. "Ex what?"

I know what it means, Warren spoke up.

He hadn't said anything since we'd gone into the crawlspace. But now he awakened, his tone as vindictive and malicious as always.

What? I said. Ex for X marks the spot?

Cute, Lefland, but not cute enough. Look at it again.

Don't those first set of letters resemble part of a word? Fill in the empty space. There aren't too many choices, are there?

I needed paper and pencil, and so Quinn and I hurried downstairs to my room, where I sat at my desk and carefully copied out everything that was visible on the scrap of paper.

*EX D 205. LLV 2011.*

"Does that look like anything you've seen before?"

"Start putting letters in between," Quinn suggested.

I was halfway through the alphabet when my sister suddenly clapped her hands in excitement. "It's the Bible!" she cried out. "It's short for Exodus, chapter and verse."

"But what about the LLV?"

"Maybe they're someone's initials."

"No, I don't think so." I picked up the slip of paper and held it under the desk lamp, slowly turning it from side to side to illuminate it as fully as possible. "Wait a second, isn't that another mark there?"

"That little scratch?" she said doubtfully.

"Sure it is. And that dot right next to it. It's all part of the same letter."

"You mean it's not an L?"

"No, look carefully, Quinn. See? The second letter's not an L, it's an E! And I bet LEV is another part of the Bible, chapter twenty again, verse eleven."

The two of us couldn't get downstairs fast enough. As soon as we snuck into the study, Quinn ran over to the wall of bookshelves nearest the fireplace. The Lefland family Bible was a big weighty affair bound in hand-tooled leather. It had been passed down from one generation to the next, and in the back there was a record of births, deaths, baptisms, and marriages. Quinn pulled it off the shelf and began to hurriedly flip through the pages.

"Here it is, Exodus," she said a moment later. She

turned to chapter twenty, then moved her finger down the closely written page until she came to the small number 5.

I was afraid to ask what it said, but by then she had already begun to read it aloud.

" 'For I the Lord thy God am a jealous God, visiting the iniquity—' What does that mean?"

"Wickedness. Sins," I whispered, and I could feel my stomach drop, and Warren clutching my shoulders as if he were trying to prepare me for the worst.

". . . visiting the iniquity of the fathers upon the children.' " Quinn raised her eyes and looked at me in fear. "I've heard that before, Jason. We both have. It's what those notes said, the one I found the night the diary was stolen, the one you got the night Har—"

I put my finger to my lips and motioned in the direction of the study doors. "Yes, I know. Go on, Quinn, might as well read the rest of it."

" 'For I the Lord thy God am a jealous God, visiting the iniquity of the fathers upon the children unto the third and fourth generation of them that hates me.' " She took a deep breath, then plunged ahead, searching for the part of the Bible where the letters LEV would apply.

Didn't I warn you? Warren spoke up. Didn't I tell you not to go in there? But no, you wouldn't listen to me, Lefland, would you? You had to get your way to prove you were stronger than me. But how can you be stronger than yourself? You can't, and now it's too late.

"Leviticus!" Quinn said excitedly. "That's what the letters mean, an abbreviation like EXOD. Chapter twenty again. Wait, wait, here it is. Number . . . eleven."

She stabbed her finger down on the page. But before she had a chance to read the passage aloud I grabbed the Bible out of her hands and read the verse quickly to myself.

I was being watched again, not just by Warren but by all of them. The room was alive with whispering voices, and in every corner and behind every shadow a Lefland stood and pointed a finger at me, accusing me of wickedness, of acts so vile they dared not speak their name.

Quinn looked at me with wounded innocent eyes. "Why did you pull it away from me? I would've given it to you. All you had to do is ask."

"I guess I got excited, that's why," I said hurriedly. I tried to close the Bible, but Warren wouldn't let me.

Go on, he said. Read it, Lefland. He was gloating, and I could feel his spiteful presence along with all the others. It's time you faced reality, my little friend.

No, reality was too painful, and what's why I had Warren to talk to, instead of myself. I wanted to turn and run, never look back, leave the Valley like Orin Lefland had tried to do.

Tried, but he didn't quite make it, did he? Warren said with a snicker.

"Go on, Jason, what does it say?"

"Nothing. Honest, it's not important."

"I thought we weren't going to have anymore secrets between us, Jason. I thought that's what love was all about. Total honesty. The freedom to bare our souls to each other."

"Baring our souls has nothing to do with it, Quinn."

She loves you, dummy! shouted Warren. Tell her the truth and get it over with!

How can I? She'd never understand.

Why don't you let her be the judge of that? You took her innocence away from her, made her a woman, but now you want to treat her like a baby. You can't have it both ways, Lefland.

I looked down at the page, feeling my sister's eyes burning into me. My voice cracked as I began to recite the verse. " 'And the man that lieth with his father's wife hath uncovered his father's nakedness: both of them shall surely be put to death.' ''

Quinn stared at me blankly. She still hadn't figured out what this was all about, that the skeleton we had discovered behind the attic wall had been condemned to death for a crime against God and nature. I thought of Orin Lefland, the son who had mysteriously disappeared, never to be seen or heard from again. My hands were shaking uncontrollably as I turned to the back of the Bible, where the records of our family had been dutifully maintained.

There it was, all right, staring at me just as boldly as Quinn was doing.

*Orin Benjamin Lefland, b. 1869, d.*

There was no record of his death, just a blank space on the page.

''What are you looking for?'' Quinn asked.

''An answer. Maybe the one answer we really need.''

I studied the remaining records. When I discovered that his mother had not been Hepzibah, but another woman who had died at approximately the same time Orin had disappeared, I realized the mystery was all but solved.

For the terrible sin that young Orin had committed, his father had seen fit to act as both judge and executioner. I could even see them enacting that age-old ritual, a Biblical judgment passed down through untold generations. Josiah had discovered the boy's iniquity and had condemned him to death. He had dragged him up the stairs to the attic. Perhaps Orin had struggled to escape, but somehow I couldn't picture him being anything but resigned. With wooden, lifeless steps he followed obediently after his father. The molding twisted according to its awful design, the panel slid back, revealing an opening in the wall. Josiah must have ordered him to walk on ahead until they reached that hidden room, perhaps a room Great-grandfather had built expressly for this purpose.

Seated in the plain wooden chair, Orin had said nothing, making no effort to defend himself. The Lefland stubbornness perhaps, or maybe it was pride, and a willingness to accept the dreadful consequences of his act. His father had strapped him to the chair, controlling his rage long enough to write out the message that we, generations later, would end up discovering. Then he had locked the door behind him and retraced his steps.

Had Orin begun to scream, begging his father for mercy? Had his voice echoed through the house, a shriek of terror that grew weaker by the hour? Had his mother tried to rescue him? Had Josiah flung her down the stairs, condemning her to death just as moments before he had condemned their son?

And what of Alethea of the next generation? Had Grandfather Ephraim's first wife reenacted the Lefland curse, so that she too had lost her life for the weaknesses of the flesh? I looked down at the record of births and deaths, and when I once again saw what I'd suspected, I wasn't even surprised.

Alethea's first-born, Charles Jared Lefland, was just a year older than me when he had died at the age of fifteen. The family records revealed that in that same year Alethea too had passed away, and by the following spring Grandfather had remarried.

So there it was, a record not of triumphs and tragedies, but of sin and judgment, wickedness and retribution. And as the Valley itself had been passed down through the years, so too had the incestuous curse that still haunted the Leflands. For the sins of the fathers were visited upon the children. And we, Quinn and me, we were the children of the fourth generation.

Now do you remember? Warren asked.

I think so, a little bit at least. Pieces of it. It's beginning to make sense again.

Quinn had stood there all this time, but now she broke her silence, wanting to know what it was that I had learned. It was so complicated, I thought, and if I told her it would only cause her unnecessary pain. Even Warren agreed, and that struck me as very strange because he was suddenly beginning to sound like me. Maybe I wasn't such a bad person after all. Maybe he was learning to like me, and accept me for who I was. I didn't want to hurt anyone, and certainly not Quinn. Warren must have realized that, because he didn't try to make me tell her what I knew, tearing the words right out of my throat the way he had done before.

I tried to sound calm, level-headed, completely in control of myself. "Please don't ask me to explain, Quinn. I will, in time, I promise. But I have to get everything straight in my mind first. You know the old expression, 'the light at the end of the tunnel'? Well, I see it for us, I really do, and it's getting brighter all the time. I have plans for us, Quinn, wonderful plans."

"But what good are plans without Mother? What good is anything if she's not here to share it with us? Someone's trying to frighten us off with notes and threats and God only knows what else. Is that skeleton up there Great-uncle Orin? And if it is, why was he murdered like that? What are the sins of the fathers that we're being blamed for?"

All the answers to her questions were in the letter I'd written her the night before. I could feel the folded sheets of paper in my back pocket, and I wondered if now was the time to give them to her. But before I had a chance to make up my mind, one way or the other, I began to feel all itchy and uncomfortable, almost as if I were having some kind of allergic reaction.

I tugged at the collar of my shirt, trying to loosen it. What was happening to me? What was wrong? The shirt was too tight, like it had shrunk to fit someone half my size. I wondered if they were trying to trick me again. I bet they are, I told Warren. I bet they're substituting my clothes for someone else's.

"Shirt's so tight I can't breathe," I complained. "Jeans don't fit right, either. Can't you see how short they are?"

"They look fine, Jason."

Her eyes were crawling all over me. I had to look away.

"They aren't," I insisted. "They feel tight and itchy and don't ask me anymore questions, Quinn. I keep my promises, you know that. When the time is right you'll know everything."

"And when do you think that'll be?"

She sounded real snotty and Warren wanted to slap her for being fresh. But I begged him not to, saying she didn't mean any harm.

"Soon, I swear." I heard the letter crackling like fire in my back pocket. But now I was too scared to give it to her, and I backed away. "Before Dad gets back, I promise you'll know everything."

Famous last words, Warren giggled.

Without any warning, he stuck his fingers in my eyes, trying to blind me. I cried out in pain and staggered back.

"Jason!" my sister said in alarm.

And if a man shall take his sister, and see her nakedness, and she see his nakedness; it is a wicked thing; and they shall be cut off in the sight of their people, Warren recited. Leviticus, Jason. Chapter twenty, verse seventeen. Shall we say it together, my friend, memorize it so we won't ever forget?

"No!"

Quinn was shaking me, begging me to tell her what was wrong.

"We're cursed," I groaned. "It's in the blood, Quinn. Always has been. It can't ever go away."

"Cursed for doing what? Caring about each other, trying

271

to help our mother? That's not a curse, Jason. That's a gift. That's part of loving one another, and it's the most wonderful thing in the world.''

She put her arms around me, trying to share her strength with me. But I was afraid Warren would try to hurt her the way he was hurting me, and I pushed her away before he could get his filthy hands on her.

''Burn for your sins, Jason Lefland!'' shrieked the voices of my ancestors. They were calling out to me, all of them. Leflands long dead and buried. Leflands walled up in hidden rooms. Leflands murdered in their beds, smothered and knifed and buried alive for a seed of passion so corrupt as to defile the very name of God.

''I'm good!'' I cried out. ''I swear I'm a good boy, I swear it to God and the baby Jesus and everyone!''

''Jason, don't, they'll hear you,'' Quinn warned. ''We can't let them know.''

What did it matter when I was already condemned? They had sent Warren as their emissary, that was the fancy fifty-dollar word. He was their emissary of death, sent to destroy me, to twist my thoughts around and turn them inside out until I couldn't tell right from wrong, reality from fantasy. They'd stolen my clothes and soon they'd try to steal my body, too. They were clever, these people who hated me, Dad and Aunt Gwen and the Darbys. It was a much subtler form of retribution than being strapped to a chair and left for dead. It was crueler and far more painful. But God approved. He looked down from heaven and said I would be put to death so that the seed of corruption would die with me, never to bear fruit again.

Should've ripped him out of her womb, strangled him in his crib.

Clothes didn't fit.

Head hurt.

Warren was trying to tear my arms off, my legs, give them to someone else.

Quinnie shook me and shook me but she couldn't shake out the poison.

Room was getting dark.

Warren was blinding me, that's what he was doing. He was sewing my eyes shut and I could feel the needle going in and out, in and out, every stitch nice and even. I screamed and screamed and Quinnie shook me. The door suddenly flew open. Who was that? Who was standing there, watching me, staring? Was that Mom? Was that finally Mom?

"My God, what's going on in here?" cried the voice at the end of the tunnel.

Josiah Lefland, that's who it was. He'd lock me up, throw away the key. I had to get away, had to run. He tried to grab me but I lunged out of his way. Why did Josiah look like Gwen? I didn't know but I had to escape. So I ran, so hard and so fast I knew I was flying.

The hills!

Yes, that's where I'd go, up into the hills where Mom would find me and tell me it was okay, I was safe, a good boy. They wouldn't hurt me anymore because she wouldn't let them. We'd protect each other and Quinnie, too. No one would ever hurt us, and everything would be all right again.

NO MORE HURT! I screamed. NO MORE HURT NOT EVER AGAIN!

# 17

"**L**et him go!" I shouted at my aunt when she tried
to chase after Jason. He'd barreled his way past her, nearly
throwing her down to the floor. Now, Aunt Gwen stood
there in shocked silence as my brother flung the front door
open and raced out of the house.

"What happened?" she said. "What was all that screaming about?"

I was trembling, but I knew I had to regain control of
myself if I was ever to help my brother. So I tried to push
the anxiety I felt down into the pit of my stomach, hoping
my aunt wouldn't notice how upset I was.

"We had an argument, that's all. I guess he overreacted."

"Overreacted?" said Aunt Gwen, and her carefully pen-
ciled eyebrows shot clear up to her forehead. "I'd call that
an understatement, wouldn't you?"

"Jason likes to be dramatic, you know," I said hurriedly. "I better go apologize."

I walked past her, smiling pleasantly and trying to act as
nonchalant as I could. But as soon as I was out of her sight

I began to run, tripping over myself in my haste to get outside. I raced through the garden, calling to him over and over again. But he was nowhere within earshot, so I made my way down the path toward the Bottom, looking back over my shoulder just to make sure Aunt Gwen wasn't following me.

It was a hot, muggy day, and the hills that ringed the Valley were the color of oatmeal. The grass was like straw, and dust devils swirled down the road, turning and twisting with each stray breeze.

I looked for Jason's footprints but I couldn't find them. Perhaps he'd steered clear of the road for just that reason, afraid that either me or Aunt Gwen would try to follow him. Hoping he'd headed for the Temple, I made my way in that direction, wondering what I would say when I found him. He was so troubled that I wasn't sure I could even be of help. But I knew I had to try, or else he'd end up destroying himself.

What were the sins of the fathers? I wondered again. And what did the verse from Leviticus have to do with what had happened to young Orin Lefland? *And the man that lieth with his father's wife* . . . Did that mean his stepmother? Or could it mean that his mother had been in love with another man, and Orin had tried to keep it a secret from his father? Yes, maybe that was it. Maybe Orin knew that his mother had a lover (Jason's word, but I guess it was the right one), and when Great-grandfather discovered her infidelity, he blamed his son for trying to conceal it from him.

But even more important than the verses cited in the note was my brother's reaction to all that had taken place. When he had insisted we were cursed I was sure it was because he felt guilty for what we had done together. Perhaps that was a natural reaction, but then to moan in pain, to start screaming as if someone were actually torturing him—I just couldn't figure it out. If only he could remember what had happened the night they had taken Mother away. If only we could find her and ask her ourselves.

When I reached the Temple I knew right away that he had already been here, for the door to the playhouse was ajar. I called to him because I didn't want him to be frightened or surprised. But he didn't answer. So I knocked on the door and stepped inside.

One look and I wanted to go running out again. The portrait of our beautiful mother had been slashed beyond recognition, the painting little more than shreds of canvas, torn and hacked at again and again. As for the blessed instruments of our faith, these too had been destroyed, smashed and broken and hurled in every direction. The bottle containing the fragrance of remembrance was in pieces too, and the scent of Mother's perfume was so heavy it was almost cloying.

But perhaps the most frightening thing of all was the pile of tiny arms and legs that lay in a heap on the altar. They were the dolls Father had given me for my birthday, but now they were merely a collection of disjointed limbs and twisted torsos, completely dismembered and left there like some kind of grisly offering.

With trembling steps I crossed the room, feeling my stomach suddenly clench so tightly I doubled over in pain. What had happened? Who had done this terrible thing? Was this Jason's work, or was it Mother's, I couldn't help but wonder?

The clothes had been ripped off the dolls, the flesh-colored plastic looking so real that for a moment I was afraid to touch it. I reached down and picked up one of the broken legs. It was wet, sticky. Even as I looked at it blood was dripping onto my hand. I flung it to the floor and backed away, sickened by what I saw, this incredible outpouring of mindless rage, hatred that filled the air as suffocatingly as Mother's perfume.

Why was there blood? Why had Jason run shrieking from the house, moaning of a curse we were powerless to defend ourselves against? Did the dolls represent us? And if they did, did that mean we too were marked for death?

I sank down onto my knees, gazing up at the tattered canvas that had once been a portrait of a woman I had come to worship. Was God angry at me for sending my prayers to Mother, and not to Him? But surely He understood how much I missed her, how much my brother and I needed to have her back again.

I thought of poor Harry with his beautiful hair and smoky-gray eyes, lying there as broken as the dolls. I thought of Great-uncle Orin, and the diary of the little girl whose father had beaten and raped her. Why couldn't I just go back in time, to when everything was perfect for us, and Mother was always there when I needed her?

The ivory nightgown I had worn for Jason lay in a crumpled heap on the floor. It too was stained with blood, and when I picked it up I saw that it had been slashed as mercilessly as the portrait. But there was something else, for I found a bunch of papers hidden beneath it. Across the top sheet was written "For Quinn," and I could see right away it was in Jason's hand.

"Don't be afraid of me, Quinn," I could hear him saying. "And don't be afraid of love, either."

He would never hurt me, neither with words nor deeds. Angry at myself for ever doubting him, I sat there on the floor and began to read the letter he had left for me.

"My dear dear Quinnie," it began. "This afternoon I knew you as no one else has, and tonight, sitting here in my room, I can feel how close you are to me as you lie asleep next-door. I'm afraid of so many things, Quinn, but I'll never be afraid of you. It's the truth that's scary, and so that's why I'm writing this instead of telling it to you. I don't want to see the look in your eyes when you finally discover the terrible secret I've been keeping from you.

"Secrets are like weapons, I've always thought. You can use them to defend yourself or you can use them to inflict pain and hurt. But I love you so much I can't bear to think of causing you anymore unhappiness. Even though we try to act like grownups, I guess we both realize we're still children. Childhood's supposed to be this real terrific time in our lives. Only it hasn't been, Quinn. Even the last few weeks, when I've felt closer to you than ever before, I've still had to wrestle with all this guilt and anger that keeps boiling up inside me.

"You said that Aunt Gwen told you Mom was crazy. Maybe I'm crazy too, for thinking we could love each other like husband and wife. Maybe we still can, though that's something we'll only be able to discover in time. But that's not what I wanted to write to you about. It's the secret I've kept from you, a secret that's tortured me for so many months now that maybe if I explain it, get it all off my chest, I won't be crazy anymore. I'll just be Jason again.

"I'd had a nightmare, that's how it started. Mom must have heard me crying in my room, because she came in to see what was wrong. She was wearing that long ivory nightgown I liked best of all. She sat down on the edge of my bed, brushing my hair back with her fingers, telling me it was all right, it was only a bad dream.

"I'd just turned twelve, because I remember it was a few days after the party we had for my birthday. I didn't realize there was more to the dream than fear, then running and running because someone was chasing me and I had to escape. But then Mom started looking at me, Quinn, different from the way she'd ever looked at me before.

"This is hard now, but it has to be said. Just don't hate

us for it, that's all I ask. You see, when she looked at me she stared at the front of my pajamas—I was still wearing them in those days. When I realized what she was doing I got so embarrassed I guess I started to cry all over again. 'Lefland men never cry,' she said. Those were her exact words, Quinn, and I started feeling better right away, because I liked the way she'd called me a man, and not her little boy. Then she reached inside my pajama bottoms and tickled me like she used to do when I was real little and there wasn't very much there to tickle. Only the way she touched me wasn't the same. It was totally different, Quinn, and I knew it and she knew it, too.

"That was the first time, just the tickling and the way she looked at me and didn't say anything. Days and days went by and I was sure she'd talk about it. But she never did. Her eyes avoided mine it seemed, or maybe mine avoided hers, like boxers in a ring circling round and round each other, each unwilling to throw the first punch.

"Then, one night a few weeks later when Dad was away—and I don't need to tell you how often he left on business, so maybe that's why this whole thing started—it happened again. This time when she came into my room she didn't even bother to knock the way she usually did. I was scared, Quinn. I just didn't know what to do. But she told me there was nothing to be afraid of because she was my mom and she knew what was best for me.

"Anyway, I guess you can imagine what happened. She kept her hand there, under the covers, until it felt so good that I couldn't stop it from happening. I'd had dreams that felt the same way, and I even had a special word to describe it. I called it the feeling-good, because I didn't know the real word for it. Dad hadn't made any effort to tell me about the facts of life, ejaculation, masturbation, and all the other 'ations' grownups know so much about. I don't think he's ever cared very much for me, Quinn, and maybe that's why I let Mom do this to me, because I didn't think Dad loved me.

"She told me I mustn't be frightened of pleasure, and then she began to teach me everything there was to know about it. Do you know what I'm saying? Do you understand now, do you really understand what happened? It was sex, Quinn. Intercourse. She took me into her bed, and I couldn't help but like it. But she warned me that we had to be very careful. And that's when I really knew it was wrong, because if it was right she wouldn't have cared if anyone found out. But no, it had to be a secret, the biggest, most serious secret I'd ever had to keep. She told me Dad wasn't to be trusted, that if he knew how much she loved me, he'd send me away, so far away we'd never see each other again. And I believed her, Quinn, every word of it. And I guess I still believe it to this day.

"Mom said that since I had come out of her body, her womb was the way she put it, I was still a part of her. She said we were of the same flesh, and that how could there be anything sinful in the love of a mother for her son? I knew what the word was for what had happened between us, because Mom herself used it often enough. It was incest, just as it was incest when her father took her down to the cellar.

"I guess the big difference is that Mom loved me, whereas Grandpa Howe did it because he was sick and evil. And besides, how could I have disobeyed her, Quinn? I always did exactly what she asked, even when it seemed wrong. Mothers couldn't be wrong, she used to say. Mothers were always right, and that was something I'd just have to learn to accept.

"So now you know the awful truth. I just hope you don't think it's *so* awful that you'll hate me and Mom for it. She didn't mean any harm, Quinn. She was lonely and they weren't getting along, just like Gwen told you. As for what happened that night, I know I was in their bedroom when it all started. But I swear to you I can't remember what took place. I've tried, Quinn, but there's just this big empty space where the memory used to be. They must have been talking about Dr. Warren though, because I don't think I'd heard his name mentioned before then. But I don't know what happened after that.

"When we find her, Quinn, and I swear to you I won't give up until we do, I promise I won't let it happen again. Maybe it all started because she was depressed, having those terrible sick headaches and all. But we can't hate her for that. We'll get her help, that's what we'll do. And she'll get well again, Quinn, and then we'll all be together. So please don't be mad at me. I made love to you not because I was trying to pretend you were Mom, but because I needed to know you cared about me more than you cared about anyone else."

Jason had signed his name at the end of the letter. But then, in a shaky handwriting that was barely recognizable, my brother had scrawled the following postscript:

"I didn't do that to the painting or the dolls, I swear. Someone's in my head. Can't write. Going to find her. Love you always."

This was followed by a jumble of letters, and when I examined them closely I saw there were two names, one written over the other. The more prominent and legible of the two spelled JASON, while the one buried beneath the jerky swirls and loops of his handwriting started with a W, and ended with an N.

I spent the remainder of the day trying to find my brother. We had both talked about going up into the hills to search the numerous shallow caves where we had often played at Tom Sawyer and Treasure Island when we were younger. Sometimes Jason would pretend to be Captain

Kidd or Blackbeard the pirate, and I would be his fearless first mate. Other times he was a swashbuckling prince and I was his consort, the two of us kidnapped by Long John Silver, forced to help him find Captain Flint's treasure. Or he would be Tom Sawyer and I'd be Becky Thatcher, searching for the treasure left by Injun Joe.

Thinking about the innocent fun we used to have, the fanciful costumes Mother helped us create to add a note of authenticity to our games, left me with a sad, aching memory of childhood. In just a matter of a few short weeks I had been forced to put all that behind me, the fantasies of girlhood, the dolls and tea parties, the games of make-believe and all the laughter and high spirits that went along with them.

Now, life had taken on a sense of dread and urgency, as if time itself were running out not only for me, but for all of us here in the Valley. Even if I spent every waking hour searching for Quinnie, I would never find her again. I was Quinn now, just as my brother had said. I had experienced what it was to be a woman, had watched a young man die. And then to read Jason's letter, to finally learn what it was that he had managed to keep secret for nearly two years, was more than I was able to comprehend.

There were so many unanswered questions that hardly anything made sense anymore. One thing I did know, though. Jason needed me, needed me as perhaps he had never needed anyone before. Something or someone had crept into his thoughts. This presence or whatever it was he had created for himself, this spiteful Warren he kept speaking of, was trying to play havoc with his mind and drive him into a world of madness and unending despair. I had to save him from that, even if it meant saving him from himself.

So I trudged up into the hills, where the afternoon light

scattered purple shadows across the thorny chaparral, and hawks wheeled in the cloudless sky. Sparrows flitted nervously through the scrub, their twittering calls dogging my steps as I made my way up toward the hills that pockmarked the rim of the Valley.

The sun had begun to set by the time I was forced to give up my search and head back home. I had found nothing to indicate that either Jason or Mother had been here. The long-awaited reunion I had prayed for never took place, and it was with a growing sense of helplessness that I returned to a house that had become cold and forbidding. Here I had lived out the dreams of childhood, never aware of the madness whose seed, once planted, can never be uprooted. All of us were touched by it now, and whether it was a family curse or merely the act of one person, repeated from one generation to the next just as wars are repeated, mattered little. The deed had been done, and now Jason and I had to deal with its dreadful consequences.

Aunt Gwen was waiting for me when I returned, her anxious expression making it clear that my brother had not preceded me. "Well, what happened?" she said impatiently. "Did you find him? Did the two of you settle your differences, or what?"

What, I thought. Yes, that was perfect. *What* exactly.

But if I told her I hadn't been able to find him, I was afraid she might lose her head, call the sheriff in Juniper City and ask for his help. I could picture low-flying helicopters swooping across the Valley, their powerful searchlights crisscrossing the darkness, amplified voices booming out of the night. So I lied to her, knowing it was so much simpler to say that Jason wasn't very hungry, and he was watching the owls teach their young to fly, and he was studying the constellations, and whatever other likely projects I could think of.

I don't know if my explanation satisifed her, but she went into the kitchen and told Anna he wouldn't be joining us for dinner, and she should keep a plate warm until he returned.

I was about to turn away and go upstairs, when I heard something that made me freeze in my tracks. I edged closer to the kitchen door and listened intently.

"I checked the study very carefully," Aunt Gwen was saying in a whisper. "The Bible was the only thing that was disturbed."

"What do you suppose they were looking for?" Mrs. Darby replied.

"Your guess is as good as mine," said my aunt.

"That child's far too clever for her own good. Go out and see if she's eavesdropping. We've taken enough chances as it is."

There was no place to hide, no time to run. I pressed my back to the wall, holding my breath as the door connecting the kitchen and dining room swung back. If my aunt bothered to check behind the door I was done for, but luckily for me it never occurred to her that I might be standing there. A moment later the door swung shut again.

"She's probably gone upstairs to her room," I heard her say to Mrs. Darby. "Surely you don't think she suspects, do you?"

"That was Harry's job to find out, and now that he's gone we've lost a valuable set of ears. Damn that boy for being so irresponsible. He doesn't take after my side of the family, I can assure you. But I hid it good though, never you mind."

"You mean you didn't destroy it?" Aunt Gwen said with alarm.

Anna didn't answer right away. She moved off, and I could hear her at the stove. The lid of a pot went clang, and then the over door opened and closed, the aroma of roast chicken drifting back into the dining room to remind me that it had been hours since I'd had anything to eat.

"But why didn't you get rid of it when you had the chance?" asked my aunt.

"Because that decision wasn't mine to make," Mrs. Darby declared with a note of defiance. "Besides, Mr. Bennett didn't tell me to throw it away, so I just hid it in my room. And you know as well as I do that even if you destroy words, you still can't destroy the feelings that brought them into being."

I didn't have to hear anymore, because by then I was certain I knew what they were referring to. So it was Mrs. Darby who had snuck into my room to steal the diary, part of the conspiracy Jason had suspected from the very beginning. Everything he had said was coming to pass, and with that realization I didn't hesitate to hurry upstairs, not stopping until I reached the third floor.

"Will?" I called out softly. "Will, are you up here?"

There was no answer, and I knew I had to work quickly lest Anna or Aunt Gwen discover what I was up to. So I snuck into the Darbys' sitting room, calling out Will's name just in case he was in the other room taking a nap. But when I opened their bedroom door, I found it empty.

Just then the telephone rang, startling me so that I nearly gave myself away. Someone picked it up on the third ring, but I didn't have time to listen in on the conversation. Instead, I started going through every dresser drawer, searching for the slim morocco-bound diary Mrs. Darby had stolen from my room.

So they didn't want me to know the truth, did they? They all thought they were so clever, but now I'd show them that I was fully their match, just as capable of ferreting out the truth as they were at concealing it. What amazed me more than anything else was Mrs. Darby's participation in everything that had happened since the night they had taken Mother away. I'd never dreamed she could be so deceitful, nor did I ever suspect how intimately involved she was in the private affairs of our family. Obviously, Father placed a great trust in her, and so she had taken it upon herself to spy on me. The unfortunate result was that she had discovered me reading the diary, and the moment I went into the bathroom she slipped into my room and snatched it off my bed.

But then why had she left such an ominous and threatening note? Surely she didn't bear me ill will. Surely she didn't mean to cause me any harm. But what if she did? What if she really knew what had happened to Harry? And what if the conspiracy Jason had spoken of was far more complicated than either of us had imagined?

The dresser drawers yielded up nothing but piles of neatly laundered clothes. I looked frantically around, trying to second-guess her. What would be a likely hiding place? I kept asking myself. I had hidden the diary in the back of my bookcase. But the Darbys only had a small collection of paperbacks, and though I pulled every one out, there was nothing behind them, not even dust.

I went back to the door, opened it a crack, and listened carefully. There were no footsteps on the stairs, though I was afraid any moment I'd hear her calling me to dinner.

There were two closets in the bedroom, and in one of them I found a pile of shoeboxes stacked on the floor. In the first box lay a pair of fancy pumps wrapped in tissue paper. In the second a pair of dress shoes Will had worn at the funeral. But in the third I didn't find shoes at all. Instead, there were papers, old bank books, canceled checks, and under all of these the record of suffering my mother had set down in her own hand, more than twenty-five years before.

I put everything back the way I'd found it, then left the room as silently as I had entered. With the diary stuffed inside the waistband of my jeans, I raced downstairs to my room. No sooner did I close the door behind me when I hurriedly turned the pages, looking for the last entry I had read.

*"January 11.*

*". . . called me. Becky-wecky your Daddy-waddy is here honey. He touched me in that place. I was scared terrible. Miss Blair said it was wrong and evil. Also a big sin. He didn't care he did it. First with his finger like tickling. Then the other part that he has. It hurt terrible but he put his hand over my mouth and said don't you cry or I'll make it hurt worse. He was heavy too on top of me. It hurt and hurt and wouldn't stop.*

*"January 13.*

*"After school was over today me and Miss Blair my teacher had a long talk together. I was shamed to tell her what happened but it hurt so bad between my legs I did anyway. She looked so serious at me I was scared she would be mad but she wasn't. She said you are a brave little girl Rebecca and I am going to take you home and speak to him myself. I said please don't Miss Blair. He will hit me worse than ever & my sister too if he knows I told you the secret. She said she had to or else I would be something for life. Scared or scarred I can't remember.*

*"We went home together and talked a lot and it was nice. I like Miss Blair a lot and always will. She is good to me and listens hard to what I say. Mama was there and Gwennie too. They made me go out to play when they talked. I waited on the stoop with Gwennie. After a while Miss Blair came out and said come in Rebecca your mother wants to speak to you. I was scared Mama would hit me but she didn't. She*

*said I was telling lies. Papa was good to me and bad
girls who told lies went to jail. Miss Blair said a
child doesn't make up stories like that Mrs. Howe.
Mama threw Miss Blair's coat at her and said get
the HELL out of here you trublemaker you. Miss
Blair said don't worry Rebecca I am going to speak
to the socill worker you just trust me.*

*"January 14.*

*"I heard Mama and Papa talking in the kitchen.
Mama told about Miss Blair and said to Papa you
are a pig and always will be. You'll never change. I
should throw you out on your ear you G\*dam bastard you. Papa slapped her she was crying real
hard. But Diary I didn't care I was glad. She deserved it a lot for being mean to me and Gwennie.*

*"January 25.*

*"Dear Diary, Lots of People came all week. Mama
made the house shine and I had to help her. It was
real hard work. She called me names and said I
didn't deserve to be born I was a rotten little girl
from the word Go. What did that mean?? I don't
know but she slapped me too and said if I told
anyone Papa and Miss Blair expecilly she'd make
me pay for it. How?? I still have the silver doller
Mrs. Stern gave me. Will that pay for it? I don't
know. Anyway Diary, people came from the City,
men and ladys both. I think they were socill work-
ers. I don't know what that means but they talked to
all of us, Gwennie and Papa too.*

*"They said we will give you another chance Mr.
Howe. You are making a great effort we are awear
of that and appreciate it too. They left and I thought
it was over and he would be good and nice to me.
But he wasn't. He didn't change. He was the same.
MEAN MEAN MEAN!!! He came into my room at
night and made me touch him in that place again.*

"*February 3.*

"*Dear Diary, I didn't write till I knew for sure if Papa would be mean like he promised not to. For one week all 7 days I counted he didn't hit me. He just made me touch him there 2 times. It was once on a Monday and once Friday. But yesterday Mama went shopping for food it was Saturday. As soon as she left he took me down to the celler. He tied a rag on my mouth so no one would hear not even my sister who was playing in the living room with her dollie.*

"*When he did that thing to me I prayed & prayed to GOD but he didn't answer. No one can help me. Not Miss Blair my teacher or the socill worker from the City or Mrs. Stern the nice lady who gave me the doller. I called her one day she wasn't home. I bet she moved away. He didn't hit me this time. He just did that thing putting it into me.*

"*I got sick and prayed to GOD and the BABY JESUS they would take me up to Heaven so I would die and be an angel with wings. But when I prayed they didn't answer and he kept doing it worse than ever. When Mama came home I told on him. But she didn't believe me and hit me hard on the face and hands and said I was a evil child a big liar even HELL wouldn't be good enough for me.*

"*February 5.*

"*I know what I will do to them, Diary. I had a dream and GOD said Rebecca it is all right go and do it they do not love you they never have. The can said lighter fluid. It was blue and yellow. I waited till they were sleeping in their room. Then I got out of bed & used the lighter fluid squeezing it under their door. Matches too I had from the kitchen where I found them in a draw. I squirted it in the living room and everywhere else until there wasn't any left and the can was empty.*

*"Then I lit it with the match, Diary. I had to. GOD told me it was all right Rebecca they are sick and evil. They deserve to be punished and burned for their sins. I woke up Gwennie and took her with me. She is the only one I love. Also Miss Blair & Mrs. Stern. Gwennie cried and cried when she saw the fire. It was everywhere. We ran outside and down the St. it was cold. No one saw us I don't think. But I will lie if they ask. I will say the door was locked and Mama & Papa wouldn't answer when I called to them to wake up.*

*"April 17.*

*"Dear Diary, I am happy now and Gwennie is happy, too. We are together and they are dead in HELL where they deserve to go. We are living with Mrs. Stern the nice lady from before. She is so good to us, Diary. We are orphans. She calls us that and says we are safe now because she loves us. But I killed them dead and burned them all up. Now I get scared specially at night. I have bad dreams . . ."*

"So you couldn't leave well enough alone, could you, Quinton? You had to find out, didn't you? You had to sneak into my room like a common thief."

With a gasp of surprise I jerked my eyes toward the door. Mrs. Darby was standing there, and the moment I saw her I jumped up from where I was sitting on the bed and backed away, suddenly so frightened I couldn't even think straight.

I had the diary clutched to my breast. There were several pages left unread, but I already knew what Mrs. Darby had tried to prevent me from discovering. Mother had murdered her parents, had set fire to their house, had fled in the middle of the night, clutching her little sister's hand as flames shot up all around them. But they weren't parents. They weren't even human. They were monsters who deserved to die as painfully as they had. If Mother hadn't stopped them when she did they might even have tried to kill her and Gwen. No, I could never blame her for what she had done, nor could I feel anything but the utmost contempt for my Howe grandparents, grandparents I was grateful for never having known.

"Give it to me, Quinton," Mrs. Darby said angrily, and her breath rattled in her chest like beans in a sack. "Give it to me this instant!"

"I won't and you can't make me," I said, trying to sound much braver than I actually felt. "It's not yours, Mrs. Darby. You had no right to steal it from me. You're the big thief around here, not me."

"So you've read it all, haven't you? You know what happened then?"

"Yes, I know how she suffered, how he wouldn't leave her alone. They were sick, the two of them. The mother ignoring her, pretending everything was normal. The father doing . . . you know what he did, those awful things to her, torturing her that way. They were evil, the both of them, and I'm glad she did it. And you're evil too, leaving horrible notes for me, trying to frighten me half to death."

Mrs. Darby looked at me in confusion, unable to understand what I was talking about. "What notes?" she asked. "I never wrote out a note, Quinn. What in the world are you talking about?"

"I'm talking about this," I said, and I rummaged through the top drawer of my desk until I found it. "You came into my room, you stole the diary, and then left this behind to scare me. Well, you can have it back for all I care because you can't frighten me anymore, Mrs. Darby. The truth isn't scary. It's the lies that are, and there won't be anymore lies in this house!"

Mrs. Darby stepped closer, snatching the note out of my

hand. She read the crumpled slip of paper and suddenly all the blood began to drain out of her face. With a gasp of horror she looked up at me.

"My God," she kept whispering. "Why didn't you tell your father about this? Or tell me, or your aunt? Why did you keep it a secret, Quinn?"

"Because everything around here's a secret, more secrets than I know how to deal with," I cried. "And what are you getting so upset about, anyway? You were the one who left it for me, weren't you?"

"No, child, I'd never harm you, not in a million years." She reached out, trying to cup my face in her hand. "But there are others who would, others who aren't well, who don't know their own mind."

"Who are you talking about?" I demanded. I wasn't scared of her anymore, and I guess I even believed most of what she had said. But I was still afraid to trust her, knowing that she had been a part of the dreadful conspiracy to do away with my mother.

"Too late," she said softly. Her eyes roamed restlessly about the room, finally turning back to me. "Where's Jason now, do you know?"

"He's . . . he's out somewhere," I stammered, still unwilling to be completely honest with her.

"And did he get a note, too?"

"Yes," I murmured. " 'For the sins of the fathers you, though guiltless, must suffer.' "

Another gasp of either fear or panic flew from her lips. "When?"

"Just . . . just a few days ago, I think."

Mrs. Darby turned abruptly away and hurried from the room. I ran after her, wondering what she was so upset about, and why she was in such a great rush.

"What are you going to do?" I called after her.

"Try to get ahold of your father. I have a number where he can be reached. We can't wait till the end of the week, especially since Will and I have to go down to Los Angeles tomorrow."

"But why? What happened?"

"A telegram arrived just a few minutes ago."

"You mean the phone call?"

She nodded, and even from a distance I could see how the color had yet to return to her cheeks. "It was from Harry. He's in big trouble, needs his father and me to bail him out. Wouldn't say what it was, only where to meet him. We have to leave in the morning."

"Harry?" I whispered, trying desperately not to give myself away.

Mrs. Darby's little gray eyes seemed to pierce me to the quick. "Do you know what it's about, Quinton? Because if you do you'd better tell me. Is that why he ran off like he did?"

"I . . . I don't know, Mrs. Darby. He never said anything about it. I didn't even know he was in trouble, I swear."

I wasn't certain if she believed me. But rather than stand there and question me further she started down the stairs. I went back to my room, positive it was my brother who had sent the telegram. He'd probably hitched a ride into Juniper City, then called Western Union from a pay phone. But I had no idea what was behind it all, and why he had gone to so much trouble just to get the Darbys to leave the Valley.

Something was about to happen, something which he didn't want to involve them in. But what? And who had Anna been referring to when she read the note I had found under my door? Who were the others who weren't well, who didn't know their own mind? Could it be possible that my mother had been lied to as a child, told she was an orphan when in fact she actually wasn't? Were the Howe grandparents really dead, or had they risen like the phoenix from the ashes, hideously scarred from their fiery ordeal, but very much alive?

If only there was a lock on my door. But there wasn't. If they wanted to they could barge right in, and now I was terrified that was just what they would do.

# 18

**N**o more hurt, not ever again.

Warren agreed.

We made a truce. He would stay up there between my ears because he didn't have any other place to go. He was part of me, even if I didn't want him to be. I hadn't made him up like I used to do when I was a little kid, talking to imaginary friends that only I could see. No, I'd given Warren his name but he'd always been there, nameless maybe, but he was still inside my head just waiting to make himself known.

No more hurt.

That was the pact.

I guess he realized that if he hurt me he'd only end up hurting himself. Only this one body, know what I mean? If he ruined that he wouldn't have any place else to go. He wouldn't *be*. And he wanted to be. He wanted to be real bad. Life was everything to him, so he made a pact with me. He wouldn't try to hurt me so long as I didn't try to get rid of him. I didn't know how I could, anyway, but I didn't tell him that. I said yes, sure, whatever you say, Warren. And he said, I mean it, honest, Lefland. This time I'm not lying. It's the truth.

Truth. Isn't that the sickest joke you ever heard?

I ran out of the house because of the truth, ran to the Temple because of the truth. I saw everything ripped and smashed and bloodied and that was truth, too, truth she had her Warren just like me, the demon who lived beneath her golden hair. She had her gremlins, same as her son. And that—THAT!—was the awful truth Dad didn't want anyone to know about.

I got to the Temple and it was terrifying. The painting was slashed, clothes were ripped, Quinnie's dolls torn apart because she couldn't get her hands on the real thing. It wasn't Warren who did it, though I knew he would have liked to take the credit. It was Mom, Mom's gremlin that is, the hideous beast who lived in her brain and wanted to get out in the worst way imaginable.

But they'd already fled, the two of them who lived as one. I left the letter for Quinnie because she deserved to know everything and I couldn't lie anymore, not ever again. Then Warren and I went up into the hills looking for her.

I knew she was up here. I could smell her too, only it wasn't rose perfume. Unwashed. Dirty. Long matted hair. The poor beast in her trying to break out, getting stronger by the day while she and the baby inside her got weaker and weaker.

She wouldn't answer. I called and called, screaming through the hills, Warren and me both because he missed her just as much as I did. He was her son too, don't you see? Flesh of her flesh. Out of the bloody womb we marched arm in arm, destined to spend the rest of our lives together.

But we knew she was somewhere nearby. That was the

important thing. And if we found her and brought her back to the house, with Anna and Will around it would only make everything twice as complicated. It would be the three of us against the three of them. If Quinnie found out what was going on, she might not go along with the plans I'd already made. I couldn't take a chance, so Warren and I thought and thought and were a real team for a change.

That's when we came up with our scheme to take care of the Darbys. A truckdriver gave us a ride into Juniper City. Luckily, we had money in our pocket, though I guess the owner of the general store would have loaned me a few dollars if I needed them. Anyway, we called Western Union, and pretended to send a telegram from Harry. COME QUICK! IN BIG TROUBLE! NEED YOU AND DAD! A little less dramatic than that, but it got the point across. I guess they phoned the Darbys right after, because they don't hand-deliver anymore like they used to.

Then we hitched back the way we had come, knowing it was time to start looking for Mom again. Warren reminded me about the old abandoned shacks at the west end of the Valley, about as far from the house as you could get without actually going up into the hills. They were like houses made of playing cards, just a collection of weathered boards and not much else. Quinnie and I sometimes went there to play, and the year before it was where we'd seen that bobcat we told Gwen about.

But though we checked carefully, making our way from one ramshackle hovel to the next, there was no sign of Mom anywhere. She hadn't been here, but maybe somehow she was watching me, the poor thing scared out of her mind.

I called to her again. "Mom, it's me, Jason. I didn't tell anyone. The Darbys are leaving tomorrow morning. The only ones left will be Quinnie and Aunt Gwen. Dad won't be back till the end of the week. We'll take care of you, Mom. We'll escape, the three of us.''

The four of us, said Warren.

"So don't be scared of me. We only want to help you."

Silence, awful dead and dismal silence. The wind picked up, scattering balls of sagebrush across the Valley floor. Stars came out one by one. Owls called. I saw a bat gobbling up insects on the wing. I saw two falling stars and a ring around the moon. And still she didn't come. I didn't want to try to make a fire in case they were out looking for me. So I scrunched myself up into a corner, knees to chest, arms around knees, and tried to stay warm.

And Warren gave me a dream.

Quinnie's bone-handled dirk flashed in the darkness. Blood thick as pudding poured slowly through the nooks and crannies of my mind.

"Come to me, my precious," I could hear her whisper. "Mother's so lonely tonight. She needs you, Jason."

"More than Dad?"

Mom laughed and laughed. "He can't compare, my darling, he never will."

The tingles all over. The feeling-good dreams even when I was wide-awake. The shudders and the falling over the edge.

"Come to me, my darling, my precious, Jason the smartest, cleverest boy in all the world."

"I'm here, Mom!" I called to her, shouting through the blood-red darkness.

But instead of her voice, I heard Dad's. "It's starting again, Rebecca. You can't help yourself anymore. You're sick, and it's getting out of control. You want the boy for yourself, don't you? You want to destroy his life, just the way you're destroying your own life. Do you remember what your friend said the last time?"

"Friend!" Mom shrieked, but she was faceless, just a

voice that tore through my dream like a wind out of hell. "Dr. Warren isn't my friend, Bennett, he's my shrink. You men are all alike, anyway. Expect me to sit at home and be a perfect wife and mother while you fuck your brains out with every cunt that crosses your path."

"I don't like it when you talk that way."

"Tough shit, Benny."

"Have you done it yet, Rebecca?"

"That's for me to know and you to guess."

"Don't toy with me, Rebecca. We're talking about someone's life now, someone we brought into being. Have you done it or haven't you?"

"And what if I have?" Mom said. "After all, he's more of a man than you'll ever be. You've been a big fat zero in my book for so long now your feelings don't mean shit to me."

"Feelings?" Dad replied. "You don't have any, Rebecca. You're like a black widow spider, and now that you've caught him in your web you won't let go. And you call yourself cured? You're sicker than you ever were. Only now you've infected him with your madness. Is this what you call being a mother? Is this your idea of love, devotion? It's a way of killing him, Rebecca. It's like a worm burrowing through his soul, and you're the one who planted it there."

"The gospel according to St. Benny," said Mom, and she hurled laughter in his face and it was like thunder and lightning and the rage of demons. "Only it's a bit too late, darling. The spider has spoken to the fly and he's come into my parlor and he can't live without me now. And if you want to know the truth, Bennett, I can't live without him either."

"You're going to have to learn to be without all of us, Rebecca, because I can't take it anymore. They're too important to me. They're all I have now, and if it means protecting them from you, then that's just what I'll do.''

"Liar!" I screamed, and I was running and running, racing down hallways, up stairs and down stairs, racing and searching and never finding her. "You took her away! You murdered her and the baby!"

"He didn't, Jason. We escaped."

"Mom, is that you, is that really you?"

"Yes, my darling. And I won't leave you, I promise."

"And there'll be no more hurt?"

"No more hurt and no more pain. Not ever again."

I opened my eyes and Warren opened his eyes, too. It was dawn, and the air was as sharp and tingly as a feeling-good dream, as the blade of the bone-handled dirk I had given Quinnie for her birthday. The light was thin and hesitant, unsure of itself. I looked up, watching the sky drift down through the open roof of the shack, streaked with the colors of honey and rose petals. A beautiful morning. A perfect morning.

And I could smell her. And it was the smell of fear, a trapped, haunted smell that made me edge back until I was pressed up against the wall and I could go no further.

She watched me, her ice-blue eyes glinting with terror and suspicion. Her beautiful golden hair was a mass of tangled, filth-encrusted curls. Her skirt and blouse were little more than rags. She was barefoot, her feet covered with scratches and sores. She picked something off the back of her neck, a tick I guess, examined it between her cracked and blackened fingernails, and rubbed it against the floor.

"I watched you," she said. "All night."

I wanted to run to her and bury myself in her arms, the warm safe hollow between her breasts where I had laid my head so many times before. But I couldn't move, and

Warren couldn't move, either. We just sat there, joints all stiff and achy and the breath frozen in our lungs.

"I watched you," she said again. "I saw you in the playhouse. Count the strokes like a good boy, and you did. I saw you in the attic, called to you but you didn't hear. Why did you steal my diary? I was saving it for the baby. Why did you steal my red diary? I didn't want Dr. Warren to see it. I didn't want him to think . . . you stole it away from me, Jason. I went looking for it and it was gone. You stole it and you wouldn't give it back to me. I left you a note. I warned you, but you still wouldn't give it back. But it's not yours. It's mine. Mine!"

Her scream roused me from the nightmare that was no longer a dream. Her eyes darted every which way at once, as if she were trying to make sure she knew the way to escape. But I couldn't let her go, and Warren agreed. She had come to us because she needed our help, and now we weren't going to let her down.

So I got slowly to my feet, trying not to frighten her with any sudden moves. "I love you, Mom, I always have. Quinnie loves you, too. God, we've missed you so. We knew you were alive, we knew it all the time. Even when Dad made us go to the funeral, we knew he was lying to us and it just couldn't be true."

"What funeral? The baby didn't die. The baby's right here, safe inside me." She looked down and patted her stomach, and it was then that I noticed how much larger her belly was. When I had seen her last she was hardly showing. But now I could tell the pregnancy was very far advanced.

"When is the baby due?" I asked.

"Soon. Very, very soon."

"But I thought you'd just found out yourself."

Mom giggled softly to herself. Although I wasn't sure why, the sound gave me the chills. "Lied to him. Lied to my Benny boy. Wore loose dresses. Didn't let him touch me. Kept it a secret, Jason. A big, fat secret.''

"But why?"

"I'm hungry," she said. "We'll go to the house and get food.''

"No, you can't, not yet," I said in alarm. Hurriedly I began to tell her my plan, how the Darbys would be leaving in just a couple of hours, and that it was very important to stay out of sight until then. "But as soon as they're gone, there won't be anything to worry about. We'll be able to take care of Aunt Gwen with no trouble at all.''

"Is that cunt still around? That bitch wants to marry him," Mom said. Her voice got all harsh and gravelly, so I knew it was the gremlin who was doing the talking, and not her. "He told me so. He said Becky-wecky Daddy-waddy's gonna get married, gonna get married, gonna marry your baby sister," she sang.

It was the same lisping baby talk she had used the day I'd heard her arguing with Dad, only now I don't think she could have stopped it even if she wanted to. She rocked back and forth, moving her arms as if she were cradling an infant and singing it to sleep.

I tried to help her to her feet but she shrank back in terror. From the look in her eyes I could tell she was having difficulty remembering who I was.

"I'm Jason," I said. "Jason, your son. I only want to help you, Mom.''

"Jason was the smartest, cleverest boy," she murmured. "Jason loved me best of all. I said, 'Jason, it's a curse, it's in the blood, I can't help myself.' And Jason said, 'It doesn't matter, Mom, because we love each other, and love is everything.' But Benny found out, didn't he? He caught us together. He said, 'Becky-wecky you're a very bad girl and Daddy-waddy has to take you to see Dr.

Warren.' I said, 'I'll kill myself first. I will, I really will. You won't put me there like you did the last time.' Remember, Jason?''

"No," I whispered.

"But darling, you were there, right there when it happened. You know what he tried to do. I couldn't let him get away with it, don't you see? I had to protect the baby."

She almost sounded normal then, so convincing, her voice so sweet and melodic. I believed her, and yet I was scared too, scared she'd try to hurt herself again. I glanced down at her hands, her fingers nervously twisting the buttons on her grimy blouse. A filthy bandage was wrapped around her wrist.

I tried to remember. I closed my eyes and tried to squeeze the memory out like toothpaste from a tube. I worked at it so hard that tears began to trickle down my cheeks. But nothing happened. It was all a blank.

"I'm hungry. The baby needs good food. I want it to grow up to be strong. Then I'll teach it to hate him, my sister too. I'll have the baby follow them wherever they go. I'll give it a big can of blue and yellow and then they'll be sorry. They'll be very, very sorry Becky-wecky wouldn't forget how much they hurt her.''

I didn't know what she was talking about, but I knew that if I asked she probably wouldn't be able to tell me. To see her this way, to know her mind was somewhere else, the gremlin having succeeded in taking her place, made me want to cry like I hadn't cried since the night . . . the night . . .

Hard as I tried, I just couldn't remember. But now I had Mom to take care of, and that was the most important thing. As soon as the Darbys left, I'd take her home, see that she had a good meal, a bath, then a bed with clean sheets to lie upon. And as for her sister Gwen, the one who wanted to take her place, she'd get what she deserved too, but all in good time.

I told Mom that, pleading with her to listen to me, I knew what was best. I wasn't sure if she understood, but when I reached down to try to help her to her feet, she didn't pull away like she had the last time. The smell she gave off was nearly as frightening as her appearance, but I knew it wasn't her fault. That she had managed to avoid being caught for as long as she had was a credit to her ingenuity and resourcefulness. Even though her gremlin had gotten the upper hand, it still knew how to protect itself, protecting her at the same time.

"Where are we going, Jason? I'm hungry."

"I know, and I'm going to get you food. But I can't bring you home till the Darbys leave."

"Where's Quinton? Where's your sister?" she suddenly asked. She looked all around as if she expected Quinn to burst out of hiding and throw her arms around her. "Doesn't she love me anymore?"

"Of course she does, Mom. She loves you just as much as I do."

And maybe even more, Warren snickered.

I told him to shut up, if he didn't have anything nice to say he shouldn't say anything at all.

"Then where is she? Why isn't she here? Doesn't she love the baby?"

"She's back at the house. If both of us were gone they'd get suspicious. I'll hide you nearby and bring you food. Then when Will and Anna leave we won't have to keep you a secret anymore."

"Secret?" she said, her eyes sharp and accusing. "Did you tell her, Jason? You promised you never would. It was our secret, and you know baby Jesus would punish you if you told."

I could lie, but I was afraid to. She'd have to know

sooner or later and maybe it was better this way, just getting it over with.

"I had to. But she's not angry, Mom. She understands. She's a woman now, she's not a child."

"She doesn't hate me?"

"No, of course not. She loves you with all her heart."

"My sister hates me though. But the bitch is going to be surprised, isn't she? Gwennie's going to be surprised, Gwennie's going to be surprised," she started to sing. "That's because she hates me, Jason. Even when we were little and I saved her life—I did, lots and lots of times— she still hated me for what I did to them."

Who was she talking about? I asked, but she wouldn't tell me.

"But you know what? I hated her, too. So now we're even." She put her hand over her mouth and began to giggle uncontrollably.

It was mad laughter, but it was laughter nevertheless. Warren and I were just glad to be with her, grateful she was still alive. We'd find out why Dad had lied to us, why he wanted us to believe she was dead. And then we'd punish him. We'd punish him good.

So I took Mom's hand in mine, and she held on so tight it began to hurt. She needed me, that was the important thing. She needed Warren too because he was being a good boy, behaving himself and not doing nasty things like trying to stick his fingers in my eyes or pinching me or telling me I deserved to burn in hell for being bad. But how could I be bad when I was saving Mom?

"I'm still your good boy," I told her. "And we're going to get back at them for being mean to you."

"He hates you, Jason. He always has."

"Yes, I know."

"Where did he go?"

"He went looking for you. How far away is Dr. Warren's hospital, do you remember?"

"Up north . . . no, south, near San Diego."

"How did you manage to escape?" I asked.

"Stole the nurse's keys. Got a ride in a big blue truck."

I asked her how she'd survived all this time, where she had slept and what she had eaten. It was hard to make sense of what she said, but I pieced together a frightening story of day-to-day survival. She stole food from the house, as Quinn and I had suspected. She lived up in the caves where I'd gone looking for her, and even spent several nights hidden in the basement of the house. She had used the Temple too as sanctuary, observing us from afar on many occasions.

But then she grew tired of answering my questions, and began to sing a little song, a lullaby I hadn't heard in so many years I'd forgotten how she used to sing it every night when she put me to bed.

We walked down the dusty trail that led back to the house, me and Mom and Warren, the baby too. Dad had wanted her dead, but now he'd have to answer to all of us, Quinnie included, and God and the baby Jesus who looked down from heaven and knew he was the sickest, evilest one of all for trying to take her away from us.

"I did what you told me to," I said. "I made Quinn a woman, just like you said I should."

But she wasn't listening. When the song ran out she started all over again, humming the tune softly to herself. Suddenly she paused in the middle of the road, scratching her head as if she were trying to remember something.

"It's like a lion at the door," she began. "And when the door begins to crack—"

"It's like a stick across your back," I said with a grin, remembering the nursery rhyme she used to have me recite when I was little.

308

"And when your back begins to smart—"

"It's like a penknife in your heart. And when your heart begins to bleed—"

Mom clapped her hands together and started to laugh. "You're dead, and dead, and—"

"Dead indeed!"

"Then that's what we'll do, Jason," she said, speaking in her own voice now, and not the gremlin's. "Yes, my precious, that's just what we'll do."

I hadn't expected Mrs. Darby to be up so early, but she was. She looked at me and Warren and pretended not to recognize us. "Your aunt was worried sick," she said.

Poor thing, too bad she didn't worry herself to death, snickered Warren.

"Why?" I asked.

"You didn't come in all night. What were you doing out there?"

"I came in. It was late, but I came in. And I left early."

"Don't lie to me, Jason. I see right through your shenanigans. When your father comes home this evening you can answer to him."

"What do you mean, he's coming home?" I said in a panic. "He's not supposed to be back till the end of the week."

"There's been a change of plans," explained Mrs. D. "As soon as everyone's had breakfast, Will and I have to get on our way."

"Where are you going?" I asked, trying as hard as I could to sound surprised.

"To Los Angeles. Harry's gotten himself into a mess of trouble."

"Gee, I'm sorry to hear that. Guess you'll be gone a couple of days then, right?"

"I just don't know," she said, her voice filled with

sudden pain. Then she swept past me, hurrying on into the dining room to set the table.

Mom was waiting for me in the toolshed, and if I didn't work fast I had a feeling she'd just wander off, not even knowing where she was going. I would have hidden her in the old carriage house which was much bigger, but Will kept his pickup there and I knew he'd be needing it. So the moment Mrs. Darby left the kitchen, I grabbed a grocery bag from where she'd laid in a year's supply, then began to toss in whatever food I could find in the fridge.

Suddenly the door swung open and I thought I'd wet my pants.

"Jason!" my sister cried out. "Where have you been all night?"

I put my finger to my lips, then pointed behind her to the door. Quinnie read me loud and clear, and rushed after me as I took the back way out.

"What's in the bag? Where are you going?" she wanted to know.

I had to tell her, though I'd planned it a little differently, more like a surprise like when she had her birthday party.

"I found her, Quinn. Or she found me."

"Mother?" she gasped.

"Yes, but keep your voice down. We can't let anyone know. As soon as the Darbys leave we'll bring her in."

"I figured you were the one who sent the telegram," she replied. "But how is she? When can I see her? Is she all right?"

This was going to be very difficult, but it had to be done. So I told her the truth, not sparing her any of the gory details. But Quinn was very brave, and took the news even better than I expected.

"We'll see that she gets help, that's what we'll do," she said after I told her about Mom's state of mind.

310

"Maybe it was all brought on by what happened, running away and all."

"Maybe," I said. "Though I have a feeling it's been building up for a long time. But Anna said Dad's coming back tonight, so we'll have to work fast."

She looked at me in confusion. "We're going to tell him she's come back, aren't we?"

I didn't want to get into a big discussion right there in the middle of the yard. So I told her I had to bring Mom her food before I did anything else. Then we'd talk about what had to be done once the Darbys were gone. As I turned away and headed back to the toolshed, she called after me.

"Jason, I read the letter." She looked down at her feet as if she were suddenly feeling guilty.

"I figured you had. That's why I left it." I smiled nervously and waited for the punch line, wondering if she hated my guts.

"I think what she did to you was wrong, but I don't think she did it to be mean or destructive or anything like that. But what happened between us was different. And I'm not sorry about it, either. In fact, I'm glad you were the one who showed me about love, and not someone else. And Jason, there's one other thing."

I watched her silently, afraid of what she might say next.

"When this is all over, and we find out why Father did this terrible thing, what he hoped to gain by it, we'll still have each other. That's the way I want it to be, okay?"

She was telling me she loved me. I nodded and couldn't help but smile. "The other stuff," I said, "between Mom and me, that's all over now. She's not well, and even if she gets better, and I pray to God she does, it'll still be over. But I don't want it to be over between us."

"It won't be." She was blushing, and when she spoke

her voice quivered with emotion. "We're Leflands, remember? And Leflands just aren't like other people. Maybe what everyone else thinks of as a curse is actually a blessing. Who's to say?"

There was no time to respond. I had to get back to Mom, and so I blew Quinnie a kiss and rushed off to the shed. The moment I stepped inside Mom grabbed the bag out of my hand and started bolting down the food as if she hadn't had a decent meal in weeks—which I guess she hadn't.

"Not so fast, Mom. You'll get sick that way. No one's going to take it away from you."

But I could have been speaking to myself, because she didn't pay any attention. Food dribbled down her chin. She was ravenous, a wild animal staring at me with her haunted icy eyes.

"Hungry, so hungry," she muttered through a mouthful of food.

I thought of Mrs. D. complaining food was missing, how Mom had snuck back into the house time and time again, always managing to slip away without being seen.

"You won't be hungry anymore," I promised. "And you won't have to hide from anyone, either."

Then I pocketed a pair of wire clippers and told her she had to stay here just a little while longer. I'd come and get her as soon as the coast was clear.

"Do you understand what I'm saying, Mom? You can't go wandering off again."

She looked up at me, wiping her mouth with the back of her hand. "Bastards tried to get rid of the baby. Wanted to rip it out of me. Lock me up and throw away the key, that was their plan. Know what electroshock is? Fries your brain, sweetie-pie. But Becky was too damn clever for them. You're clever too, you sweet boy. You love your

312

mother, don't you? You won't let that lying bastard put me away again, will you?''

''No, of course not. I'll take care of him, I promise.''

''And little Miss Perfect too, the jealous bitch like to tear her eyes out.'' She was raising her voice and I was scared they'd hear.

''Shh,'' I said, ''it's okay, it's all right, Mom. You just stay here and finish eating and I'll take care of the rest. As soon as they leave I'll come and get you.''

I made her repeat that to me, word for word, till I was certain she understood what I was talking about. Then I slipped out of the toolshed and made my way back to the house. But before I went in for breakfsat I made sure to cut the telephone wires.

Oh yes, today was definitely going to be my day.

# 19

The secrets that had surrounded me for so long now were all but solved. The web of deceit and cruelty Father had spun was about to ensnare him, and I could not help but feel that he deserved whatever my brother was planning. How could he have done this to us? How could he have done this to Mother?

I thought of all the pieces of the puzzle I had tried to assemble, the conversations I'd overheard, the clues I'd discovered. At long last they were beginning to make sense.

*The boy suspects* . . . you killed your parents.

*Gwen remembers* . . . what happened that awful night you set the house on fire.

*Will they ever forgive me, Gwen?*

No, we'd never do that, for he had taken her away from us, told us she was dead when in actuality he'd shut her up somewhere, handing her over to doctors who cared nothing for her feelings and even less if she lived or died.

*Why didn't I see it earlier?* Father had said. *Why was I so blind to the truth?*

No doubt he had discovered the incestuous relationship between Mother and Jason, how in her loneliness and despair she had taken my brother into her bed.

*We have problems here, big problems,* I could hear Anna saying.

And now I knew what those problems were, and knew that she had been a part of Father's elaborate scheme, a plan that had gone completely awry.

But all I could think of now was seeing her. Although I had a million questions to ask my brother, I knew they could wait, for the most important thing was to help Mother, and see that she got the care and love she desperately needed. Barely able to contain my impatience, I somehow managed to sit through breakfast, even going so far as to be polite to my aunt.

"How are the owls getting on?" she asked my brother.

"The what?" he said.

"The owls. Quinn said you were watching them teach their young to fly last night."

He glanced at me and I nodded as imperceptibly as I could. "Oh, *those* owls," he said. "They were great, just terrific. Can I get you some more coffee, Aunt Gwen?"

"Just half a cup, thank you, Jason."

Anna came into the dining room, more dressed up than I'd seen her in years. She wore a severe looking black suit, and a single strand of turquoise beads I recalled Mother having given her for Christmas the year before.

"Well," she said, "looks like we're off. I've left a casserole in the icebox. It just needs reheating. There's a roast beef in the freezer and several chickens. I don't think you'll starve."

"Oh, I'm sure we'll be quite all right," Gwen told her.

"Come on now, Mother, we'll be late," Will said. He

stubbed out his cigarette, gave a cough in lieu of a good-bye, and carried their bags out to the truck.

Just a few more minutes, I kept telling myself, and then we'll be together again.

Aunt Gwen wiped her mouth daintily with a napkin. "I spoke to your father, Jason," she announced. "He'll be coming home this evening."

"Yes, Quinn told me. We'll be very glad to see him, won't we, Quinn?"

"I can't wait," I said, trying not to choke on my words.

"Have you given any more thought to that trip he wants to take you on?"

But Jason didn't bother to answer. Abruptly, he got up, and without even bothering to excuse himself—Aunt Gwen was a stickler when it came to good manners—he rushed out of the dining room. She followed him with her eyes, then looked at me questioningly.

"Wasn't he in a big hurry," she remarked.

"He has a surprise for you, that's why."

"Oh, really? How lovely."

I didn't think "lovely" was the word for it, but I didn't tell her that. Instead, I pushed my chair back and came to my feet.

"You just sit tight, Aunt Gwen. We'll be right back."

I wanted to see Mother first, of course, wanted to be alone with her even if only for a few minutes. By the time I got outside Will and Anna had left, though I could still hear the pickup off in the distance.

"We're here, Quinn. Over here," Jason called.

It was then that I saw her, and it was then that I began to cry. I could barely see through my tears, but I just started to run, crying out her name as she stood there next to my brother. As different as she was, not just her terrible appearance but the frightened, sick look in her eyes, it didn't matter, so long as we were together again.

"The baby's gotten so big," I said, and I tried to laugh. Only I couldn't, and the tears kept streaming down my cheeks.

"Quinton?" she said. "Is that my little girl? You're not so little anymore, are you, darling? Come, give Mother a kiss."

I didn't care how she smelled, didn't care about anything but that she was alive, standing there with her arms outstretched to greet me. I just held onto her and wept and wouldn't let go, knowing the nightmares were over, and at last we were a family again. When I finally stepped back, she smiled like Mother had smiled of old. For that moment at least, that split second of recognition, I knew that she loved me, and always would.

But by then her attention had strayed. She was looking beyond me, and even as I watched her a dreadful mask slipped over her face, obscuring her features and transforming her into someone I barely knew.

Her lips curled back, exposing a chipped tooth and raw, swollen gums. "You bitch!" she shrieked, and it was more of an animal's snarl than human speech.

I looked over my shoulder. Aunt Gwen was standing behind me, her face chalk-white, her mouth hanging open, loose and slack with utter astonishment. She just stared and stared, unable to stop trembling. A single tear began to make its way slowly down her cheek, yet there was nothing even faintly remorseful in her expression. Rather, she seemed to be trying to overcome her panic, for when she finally ran towards us, it was with a joyous grin that bore no relation to the real thing.

"Fucking cunt, lying bitch," Mother hissed. She raised her hands, the fingers curled menacingly as if they were equipped with claws. "Don't you touch me. Don't you come near me. They know what you did. My babies know, my precious babies who never gave up looking for me.''

"It wasn't like that, Rebecca, it wasn't like that at all,'' whimpered Gwen. "We'll clean you up, sweetheart. We'll take care of you again.''

"No, little sister, little Gwennie the goody-goody. This time we're going to take care of you.'' Mother lunged forward, trying to grab hold of Gwen's hair. But suddenly she stiffened, and looked at each of us in confusion. A gasp of surprise spread across her lips.

Liquid began to trickle down the inside of her legs. I thought she was wetting herself because she was so enraged, and I turned in horror to Jason, not knowing what to do.

"My God, she's losing her water!'' Gwen cried out.

What did that mean? I didn't understand. I thought Mother was urinating but no, Aunt Gwen said it meant the baby was coming, and we had to call a doctor because Mother was going into labor.

"I don't want to lose this baby, I don't want to lose it,'' Mother kept saying. She could barely stay on her feet, and Jason helped support her as he led her into the house.

"I don't even know who to call,'' Aunt Gwen said in a panic.

I gave her the name of the family doctor we'd occasionally used. He lived in Juniper City and it wouldn't take him very long to get here. But when she picked up the phone she couldn't get a dial tone.

"Operator, operator!'' she shouted into the receiver. "Operator, can't you hear me?''

"What's wrong?''

"The phone's out. And we don't have a car.''

"I can always hitch a ride into town,'' I said.

Jason was about to help Mother up the stairs, but now he stopped short, his face filled with the same kind of mindless rage Mother had shown just a few moments earlier. "No!" he shouted. "You're not going anywhere, Quinn. We'll do this ourselves."

"But you have no idea what it entails," protested Aunt Gwen.

"Then you'll just have to help us, won't you?" he said grimly. "After all, you're a woman, and women are supposed to know all about these things."

Aunt Gwen was so frightened and beside herself at this point that she didn't know what to say. She asked Mother if she was early, because if the baby was premature we'd never be able to keep it alive without proper medical care.

"Eight months," whispered Mother. She started to double up in pain, and Gwen said it must be a contraction and we'd best get her into bed while there was still time.

So the four of us slowly made our way up to the second floor, then down the hall to Mother's room. She expressed no surprise when she saw how empty it was, stripped bare of all her personal belongings. It was then that I began to suspect that she was responsible for the destruction at the Temple. But why did she hate herself so? Was it because of what had happened between her and Jason, or was it something even more disturbing than that?

I hurriedly ran off to get linen to make up the bed. A short while later Mother lay upon the clean sheets, taking deep breaths and trying to overcome the pain as the contractions began to occur at shorter and shorter intervals.

Aunt Gwen took charge of the situation, more level-headed than I would have expected. I rushed downstairs to bring her towels and a bowl of warm soapy water. Although she started to tell Jason to leave the room, she wanted to get Mother undressed and washed, he refused. I was sure he was about to tell her that he had seen Mother without her clothes on many times before, but he never did. Instead, he got right to work, bathing her as best he could as she lay there on the bed, whimpering in pain.

I guess for a moment I was embarrassed, but then the fact that Mother was naked no longer seemed of any importance. I had never seen a pregnant woman before, and it amazed me how large her abdomen was, a complex network of blue veins showing like a map of rivers across her stomach. I held her hand tightly in mine, gently washing her face with a damp cloth.

"Let's just pray it's not a monster," I heard Aunt Gwen mutter under her breath.

How could she be so cruel and unfeeling? I wanted to grab her in my arms and shake all the meanness out of her, for if anyone had contributed to Mother's fragile state of mind it was her sister.

"How can you even say such a thing, knowing what you've put her through?" I demanded.

"Me?" replied Aunt Gwen, sounding affronted by my accusations. "I didn't put your mother through anything, Quinn. She brought it all on herself."

"Liar!" I shouted. "You and Father planned this from the very beginning. And when it was over you thought you'd marry him, didn't you?"

"And why shouldn't I?" she spat out. "Just look at her; it's enough to turn anyone's stomach. She's sick and she's evil and the things she's done even God wouldn't forgive."

I raised my hand to slap her for daring to speak such filth in Mother's presence. But Jason got between us, and with both hands he shoved Aunt Gwen aside.

"You want to know who the monster is?" he said. "It's Bennett Lefland, that's who. Only a monster could treat someone this way. She's carrying his child and all he could think of was getting rid of the two of them."

"Is that what you really believe?"

"It's not just what I believe, Aunt Gwen, it's what I know."

"But you don't. You don't know the half of it, Jason. He tried everything he could to keep it from you because he loved you so. But now it doesn't matter, does it?"

"What are you talking about?" I said.

"I'm talking about your mother, Quinn. I'm trying to tell you why your father wanted the child aborted."

"He didn't love her anymore, that's why!" Jason shouted.

"No, that's not it at all. I don't think there was another man in all the world who could have loved my sister as much as your father did. She was everything to him, but that didn't matter to her, that didn't matter in the least. The sickness just grew and grew like a cancer until it infected everyone. Whose child do you think she's carrying? Do you honestly believe your father would try to murder his own flesh and blood? My God, how little you know him. How little you understand."

"Don't listen to her, Quinn. She's making up lies again, that's what she's doing," Jason cried. "Isn't that so, Mom? Isn't she telling lies again to get us into trouble?"

"No, I'm telling the truth," Gwen murmured, and where I had seen vindictiveness and hostility a few moments before, I now saw sadness, deep and heartrending.

"He tried to kill her! He tried to kill his own baby!" my brother shrieked.

"No, he tried to kill your baby, Jason. You're the father of this child."

I was standing stock-still, and yet it felt as if a wind were howling all around me and I was being shaken and torn up by my roots. *His* child? *Jason's* child? Was that the Lefland curse? Was that the reason for the skeleton strapped to a chair, and Mother dragged screaming down the stairs? But it was still a life, wasn't it? Love had brought it into being, however twisted that love might have been. Two people whom I cared about more than

322

anyone else in the world had come together to bring this new life into existence, and now I wasn't going to stand here and pass judgment on their union, or call the offspring of that love a hideous monster that deserved to be murdered as punishment for their sins.

Love wasn't a sin. It couldn't be, not ever.

"I don't care what anyone thinks," Mother whispered. "This child is going to live. This child is going to know how much you despised me, Gwen, you and Bennett both."

Suddenly her hands clenched into fists, and she half-rose up off the bed. A feverish look came over her, and the cool, crystalline blue of her eyes shone hotly like the blue of a flame. A few seconds later the contraction passed, and she fell back with an exhausted sigh.

"They're coming closer together," Gwen said.

Jason knelt by the side of the bed, stroking Mother's hand as if he were afraid to ever let go. "We're here for you," he told her, repeating that phrase like a litany. "Nothing's going to happen to the baby, I swear."

"Ours," whispered Mother.

"Yes, of course, yours and mine, and Quinnie's too because she loves you so, Mom."

Mother's eyes found me, and I saw pain in them and heartbreak, so many things left unsaid, so many promises that couldn't be kept. "You're not angry?" she started to say when another labor pain hit her and she arched her back, clutching Jason's hand as the contraction brought tears to her eyes.

I glanced at my aunt, hating to ask for her help but knowing we had no other choice. "What do we do, just wait? Can't we help her? She's in so much pain."

"Help it along, Rebecca," she said. "Push down. That's it, it'll come."

Then something began to go wrong, something none of us were prepared for.

I ran over to the phone and tried to get a dial tone, but the line was still dead. Mother had begun to hemorrhage, and the pain she was experiencing was far more intense than it had been before. Although we could just about see the baby's head, there was so much blood I was terrified it might be stillborn.

My aunt was now as panic-stricken as the rest of us, not knowing what to do. She kept running back into the bathroom to bring clean cloths. But each time she swabbed Mother dry the blood kept flowing, soaking into the sheets.

Mother was groaning terribly now, writhing from side to side as Aunt Gwen kept telling her to bear down, bear down harder she was almost there. As for my brother, he just kept walking in circles it seemed, not knowing what else to do.

By now, Mother was so weak she could barely move. Aunt Gwen was cupping the baby's head in her hands, but I didn't know if it was alive or dead. There was so much blood it obscured everything, and when she finally held the child in her arms and I saw that it was a girl, it lay there lifelessly, yet to utter a sound.

Hurriedly she instructed Jason how to cut and tie the cord, then turned the baby over and held it by its legs, dangling it in the air. Before she could even slap it, for that was what I imagined she was about to do, it gave a raspy cry. Then it began to squall in earnest, its little fists flailing at the air.

I was laughing through my tears, but Jason suddenly began to sob uncontrollably. When I jerked my eyes over to the bed, he was holding Mother in his arms and shaking her back and forth.

"You mustn't, you mustn't," he kept moaning. "No, please, don't, you can't!"

Her head fell limply against her chest, but as I started

toward her, Aunt Gwen grabbed me by the arm and spun me around.

"Wash the baby with warm water, Quinn. Then make sure she's dry," she said in a voice thick with grief. She handed me the quivering bundle that had won the battle for life as Mother had not.

The sound of Jason's anguish followed me from the room. I sponged the baby down until her pink skin glistened, then dried her thoroughly before swaddling her in a clean sheet. But whatever I did I did mechanically, hardly knowing where I was or even what had happened.

When I returned to the bedroom Mother looked so peaceful I was sure she was only asleep. They had drawn the bedcovers up to her neck so that only her face was visible. Her eyes were closed, her lips curled in a sad little smile. It was as if she knew she had gotten her way, having succeeded in bringing this life into being against the most impossible of odds.

"Look at your daughter, Jason," I said softly. "Look how beautiful she is, perfect in every way."

He held the infant tenderly in his arms and began to hum a lullaby Mother had often sung to us when we were very little. "What shall we call you?" he asked, trying to smile though his face was streaked with tears. "I want you to decide, Quinnie. After all, you're going to be her mother now, so it's only right you choose her name."

Aung Gwen backed away from us, her eyes as frightened and haunted looking as Mother's had been when I first saw her standing there in the yard, arms outstretched to greet me. She made a funny gurgling sound in the back of her throat and I knew she was going to be sick. But I didn't care.

I looked down at the baby, this helpless angel now sleeping peacefully in her father's arms. "We'll call her Becky," I said.

"Becky what?"

"Becky Hope Lefland."

Jason smiled and kissed her lightly on the forehead. "Becky Hope," he whispered, his voice filled with love. "You're Daddy-waddy's best little girl. You're his Becky-wecky, and he'll love you till the day he dies."

# 20

Now there'd be no end to the punishment, no stopping the retribution. Her death would be avenged. They'd pay for her suffering, and Warren and I weren't going to wait the rest of our lives to see that they got what they deserved. No, we'd do it now, right now, right this very minute. But Quinnie was afraid, terrified I guess, and begged me to reconsider.

When she saw me rush down the hall after Aunt Gwen, she ran after me, still carrying our dear sweet little Becky in her arms. "Jason, where are you going? What are you going to do!" she shouted.

She must have known. She must have seen the rage in our eyes. She wanted to stop us, too. But we couldn't let her. We had to get our way because it was the only way that was right and just. Aunt Gwen must have sensed what I was thinking too, because she started to scream, and wouldn't shut up even when I wrestled her down to the floor, clamping a hand over her evil lying mouth. Behind me Quinn was still shouting, begging me to stop before it was too late.

Too late for what? It was too late to save Mom, but not too late to punish her evil sister. Besides, I wasn't going to kill the bitch. I was just going to make sure she suffered a little, that's all.

"Either you do what we say, or get the hell out of here," I told my sister. "We don't want any interference, do you hear us, Quinn?"

"Who's *us*, who's *we?*" she whimpered.

"You know damn well I'm talking about Warren," I said angrily. I could see him smiling up there between my ears, pleased-as-punch that I was finally admitting we were a team and always would be.

"Warren's a psychiatrist," Quinn said. "Jason, you don't know what you're saying. You're not well."

Aunt Gwen was making gurgling sounds behind my hand, trying to put her miserable two cents in. I wanted to slap her across the face, but Quinnie pushed me back, screaming at the top of her voice now as she held the baby in one arm and me in the other. The cold-hearted bitch that was Mom's bad sister scrambled to her feet. I pulled free of Quinn, and raced after her, catching her just before she reached the stairs.

"You're coming with me," I said. I started to drag her up to the attic, Warren right there inside my head to help me every step of the way.

Behind me my sister's shouts grew louder and more desperate. She followed after us, clutching the baby in her arms. Gwen was trying to kick free, and her screams were like music rising up into the air. But she had to be punished for what she had done. She had to pay for her treachery, and nobody—not even my beloved Quinn—was going to stop me or stand in my way.

"Where are you taking me? What are you doing?" Gwen was yelling. "Let me go! Stop him, Quinn! Stop him before it's too late!"

"He won't listen to me," she cried.

"Jason, don't," Gwen begged. And when I ignored her plaintive moans, and managed to haul her from the second floor to the third and then up the last flight of stairs to the attic, she changed her tune and got mean and threatening. "Your father will hear about this. I'm going to tell him everything."

That made us laugh. Warren said what fun this will be, the most fun we've had in years. "You're not going to tell anyone, except maybe Great-uncle Orin."

As soon as Quinn heard that she raced on ahead of me. The baby was crying as she stood before the attic door, trying to stop us from entering.

"Get out of the way, Quinn. If you don't want to be a part of this, then go downstairs and leave us alone."

"Jason, I beg of you. You don't know what you're doing."

"Oh, we know all right." I tightened my hold on Aunt Gwen, and once again ordered my sister to move out of the way.

Tears were dripping down Quinn's cheeks, but it was too late to stop us. Warren had to have his way, and so did I.

"Listen to me, Jason. She won't tell on you, I promise. Will you, Aunt Gwen?"

"No, of course not," Gwen said, her voice cracking in fear.

"See? It'll be our secret, Jason, just the three of us."

"Get out of the way, Quinn. You've never betrayed me in the past, so don't start now."

Perhaps she was afraid I might hurt the baby, though I knew I never would. But she finally stepped aside, and I threw open the attic door and shoved Aunt Gwen inside.

"Call the police, Quinn!" she screamed.

"The phone is out," I laughed. "Warren and I cut the wires. Didn't we?"

That's not all we'll cut if she doesn't shut her fucking trap, Warren replied.

"So you'd better watch yourself, Aunt Gwen. Warren's stronger than me. And he doesn't like you one bit."

They didn't know what I was talking about, but I really didn't care anymore. I dragged Gwen along the floor in the direction of the chiffoniers, thinking of poor skin-and-bones Orin, and how he'd really enjoy having some company for a change.

"Jason, please, don't hurt me," Auntie groaned. Tears like droplets of clear syrup dripped slowly down her cheeks. "I didn't—"

"Didn't what?" we shrieked, and our voice went booming through the attic. Quinn shrank back into a corner, terrified by what we were about to do. "Why did you lie to us? Why did you tell us Mom was dead when you knew she wasn't?"

We were still holding onto her, our fingers tight around the neck of her blouse. But now we let go, just long enough to push the chiffoniers out of the way. She tried to escape, but that didn't surprise us. We knew Gwen was a coward who'd never admit her guilt. But though she reached the door and flung it open, we caught her before she could get outside.

Warren wanted me to drag her back by her hair. Instead, we pulled her by the arm. Quinnie was still standing there in the corner, acting as if she were being punished. But suddenly her knees began to buckle and her legs gave way beneath her. She slipped down to the floor, whispering to the baby and behaving as though she didn't even know where she was or what was happening.

"Quinnie, are you all right?"

But she wouldn't answer us. She just kept whispering,

humming a little tune like Mom had done. Shock, was that it? We didn't want her to act this way, and Warren said that if she freaked out on us we'd never be able to escape. But we still had Aunt Gwen to contend with.

"You still haven't told us," we reminded her. "But that's okay. Just take your time, Auntie. We have all the time in the world, Warren and me."

"You keep mentioning Warren," she replied, and fear turned to confusion, and confusion melted right into desperation. "You mean you knew?"

How dumb did she think we were? "About Dr. Warren? Of course we knew. We knew everything. We knew the coffin was filled with stones. We knew how you'd slept with Dad, how you hated Mom's guts. What we didn't know was why you lied, especially since we were old enough to take the truth. Isn't that right, Quinn?"

But we still couldn't get her to answer. Instead, she whispered to the baby, sung to it, rocked it back and forth in her arms and looked right through us as if we weren't even there.

So we answered for her, saying, "Yes, we knew everything, and now you're going to pay for your lies."

Poor Gwendolyn Howe, face covered with glycerin tears, groveling before us. "It's not . . . I mean . . . your father should've . . .."

"Slowly, Aunt Gwen," we giggled. "Take your time. Dad won't be here for hours and hours. And Orin's in no hurry. After all, he'd been looking forward to meeting you for nearly a hundred years."

Aunt Gwen took a deep breath. She seemed to be trying to overcome her fears, or maybe just put her thoughts in order. "You see, I didn't know, what he'd decided, I mean," she began, struggling to get the words out. "When he called me and told me I wasn't even sure if he should."

"Should what?"

"She . . . your mother, my sister . . . Dr. Warren said she was incurable. Schizophrenic, something like that. I can't even remember the exact term he used, but she was so ill she wasn't ever going to get better. They'd tried everything over the years. Shock treatments, lithium, endless combinations of drugs. And then . . . when your father discovered what had happened, he just couldn't . . ."

"Discovered what?" we asked.

"You know what it was, Jason." She couldn't even look me in the eye. I wanted to slap her across the face, but Warren said to hold on, be patient, Lefland, we've got plenty of time. "It was . . . between you and your mother," she went on. "He didn't blame you, honestly he didn't. He knew it wasn't your fault, Jason. But then, when he discovered that she was pregnant, and he knew it couldn't have been his child because they hadn't . . . that is to say they weren't . . . you know . . ."

"Fucking," we said, howling with laughter because she was so frightened of us she couldn't even think straight.

"He wanted you to have a chance, you and Quinton both. He thought it would be easier for you if you grew up thinking your mother had died a natural death, not to know she was institutionalized somewhere, hopelessly insane."

"But she escaped from the hospital," said Quinn, speaking so faintly that for a moment we weren't even sure if we'd heard her.

"Yes, and he went looking for her, never thinking she could have made it back home. But she did."

"Because she was brave," Quinn replied. She was still sitting in the corner, back to the wall and the baby asleep in her arms. "And she loved us so much she couldn't live without us."

"But you can't blame him for trying to protect you,"

Gwen insisted. "He did it out of love, not hatred. You're his whole life, children. You're everything to him."

"No, we're nothing to him," we said. "He only thought of himself, not anyone else."

"That's not true!" cried Gwen, "Your mother was terribly ill. She was destructive to all of you, only you still can't see that because you loved her so much. But what woman in her right mind seduces her own son, throws it up to her husband as if it's the most wonderful thing in the world, and then tries to have the child? It goes against everything we stand for as civilized human beings."

We'd heard enough of her speeches and fancy excuses. We were bored with her lies, the way she'd say anything to save her skin. "It's time to meet Orin, Auntie," we snickered. "You're no use to us now with your talk of morality and good intentions. You had your chance to help us, and you blew it. You could've told Dad he was wrong, no one's incurable. Even if it took ten years to make her well, or even twenty, we still would've waited."

"But you can't make a schizophrenic well, Jason!"

"That's your opinion, not ours. But you can discuss it with Orin. He's not very talkative, but he makes up for it by being a terrific listener. Shall we, Quinn?"

I looked across the attic, hoping she'd come to her senses and realize that what we were about to do was only fair. But she wouldn't answer me. She wouldn't even look up and acknowledge I was there.

"Quinnie, please, help us," we begged, Warren and I speaking in one voice because we were now the best of friends, as inseparable as Siamese twins.

"I can't," she said in a voice that sounded lost and distant.

"Help me!" screamed Aunt Gwen.

"I can't. I can't do anything."

There was so much grief and anguish in her voice that

for a moment I even began to reconsider what I was planning. But then Warren reminded me that his opinion counted just as much as mine, and he wasn't about to offer mercy to Aunt Gwen when she had never offered even a shred of compassion to Mom.

"Quinn, please, just this once," we pleaded. "You have to help us. We can't do it on our own. Quinn, she's responsible for Mom's death, she and Dad both. Don't you see that? She's as much to blame as he is."

Quinn came slowly to her feet. I thought she'd turn away and leave us alone in the attic. But no, she put the baby down and slowly made her way toward us. Her eyes were dull and glassy, her expression as faraway as it was forlorn. She seemed in a daze, barely knowing where she was or what she was about to do.

"Help us," we said again, Warren and I begging her as we'd never begged before.

She said nothing. But when she reached down and took hold of Aunt Gwen's arm, I knew she wasn't going to turn her back on us, not when we needed her most. So between the three of us, meaning me and Warren and our sister, we dragged Gwen along the dusty attic floor. As soon as we managed to get the panel open, the smell of the opossum, rotting and maggot-ridden, rushed down the passage to greet us. Gwen gave a last fitful scream, and then vomit started to dribble out between her lips.

"Wipe her mouth dry. It makes us sick to look at her," we told Quinn. If she heard the "us," she didn't say anything about it, so maybe she and Warren had already made their peace. I didn't bother asking him because there was too much to do. Aunt Gwen had a date with Great-uncle Orin, and I didn't want her to be late.

Halfway down the crawlspace, Mom's evil sister made a last-ditch effort to escape. But once again we managed to stop her, tackling her before she could get away.

"No, please, I didn't hurt anyone," Gwen was whimpering while Warren and I got her down on her back, pinning her arms down with our knees.

"Mom would be alive today if it weren't for you," we told her. Then we pulled her along like a sack of potatoes. Every time she tried to slip free of our grasp I wanted to kick her, but Warren said no, we'll tie her up next to Orin and that'll be punishment enough.

"Can't you see he's not well? He's as crazy as she was!" Gwen shrieked at my sister. "Don't you realize what's going on, Quinn? He's disturbed, he's hallucinating, he doesn't know what he's doing."

"He knows," whispered Quinn, sounding so withdrawn her mind seemed to be somewhere else. "He's my brother and I love him. And I can help him, too."

"But I didn't hurt anyone!" she shouted.

We didn't answer her after that. We hauled her down the musty dusty passage that reeked of dead meat, rotting and putrid. Vomit dribbled down her chin. Tears drenched her cheeks. Her chest heaved and her breath came in short, strangled gasps. And words, an endless uncoiling of words like a rope to hang herself with. She called us sick, disturbed, perverted, depraved. They were nasty, ugly words that should never have been uttered, but Warren said don't listen, Lefland. Just pretend you're deaf.

We turned the bend in the passage and Quinnie said she felt sick. We told her to breathe through her mouth, it was just a few more feet and then we'd be there. And when we finished with Mom's evil, lying sister we'd go downstairs and feed Becky-wecky.

"With what!" screamed Auntie. "You don't have formula. You don't have anything for her. You can't take care of that infant without my help. You don't know the first thing about it. Let me go, Jason, and I'll help you, I promise. Think of your daughter!"

"Think of our mother."

Our words were like stone blocks. We'd build walls around her, seal her in for all eternity. We had rope with us too, everything we needed. The broken door to the hidden room where poor dead Orin stared into the black face of fatherly rage was right before us. We kicked it open with our foot. Then we whipped out the flashlight from our back pocket, and shone it right in Gwen's frightened eyes.

Silence then. She wasn't saying a word, just choking and gagging from the smell. But it didn't matter, because words were useless now. We didn't care if she kept calling us names, saying God would punish us for sure. He wouldn't; He'd punish her. Then we showed her Orin, his blind eyes and empty sockets, the poor dead son who loved his mom just like me.

Her screams rose in the air. Warren and I could have cared less. We shoved her down on the dead man's lap that was nothing but rattling bones, then wound the rope around her, lashing her securely to both Orin and the chair.

"Don't let him do this to me, Quinn," she moaned.

"I can't stop him anymore," whispered my sister. Abruptly she turned away and rushed down the passage.

"Dad will come and get you when he's good and ready," we told Gwen when we were alone. "Providing of course you don't die of fright. But in the meantime, you and Orin have a nice pleasant chat."

We knew she'd keep on screaming, so we ripped her blouse off and stuffed it into her mouth, tying it good and tight to keep her quiet. Then we stepped back, eying her for a moment and liking what we saw. Her eyes were so wide they looked like they were about to pop right out. The terror that Mom must have felt being locked up in the hospital was now Gwen's to experience, to savor for her very own.

336

"You're getting off lucky," I told her. "Warren wanted me to kill you, but I wouldn't let him." Then we closed the door and made our way down the crawlspace and back into the attic.

And now for the Daddy-waddy, Warren reminded me as we went downstairs, taking deep breaths and trying to push the dead smells out of our lungs.

But we still didn't remember what had happened that night. How could we leave here with our Becky-wecky if we didn't have the memory to take with us? We wanted to tell Quinnie that, but we were afraid she wouldn't understand. So we kept our fears to ourself, hoping that Dad would tell us since he was there when it all happened. Then, when the last piece of the puzzle fit snugly into place, we'd leave the Valley, never to return.

# 21

Of late, I often ask myself if things could have been different, if Jason's behavior was as much a reflection of my feelings as his own. Aunt Gwen's fearful cries echo in my mind like drumbeats, distant and unforgiving. Yet what choice did I have but to help my brother? If I had turned my back on him that day, a day that lives in my memory as one of birth and death, the putting aside of the old, the taking up of the new, he would have had no one but Warren to turn to. And who *was* Warren, after all? Was he an entity unto himself, driving my poor brother deeper and deeper into madness? Or was he merely a facet of Jason's personality, like a coin whose face is marred by fire, the features twisted and unrecognizable?

Yet whoever Warren might have been, he existed that summer in the Valley when Mother returned to give birth to our child, and Father returned to witness the bloody aftermath of plans gone awry, and hopes shattered in the flickering, uncertain light of a dying afternoon.

One thing Aunt Gwen had said was true though. We had

little if anything to feed our Becky. Shaken by all that had happened, Mother's death, the terrifying scene in the attic, I grabbed the baby in my arms and rushed downstairs, fully prepared to keep on running and never stop. But Becky was hungry, and Jason needed me, and it was much too late to turn my back on them. I warmed some milk, fitted one of Anna's rubber gloves over a mason jar, and put a pinprick through one of the glove's fingers. Becky sucked contentedly, though I was afraid milk might not be the best thing for her. After all, she needed formula, as Aunt Gwen had reminded us, and until we went into town, or until Father returned, we had nothing else to give her.

I took her with me into the music room, where the vases of flowers lay dying in the hazy golden light, the long shadows of late afternoon slipping silently across the floor. A mockingbird's strident cries gave way to song. It was peaceful here, and Aunt Gwen's terrified screams were like a distant memory, soon to be forgotten.

Father would come, would rescue us from all that both he and Warren had created. And in the morning after this day of unremitting pain, I would awaken to find my world as it had always been. But no, that was just a dream, another fancy of the childhood I was destined to discard forever that summer in the Valley.

I heard footsteps on the stairs. Jason, breathless and red-faced, his tousled hair damp across his forehead, hurried into the music room.

"What are you doing, just sitting there?" he said, his eyes wild and unfocused.

I tried reasoning with him, calming him down, but it did little good. He said we had work to do. We had to pack our things and get ready to leave.

"Where are we going?" I asked, and though I tried to laugh, Jason was in deadly earnest.

"We can't stay here," he said. "They'll open the coffin

and find Harry. Then they'd separate us for sure, take the baby away, never let us be a family again. We can't let them get away with that, Quinn."

He sat down beside me, watching Becky sucking on her makeshift bottle. I didn't know what to say, because if he was divided in two by Warren, I was divided in two by doubt and confusion.

"I took a pill, a little white pill I found in Mom's medicine cabinet," he announced.

"What kind of pill?" I asked, feeling panic rising up inside me.

"Not to worry, not to worry," he kept saying. "It's just to calm me down. I can already feel it working. Warren's asleep. He won't bother me for awhile."

"And when he wakes up?"

"We'll be so far away from here it won't matter, Quinn, I promise."

"And what if I said I didn't want to leave?"

I saw so many emotions pass across his face it was like a slide show, or looking through pictures in an old family album. There was rage as well as tenderness, fear as well as courage.

"Are you going to desert me, is that what you're saying?" he asked, sounding so wounded I couldn't help but reach over and put my hand against his cheek. I could feel the faintest suggestion of stubble, though perhaps that was just my imagination, and his cheek was as smooth and downy as the young boy he was trying so desperately to leave behind.

"I could never desert you, you know that," I replied.

"We'll make a new life for ourselves, Quinn, I promise. We'll take his car and we'll drive so far away from here they'll never find us. I took some money I found in Gwen's purse. Mrs. D. had some stashed away for groceries and I found that, too. We have over three hundred dollars altogether, plus another fifty or so I saved from my allowance. And Dad's sure to have money on him, so we'll have even more.''

He made it sound so simple, so easy. And even though I knew that ''easy'' was the one word that could never describe what our lives would be, I also knew there was a great deal of truth in what he had said. If we didn't leave, if we remained here in the Valley, I knew that Jason's fears would come to pass. We would be separated, the baby taken away from us. Father would send Jason away, perhaps to Dr. Warren's hospital where Mother had been dragged that terrible night that will live forever in my nightmares. But I couldn't let that happen, no matter what the consequences for me might be. There had to be an end to the madness, and locking Jason up for the rest of his life was not the solution.

So I agreed to what he proposed, though at the time I hardly realized what such a commitment would ultimately mean, and how it would change our lives forever, not just for this one summer's afternoon.

It was dusk when we heard the tires screeching along the gravel, and then Father's big cheery hello as he bounded up the front steps. We waited for him in the entrance hall, the pendants of the crystal chandelier scattering rainbows across the walls. When he came inside, hale and hearty and much taller than I remembered, I stood there with the baby in my arms, staring at him as Jason spread his rage around us like a protective shell. Father stopped dead in his tracks, and the smile he'd given us faded away like the afternoon light vanishing beyond the hills.

Though my first impulse was to run to him, and feel his arms around me, I turned away and started up the stairs. I felt drugged, anesthetized perhaps, seeing the world as if through a thick layer of cloudy glass. I knew it was time to make my good-byes, and yet I was terrified of leaving, of facing a world in which I had little if any experience. Jason too remained silent, following after me, our measured footsteps like an unspoken invitation for Father to join us.

"What in the—?" he started to say. But the words fell from his lips, blowing away like brittle autumn leaves.

Down the second-floor hall we marched like a funeral procession, heading straight to Mother's room where she lay in bed, waiting for her Bennett to return. He began to run after us then, but by the time he grabbed Jason by the shoulder we were already at the end of the hall. I opened the bedroom door and stepped inside, little Becky with her pink porcelain cheeks asleep in my arms.

"Oh my God," whispered Father when he saw what I had been unable to stop my brother from doing.

Mother was sitting up in bed, lipstick and rouge and eye shadow turning the dead gray skin back to life.

"Oh Jesus," Father whimpered, and he buried his face in his hands and began to weep.

I watched him, wondering if the grief he was showing was all an act, and if he really cared if Mother was dead or alive.

"But how? When?" he stammered. Then he pointed at the baby and seemed to understand.

"Yes, it's our child now," said Jason. "Mom's dead because of you. It's just a miracle the baby didn't die, too. This is Becky, Becky Hope Lefland, and as God and the baby Jesus are my witness, you're never going to hurt us again."

"She was ill, she was so terribly ill," Father said. He rubbed the tears from his eyes, pleading with us to listen to what he had to say. "I didn't want you to know her that way, incurably insane. It would have haunted you all your

343

life. Wasn't it better to think she wasn't disturbed? Wasn't it kinder? I did it for you, for the two of you.''

"And the baby?'' Jason asked.

Father looked down at his feet, unable to meet Jason's accusing glance. "The baby shouldn't have been born,'' he said sadly. "You know that as well as I do.''

"See, Quinn, he wanted her dead. Baby-killer, that's what he is. But you didn't get your way this time, because here she is. And she's beautiful, and healthy, and perfect in every way.''

"Jason, Quinn, please, just listen to me for a moment. I was only thinking of your welfare, believe me. I don't blame you, son, for what happened. Your mother wasn't well. She was two people, don't you realize that, two people who kept splitting her right down the middle. She tried to kill you, Jason, don't you remember? She tried to murder you, for God's sake!''

What was he saying? Was this just another lie to convince us he had only done what he'd thought best, sparing us the pain of Mother's hopeless insanity? Startled by what Father had just said, I looked at Jason in confusion, asking him if it was true.

"Of course it's true!'' Father cried. "I was there the night it happened. I saw the knife. I saw the blood. She tried to kill your brother and I couldn't . . . I just couldn't . . .''

He broke down, begging us to understand, to forgive him. But though I was beginning to waver, one look at Jason and I knew there was blood in his thoughts. My brother stared at Father as if he were a stranger. Or worse, a murderer.

"She took that knife you gave Quinn. She cut you with it,'' Father went on. "Then when you were trying to get away from her she started to cut herself. She just slashed at her wrists, hacked at herself. She didn't know what she was doing."

"Yes, I remember now," Jason replied. There was something in his voice that made me realize it was my brother who was talking, and not the spiteful Warren with whom he was forced to share his thoughts. "There was blood on the walls, the mirror, the floor. The blood spurted from her wrists and it was bright red and oh, how I laughed, holding my hand over her mouth, that sweet red mouth of hers so she wouldn't scream."

"Jason, don't, you don't know what you're saying!" I cried out. "You're making this all up, you know you are!"

"No, it's the truth," he whispered. Then he looked over at Father and raised his voice, speaking with the utmost conviction. "It was wrong, wasn't it, what she did to me, taking me into her bed—your bed, really. She thought it was a game, but I felt dirty afterwards, used. I hated her for loving me that way. I hated myself for not understanding, but I couldn't. And I couldn't say no to her either, even when I wanted to. She was Mom, don't you see? I had to stop her, I just had to. She was making me do things, and she said it was my baby and you hated me and you were going to rip it out of her womb and kill me because that was the Lefland curse and you wouldn't be able to stop yourself."

"Son, it's all right, it's all right, we understand," Father said. He started toward Jason, but my brother backed away.

"You were downstairs in the study, working late. She came to my room and told me to come with her, she needed me. I followed her into the bedroom, and she told me how much she wanted me, saying dirty things that were wrong. I knew it and she knew it, too. She said other things, I can't remember all of them. But I had the knife with me and I knew it was time because Warren told me it was.''

"Warren? What does Dr. Warren have to do with this, son?''

"A different Warren. The Warren who lives up here," he explained. He tapped his finger against his head and told us that he saw it all, the explosion of blood as he drew the blade across her wrists, first one and then the other.

I wanted to run to him then, hold him tight and safe in my arms. But he wouldn't let me.

"But then you came into the room, remember?" he asked Father. "And remember how you saw the blood and I screamed she was trying to kill me and now she was trying to do the same thing to herself. It was a lie, but you believed everything I said, remember? You pushed me out of the room and warned me not to say a word about it to anyone, especially Quinn. Remember, Dad? Do you remember?" he cried. "Because I do. For a long time I couldn't recall what happened that night. It was just a blank space in my mind, all dark and empty. But now it's back. It's all in my head and it won't go away.''

Father was weeping then, and he said, "Jason, don't worry, we'll get you help. We'll make you whole again, son, I swear." He glanced at the bed, shouting, "Oh God, Rebecca, look what you've done. Look what you've done to us!''

I rushed to Jason's side, but his eyes told me no, it wasn't over yet, there was still more to be done. But when Father put his arms around my brother, he didn't pull back, shying away at his touch.

"You're safe now," Father said, kissing the top of Jason's head as his arms held him close in his embrace. "Your Dad's here and you'll be all right. You'll be okay, son. The worst is over.''

But it wasn't. It had only just begun because Father

suddenly stiffened, and his arms fell away from Jason and he staggered back, turning to look at me with sad, disbelieving eyes.

"Jason, what have you done!" I screamed.

Blood seeped through Father's white shirt. It looked like red ink, so thin and watery it couldn't possibly have been real.

"Just a cut, just a little cut," Jason said in a gruff, husky voice, a voice that surely had to be Warren's and not his own. "Not too deep, not too dangerous. He'll live. Leflands always do. They go on and on and on, murdering their sons. Only now the curse is over. Finished, Quinnie. Done with."

Father tried to straighten up but he couldn't make it. He slumped to the floor and I put the baby down and rushed to help him.

"A surface wound, no big deal," Jason was saying. "It looks worse than it is. He'll live, but he won't be in any shape to follow us. We'll send a doctor over as soon as we reach town. But now we'd better get going while we still have the chance."

"Don't listen to him, Quinn," whispered Father. "He doesn't know what he's saying. The only way to help him is to help me."

I didn't know what to do. There was Jason, standing by the door, smiling at what he had done, wiping the blood off the bone-handled dirk he had given me for my birthday. And there was Father, stretched out on the floor with his bloodstained hand covering the wound in his side.

"He's a liar, Quinn, a filthy liar!" Jason suddenly screamed. "He'll send me away, lock me up and throw away the key. He'll take Becky away from us and we'll never see her again. Mom's dead because of him! Look at her, Quinn. She's dead, and it's all his fault!"

Jason hauled me to my feet, grabbed my chin in his hand and forced me to listen to him.

"But now we have our little Becky to take care of," he said, "and we're going to teach her what hate is." He looked down at Father, his lips curled back in contempt. "When she grows up she'll know what a monster you are, you and Aunt Gwen both. Oh yes, she's still here, up in the attic, behind the wall. She'll be very glad to see you, if she hasn't died of fright by now."

He bent down and began to go through Father's pockets, removing the car keys as well as his billfold. Then he glanced over at the bed where Mother watched us with dead, unseeing eyes.

"It's what you told me to do," Jason said to her. "Now you can rest, can't you, Mom? Now you can rest easy, knowing he's been punished."

"Quinn, please, don't listen to him," Father begged, gritting his teeth as he tried to bear up to the pain. He still had his hand over the knife wound, trying to stanch the flow of blood. But it seeped through his fingers, dripping to the floor.

I see it then as I see it now. A choice. A fork in the road. If I turned one way, I would leave my brother behind. If I turned another, I would leave Father and the Valley, never to see them again. A choice. A fork in the road. The past is irrevocable. The decision was made, and now I can only recall what I said and not what I thought that summer's day, when twilight darkened the sky with the color of blood.

"He doesn't know what he's doing, Quinn," said Father. "Please, your brother's not well."

"Then I'll make him well because I love him," I replied. "You would send him away just like you sent Mother. You'd keep us apart for the rest of our lives. But now we'll be together because we love each other, and our love is much stronger than your hatred."

I picked up the baby, then reached for Jason's hand. As Father called after us, a last futile effort to get us to listen, we turned away and left him there, lying on his side in an ever-widening pool of blood.

I see it then as I see it now. A choice. A fork in the road. Years have passed, and Becky is nearly six years old, and there is still so much more to tell. But I shall save that story for another day, when the air is warm with the scents of summer, and the Valley shimmers in the golden afternoon.

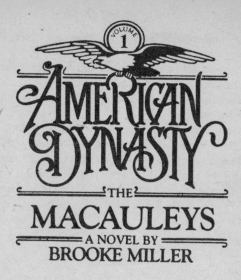

# AMERICAN DYNASTY

## THE MACAULEYS
### A NOVEL BY
### BROOKE MILLER

Disinherited by one of the nation's most powerful families, Marshall Macauley gambled on a ruthless country, fought for an impossible dream, and founded an American dynasty.

**A June 1982 title from DELL/EMERALD**     06099-0

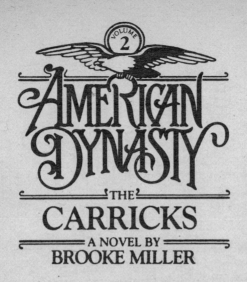

# THE CARRICKS

## A NOVEL BY
## BROOKE MILLER

Patricia Carrick, beautiful and brilliant,
came out of a mill town to create a finan-
cial empire, risk it for a reckless love, and
continue an American dynasty.

An August 1982 title from **DELL/EMERALD 01413-1**

VOLUME 3

# AMERICAN DYNASTY

## THE
## STERNS

### A NOVEL BY
### BROOKE MILLER

Scorned by her family and rejected by the man she adored, Rachel Stern surrendered everything to save a son whose exploits would astound turn-of-the-century New York. From the ashes of a forbidden love, Rachel Stern founded an American dynasty.

**An October 1982 title
from DELL/EMERALD**

07639-0